Praise for *The Pleasure Seekers*

Shortlisted for The Hindu Best Fiction Award 2010

'A family saga that reads more as a personal odyssey. It convinces, entertains and, at times, reminds the reader of how tough it is to be human … This big-hearted, engaging novel will appeal to as many readers as there are lovers; winners and losers; dreamers and survivors' Eileen Battersby, *Irish Times*

'I read this book almost in one sitting, and became completely engaged by the characters' Louis de Bernieres

'Flecked with tragedy and death but *The Pleasure Seekers* soars with a forceful paean to the human spirit' *Metro*

'The writing is assured and vivid and there is warmth and a great tenderness about the portrait of this unlikely marriage, which wins the reader over' Susan Hill, *The Lady*

'A post-colonial family saga, written with warmth and empathy for all the characters' *People*

'Charming and largely poetic, the book is emphatic in its portrayal of familial relationships and the search for love' *Harper's Bazaar*

BY THE SAME AUTHOR

Countries of the Body

ABOUT THE AUTHOR

TISHANI DOSHI is a poet and dancer based in
Madras, India. Her first collection of poetry, *Countries
of the Body*, won the Forward Poetry Prize for best first
collection in 2006. *The Pleasure Seekers* is her first novel.

The Pleasure Seekers

Tishani Doshi

BLOOMSBURY

LONDON · BERLIN · NEW YORK · SYDNEY

For my parents, the original pleasure seekers.

First published in Great Britain 2010
This paperback edition published 2011

Copyright © 2010 by Tishani Doshi

The moral right of the author has been asserted

Bloomsbury Publishing, London, Berlin, New York and Sydney
36 Soho Square, London W1D 3QY

A CIP catalogue record for this book is available from the British Library

ISBN 978 1 4088 0983 9

10   9   8   7   6   5   4   3

Typeset by Hewer Text UK Ltd, Edinburgh
Printed in Great Britain by Clays Ltd. St Ives plc

www.bloomsbury.com/tishanidoshi

PART ONE

Sylvan Lodge

1968–1974

1 Departures and Depositories of Deceit

In the early hours of 20 August 1968, the morning of his son's departure, Prem Kumar Patel succumbed to a luxury he had never, in all his forty-seven years of living, experienced before: he had a dream. It was a long, terrible dream that seemed to take him back to the coils of his mother's womb and hurl him to the end of his life, to a valley submerged in ice. In this dream Prem Kumar was climbing mountains, trying to find his wife and four children. They were lost to him in a strange kingdom where men carried the ghosts of ancestors on their backs and women hid in trees, throwing poison-tipped arrows. Prem Kumar, standing in front of a great wooden doorway, could hear his children screaming. Babo, especially; his eldest, who was cold and wanted extra blankets to sleep, who wasn't used to this bite in the air that was making him turn from a dark shade of walnut to a pasty pistachio. Babo kept calling out to Prem Kumar, *Why did you send me here? Why did you send me away?* And the other children – Meenal, Dolly and Chotu, cried in chorus after him, *Why did you send him away? Why did you send our brother away?*

 All morning, while on the other side of the world Soviet tanks invaded the Czechoslovak Socialist Republic, Prem Kumar Patel lay corpse-still on his back in Madras, South India, watching as his entire life passed before him in a series of silvered, fleeting scenes. He saw his white-haired mother on the front steps of her house in Ganga Bazaar, peeling mangoes

3

for grandchildren that hadn't been born yet. He saw jackals roaming the rubble-strewn streets of a city laid to waste. He saw burnings and soarings, a celestial aeroplane descending from the sky. He saw things that couldn't possibly have happened but bore a resemblance to reality that frightened him so much he had to turn to his wife lying beside him and suck on her breasts of wondrous light. He wanted to ask what these portents meant, but Trishala, slapping her husband's mouth irritably away, wanted nothing to do with it. 'Get off, get off,' she said. 'What's the matter with you? Bothering me so early in the morning.' And she pulled the sheets from him, wrapping them around the large mass of her body, preferring to stay cocooned in a dreamland of her own making.

When Prem Kumar finally woke to the event of Babo's leaving, it was with dark circles under his eyes and the wide expanse of his nose rutted with a rash of mosquito bites. From the distance, he could hear his neighbour Darayus Mazda's daily morning balcony diatribe: *Oh! They are breaking me into pieces. My family is breaking me into pieces. They want to send me to the Towers of Silence before my time. Won't someone save me from their wickedness* ... And on and on and on, till Prem Kumar, for the first time in their neighbourly association, wanted to walk over and reassure his Parsi kinsman in suffering that no one was trying to do away with him; that in fact, it was he, Prem Kumar, who was the target of a far greater suffering.

Prem Kumar was not a sentimental man, but he was religious, and he believed in retribution. For him, this event of Babo's departure was much more than just an investment in the Patel family future. It was about his personal dharma, his responsibility. Babo, who had graduated with honours in chemistry from Jain College, was going to be the first member of their community to further his education by studying

4

abroad. Babo, at the breathtaking age of twenty-one, was also going to be the first person in their immediate family to fly on a plane all the way to London.

At the beginning of the year, Prem Kumar had written to the offices of Joseph Friedman & Sons in London, from whom he imported coloured cement and raw materials, asking if his son, who was going to be taking evening classes at the City & Guild Borough Polytechnic, could get some practical training under their auspices during the day. Fred Hallworth, who was the man in charge of exports, had written back saying that they would be delighted to have young Dharmesh Patel working at their offices in Wandsworth, that they could offer him a weekly salary of £10 15s and would furthermore be able to give him Wednesdays off so he could finish his course at the Polytechnic sooner.

These provisions are more than adequate, Prem Kumar replied, *And I can only hope that with this new venture, our partnership will grow from strength to strength.* A month later, a letter arrived from the Chairman's office saying that a work permit was being organized for Babo, and that if anything else needed to be arranged, the company would be more than happy to help.

All this was cause for a great swelling in Prem Kumar's chest. Ever since the Indian government had banned imports on finished products in an effort to encourage home industry, Prem Kumar had been dreaming of opening his own specialized paint factory: Patel & Sons, where Babo, with his foreign-acquired knowledge, and Chotu, under his brother's guidance, could steer the Patel family towards a stable, lucrative future. Prem Kumar had already raced ahead in time. He could see it now: the labels on the paint cans, the logo, the motto, the workers scurrying in and out noiselessly like ants, filing cabinets filled with account books in his careful, crested handwriting, showing rising profits year after year.

Prem Kumar indulged in this dreaming even as he sat solemnly beneath the sign that he had lovingly tacked above his current desk in his early idealistic years:

PLEASE TALK OF BUSINESS,
FINISH YOUR BUSINESS,
AND LEAVE THE MAN TO ATTEND TO HIS BUSINESS.

Only later, much later, on the day of the dreaded telegram, nine months after Babo left Madras on that nearly rainy day in August 1968, would Prem Kumar begin to understand the dangerous implications of his idle daydreaming. He'd realize that he was being punished for his own duplicity: for dreaming of the future when he should have been attending to the present.

On the morning of Babo's departure, when Prem Kumar hauled his struggling body out on to the veranda to join the rest of his family, he kept quiet about his dream. He didn't tell Trishala about it – not in the months of silence during her illness, not even when she lay delirious on her deathbed, demanding to know the ways in which he'd been unfaithful to her. Because Prem Kumar didn't believe in superstitions or spiritly visitations. After Trishala died, of course, he found he couldn't sleep at nights; he was restless, doomed to listen to religious songs blaring into his ears from his Walkman because he missed his wife's extravagant presence beside him, and because, after his first and only dream, he dreaded the consequences of another.

Prem Kumar had to live with the guilt that if only he'd shared his dream with his wife, she would never have allowed their son to fly away on that fateful day. But as it was, he stood with the rest of the family, watching Babo as he walked out in his new, over-starched Jamal's suit, smiling at all the world with his jhill mill gleaming teeth, completely innocent of the tumultuous changes his departure was going to bring upon them all.

The drive to the Madras Meenambakkam Airport was mostly sullen. Chotu, Prem Kumar's youngest child, sat squeezed in the front seat between his father and the driver, sulking furiously because he was about to lose one of the things he was most passionate about – his older brother, (the other being the more steadfast game of cricket). In the back, Trishala and Babo occupied places of importance by the windows, while the girls, Meenal and Dolly, tried to find comfortable positions between them. Once in a while, Prem Kumar would yell, 'Watch out! Can't you see where you're going?' or 'Mind the cow!' to the taxi driver, but otherwise, it was all silence.

Babo, looking out of the window, was watching the patterns the recent puddles had made in the streets. It had been raining in Madras for two weeks, but this morning the sky seemed to be holding its breath, as if in reverence to this momentous occasion.

'Papa,' Babo said, as if the thought had just occurred to him, 'In England, when people ask me what caste I am, what shall I tell them?'

'You'll explain exactly what you are – that you are the son of Prem Kumar Patel, grandson of Shantilal Kumar Patel, great-grandson of Kunthinath Paras Kumar Patel.'

'And if they ask me what religion I follow?'

'Then you'll tell them that you are a dedicated and practising Jain. And just like the father of our nation, Mahatma Gandhi, you are a believer in ahimsa, and in the equality of all souls.'

Yes, Babo thought, that is what I will tell them if they ask.

'Chotu,' he said, reaching over to pat his eleven-year-old brother on the head, 'Do you think one day you too will go to England to study?'

7

'Of course, bhai. I'm going to grow up and become a paint maker just like you and papa.'

With that settled, Babo leaned back in his seat, smiling, thinking things were exactly as they should be. As they drove through the tree-lined avenues of Madras, Babo noticed how the flower-sellers were already out, stringing jasmine and marigold for the housewives who would come by after their chores to offer morning prayers at the temple. The coffee and tea makers in the little shanty stands like Balaji Snacks and Hot Point were busy too, as were the newspaper sellers and the early morning walkers. Madras was alive, singing and dancing like the oil on the surface of the low-lying puddles, quivering with delicate rainbows. Babo saw a young girl riding on the back of her father's bicycle. She wore a bright pink dress with silver anklets around her bare feet, and to Babo, she looked like a princess being guided by a troubadour through the deep forests of morning.

He watched her as he watched everything, knowing it would be a long time before he saw any of it again. But after half an hour of mustering up such an intense look of concentration on his face, Babo felt himself being assailed by a great and sudden need for sleep.

Prem Kumar, still irritated with his sleepless night, noticed with distaste that the dashboard of the Ambassador was cluttered with pictures of gods: Baby Krishna, Jesus Christ, Guru Nanak, Gautham Buddha, even Lord Mahavir – the twenty-fourth thirthankara and Great Hero of the Jain religion; they were all lined up, side-to-side, shimmering in gaudy benevolence. The taxi driver, who was obviously trying to cover all bases by appeasing the gods simultaneously, had already infuriated Prem Kumar by smoking bidi after bidi at the gates of Sylvan Lodge, leaving poor Selvam, their half-blind watchman, to pack the luggage in the car. Clearly, he was a fellow who completely lacked any grasp of Right

Thought, Right Action or Right Understanding – the basic tenets of the Jain faith that Prem Kumar had tried to instil in all his children but particularly in Babo.

Sometimes it seemed to Prem Kumar that Babo came from a different family. He never openly mocked his father or disagreed with him, but Prem Kumar knew for a fact that his son did not pray, did not recite Navkar Mantra thrice a day (which was the minimum number prescribed), did not believe in ideas of penance and certainly didn't believe in the idea of denying the self pleasure.

Once, when Babo was twelve, he rounded up all the neighbourhood children and his siblings (including two-year-old Chotu, whom he carried on his back), and walked them five kilometres to Marina Beach, thinking it would be a grand idea to go out to sea with the fishermen in their catamarans, and to swim with dolphins. When Trishala returned to Sylvan Lodge from her shopping to find her children disappeared, she began a stupendous wailing at the gates with all the other neighbourhood mothers joining in, thinking that demons and asuras had collectively carried their children away. Hours later, when Babo finally returned like Alexander the Great crossing the River Jhelum to conquer King Porus with an army of brown-faced children burned by the midday sun – their clothes wet from sea water, their pockets full of shells – Prem Kumar, who had been summoned back from work, took his son upstairs and gave him the whipping of his life. Trishala went to him later of course, with soft words, saying that as Babo was the eldest, he was the vehicle for all Prem Kumar's aspirations; it was his responsibility to guide the younger ones, not to tickle their fancies and imaginations. She tried to feed him the samosas she'd prepared for him tenderly with her fingers, but Babo became a wall of stone. He bore his grudges like a turtle – for ever. He'd pretend to shrug them off and carry on as if everything were normal,

9

but inside he never forgot things, especially actions that were charged against him unjustly. There were stores of memories just like this one, that he kept locked inside his chest, which remained like fresh wounds on the surface of his body.

Despite all their differences, though, Prem Kumar knew his son was a good boy. That at least he believed in ahimsa – non-violence to all living beings, and the idea of truth – because it was the most important idea of all. According to Prem Kumar, everyone had to find their own truth, for without it, life would remain a useless circle of deception and conflict. If one had the wisdom to follow this truth, then one could hope to break the bonds that tied one to the suffering of this world, and attain moksha – the final liberation. But the problem with the young, thought Prem Kumar, was that they were unwavering in the idea of their own invincibility.

Prem Kumar glanced back at Babo, who was on his way to finding out all these things, whose head was nodding against the glass of the window – knock knock knock. And in an extraordinarily open gesture of love, he looked at his sleeping son and smiled.

At the airport the family disembarked, carrying their allotted pieces of luggage. Dolly and Meenal stood in matching green checked maxis and blouses, holding the getting-ready-for-camera gear: talcum powder, comb, mirror, hand towel. Chotu stood separately with the basket of snacks and tea flask, staring at the ground so he would not shame himself by crying in public like his sisters. Trishala was pushing through the crowds in her new maroon sari and matching maroon glasses, balancing rose garlands in one hand and puja tray in the other, hollering at the girls to hurry behind her and stay close. Prem Kumar, pulling crisp notes out of his wallet, was lecturing the taxi driver on the ill consequences of smoking, while simultaneously keeping an eye out for another lazy, unreliable man – Lilaj-bhai, who had been hired to take photographs of Babo's going-away ceremony.

Babo was being preened, made to stand in the light for the photograph session. Meenal was fussing with his hair, trying to get his curls to stay in place. Meenal: second in line, quietest of all four children, given to short bursts of emotion and long periods of introspection, weeping copious tears, as was the tradition of all Patel women when it came to interactions with their men.

'You won't forget about us, will you, bhai?' she said, picking up his hand and stroking the chunky gold ring on his left finger, which she'd given him the night before on Trishala's instruction.

'Don't be silly,' said Babo, just as he'd said the night before when Meenal had found him on the terrace, sneaking his last fag of the day. 'I wish I could forget about you,' he'd said, 'but I've lived with you for nineteen years now, so it looks like we're stuck for life, doesn't it?'

When he saw Meenal's well-powdered face shrink like a deflated balloon, he'd immediately reached out to pull her plaits and said, 'Oy, sour puss, why all this drama bazi? Didn't I promise to write to you?'

'And to Falguni,' Meenal replied, tittering.

Babo had been thinking of Falguni when Meenal had burst in on him. He had fallen in love with her during the festival of Navratri, when for nine consecutive nights, all the people of their community, young and old, gathered in a large hall to celebrate and worship the three supreme aspects of the Goddess Durga. The religious significance was lost on Babo. For him, it was enough to celebrate. It was also one of the few legitimate ways to meet a girl.

Babo had noticed Falguni on the very first night. He'd known her for years, of course, because she was the daughter of Prem Kumar and Trishala's closest friends, Kamal and

Meghna Shah. That night, though, it was as if he was seeing her for the first time, standing next to Meenal in a bridal-red ghagra with coloured glass bangles all the way from her slim wrists to her elbows. She was a milky-skinned girl with almond eyes, a willowy waist and a thick river of black hair, which she kept demurely plaited. But her biggest attraction was the peculiar structure of her teeth which forced her to lisp her words and confuse her s's for th's. For this reason mainly, and for the fact that within the span of a few short months Falguni had developed a sizeable pair of breasts, Babo found himself hanging around her with a clutch of other admirers.

Babo had learned from the movies that the best heroes were the ones who were slick, suave and oftentimes cruel. So after his initial gaff at gawping, he whisked away one of Meenal's less attractive friends and spent the whole night dancing with her. By six in the morning, when people started heading towards breakfast places with leaden feet, Babo, continuing in his nonchalance, sat at a separate table with all of Dolly's sixteen-year-old friends, cracking loud jokes, boasting about being the first one to soon-be-getting-on-a-plane, and pretending to be bashful about his Bon Voyage picture which had appeared in *The Hindu* newspaper the day before.

Just before taking his sisters home, Falguni had crept up to him with her almond eyes brimming with tears. 'Promith me that ssomorrow you will only danth wiss me,' she said determinedly. But Babo, patting her dainty, milky hand, said nothing; gave her a mischievous wink, and left her to worry all day about his intentions.

Since then, they'd been passing secret messages back and forth through the willing and eager conduit of Meenal; the messages getting more and more fervent as the day of Babo's leaving approached. Along with Trishala's ring, Meenal had also pressed a long, tear-stained letter from Falguni, who promised that she would not *path a thingle day in happineth* till Babo returned to her from London.

Last night Babo had looked at his sister Meenal like he'd never looked at her before. She wasn't beautiful. There was nothing very special about her at all. But she had that aura that only a young woman overflowing with innocence could have. Something so heartbreaking, it made him want to reach out and claim it for himself. It was nostalgic, looking at a girl like that – her clear face and untouched body draped in a chiffon sari, the puffy short sleeves, the hair tied back in double braids with ribbons.

All these events – even this moment with Meenal, were entering the annals of *Last Times* for Babo. Months and years from now he'd think about his sister like this on the terrace, looking at him wistfully with tears running down her cheeks, asking when he would come back to be married, and what if she were married before that? He would remember the magenta bougainvillea cascading out of the terracotta flowerpots, the air mostly still and quiet, telling her briskly that nothing in the world would happen until he returned. He remembered believing it, too, while they stood there, sister and brother, their feet on the red-brick terrace – Meenal, whose temporarily waif-like frame would disappear soon after her much anticipated marriage, and Babo in his crisp white kurta pyjama, his fingernails cut and filed, his hair glistening with the coconut oil that Trishala had lavishly anointed while listing the temptations he must resist while he was away: meat, alcohol, tobacco and most importantly, women.

Lilaj-bhai was trying to get the family organized. As soon as he'd seen the Ambassador roll through the departure gates, he had walked towards it jauntily with a foxy, betel-stained smile. He knew if he played his cards right, he could make a killing with the Patel family: families were at their weakest on occasions of departure and arrival. Deaths, births and marriages figured highest on the emotional range, of course. What were photographs after all, but a desire to capture some of those emotions, trap the feelings so you could pull them out later to marvel at?

Marriage was the greatest occasion of leaving and arriving. The girl departs one house and arrives in the other, and likewise, the family of the boy is, in a way, leaving an old life and entering into another. These moments that occupied the cusp were what Lilaj-bhai lived for, because this was when human beings were willing to forget about hard things like money and expense. And this moment here, with the Patel family on the pavement of the Madras Meenambakkam Airport, was an event Lilaj-bhai could plunder.

While Lilaj-bhai set up his equipment, Prem Kumar pulled Babo aside and slipped him his most prized possession – the locket of his grandfather, Babo's great-grandfather, Kunthinath Paras Kumar Patel, whom Prem Kumar admired for two things: refusing to take up arms against the British because of his belief in ahimsa, and living a life of the highest virtue (eating only two meals a day, taking care of all the stray animals in the village and dying without any of his neighbours being able to whisper a single word of malice against him).

'Your mother wanted me to give this to you, son. I hope you will wear it with the dignity that your great-grandfather did. And I hope it will give you the strength to make the right choices.'

The locket was a platinum globe the size of a fifty paisa coin with a faded reproduction of Lord Mahavir inside. Ba, Prem Kumar's mother, and the grand matriarch of the entire village of Ganga Bazaar, had given it to him on the occasion of her husband's death. She had meant it to be a symbolic passing over of reins. It had been Trishala's idea to give the locket to Babo for good luck, and as a concrete reminder of

14

home, although Prem Kumar knew that even if the locket possessed any ability to pass on guidance and virtue to its wearer, it would be wasted on Babo, who was more likely to wear a Dev Anand-style cravat around his neck than an old-fashioned, religious pendant.

Prem Kumar, who had a penchant for sayings, had initially thought to tell his son something especially historic at the final moment of farewell: *All humans are miserable due to their own faults, and they themselves can be happy by correcting these faults*. But now that the moment was here, Prem Kumar, realizing his wife had been right after all, found the words too solemn and artificially constructed, and allowed them to slide back down his throat.

Babo, standing close to his suitcase labelled with his cousin Nat's address in London – NUMBER 172, FLAT B, BELSIZE PARK ROAD – looked at his family as though he were never coming back. Despite all his youthful inexperience, he knew that after this moment, things were going to change far beyond what he could imagine. He wanted to take each member of his scattered family and press them close to his chest, hold them there and make them realize the moment too.

Perhaps he would come back to Madras one day and everything would appear to be the same: the sky might meet the sea like an old lover; the people pushing past the railings towards their unknowable futures might still smell of dust and tobacco, rosewater and jasmine; the air clinging to his clothes might still be as heavy as tar. His family might even be lined up in a similar fashion: Prem Kumar in his beige safari suit buttoned up to the neck, Trishala in her giant-sized maroon sari flapping about like a tent in a storm, Meenal and Dolly like twin dolls in matching outfits, winking and sticking their tongues out at him. And Chotu, standing apart from them all, concentrating on the giant metal birds on the runway. They might all still be there, waiting for his return to free them. But

Babo could feel himself changing already. He knew he was going to forsake all this for something else, something larger, something which for the moment he couldn't touch.

For the moment he would stand with his family in the morning light with the sun shining through the rain-laden clouds. He would let Lilaj-bhai say, 'OK, E-sherious look now please,' or 'E-shmile please,' and take pictures of them together; stiff as dummies in a store window, arms at attention at their sides. And gradually, as they relaxed and lost consciousness of the camera, there would be pictures of Babo's gleaming teeth and his family smiling along with him, as though it were the most natural thing in the world – to let this boy fly away from them for the first time in his life. Far far away. Zing zing zing in the sky.

2 Under False Skies

It took Babo three months and five days in London to forget about Falguni. There had been a lot to deal with since his arrival, and pining for a large-breasted girl with a lisp from Madras was only working as a deterrent to his ultimate goal, which was, as his father repeatedly reminded him every time he wrote or telephoned, to get the gold medal for the advanced course at the Polytechnic, and to make himself indispensable to Joseph Friedman & Sons.

In any case, Falguni's letters were getting increasingly and irritatingly sentimental, demanding replies and declarations of love that Babo, with his current schedule, just couldn't keep up with. How could he begin to describe his new life to her, or to anyone in his family, for that matter? It was all so utterly different from what he'd expected; nothing at all like the English movies he used to cut classes for and watch with his college friends in Madras. There were no Alec Guinnesses or Humphrey Bogarts walking around in London. No Gina Lollobrigidas. At least none that he could see in the London City Council hostel in Wandsworth where his cousin Nat had dumped him.

To start with, Nat and his wife Lila hadn't even picked him up at the airport. Babo had waited, holding tight to his suitcase, senses on high alert. Every five minutes he looked down at the face of his new HMT watch to see if it was still working, and finally, after confirming that he had indeed been waiting for three hours and fifteen minutes, he found a sardarji taxi driver who agreed to take him to Nat's address in Belsize Park for £3 – which was all the money he'd been allowed in foreign exchange by the Indian Government. In the forty-five minutes it took to reach their flat, Babo had worked himself into a teary-eyed rage, because he was already broke, and because to arrive in a new place with no one to greet you, was surely an inauspicious way to begin.

'Where were you?' shrieked Babo, to a surprised Lila, who answered the door. 'Didn't you get the telegram from Papa? I don't understand. You're my family! You were supposed to pick me up.'

Nat and Lila hadn't received the telegram. They'd been informed that Babo was due to arrive at some point, but the exact details of that arrival had gone astray. 'Doesn't matter,' said Nat, somewhat too nonchalantly for Babo's liking. 'You're here now, isn't it?'

Nat had grown fat during his time in London. Babo had last seen him four years ago at his wedding in Baroda, at which point he'd been a regular, plumpish Gujju boy with a regular head of hair. Now, though, he looked to Babo like a cabbage – devoid of any character, his features flattened into oblivion, and his hair, whatever was left of it, swept into a scary comb-over. To compensate for these deficiencies, perhaps, Nat talked louder and faster than before, and during the course of tea and snacks, he delivered Babo his second googly of the day. 'Well,' he said, reaching for his fifth vegetable cutlet, 'We ought to sort out some accommodation for you, don't you think?'

'What do you mean? Won't I be staying with you?'

'Look at the size of this place!' said Nat, gesturing to the grubby walls of the bedsit with his chubby arms. 'There's barely enough place for Lila and me as it is. Besides, this is England, Babo. In this country, they don't live like sardines,

18

not like back home where it's all family-shamily all the time. Day in and day out, eating, sleeping, shitting in each other's faces. You know what I mean? No privacy, only lunacy. I tell you, it's the best thing about this country. Give it a few months and you'll learn to enjoy your time alone. In fact, you'll be thanking me.'

Even though Nat eventually proved to be right, Babo never really forgave him for turfing him out of Hampstead – haven of tycoons and film stars – on his very first day, and depositing him in the London City Council hostel in Wandsworth, henceforth the LCC, with only a loan of £5 and an *A–Z* to keep him company. His room was half the size of his parents' bathroom in Sylvan Lodge, and it was windowless. If he stretched out his hands he could feel the partition cloth that separated his space from the next fellow's, and if he stretched further, he could potentially topple the glass of teeth that would surely be sitting on the side table next door, because the average age of an LCC occupant was seventy.

On his own side table Babo kept his wristwatch, locket and a limited array of toiletries (toothbrush, tongue cleaner, toothpaste, shaving cream and brush, soap and hair oil which would later be exchanged for Brylcreem). The rest of his possessions – two suits, four shirts, one pair of trousers, four pairs of underwear and socks, two ties, family photos and Falguni's letters – he fitted into his suitcase and stored under the bed. In his briefcase, he kept his passport, wallet and work papers. The one pair of Bata shoes he owned, black and perfectly polished, he removed and kept by the door as soon as he entered the room. For this room, and for a steady diet of toast, tea, boiled vegetables and custard, Babo would pay £4 15s a week, nearly half his weekly salary.

On his first morning in London Babo was up early, making his way to the communal toilets before anyone else so he could do his business in peace. He had with him the plastic mug that Trishala had insisted on packing because she'd heard that English people used scraps of paper to clean their bums instead of washing them, which Nat had later affirmed. After dressing and eating breakfast, Babo walked to the offices of Joseph Friedman & Sons according to the route he'd mapped and memorized from the *A–Z* the night before. He was so excited, his stomach kept doing jiggly-wrigglies, and halfway there he thought he might have to turn around just to use the toilet again. At 8 a.m. he arrived at the office reception with briefcase in hand and bowels subdued only to be told that no one from Exports had arrived yet. By the time Fred Hallworth finally rolled in to pump his hands up and down and say, 'Wonderful, just wonderful to meet you,' Babo had emptied and restored the contents of his briefcase a thousand times, and had started a letter to his father which began: *Dear Papa, in England it seems, the first lesson I am to learn, is the art of waiting.*

'Let's take you up to meet Joe, shall we?' said Fred, ushering a bewildered Babo all the way to the eighth floor to the chairman's office, where old Joseph himself was sitting in a swivel chair, smoking a pipe.

The chairman took one look at Babo and said, 'You've brought the Indian summer with you, Bob. Is it all right if I call you Bob?'

'Yes, of course,' Babo blinked, not knowing what an Indian summer could possibly mean, but it was something he'd hear repeatedly over the next few months.

'And when would you like to start working for us?' old Joseph boomed.

Babo stood in front of him, beginning to feel a bit hot in his blue wool suit. 'Today?'

'Don't you want to take a few days off, son? Get to know London a bit before you settle in for the daily grind?'

And that's when it all came pouring out: Babo's money woes; the cab driver, a fellow countryman who'd gypped him; his own cousin who hadn't even bothered to pick him up at the airport – all of it in clipped, heavily accented English sentences, until the chairman, grasping the breadth of Babo's distress, got up from his chair and planted fifty quid in Babo's sweaty palms, saying that this was just something to start him off – it was a lot of money, sure, but he could see from Babo's face that he was hard-working, and that he'd be nothing but an asset to the company. Furthermore, if he needed anything else, he shouldn't hesitate to bother Fred Hallworth about it.

It was a kindness Babo hadn't expected. 'I'd still like to start today, sir,' he said, before leaving the room, clutching the fifty quid tight.

Fred Hallworth turned out to be Babo's great protector and champion in London. He was responsible for getting Babo's photograph printed in the company's September newsletter, with the headline 'WELCOME TO JOSEPH FRIEDMAN & SONS DHARMESH PATEL', which Babo promptly cut out and sent home to his father, knowing that Prem Kumar would place it lovingly in his file along with his college certificates, *The Hindu* Bon Voyage photograph and the company's formal letter of employment.

There was something about Fred that was instantly likeable. He was a big, bearded man with hands like stone crushers and a voice that matched the pace and turbo of the zippy MG he tore around in, but he was also a surprisingly good listener, and in those early days, Babo found it comforting to be able to pile some of his concerns into Fred's pliant, available ears. Fred had been to India many times, and he'd been supplying cement and raw materials to Prem Kumar for so long now, Babo felt he was the one person who understood exactly where he was coming from.

Every day they ate lunch together at The Brewer's Inn, and every day Fred joked, 'Fancy a pint of bitters, Bob? Or some steak and kidney pie?' knowing that Babo would only laugh good-naturedly and say, 'Not today, Fred, I think I'll stick to my regular,' which was a cheese sandwich and orange juice.

It took Babo a long time to stop calling Fred Mr Hallworth. It was easier if they were out of the office, but in the domain of Joseph Friedman & Sons, Babo always slipped back to the well-honed show of reverence he was used to reserving for his elders. The lack of rigidity between generations in England took a while to get used to. Back home for instance, Babo couldn't imagine sharing a cup of tea with one of his professors, or addressing him by his first name. Imagine! *Oh! Hello, Harindranath. Good morning, Subramanium!* Unthinkable. More unthinkable for a teacher to light up a smoke in class, and for a student to follow. Yet, this happened regularly at the Polytechnic. Babo, despite his rebellious leanings, had at first been uncomfortable with the whole scenario because years and years of being a closet smoker had made it impossible for him to enjoy a fag in public. But, as Fred rightly pointed out, when in Rome, one should do as the Romans do. So, Babo trained himself to adopt the English custom of smoking during class until it began to seem like this was the way things had always been.

Everything was so continually surprising to Babo during those first few months in London that when he sent news home, he didn't know where to begin. *England is an amazing country*, he wrote to his grandmother, Ba, in Gujarat. *There are parks everywhere – all over the city. Sometimes, while walking to work, I get a strong smell of wet leaves, which in this season are turning colour and falling, and somehow it reminds me of Ganga Bazaar after the rains, and of course, of you, Ba.*

To his father he wrote about the preciseness of English life. *You would like it here, Papa. Life here is very orderly. Cars go in straight lines, no one uses the horn, they have zebra crossings where all traffic stops automatically so pedestrians can travel safely, and there are absolutely no animals on the road at all – not even dogs! Some adjustments are harder to make of course; the food, even English people will agree, is horrible, and the weather, I'm still finding very cold. Also, life in the LCC is very dull. It's full of old fogies who do nothing all day but play cards. There are a few young fellows who live here, but they smell unbearably because I think they only shower once a week and live in the same clothes day in and day out. Anyway, the good news is that Mr Hallworth is going to arrange accommodation for me at the YMCA in Croydon, where for only 15 shillings extra, I can get a larger room with a window and a washbasin, and the same weekly meal plan. There's also a billiards table and regular Scrabble nights, so I'm looking forward to it as I'll get to make friends my age and it will make me feel less lonely.*

Being on his own was one of Babo's biggest challenges. All his life he'd been surrounded by people – family, friends, neighbours, servants. And while technically the upstairs bedroom in Sylvan Lodge had been assigned to him, he never actually slept in it alone. Chotu invariably dragged his mattress upstairs, or sometimes shared the bed with him, and when cousins came to visit, which was fairly often, a whole gang of children would spread their sheets on the floor and keep each other awake by telling ghost stories all night.

In London, by the time Babo finished his classes at the Polytechnic at 8:30 and made his way back from Elephant & Castle to stomach a few boiled vegetables and crawl into bed, the feeling he was left with, more than any sense of moroseness, was a stultifying boredom that he'd never experienced before. The only thing that salvaged those early evenings for him was listening to the Hitachi transistor that Nat had managed to wangle from work. It was a peace offering, which Babo had grudgingly accepted, and given place of prominence on his side table. Late at night, while the geriatrics snored and rattled around him, Babo tuned into the All-India Radio Station and listened to the news and the occasional Hindustani recital, low and long, because it was the only immediate connection he had to home.

Apart from the loneliness, Babo despaired about the food. He couldn't understand how something that had been so irrelevant to him in the past could suddenly become such an obsession. The canteen ladies at the LCC felt sorry for him because he was frequently ill and getting skinnier by the day. To compensate for his meagre main courses, they loaded him up with double helpings of custard and rice pudding, but still, Babo dreamed of food. More than Falguni, more than his family, Babo dreamed of food. Every morning he'd wake up hungry, wishing it was Friday, because Friday was pay day, and Friday was when Fred took him to The Star of India for a good feed: vegetarian thali for Babo and mutton vindaloo and butter naan for Fred.

Once in a while, Babo would go all the way to Lewisham, to the house of one of his Polytechnic friends, Bhupen Jain, a fellow Gujju from Kenya, whose wife, Mangala, made the kind of food Trishala used to make at home. And at weekends he'd park himself at Nat and Lila's, where the plan was for them all to cook together, except Babo was so bad at it, they suggested he do the washing up instead.

Babo would report all this to Trishala (except the vindaloo bit, which would upset her unnecessarily) because he knew that her main concern was food: was he getting enough of it, and was he keeping healthy? It was also Babo's way of letting his mother know that people were being kind to him, and that he wasn't experiencing antagonism of any sort.

A week before he'd left for London, one of Prem Kumar's card-playing friends, Vimal-bhai, had come over and launched into a story of his own son's experiences in England. 'Babo beta,' he'd said, 'When you go to England, you mustn't worry if somebody calls you a darkie, OK?'

'Why?' asked Babo innocently, 'I am a darkie ... See!' he said, pointing to his nut-brown arms.

'But they mean it in a not-nice way, son. Anyway, you don't take it that way. You don't let it affect you. You just get on with what you're going there for. That's the only way to beat them at their own game.'

Vimal-bhai's advice had greatly agitated Trishala, who wondered whether Babo, with his over-sensitive nature, would be able to cope with any kind of aggression. But Prem Kumar had pooh-poohed her concerns, saying that Babo would have to develop a thick skin if he was going to succeed in a foreign country.

In fact, Babo had never once felt threatened in England. Everyone he'd met so far had gone out of their way to make him feel comfortable. If anything *had* been disappointing, it was Nat and Lila's lacklustre welcome, which Babo made sure to recount in full to his parents. Later, Babo would sever all connection with his cousin and his wife, but that was for a treachery that was still to come.

To Falguni, Babo's initial letters were all about how he was aiming to get rich quick by winning the football pools. The place where Nat and Lila lived was the ugliest building in Hampstead, but it was owned by an Indian who used to work in a petrol station, and had won the Treble Chance after fifteen years of playing the pools. Babo calculated that if he set aside a small amount every week for coupons, he too could eventually buy property in London. When Falguni pestered him about possible dates for an engagement, Babo felt his stomach go thud thud very dully – no jiggly-wrigglies or excitement of any kind. He responded by saying how amazing it was that so much could happen in the little time he'd been away from her.

After a while, twelve weeks and five days to be exact, Babo's letters to Falguni finally came to a stop. About the time when he moved premises to the YMCA in Croydon, something big happened in his life, and when that thing happened, Falguni, who'd been fading fast, was irreversibly dethroned. Babo's last letter to Falguni would be blunt and pitiless: *For reasons that I can't explain right now, I suggest that you forget about me and carry on with your life. What you imagine between us will never happen.* And with that off his chest, Babo made a solemn fire in the washbasin of his new room, determined to burn all evidence of his past love so he could begin this new phase of his life untainted.

What happened to Babo on 25 November 1968, when he saw her standing in the doorway of the canteen in her white mini-dress, with a twirl of red ribbon in her hair, was a familiar feeling. He'd had it when he'd seen Falguni with her newly grown breasts at Navratri, and he'd had it recently at the Dominion Theatre when Liz Taylor batted her Cleopatra eyes at him. Babo was used to falling instantly in love. It was what he'd done throughout college – run away to the movies to see Meena Kumari or Sharmila Tagore smouldering in their shimmery clothes with their kiss curls and chori chori looks, singing *Akele akele kahan ja rahen ho? Where are you going to alone?* But this was different. This was a real-life girl with the tiniest gap between her teeth, smiling at him and saying, 'So, I meet the culprit at last.'

Babo would find out that her name was Siân Jones. That she'd been working for the company for a year as one of the chairman's secretaries. That she was from a small village in North Wales. That her father worked in a limestone quarry and her mother taught at a primary school. Later, Babo discovered that Siân looked most beautiful when she was drunk. That when she thought no one was looking, she had long conversations with herself. That the reason she'd come to London with her best friend Ronda was because she wanted something bigger than what her little village in Wales could offer.

For now, though, all he could say was, 'What do you mean?'

'Well, you're obviously the reason why we're having to up our sugar ration around here,' said Siân, pointing to the over-brewed cup of tea on the sideboard, to which Babo was adding his fourth spoon of sugar.

'I've been spying on you for a while now,' she said, laughing. There were little crinkles in the corners of her green eyes. To Babo, she looked like a fashion model out of *Vogue* magazine – her lithe 5 foot 5 inch frame leaning against the doorway like a feather.

'So, where are you from?'

'India.'

'I know, silly. I saw you in last month's newsletter, but where in India?'

'From Madras. It's a city in the south, on the coast. I grew up there, but originally my family is from Gujarat.'

'Sounds lovely. You'll have to tell me all about it sometime.'

Ba-ba-boom, ba-ba-boom, ba-ba-boom boom boom.

'Hey, I have to take this up for Mr Joe, but my friend Ronnie and I are having a party at our flat this Saturday. You want to come by? It's 38 Canfield Gardens, right by the Finchley Road tube. See you there.'

And with that, she was gone, the twirl of ribbon in her hair fluttering like a red Monarch butterfly out of the canteen into some other space that Babo wanted to immediately follow her into.

That Saturday, Babo, who had never been to a proper party before, arrived at Siân and Ronnie's Finchley Road flat with a bottle of Peppermint Schnapps. 'Should I take some flowers?' he'd asked Fred.

'What? To some girl you met for two minutes in the canteen who casually invited you to a party? Erm, no, Bob. You want to take a bottle – any kind of alcohol will do.'

Babo hadn't planned on tasting alcohol that night, never mind getting drunk; it just happened. He'd been sitting on the couch, nursing a tonic water, wondering when would be a good time to leave so as to catch the last tube home, when Siân plopped down next to him and said, 'Let's try some of this stuff you brought us, shall we?'

Babo didn't have the heart to explain what he'd had to explain to so many people before: that he was a Jain; that Jains weren't supposed to eat meat or drink or inflict violence on anyone or anything; that his mother would rather go blind than see him like this – with a girl, smoking a cigarette, about to down half a bottle of Schnapps. But, 'OK,' he said, 'Let's try it together.'

By the third shot, Babo felt like he was on fire. This must be what love feels like, he thought: a burning. A burning that starts in your stomach and spreads to the rest of your body, filling you up with the smell of peppermint and making you light. Siân, laying her soft, auburn head on his shoulder said, 'You're nice, you know? Really nice. I could tell from the minute I saw you. I'm glad you came.'

Babo wished she would lean against him for ever. He wanted to reach down and brush away part of her fringe that had fallen into her eyes. 'I hope you don't think this is too forward,' he said, 'But would you like to go for a movie with me sometime?'

After a lot of back-and-forthing Babo decided on *Dr Zhivago* at the Curzon Soho. 'Are you sure?' asked Fred, 'Isn't that a bit too heavy? Wouldn't you be better off with something like *The Graduate* or *Some Girls Do*?'

Babo winced. 'No no. Omar Shariff, Julie Christie, it will be perfect.' He'd seen it the week before by himself, but he wanted to see it again with Siân just to see if she'd cry in the same places.

That evening, as they sat in the pensive gloaming of the theatre with their hands entwined like serpents, Babo felt something growing inside him. It was the city opening her arms to him at last, saying, *Welcome, welcome to London town*. And afterwards, when they went back to Siân's blue-walled bedroom to lie down on the bed and undress each other, Babo would lie there next to her, not knowing what to do, but with a feeling growing inside, filling and filling him.

He had never been this close to a woman before. The most Falguni had allowed was hand holding, and once, just once before he'd left, she'd allowed him to kiss her on the lips, but even then, she'd kept them clamped shut so his tongue couldn't explore that lovely, lisping area of her mouth. Now, with Siân lying next to him – her body, naked and white, exposed to him like a wheat field to the wind – Babo could only gape with wonder, too scared to touch in case she should disappear, or suddenly turn into sand.

Later and later, though, he'd get the hang of it. There would be fumblings and premature ejaculations. 'I'm sorry, so sorry, it's just that you're so beautiful, so incredibly beautiful. Can we try again?' And Siân would nod, guiding him, until Babo learned to hold her long and hard while the trains screeched by beneath them.

'I want to try meat,' Babo announced to Fred one afternoon. 'I'm serious. Anything. You suggest. If I want to live in this country – and I do! then I need to learn how to eat meat, isn't it? You tell me, Fred, can I afford to keep falling sick like this? Can I afford to be unhealthy?'

'Slow down, Bob. What's going on? You know I can't do that. Your father will kill me. Besides, this is your religion, your tradition. Why do you want to change anything now?'

'Because I'm in love with her, Fred, that's it. I want to marry her, and if I'm going to marry her and live here in London, then I'm going to have to live like people here. I can't keep holding on to these traditions. It's too difficult.'

Fred wasn't entirely convinced but he started Babo off with a poached egg anyway. 'Better take it slow, mate. No meat as yet, just eggs, and after that we'll raise the bar with some sausages and bacon.'

Within the month, Babo had eaten his way through the food chain, discovering that there were things that suited him better than others – corned beef in sandwiches he quite liked, and shepherd's pie with lots of gravy. Sometimes, when Fred ordered something particularly distasteful like liver or ox-tail soup, Babo would raise his head from his plate and say miserably, 'I thought eating meat would make the food better here, but it's just as bad, isn't it? All of it, whether it's vegetarian or not, it's just bad.'

'Afraid so, mate, but at least now you know you're not missing out on anything. Anyway, like I always say, you got to try, try and try again. You never know, things just might get better.'

And he was right. By the end of the year, thing were looking positively peachy. Babo had managed to gain five kilos and defy every one of Trishala's prohibitions: meat, alcohol and women – just like that.

3 All Straightness is a Lie

All her life Trishala had heard that English women were not beautiful. Nothing to worry about in that department. Babo, whose idea of beauty was Nargis – doe-eyed, lustrous and most definitely Indian – would not find white-skinned, horsy women attractive. No. She would not lose him to that.

But Trishala knew nothing about hubris, or knowing thyself, or any of the other ancient Greek wisdoms. She should have known better.

The morning she received the telegram from Nat and Lila, she'd been sitting on the kitchen floor with bitter gourds in her lap, very like how she used to sit in the first few years of her marriage, when she'd been desperately trying to conceive a child. It had been on the advice of her mother-in-law in Anjar, who suggested that holding fruits and vegetables close to the female genital area would help kindle fertility. Furthermore, if this didn't work, she was to tie a piece of red cloth around the waist of the neem tree which stood outside the bedroom, to ensure that the tree withered up and passed on its proliferating properties to her womb.

The morning the telegram arrived Trishala wasn't contemplating or hoping to conceive another child, obviously, but she was thinking of how best to prepare the bitter gourd, and also thinking how remarkable it was that the curlicue shape of the gourds reminded her so much of the new jewellery set she was trying to persuade Prem Kumar to buy for her from Bapalal's.

When she opened the telegram, she wondered at first whether she'd be able to read it with her basic 6th Standard English, or if she'd have to ask one of the children to help her. Alarmingly, the words made themselves immediately understood – loud and clear, throwing her into an irreparable state of turmoil, not unlike the turmoil she'd suffered as a young bride.

Oh, it was all coming back to mock her now. That one reckless night in Anjar when Ba asked her what good cradling vegetables in her lap for sixteen straight months had done her.

'What to do? Nothing is happening,' Trishala had said.

The problem had really been Prem Kumar. He didn't understand desire. When he returned at nights he touched her body with the same care with which he supervised the wiping down of his machines at the end of the day. He was careful with her different parts and compartments, never experimenting, knowing only what to put where and getting there in minimal time with minimal fuss. He couldn't know about desire because he didn't understand the body. He desired a son, yes; children, yes; a wife, yes; but it was the flattest, straightest desire in the world which started at a point somewhere by his toes and ran up the length of him to his head. It didn't diverge, refract, expand or explode. And there needed to be some amount of explosion if Trishala was ever going to get pregnant.

'If you are looking to hit a six run,' Ba told her, 'You're going to have to take the top position.'

So, one night, in the middle of those November thunderstorms of 1946, Trishala anointed herself with the potion of herbs and oils Ba had given her, while telling her (and this had been so unnecessary), that it would peak Prem Kumar's penetration powers. She elongated the corners of her eyelids with extra kohl to make them glisten like raindrops on the feathers of a crow. And then, when she heard the peacocks dancing on the roof, as Ba instructed, she raced out to the courtyard, opened up her nightie and let the rain fall on her breasts and trickle through the thin cotton while she danced like a siren from a legend. She even unbuttoned her nightie and stepped right out of it to make sure that the rain fell into her, making something grow in her as it did the earth.

Later, she aroused her comatose husband by placing his hand on her wet breasts and another between her wet thighs. She licked the tips of his fingers and guided them to places he'd never ventured before. She straddled him like a goddess in the throes of war and took from him the nectar that she needed.

Something had moved inside her on that November night of great passion and cunning. Trishala felt a child being conceived: a son, who would know and remember all these things; who'd believe that people were meant to love like this; to cling to a body in the middle of the night, to turn over in sleep and grope for the soft parts of another.

The next morning Prem Kumar and Trishala, both equally startled by the events of the previous night, convinced themselves it must have been a dream, and never brought it up with each other in conversation. Moreover, they certainly never attempted anything like it again. Besides, Trishala found she'd stored up enough fertility in the space of that one evening to give birth to three more children in a more conventional manner.

Seeing the telegram now, though, Trishala understood that sometimes we pay for the sins committed in this lifetime without the luxury of being able to defer them to the next. How could she be so surprised with the news that Nat and Lila sent? Hadn't she preordained this already? Willed her own Babo to stray off the path? This first-born, this child of desire – how could he have chosen any differently?

And yet, it was horrific. Impossible to bear! Trishala shut herself in her bedroom and prayed for an hour. She prayed to the adorable, the emancipators, the preceptors, the deans and the saints. She prayed for an answer to her misery, for surely this was misery, to have to trudge to Prem Kumar and show him this telegram.

Should she wait till he was home from the office, bathed and fed, settling with his betel-nut box for his one luxurious moment of the day? Drop the telegram in his lap while he was sitting cross-legged in his brown armchair and say, 'See! Read what your son has done!' Or should she run to him immediately and wail into his chest about how their beacon of light, their eldest joy, was soon going to become their greatest source of sorrow?

Trishala decided to wait.

Prem Kumar arrived home later than usual, irritated and exhausted from the daily arguments with labourers who always wanted more from him: more wages, more time off, more bonus, more than he could give. He walked in with his paint-streaked shirt, removed his chappals, marched straight to the bathroom for his evening ablutions to rid himself of the smell of turpentine, changed into his customary house clothes – dhoti and vest – placed his bottle-thick glasses back on the bridge of his fat nose, and parked himself on the kitchen floor, expectant and hungry for his dinner.

Trishala swished up to him, holding the telegram in her hands. 'News regarding your son,' she said peremptorily, plopping the telegram by his empty steel bowl.

Prem Kumar fingered the telegram with caution. He was of the idea that telegrams were dangerous things. Too often than not, they were the bearers of bad tidings, and this one was to be no different.

BABO SEEING ENGLISH WOMAN stop LOOKS SERIOUS stop WHAT SHALL WE DO stop

Trishala hovered like a suicidal moth beside her husband, waiting for his response. He looked truly surprised. Obviously, he hadn't given any thought to this as Trishala had. He'd thought of education, money, work. He hadn't set aside contingencies for emotion.

'What a fool boy,' he said simply, folding the telegram and placing it to one side. After a tense moment of silence, he snapped, 'Am I getting fed tonight or am I performing some fast that I don't know about?'

Trishala went wordlessly to the stove for the steaming vessel of dal dhokri and placed it on the hot plate. She scooped the soupy concoction into his bowl, filled his glass with warm water from the earthen pot and took her usual place by his side.

Normally, it was Prem Kumar's habit to wrinkle up his nose and find fault with whatever was placed in front of him. Melons and cucumbers made him burp; tomatoes gave him gas; too much salt gave him swollen legs; too little salt made his eyes water; food not cooked slowly enough or long enough made his fingernails develop white streaks; coconut in any form gave him a headache; and curds that hadn't set exactly right made his left eye twitch uncontrollably.

Sometimes, when his complaints became unbearable, Trishala would grow sullen and say that if he loved his mother's cooking so much, he should have married her instead. But mostly, she did things in secret, without her husband knowing – picking the best curry leaves, tempering the mustard seeds just so, carving out the rotten parts of vegetables and depositing them in the pit at the back of the house, making sure all the time not to harm a single fly or ant

35

in the preparation of Prem Kumar's meal, so they could both be righteously absolved of any wrongdoing.

Today she watched with extra trepidation while her husband ate slowly and efficiently, chewing each morsel repeatedly before slurping it down his throat. He finished the entire bowl without comment and waited. It was his habit to wait five minutes before deciding on a second helping.

'What a fool boy,' he said, again. 'Can I have some more, Trishala?'

She served him with anger this time. 'What a fool boy, what a fool boy. What a fool husband! Is that all you're going to say? Do you realize what this means?'

'Wife dear, I'm fully aware of what this means. It means that our son is incapable. That he is short-sighted and is looking only to the path on which he treads and the wall on which he leans. We will have to bring him back.'

'And what about all the money we've spent? What about his studies? What about poor Falguni?' she screeched.

'Trishala, please stop this senseless screaming. Nothing in the world means a thing if a man has no roots. Do you understand? Babo always had that streak in him. I didn't think he would act on it, but he has. He has strayed away from what he knows and accepted a different way of thinking. Once a man does that, he's already lost. But if we want to preserve any sense of respect for this family, he must come back. We've already arranged with Kamal-bhai and Meghna-behn that Babo will be betrothed to Falguni on his return. What will we say to them? We must think of family now. Nothing else. Money is not important. Education can be taken up anywhere.'

Jointly deciding that this was an emergency of the highest order, Prem Kumar and Trishala sent off a telegram to Babo the very next day.

MOTHER IN HOSPITAL stop SERIOUS stop RETURN
ASAP stop

This job done, they waited.

Babo had grown lazy about visiting Nat and Lila at the
weekends. While he still travelled the same route north every
Friday after class, instead of going all the way to Hampstead,
he got off at Finchley Road so he could spend his two free
days with Siân. Lila often telephoned at work to pester him,
'Are you really studying that hard, Babo, or have you found
yourself a girlfriend? Come over, na? We're making bhel puri
this weekend.'

Even Nat deigned to call once. 'Babo, are you all right?
Anything troubling you? Have we offended you? Done
something wrong? You'll let us know, won't you? Your bapuji
keeps writing to ask how you're getting on and I don't know
what to tell him because I haven't seen you in so long. Listen,
why don't you come over on Sunday? The West Indies are
playing Australia. I got a brand new transistor from work,
which is just A-class superb. What do you say?'

Babo went, grudgingly, out of a sense of obligation more than
anything else. Not because he felt they deserved it. No. They'd
abandoned him the day he'd arrived; he'd never forget that.
Besides, he was enjoying his 'alone' time as Nat had rightly
predicted, so why didn't they just take the hint and leave him
be? He went because he knew if he didn't, the next time his
father phoned, he'd have something to say about it. So to avoid
that headache, he turned up late on a Sunday morning and
hung around just long enough to eat some lunch, skulking and
looking at his watch the whole time. Then he dashed out of
the door saying, 'Aujo aujo, see you soon,' not even bothering
to mask the insincerity in his voice.

By the time he received the telegram from his parents
in June, Babo and Siân were well on their way. Barely a

month after their meeting, at the 'How Exotic Can You Be?' Christmas party at the Finchley Road flat, Babo had leaned into Siân while dancing to Otis Redding's 'Sittin' on the Dock of the Bay' and said, 'Charlie Girl,' (for he'd taken to calling her that), 'I hope you know that I love you very much, and that I intend to marry you.'

Babo was dressed as a prince from the Arabian Nights – moustache and beard grown especially for the occasion, and a proper turban borrowed from a Rajput boy at the hostel. Siân had come as a belly-dancer in billowy red pants and a glittery boob tube with smoky black kohl around her eyes. They made a fine picture: Babo and Siân, starkly contrasting with each other, their features neither blunt nor sharp; their full lips and soft skin.

For New Year, Fred had invited them to his club in Surrey for a dinner-dance casino night, where Babo made a killing on the one-armed bandit. It was exactly like in his dreams – money spluttering out of the machine, ka-chink ka-chink – except these were only pennies, not enough to buy himself a property in London, but enough to give his travel fund a substantial boost. 'Well, you can't stop now, Bob,' Fred had said, 'You've got to keep going. Maybe move on to Black Jack?' 'No, no,' said Babo hurriedly, collecting the coins and taking them to the exchange counter like a good Gujju boy, 'I've had enough now. I know when to stop.'

All through the New Year, Siân and Babo made plans for what they would do that summer when Babo was finally free of his Polytechnic classes. They were planning to hitchhike all over Europe, starting with Germany, because Babo had found out through his extensive network of friends at the YMCA that to get the best youth hostel discounts and cheapest train fares, you had to join the German Association. Siân found an old Baedeker's in a second-hand bookstore, which for a while became their most treasured possession. Babo and Siân spent most weekends canoodling on the couch saying *Ich liebe dich* to each other, dreaming of all the places they were going to explore together, and how they were going to be changed by these places.

On the Saturday before the telegram arrived, Babo and Siân bumped into Nat and Lila at the Everyman Theatre in Hampstead at a showing of *Guess Who's Coming to Dinner?* 'Well, hello, hello,' said Nat, trundling over and planting his arms around Babo's neck. 'You've become a stranger to us these past months, Babo, and I can see why,' he said, looking appreciatively at Siân. 'Is the lovely lady a work colleague or a college friend?'

'We work together,' said Siân, extending her hand to Nat and then to Lila. 'And you are Babo's cousins?'

'Yes yes, all in the family. So, what are you doing after the film? Why don't you come over to our house? We are only nearby.'

'OK,' said Siân, 'That's very nice of you to offer,' even though Babo was squeezing her hand desperately, trying to signal otherwise.

'Didn't you want your cousins to know about me? Is that what this is about? Am I supposed to be a secret?'

'Of course not,' said Babo miserably. 'You just don't understand. Things are so different in my family. These people are supposed to be my cousins, but they're just waiting for me to do something wrong. They revel in it – other people's miseries. Anyway, now they know, so there's nothing to do but go along with it.'

'Oh, I see. So there's something "wrong" with me now, is there? Some cause of misery. Tell me exactly what it is, because I can try to rectify it, really.'

'It isn't that. It's not about you at all. Well, OK, maybe it is. You see, I'm expected to *do* certain things as the oldest child of my family, as the son. My parents have huge expectations of me. One of the things I'm expected to do is marry this girl they've chosen for me ...'

'Ah, ah, ah,' Siân interjected, because Babo had already revealed to her in great detail the whole Falguni story. 'Correct me if I'm wrong, but you chose her too, didn't you?'

'Yes, yes,' Babo snapped. 'But that was a long time ago and so very different from anything I feel for you. I just don't know how I'm supposed to go about this. What I'm supposed to tell my parents and when, and how. I don't want that idiot cousin of mine blurting out anything before I get the chance to say anything to them directly. They'll be disappointed, of course, but they'll see when they meet you, they'll see how wonderful you are, and how right we are together, and in the end, I'm sure it's only my happiness they'll think about. I love you so much, my Welsh Valley Girl. I love you. Never doubt that.'

'Well, if that's the case,' Siân snapped, 'I suggest you write a letter to your parents explaining the situation. It's only right.'

But before Babo got around to writing the letter, Prem Kumar's telegram arrived.

Nat and Lila had correctly surmised that 2+2 in this situation added up to 10. It was Lila's idea to send the warning telegram.

'It's our duty, Natvar,' she said to her husband, who thought Babo was quite right to get some of this young-blood thing out of his system before having to go home and carry out the inevitable.

'Let it be, Lila. It will work itself out. It will fizzle like a faulty firecracker. They are from different worlds. East is East and West is West and never the twain shall meet. Why should we involve ourselves?'

'Don't East is East faulty firecracker me! I'm going to send a warning to Trishala-behn because I couldn't bear it if we were accused later of failing in our duty.'

'Oh, duty-shmooty,' Nat muttered. 'Fine, you send it. Do your duty and then come and rub your husband's legs. That's your duty as well.'

Nat was the first person Babo telephoned when he got his father's telegram. 'Nat, I have to go home. Ma isn't well. I got a telegram from Papa today but he doesn't say anything about her condition except that it's serious and I'm to go home as soon as possible.'

'What? What do you mean, "condition"? You mean to say Trishala-behn is sick?'

'Yes,' shouted Babo impatiently. 'It's serious. Papa doesn't say what it is or how serious it is, but only that I'm to come home right away.'

'Arre, relax, Babo. I'm sure it'll be OK,' said Nat, in that too-nonchalant way of his that so irritated Babo. 'Bapuji is probably overreacting, but anyway, we should arrange a ticket for you right away. Shall I call my friend Somnath, who works for Air India? He can try to get a good ticket for you. Do you want me to do that?'

Later that evening, Babo skipped his class at the Polytechnic for the very first time and went straight home with Siân after work. 'It's always the fear, you know?' Babo whispered as they lay in bed together. 'That something will happen when you're far away. Don't you worry about it? That something bad will happen to your family when you're too far away to do anything about it?'

'There's no point beating yourself up about it, my love,' Siân said, stroking the taut brown canvas of Babo's back. 'You'll just have to wait till you get home and see how things are then. Don't worry about me, darling. We've got our whole lives to go travelling together. You just get home soon and be with your family. They need you now.'

4 Sad to Say I'm on My Way

Babo's departure from London was as unobtrusive as his arrival. When he left, it was on a day of pouring rain. There were no photographs, no garlands. There was only Siân in corduroy bell-bottoms and a rust orange shirt, her small rounded breasts heaving against the wall of his chest, her bony shoulders and arms flung around his tangle of curls.

'Here,' Babo said, pushing a bottle of Chanel No. 5, which he hadn't had time to wrap, into Siân's hands. 'I wanted to give you something,' he said, looking embarrassed because he'd never bought anyone a present before.

The prodigal son had exactly the same luggage he'd started with (minus a few letters, plus a pair of Wrangler jeans). On the journey back, though, hanging awkwardly around his neck, was his great-grandfather's antique locket, which Babo held as if it were an amulet, capable of bestowing wonders. On the flight home Babo was tense. He paced about at the back of the plane smoking cigarettes, thinking about his mother lying in some hospital bed in some awful pea-green operation gown, her eyes cleared of kajal, the bindi from the centre of her forehead rubbed away. He thought of her dying of some horrible, unnameable disease, and out of pure desperation, he held the locket close to his chest and began chanting the prayer he'd given up on a long time ago: 'Namo Arihantanam, Namo Siddhanam . . .'

By the time he arrived in Madras he'd been travelling for over twenty-four hours. He didn't know what time or day it was. His nails were gnawed down to the nub and his eyes looked like a watercolour version of their usual metallic grey. When he saw his father at the arrival gates, grim-faced, and in the same beige safari suit he'd worn to drop him off nine months ago, Babo wondered how he could look exactly the same when so much in their lives had changed.

'Papa,' he said, bending to touch Prem Kumar's feet, tears sliding down his face.

'So, you've come home, son,' said Prem Kumar, touching Babo's head and then taking his luggage purposefully over to the taxi.

Babo asked, after what he deemed a reasonable time of waiting, 'How's Ma?'

'She's much better. We didn't know how she was going to be for a while, but she's much better now. News of you coming home has helped. She hasn't talked of anything else for days.'

'You mean she can talk?'

'Of course, what did you think? That she was lying in a coma somewhere?'

'Well, no. Well, yes. I thought she was very ill.'

'It's nothing that a doctor can't cure.'

'Oh, thank God,' said Babo, as he began to look outside with eagerness for the first time.

Madras looked overgrown, like an adult man insisting on wearing small-boy shorts. After his months in London, it seemed dirtier, shabbier. There were new billboards and glossy storefront windows, but the flowers on the roundabout were dying and the trees were gasping for air. The traffic was moving of its own accord without paying heed to the coloured signals or the khaki-clad policemen waving their arms frantically at the intersections. And the people! There were people everywhere, slipping in and out of their lives for everyone to see. Babo, watching them as if for the first time,

43

saw how far he'd travelled, how it was no longer possible to be one of *them*.

Finally, they were driving down Sterling Road, past Taylor's Lane, where Babo used to play cricket and kabadi after school, and the Railway Employees Compound, where he first started smoking cigarettes with his college friends. Sylvan Lodge sat at the corner of the street, surrounded by droopy ashoka trees, perched like a wedding cake jhimak-jhimaking in a bright new coat of pista-green paint.

Trishala was standing at the gate with Meenal, Dolly and Chotu. They had been told nothing of their brother's affair. As far as they knew, Babo was coming home for the summer holidays. Selvam was looking on from his usual post, leaning on his cane stick, a red towel wrapped around his bald head to keep the heat away. Trishala was tugging him away from the gate because he was blocking her view. Babo thought how well she looked, not at all as if she'd suffered or was suffering from any illness. If anything, she looked a little haler and heartier than when he'd left.

When Babo got out of the car, Trishala, who had been smiling unrestrainedly until then, let out a towering scream. 'Look how thin you've become! Haven't you been eating anything? Didn't they feed you in that country?'

Meenal and Dolly stood around him shyly, as if he were a stranger who had briefly borrowed their brother's form. He looked different now that he was foreign-returned. His hair wasn't pasted down like before, it was more modern – a bit puffy, like a film star's. And his face looked different, too, leaner. That thin boyish moustache had been replaced with a French goatee, and his eyes were filled up with something – God knows what – but they weren't as soft as they used to be. Only Chotu pushed through boldly, demanding that Babo throw him up on his shoulders as he used to do. 'Oof, you've grown big,' said Babo, feigning hardship. 'Ma, why do you worry about my weight when you already have one son who's a heavyweight champion?'

Inside his mother's kitchen, Babo sat unsuspectingly with his siblings on the floor, eating all the things he'd dreamed about since leaving. From time to time his mother would stuff something in his mouth – a sugary yellow penda here, a deep-fried chilli bhajjiya there. Babo chewed, sitting cross-legged, using his fingers, savouring all the different tastes exploding in his mouth: pungent raw mango coated with lime, warm ghee-spattered chappathis hot from the tava, spicy mushy cauliflower stalks and jaggery-sweet dal.

As Babo felt the strength of his mother's wholesome food pass through his body once again, he tried to explain how vegetarianism was a strange concept in England, and Jainism as a religion, stranger still. He told them all about his saving graces – Fred Hallworth and Bhupen Jain, his friend at the Polytechnic, at whose house he enjoyed many a home-made meal. He said nothing of what the doctor had told him: *Son, if you want to survive in this country you better start putting a bit of meat into this body.* Nothing of how he desperately needed to survive in that country because he'd met someone in whom he'd found himself. He could talk with her about the injustices of war, the necessity of revolutions, and she could turn them into something as light as a summer breeze moving through a luminous green paddy field. He said nothing of how he'd begun his intoxicating and carnivorous adventures, or how he'd persisted with smoking.

And love? Babo said nothing of love. He sat basking in the comfort of his family – his opaque eyes shining and careening, careening and shining – while Prem Kumar, rummaging through his son's briefcase in the hall, removed his passport and hid it high on the cupboard shelf for safe-keeping.

On his first morning home, Babo was still disoriented from the journey. His dreams had been hurried and forced, and Siân had

45

been in them all, calling him back to her. Babo hadn't thought that coming back would make him feel this way; that after months and months of longing, he could find so little to call his own, as though his whole earlier life had belonged to someone else. All he could think of were Siân's green, saucer eyes, how he'd been accustomed to losing himself in them the minute he woke up. He wondered how home could feel like such an alien place when only a year ago all this had been his only reality.

Seeing his little brother, though, standing in the doorway with those broomstick legs and that matador middle parting with the flicks going to each side, managed to start a thump-thumping in his heart.

'Were you scared when Ma was ill?' Babo asked, patting the bed as a sign that Chotu should crawl up and join him on the bed, rather than hover in the doorway like a stranger.

Chotu looked at him blankly. 'I've grown three inches since you left and Papa says that before he knows it I'll be going to the factory with him. But bhai, tell me about the aeroplane flight. What does it feel like to be so high in the sky?'

Chotu ventured up to the bed and sat on the edge. When he saw Babo's suitcase lying open with the last-minute bars of chocolate thrown on top, his eyes widened quietly, patiently.

Babo tried again. 'So, when Ma was ill, did Meenal and Dolly look after you?'

'Huh? Bhai, what do you keep saying about Ma being ill? The last time was when she ate all those puris on Diwali at Meghna-behn's house. Thirty-seven puris she had and then she came home and vomited all night. Ha ha ha.

'Anyway, listen, do you know that Papa has found a husband for Meenal? He lives in Bombay, and he's a shipbroker.'

'Is that so?'

'Yes, bhai, but this is the funniest part – Papa hasn't said OK yet because his informant in Bombay told him that the shipbroker might have a limp.'

'What do you mean?'

'You know – he's langda in one leg, but he hasn't said anything about this in any of the negotiations. Naturally, Meenal doesn't want to get married to a langda fellow so she's been crying everyday. The Bombay informant is sure that he has a limp, though.'

'Don't be ridiculous.'

'God promise, bhai! I heard them talking about it during Sunday cards session. Vimal-bhai suggested that Papa go to Bombay himself and spy on him while he's doing puja at the temple. That's the best time to find out, no? When he's wearing a dhoti – because then his legs will be exposed, and Papa can tell immediately whether he's a langda or not. Can you believe it? Papa is going to Bombay and he's going to stay in a hotel and spy on him. I wish we could go too.'

Prem Kumar hid behind the door, watching his two sons, wondering what his next tactical manoeuvre should be. He had let Babo sleep his first night in innocence, believing that everything was as it should be, that his family were ignorant of his misdemeanours, while he had lain awake contemplating the roads and roads of untravelled path that were stretching out before him. These were hard times, and he had to prove to his family that he was capable of steering them through. Most importantly, he had to guide his son back to the three jewels of Jain wisdom.

Through the slim crack in the door, Prem Kumar could see Chotu's spindly legs dangling over the side of the bed, and he could feel Babo filling the room with the force he had carried from birth – as if he were the most important person in it. Prem Kumar still didn't know what he was going to say to his son. He had woken early after his restless night, taken the neem stick outside to clean his teeth, attended to all his toilet functions, recited Navkar Mantra twelves times, and was at the door of his son's bedroom at the appointed hour of 8 a.m.

'Chotu,' called Trishala. 'Go with Selvam to pick up iddlis from Hotel Annapurna for breakfast. Hurry up. Go.'

As Chotu disappeared down the stairs, Darayus Mazda's daily lament filtered through the air. *Oh! My family is breaking me into pieces. Oh! Here comes the great cloud of my family wanting to pick my bones and offer them to the vultures before my time . . .*

Prem Kumar, listening to this wailing, felt again a brotherhood with his Parsi neighbour. He understood too, the endless weight of suffering a family brought; the eternal ties that bound one to one's wife and children, and which obstructed the way to Enlightenment. But nevertheless, he thought, *Duty is Duty*, and muttering these noble words, he walked into his eldest son's room and froze.

'Papa?' Babo asked hesitantly. His father hadn't entered his room since? Since he couldn't remember. It was not a thing he did.

Prem Kumar felt like he was in one of those Hindi films that Babo loved so much, where someone was always dying or fighting or falling in love. In this film the father was entering the son's room, and each step forward was like a knife wound to the stomach. Tears were threatening Prem Kumar in a very real way and he struggled to fight them, because to go into battle with tears streaming down your face was a sure way to lose it. He had prayed in the morning, not for any favours, for it was against the Jain religion to pray for favours. He'd prayed for insight and the strength to rid his soul (and Babo's) of the thorns of deceit that had lodged themselves deep into their skin.

'Son,' he said, in his most solemn voice. 'We know about the girl. Natvar and Lila have told us. Why have you kept such a secret from us?'

In all families there is a time of awakening, when the self is detached from the body and one can experience one's family without actually being a part of it. Babo, because he was jet-lagged, and because his ideas of love were stronger than anything he'd ever had in his life, was experiencing such an awakening on the first morning of his return to Madras.

Here was his father, who'd always been a distant figure – a person who was never questioned, never touched. Here was he: raw and brash. There was no doubt in his mind of his righteousness, his love, his complete consternation at his bloody cousin who had done the unspeakable by snitching on him. Oh! The grudges were accumulating in Babo's mind like building blocks. They were falling one on top of the other – dhishoom dhishoom, crashing and colliding, leaving no room for anything else in his brain.

'There's nothing to explain then, is there, Papa?' said Babo. 'Except that I am going to marry her.'

Trishala, who had been perched outside the door all this time like an elephant trying to hide behind a potted plant, let out a squeal: a high-pitched, wronged-mother squeal. Bursting into the room, not on her cue (her cue came later in case Babo should need consoling once Prem Kumar had shown him the error of his ways), Trishala marched up to her son and gave him a resounding slap across the face.

'What about Falguni, huh? What about her, you selfish boy? Do you think of no one but yourself? What about Kamal-bhai and Meghna-behn whom we've promised ... Don't you deny it, you scoundrel, you knew that this was waiting for you. And now, and now ...' she spluttered, 'You go and find some white woman, some girl from God knows where to fall in love with, someone who doesn't know anything about us, our customs, our culture, nothing. Someone who is not even' (and here she paused for dramatic effect) 'a Jain? How can we accept it? You tell me, how can we accept it?'

Trishala was about to launch into another session of breast-beating when Prem Kumar stopped her and motioned her to sit on the bed. 'Your heart, my dear, please take care of it and sit down.'

Babo was suddenly empty. All the air had been sucked out of him. This is what it felt like to be turned inside out and thrown into the heart of a tornado. But he was strangely calm as well. Everything was out in the open now. Everything was ready to begin. He was tempted to launch into his own tirade. He had many tirades stored up for such days about parochial-mindedness and about God, but this wasn't the time or place to enter those murky territories. His argument was very simple. He was following everything his faith had instilled in him: maitri, pramoda, karuna, madhyastha – love, joy, compassion, tolerance. Ultimately, wasn't the purpose of life according to Jainism to realize the free and blissful state of our true being? To remove all bondages in the process of purifying the soul? Didn't his love for Siân purify his soul? Hadn't she put him in the most blissful state of his life?

'I want you to know that I'm going to marry her. No matter what you say, I'm going to marry her. You've already lied to get me here, you can do anything you want, but you can't take away how I feel for her. Her name is not white woman, it's Siân. I love her and I'm going to marry her and that's all there is to say about it.'

Prem Kumar felt the world loosening around him. From the moment Trishala placed that blasted telegram in front of his plate, and from the moment of waking from that first and only dream, he'd known that this business wouldn't end well. And because there was loosening, there was need for immediate hardening. Rock-stone-hardening.

'Fine, then, if that's the way you want it. But I've taken your passport away, so you can forget about going back to that godforsaken country of colonizers. Let's see how long this great love of yours lasts while you're on the other side of the world.'

With that said, Prem Kumar yanked Trishala off the bed by one flabby, bangled arm, and led her out of Babo's room, into the obliterating silence of Sylvan Lodge.

5 God Made Truth with Many Doors to Welcome Every Believer Who Knocks on Them

Barely a week after the passport palaver, the entire Jain community in Madras had heard about Babo's failure to keep good on his betrothal with Falguni Shah. News travelled like a virus, rapidly and insidiously, so that even Babo's grandmother, Ba, all the way in Anjar, had already heard some version of the white woman story before Babo got a chance to tell her himself.

Babo decided that the only place he'd rather be, other than back in London with Siân, was at Ba's house in Ganga Bazaar, where he'd spent all his childhood summers. To make this announcement, he marched downstairs at 8 a.m., where his family were gathered, putting on their assorted footwear for the day, and announced in his most self-righteous voice, 'I'm leaving tomorrow. There's no point trying to talk me out of it. I'm going to stay with Ba.'

To Babo the village of Ganga Bazaar in Anjar had always been a magical place where time ceased to have any meaning. He remembered going there as a child with his mother; taking the train to Bombay and then an onward train to Navlakhi Port, where they'd climb on to a dhow and cross the open mouth of the Gulf of Kutch until they hit the shores of Kandla. In his parents' time they had to take a bullock cart from Kandla to the village of Ganga Bazaar, but Babo only ever remembered taking a bus or a taxi for that final, exciting leg of the journey. The journey from Madras to Anjar took so long, and was so full of adventure, that Babo, thinking about it now, was filled with the idea that anything he wished for could happen.

It was exactly what he needed now. He was going mad in Madras. His father refused to speak to him, and had instructed the whole family to do likewise, although they flouted the rules when Prem Kumar was out of sight; Trishala especially, who waited till the house was empty before she settled in for her daily attempt to knock sense into her son.

'Beta, why don't you see Falguni one more time? Maybe if you see her, everything you once felt for her might return? It's been a long time. There's no harm trying, is there? You never know what can happen. Shall we do that? No need to tell Papa or anything. I'll just tell Meghna-behn to bring Falguni over, and if you still think it can't work out, then we'll forget about it.

'Do you want to see some photographs of other girls? Much prettier than Falguni, and cleverer too. See – how about this one? Pretty, no? Just like Saira Banu, her eyes are.'

And when all this judicious coaxing failed, 'Look, Babo, you can't sit like this for ever doing nothing and saying nothing.'

But Babo intended to do precisely that. He was building a wall around him to preserve his memories. Already, the picture of Siân in his head was slowly disappearing. It was hard to believe that not so long ago they'd been lying in bed, naked – Siân utterly touchable and sha-bing sha-bangable – talking about what they were going to see in Germany and beyond. And now, Babo was reduced to solitary pleasures in the bathroom with the help of his trusty hand, which offered temporary relief, but was nothing compared to the bliss of Siân's body.

He'd written to Siân every day, *every single day*, explaining the situation at home and reassuring her that he was steadfast in his love. But it would take two weeks before any of his letters reached her, and possibly a whole month before he heard back. Who knew what could happen between now and then? She might decide it was all too complicated. She might decide that Merv the Perv, the other curly-headed boy in the office, who was always flirting with her, or her ex, Clive the carrot-top, who was always sending her soppy letters from Nercwys, could do for her what Babo, so many thousands of miles away, could not.

Babo wished there was a quicker way to contact her. If he could just book a trunk call and hear her voice, he could let her know that he was thinking of her constantly, that their love would prevail. But Prem Kumar had unplugged the telephone and locked it away in the cupboard along with his passport. So Babo was left to do the thing he hated most: to wait. In a neither-here-nor-there limbo land, he was forced to wait.

All that remained in Babo's control were his letters. He armed himself with packets of foolscap paper and a dozen bottles of blue Brill ink, and locked himself in his room, where he wrote not only to Siân, but also to Fred, Bhupen and his friends at the YMCA, who were anxious to hear news of his return. There were projects waiting for him at Joseph Friedman & Sons, and a gold medal waiting to be claimed at the Polytechnic. There was an entire life which he had meticulously created in London. Babo wasn't about to relinquish that life so easily.

To combat his parents, Babo took on a mode of defiance they had never encountered in him before: he refused to cut his hair or shave his beard, boycotted meals, lounged about in his kurta pyjama all day, and sent Selvam out to buy packets of Gold Flakes which he smoked flagrantly on the terrace at all hours so the neighbours would be sure to see. He did all this, not only as a form of protest to his parents' foolish objections, but also to prove the determination of his love for Siân.

Only Chotu managed to penetrate Babo's stubborn walls. At night, he came upstairs with his pillow and blanket, and waited patiently outside the bolted door until Babo relented.

'Bhai, what are you doing? Can't I come in to sleep with you?'

'I'm writing. Go away.'

'But I won't disturb you, bhai, promise. I don't want to sleep with Meenal and Dolly, they ghus-phus the whole night and I can't get any sleep. Pleeeez?'

Finally, Babo would unlock the door and allow Chotu inside, but only if he agreed to sit in the room quietly with his lip zipped. Chotu watched in fascination as his brother, a whole ten years older than him, and with a life clearly more interesting than his, lay sprawled out on the bed filling pages and pages with his untidy handwriting, his hands smeared all the way up to his elbows with ink. What could he be writing to his girlfriend for so long? Chotu wondered. How many possible ways were there to say I love you?

A million, clearly, and Babo was going to find a way to say them all.

After a week of Babo's dissident behaviour, Prem Kumar and Trishala, realizing that their son meant business, negotiated a deal.

IF after six months Babo *still* wanted to marry Siân, they would accept her with open arms, provided they stayed in Madras, in Sylvan Lodge, for a period of TWO YEARS. After which, IF they wanted, they could return to London. And IF after six months, for whatever reason, things didn't work out, Babo would have to marry a girl of his parents' choice, and this subject would never be raised again.

'Are you sure about this?' Babo asked his parents, who were

staring at him like two owls on the sofa. 'No hanky panky, and backing out on your word if it goes my way?'

'No hanky panky,' Trishala repeated solemnly.

'And you'll welcome her with open arms? You'll treat her as you should? Like she's a princess who's coming to stay in your home?'

'Like a princess.'

'Fine,' said Babo, marching back upstairs, allowing himself the tiniest crack of a jhill mill smile. 'It's a deal.'

Prem Kumar would have the last word that night, though. Not spoken words, as he still wasn't speaking to his son, but written words, pious words, copied out from the Bible no less, to prove that he was a fair and open-minded man:

IN THE LAST DAYS, MEN WILL BE LOVERS OF THEM-SELVES, LOVERS OF MONEY, PROUD, DISOBEDIENT TO PARENTS, UNTHANKFUL, UNHOLY LOVERS OF PLEASURE RATHER THAN LOVERS OF GOD.

This, he copied out in terse, black capitals and slipped under Babo's bedroom door on the night of his second departure.

In the house of Prem Kumar's birth in Ganga Bazaar, Anjar, the doors were always open. It was a house without furniture, without clocks, where instead of chairs, wooden swings hung from the ceiling, and instead of tables, meals were eaten cross-legged under the shade of the jamun tree on the veranda. In the evenings, when visitors came to see Ba, jute mats were spread on the black stone floors in the room of swings to accommodate them all, and at night, after they left, Ba would lay her cotton mattress down either inside or out, depending on the time of year. Red garoli lizards lived and died on the walls of this house, chewing plaster, plop plopping softly, while peacocks howled on the tin roof above. It was a child's paradise, and at one point early in the century, fifteen people had lived in this house, but for some years now, Ba had lived here all alone.

Ba had been able to smell Babo all the way from Amroli. It was a special talent that had come to her in her fifty-third year when she lost her husband to tuberculosis and her knee-length hair turned white overnight. She discovered then that she could smell human defilements and devotions from over the hills and far away, which was a good thing, because she was an old woman now, severely diabetic, and her once bright, black eyes were slowly going blind. Ba believed it was life's way of compensating: to take with one hand and give with the other. This was the law of the universe – to remain in constant balance; which is why, no matter how many hardships she'd had to face, and there had been many, Ba had remained a true seeker, believing that no matter how bad the situation got, around the corner, salvation would appear.

'Tell me,' she called from her place on the front steps, 'About this English girl that has made a tyre puncture in your heart. Is she beautiful?'

Babo walked up to his grandmother and touched her feet to ask for her blessings. It amazed him, as it always did, how she had not changed since he'd last seen her. Ever since he could remember, his grandmother had looked exactly the same. 'She's not English, Ba, she's WELSH.'

'Welsh,' Ba repeated softly, savouring the foreign word on her tongue. 'Welsh. It sounds like a kind of wind – a wind that rushes through the forests and shakes all the leaves off the trees.'

Now that Babo was close to her and she could see him better, Ba touched his head and said, 'What's this? Is this the new fashion in England? To walk around like a jungli with uncombed hair? And this?' she said, tugging his beard, 'Is this the fashion too? Or is this what WELSH girls like?'

'It's my sign of protest,' said Babo proudly. 'I've taken a vow for six months that I won't cut my hair or shave until I see Siân again.'

'Oh! So you're on strike. Very good. But why do we have to suffer just because you are suffering?'

'Because I'm your favourite grandchild?'

'Oh yes, there is that. There is that indeed. Well, tell me. Tell me from the beginning. I want to know everything.'

Babo, on the first night of his self-imposed exile in Ganga Bazaar, told his grandmother the story of his last nine months in England. He told her about the meeting in the canteen and the gap between Siân's teeth which he'd wanted to disappear into for ever; about how his life in London, which had been quite difficult at first, had changed the minute love entered: it had suddenly become light and fragrant, like rose petals constantly falling around him from the sky. He told her of the conspiracy and lies spun between Nat and his parents to get him to come back home; about how every day spent away from Siân made him feel like he was shrinking into a handful of molecules, smaller and smaller, until he thought he might just vanish.

Babo laid his head down on his grandmother's lap – a childhood position he returned to with ease, and talked and talked while Ba, leaning against the walls of her house, murmured 'Mmm' and 'Then?' intermittently, her moon-white hair shining in the night.

That night, everything around them was silent. It was as if all the animals and trees that normally sprang to life after the sun went down, were waiting to hear what would unfold next in Babo's story. Babo and Ba stayed like this for a long time, building a bridge of remembrance between them, until at some point after midnight, Ba smelled the rain coming. 'We better get inside,' she said. 'You've brought us thunderstorms for the next three months.'

* * *

In Madras Prem Kumar was getting increasingly impatient. He lay awake at night, wondering if he'd done the right thing by allowing Babo to go to Anjar. He wanted his family as it used to be: seamless. And he wanted Babo returned to them, flaws and all, as he was in the past, because this new Babo had torn the space around them, shown his family the door. Prem Kumar, facing the obstinacy of this door, didn't know if he must stand still and wait, or push it open and make some noise.

He wrote what he thought was a conciliatory letter to his son, telling him that there was a polish for everything that became rusty, and that the polish for the heart was the remembrance of God. Babo did not respond. If Prem Kumar had had any inkling of the kind of talks that were taking place between grandmother and grandson, he would have quickly summoned Babo back. But as it was, he was unaware, once again, of how a woman continued to bend Babo out of shape.

Babo's mornings in Ganga Bazaar were spent in Anjar's only hotel, Zam Zam Lodge. Every day, before walking over to Zam Zam with his writing materials, Babo went to the courtyard in the back, drew a bucket of water from the well, stood in his VIP briefs and used whatever concoction of turmeric and hibiscus flower Ba had left out for him to wash with. Ba was always up at four, bathed and dressed in her staple white widow's sari. She swept and swabbed the house, clearing away the red, rubbery garoli lizard skins and the blue-green peacock feathers. By the time Babo emerged from his deep, dream-ridden sleep to offer his services, she would have already decorated the entrance to the house with powdered rice flour patterns, tended to her plants and prepared the food for the day. 'Go, go,' she said. 'Go write your love letters. There's nothing to be done around here.'

Babo walked quickly through the small lanes of Ganga Bazaar so as to avoid being waylaid by a well-meaning neighbour. At Zam Zam he sat at the table reserved for him, chain-smoking and drinking endless cups of sugary tea, filling at least ten front and back foolscap pages with heartfelt declarations. He pressed frangipani petals between the pages or sprigs of tulsi, and wrote day after day of their enforced separation because it was the only thing that kept him going. Siân in return wrote back, not quite as profusely as Babo, but more poetically, in neat blue aerogrammes that the postman Neeraj-bhai delivered.

Some days, when Babo was feeling particularly morose, he went wandering the poorer parts of Anjar, trying to convince himself that there was greater suffering in the world than his. He told Siân of all this, too: of the destitute beggar woman who sat outside Zam Zam with no one in the world to look after her, and the toothless men who sat under the trees, watching the world spin by from the tops of their rolling eyes. It terrified him to see people this way: old and alone, without the slightest trace of happiness on their face. *How do human beings lose themselves so entirely?* he wrote to Siân, and then proceeded to try and answer his own question.

For Babo it was simple. He needed to be with Siân and wake up with her every morning. He wanted to be light and free like they'd been in London, skipping down to the cinema if they felt like it or spending all afternoon in a sha-bing sha-bang haze. Mostly, he didn't want his life to slip by him. He didn't want someone telling him how he should live. He wanted a life that would be like lightning, striking the surface of water – joyous and ethereal. He wrote pages and pages like this. And Siân, from her Finchley Road flat, responded in simple, inky words: *Dreamed of you last night. You came to me and we washed together before eating in the light.*

When Babo walked back to Ba's house in the afternoons, he let the rain soak through his skin, holding his writing materials and Siân's letter for the day secured in a plastic bag against his chest. If it was a good day, Neeraj-bhai would hand over one of Siân's aerogrammes with his 100-watt smile, and Babo would take this to the back of the house, where a bamboo grove had sprung up in the recent showers, and stay there, turning the sheet of paper over and over in his hands until he had memorized every word.

Some days Siân's letters went missing in the entrails of the Indian postal system, and then, Neeraj-bhai appeared at the door with a hangdog look on his face and each of his triple chins juddering, to say, 'Sorry, boss, no luck today, maybe tomorrow?'

In the evenings the ladies came in all shapes and sizes to sit around his grandmother like a fanfare of trumpeter swans. Every day they had a different project: Mondays they cooked in giant steel containers to feed the poor at the Amba Mata temple; Tuesdays they powdered red garoli lizard skins so they could make tie-dye scarves for themselves; Wednesdays they made pappads for Poppat-bhai's shop; and so it went. Through the week there was talking, singing, wailing, complaining – a real hullabulla of voices and competing emotions. But rising above them all was always Ba, with that girlish voice of hers, her laughter tinkling over them like bells.

When the women of Ganga Bazaar saw Babo spying on them through the window grills, they shouted, 'Ey, Babo, come and sit with us! What's the matter? Are you frightened of us? Or is your heart breaking too much?' And Babo, without so much as a *hello–goodbye excuse–me–please* turned from them and disappeared into the back room to revise the chemical formulas and equations he'd learned at the Polytechnic.

Only after the women left, and the jute mats had been rolled away, did Babo venture out to Ba. They sat together with their dinner under the early stars, talking above the sound of the crickets in the undergrowth. Ba told him stories of the ancestors Babo knew so little about. She related all the love-marriage scandals she knew of, including her own sister's story – how she ran off with a Muslim boy from the neighbouring village never to be seen again, and the story of Kanta-behn's son, who fell in love with his dark, pockmarked cousin, Damyanti. Babo listened intently, secretly believing that his love-story scandal was going to be the most beautiful of them all.

'Did you love Bapa?' Babo asked one night, during the week of the British postal strike, when there had been no news from Siân for ten days. 'When he died, did you ever feel like you would die too because he was gone? Did you miss him in that way?'

'It wasn't like that for us, Babo. There are so many ways of loving a person. With us, it was a gentle thing, nothing like what you're feeling now. What you have, it's something rare. We call it Ekam. They say that you may experience it once in your life or not at all. Some have described it as entering into a dark cave with no beginning or end. Some have said it's like feeling your heart burn on a slow fire. This Ekam, once you have it, you'll believe that you can eradicate all the guilt in the world, all the pollution and misfortune.'

'Did you ever feel this Ekam with anyone else?'

'No,' said Ba wistfully, 'That remains for me in another lifetime. But your other grandparents – your mother's parents – they had this special kind of love. The people in Ganga Bazaar still talk about it – the love between Ravi Lal Mehta and the temple cleaner Gurvanthi. It ended in tragedy, though. She died giving birth to your mother, and he went a bit mental after that.'

'Wonderful,' said Babo. 'What if my love ends in a tragedy too? What if she grows tired of waiting, and I'm left with this feeling, my whole life unfulfilled. I will die, surely I will. Tell me, Ba, can you die of sadness?'

'You can die for all sorts of stupid reasons, including a scorpion bite,' said Ba, gently leaning over to flick away the scorpion that had been edging closer and closer to Babo. 'Now go to sleep. You've found what most people never find. Be happy. And Babo,' she said, before turning to blow out the lantern, 'You really must stop watching so many movies. You're getting very filmy these days.'

'It's a burning, Ba,' Babo whispered, before falling asleep. 'Love is definitely a burning.'

As Babo slept, Ba stroked his curls and thought of her husband, who had died early of a disease they had no names for then, and her son, who seemed to have entered the world with a set of values and a consciousness she'd played no part in shaping. These were men she should have loved, but in reality, their absence or presence had played such a peripheral role in her life. This grandson, though, with all his desires – he stood at the centre of her world, and she wanted him to be released. She wanted his love for the Welsh girl to unfold like a lotus and gleam. It would happen. The girl would come. But until she did, Babo would have to wait, and Ba would wait with him; standing, breathing, knock knock knocking beside him.

6 This is the World. Have Faith

38 Canfield Gardens,
London
15 October 1969

Darling,
  I received your letter dated 28 August only yesterday! I hope you've managed to sort out the beard situation by now! I can't believe you're being so stubborn about this, love. I mean, hasn't everyone already accepted that I'm going to be in India by the end of the year, unless something dreadful happens between now and then – like one of us dies or something? There's no need to keep your vow – which was, in any case, something to antagonize your parents with. I think Ba is quite right in saying that if you're going to persist with this beard business you must take care to groom it instead of letting it go helter-skelter. I must admit, though, I would love to see what you look like now. I can just picture you two under the trees – Ba oiling your beard and then plaiting it up! What a sight you must look. My own little sadhu.
  What very different lives we're leading at the moment. In some ways, I'm jealous of you. You're cocooned in some magical place, buoyed up with this incredible love that your grandmother seems to emanate. Meanwhile, I'm in London – and the talk here is WAR. All the time. Vietnam, the Middle East. I'm sick of it. Nixon and Spiro and that fool Harold Wilson. Shameful. There's a National Moratorium anti-war demonstration taking place in

Washington DC today – I'm sure you must be getting regular bulletins even in Anjar – so I won't prattle on except to say that it continues, this unrelenting greed and violence.

Otherwise, though, I'm exactly where you left me. Commuting between Finchley Road and Wandsworth. In some ways, the routine of the week helps keep my mind occupied so there isn't much time to brood. It's the weekends I dread. And to think – that used to be 'our' time, our special time. Ronnie tries to get me to go out on a Friday night, or at least on Saturdays, because I've stopped letting her have parties at the flat – mean, I know, but I can't cope with parties at the moment. The most I can manage is a quiet meal or a movie. Otherwise I spend all my time in the room reading or taking long walks on the Heath. Ronnie has been great, though, my all-in-one support system. She bought me the new Beatles LP the other day – Abbey Road – which is fantastic, and has been consoling me no end.

I miss you, my darling. What can I say? It's been three long months and I thought it would get easier. I thought knowing I was going to fly over to India in December would settle things down. But there's so much uncertainty; so much that still needs to be said. I suppose the main issue for me is my parents. They haven't yet replied to my letter of a month ago, so I'm going to call them this Sunday. I should have called them in the first place. I was just being cowardly, thinking I could ease them into the situation with words. Who knows what they think about all this? They've always been so cryptic, anyway, so closed with their emotions. It's the Calvinist way, I suppose, and they've trained me to be the same. But sometimes I just wish we could scream whatever we had to say at the top of our lungs. It would be better instead of all this tight-lipped nonsense.

I've decided to hand in my notice and go to Nercwys as soon as possible. No doubt there will be active attempts once I'm there to change my mind (smallpox reports and Christians killed by tribals and whatnot) but I really want to spend some time with my family before I leave. Who knows when I'll see them again? I had lunch with Fred yesterday (who sends a big bear hug your way). We went to the Brewer's Inn – your old haunt – and I even ordered a cheese sandwich and orange juice in your honour! I thought if I'm going to live with your parents in an all-vegetarian household for two whole years, I'd better get some practice in.

Oh, love! It's so difficult. So incredibly difficult. I thought I'd be better at this. I mean, I'm the practical one of the two of us, but it's been impossible. I hear you in the flat all the time. Sometimes, I really think I'm going mad because it sounds like you're calling me from another room – and of course, I foolishly run to follow the voice only to be confronted with emptiness. More and more emptiness. Whenever the doorbell rings I think it's you – come back to surprise me, all the way from India. All I have are your letters and the few photographs we took while you were here. My favourite is the Christmas party one. The way you're holding me – your arms around my waist and your cheeky turbaned head poking over my shoulder, smiling so brightly at the camera. It feels so long ago that you held me, that you were here, and our life was moving beautifully along.

I guess the part that hurts most is how you were wrenched away. How upset your parents must have been to make up a lie about your mother being ill. ALL just to get you home! Taking you away from your studies and work, just to make sure you don't get more entangled with ME! I can understand their concerns, that they want you to marry someone from the same background and culture – my parents have similar concerns – but still! I do wonder how I'll fit in when I come to India. I worry about so many things – the language, for a start. I know you said that everyone else speaks English, but it's your mother I'm going to be spending a lot of time with – and how's that going to work if we can't even speak to each other? I suppose I'll learn a bit of Gujarati along the way if I'm hearing it all the time, but how's it going to be for your family, who have to open their house to me, who have to like me? It's just not part of my world, you understand? It all works very differently here, and frankly the idea of living with them is a bit terrifying. It would be OK if we just had to see them once in a while, and if we had our own little place, just for the two of us. But this way there won't be any relief. I'll feel like I'm on display all the time . . . Here I go, being negative again. I'll stop.

Guess what, though? There is some good news to report. The Polytechnic had their annual award thing the other night and I went along because Bhupen and Mangala said of course I must come, especially since YOU won the gold medal for the term, DESPITE having missed the last two weeks of it! I'm so proud of you, darling. Your professor – John Campbell, was it? The mousy one who's always smoking? Well, anyway, he came up to me afterwards and raved about you. They announced your name and said you weren't able to attend as you were out of the country, which made you sound very exotic and important indeed, and Bhupen accepted it on your behalf as you wanted. Anyway, it's lying in my knicker drawer now, so I'll be bringing it with me when I come. That should give your father something to smile about.

Let me know if you want me to bring anything else. You left in such a hurry, it's a shame you didn't even have time to take presents back for everyone. You must tell me what to get for the girls. I know you said that Meenal's favourite colour is pink – she sounds like a real 'girl' to me, and I think we'll get along just fine. But what about Dolly? What colour does she like? And what's she interested in other than playing in your mad neighbour's garage? She's seventeen now, surely she must be out of her tomboy phase! And Chotu . . . do you think he'll be awfully reluctant to share his treasured big brother with a woman? I've bought him some of those model aeroplane books that you said to get him, so hopefully that will divert him for a while.

Well, my love, it's late, and I'm beginning to feel the cold with no one to warm me up. Ronnie is yelling from the kitchen. It's another baked beans on toast night because neither of us can be bothered to cook. She sends lots of love, by the way, and says that while she may not be able to attend our wedding in India, she's going to organize a whopping party when we get back! She's been a real help – the only help, in fact. I've had no one to encourage or pamper me. Not like your Ba, who sounds amazing! I can't wait to meet her. Did she really say that to you the other day? That she thought she could smell me, and that I smelled like freshly cut grass? The Nercwys fields, no doubt. And did you tell her that you thought otherwise – that I smelled like the ocean to you? Maybe I smell of both? Who knows? I do know that if I don't have a bath and get changed soon, neither of you is going to want to get near me!

   All my love always,
   Your Charlie Girl

PS London sends its love too. It's not the same city without you.

She waited till four o'clock on Sunday to call. Her parents would be home from church and finished with lunch. Bryn would be sitting in his favourite armchair, contemplating *The Doctrines of Grace* or the crossword. Nerys would be out in the garden if it was a fine day; or if there was a spattering of rain, not unusual for this time of year, she'd be inside with her knitting, muttering to herself between the clack clack of her needles. If her brothers Huw and Owen were home, there'd have been proper Sunday roast with rhubarb crumble for pudding. If not, Nerys and Bryn would have made do with a few pieces of toast with grilled cheese and onion.

Siân tried to picture her parents in Tan-y-Rhos – the house she'd spent her whole life in until Ronnie and she had come away to London. Number 10 Tan-y-Rhos. It sat dead centre on the one street that ran through Nercwys; nothing to distinguish it from any of the other houses except for the front garden full of Nerys's prize-winning roses. Inside, it was the same as Aunty Blodwyn's and Aunty Carys's on either side. Same as Uncle Rhys's down the street and Aunty Eleri's at the top of the village. Same sitting room and kitchen plan; same three bedrooms and bath upstairs; same outhouse converted to coal shed in the back yard; same wooden gate; same windows; same view.

Siân had been trying to escape this sameness since 1962, when she'd sneaked off to the dance hall in Mold with her friends Ronnie, Gwenyth and Dee. There had been a band from Liverpool playing that night – four young lads with pageboy haircuts. Siân had danced right up close to them in her new tulle ribboned dress, and one of the singers, the sweet, serious-faced one, had winked at her while singing a song called 'Love Me Do'. Those boys would later become The Beatles, but for that night, they belonged to Siân. They were like beacons, all four of them – standing on top of a hill, light shining from them, willing her to fly, fly away, and Siân, looking around, had wondered where she could possibly go to.

And that's when the dream of London began. Because she held her whole life in one clenched fist: the fields and woodland paths, the streams, The White Lion, the post office, the village school, the battalion of aunts and uncles. And it wasn't enough. It just wasn't enough any more to let Clive, her red-headed boyfriend, touch the inside of her thigh while they sat at the newly opened Gateway Theatre in Chester, or to smoke hand-rolled Turkish cigarettes with her friends. Something had started growing inside her, something like a huge, teeming city with millions of people milling about in it.

This thing taking up space in her abdomen continued to grow until it felt to Siân like a sadness, old and displaced from childhood, come back to haunt her, like her brothers running ahead of her on a winter's night yelling, 'Come on slow poke,' leaving her to make her way back in the terrifying dark. She'd been waiting for this thing to reveal itself to her for so long now, for something to happen, for someone to say, *Come, come to where I am. Let's begin our lives.* And she would go. Because she hadn't begun her life. Not yet. Not here in Nercwys.

So when the letter of employment finally arrived from Joseph Friedman & Sons after months of conspiring and planning, Siân had been able to sit down with her family at the table and say, 'I've got a proper reason to go now, haven't I?'

Huw and Owen with their shirtsleeves rolled up to the elbows – their bodies short and stocky like Nerys, their faces spitting images of their father. 'Don't be daft,' Huw had said, 'How're you going to manage on your own?' And even Owen, who usually kept his own counsel: 'You and Ronnie are going to play house in London? This I have to see!'

'What I don't understand,' Nerys chimed in, with that tea-kettle boiling voice of hers that escalated whenever she was extra excited or nervous, 'is why you've got a bee in your bonnet about this, girl. What's the point?' And then she turned to Bryn, who had been impassive throughout. 'You talk to her. She'll only talk sense to you. Just ask her what's the point of it all?'

Bryn had seen it coming. For years he'd seen it coming. He hated the idea of Siân going off just as much as anyone, especially to London – a city he imagined to be full of sin and lost souls. He'd wished differently for her, of course, what father wouldn't have wished for his only daughter to remain in the village and fall in love with one of the local boys – a quarry worker like himself, or even one of those modern men with office jobs who commuted to Mold every day. He'd hoped that she'd get married in the chapel, buy a house nearby and raise children who'd come running to sit in his lap like sunbeams. But it wasn't going to be that way with Siân, was it? And part of him understood that it had nothing to do with her free will; that it was a grace calling to her.

Bryn understood all about the penalties of mankind's sin. He knew that the mysteries of being chosen didn't stem from any individual heart, but from the heart above. He tried convincing his wife that it wasn't such a bad thing for their only daughter to go out journeying. This had been the natural state of man since his Fall, after all: to seek out his ultimate purpose. And as long as Siân remembered that the primal source of all these things lay in the infinite and immutable love of God, she'd be all right; better still, she'd be saved. So he put his arms around his daughter that evening after supper, saying nothing, but meaning all of these things, giving her the release she needed.

And so she'd gone. Gone off to London and promptly fallen in love with a boy from India.

What was she going to say to them this time? That she'd be back after two years? That she was going to marry a man she'd known for six months? A man whose family had tricked him into going home and were none too pleased about Siân's existence on the planet. A man she couldn't imagine living without, but with whom she hadn't been able to share her fears. She hadn't told him, for instance, that she got jolted out of bed some nights, as though a charge of electricity were being passed through her – thinking *what if, what if* it is all a terrible mistake? What if she went to him and regretted everything? What if he tried to show her his life and she just couldn't see it? What if there came a day when she no longer lived inside of him, and she had to return, and there was no place to return to? Wouldn't it be awful to be saddled together? To have made such a hue and cry, only to let it go? And weren't they both too proud anyway, to allow people their sanctimonious we-told-you-sos: *We knew it wouldn't work out in the end. Like chalk and cheese. No chance of that lasting.*

No, there was no easy way to say it except to say it. The only thing to do was to call and hope it wasn't raining, so Nerys would be outside, and Bryn would have to be the one to raise himself from the armchair and pick up the phone. And then, Bryn, cradling the telephone receiver as though it were a small, dying bird might say something like, 'But we won't hardly get to see you, love.' And this, Siân thought, she could just about bear.

You must picture this: the wooden gates, the row of houses with the postage-stamp-sized lawns. A young woman standing at the gates with auburn hair blowing behind her, looking into the fields ahead of her as though this were her last chance, her only chance of making things right in her life. And she was going to go the other way. She was going to chase the pleasure.

The crash-bang feeling of home. Old skin waiting to be filled.

Siân, standing at the door to Tan-y-Rhos, surprising her father's sister, Aunty Eleri, who relished other people's problems like honey in her thumbs, who thought Siân was in over her head. Poor Aunty El, who'd come by for a cup of tea with her dog, Gwythur, whose eyes nearly fell out of the back of her head when she saw Siân standing there, pleased as pie. Her brother's last chick who she'd heard had a place in London and was making big city money, had given all that up and was now saying, 'Didn't Mam tell you, Aunty El? I'm going to India to get married.'

Every time she told that story later in her life, Aunty Eleri's doughy face would pinch up into disbelief; her eyes would roll full circle and then she'd say it, 'Just like Siân to do something like that. Standing there sure as eggs, as if it was nothing. Telling me she was going off to India to marry some bloke no one had ever met, as if it was the simplest thing in the world.'

It was Aunty Eleri who would soothe Nerys when Bryn and Siân couldn't find ways to reach her. It distressed her to see her sister-in-law like this: shocked beyond anything she'd had to survive so far. And she'd survived a lot: two world wars, the loss of five siblings out of fourteen, three stubborn children. But this, Nerys could not endure. Somehow, this only daughter deciding to abandon them made her so angry, she was afraid if she gave vent to it she'd never be able to speak again.

So there was a silence that weighed Siân down in Nercwys like never before. Only her father helped her escape. Together, they made day trips to Conwy Castle and the Valle Crucis Abbey to sit among the ruins as they used to do when she was a child. They packed egg sandwiches and coffee in flasks and drove off in Bryn's Morris Minor to sit under a poplar tree in some nameless valley where they read poems from Bryn's old, leather-bound volumes. And later, when Bryn read his daughter's letters about Madras, he would always picture it something like Swansea, the town Dylan Thomas called the most romantic town he knew – '*An ugly lovely town . . . crawling, sprawling, slummed, unplanned . . . smog-suburbed by the side of a long and splendid curving shore.*'

This is how it went. Six months of waiting. Six months of understanding the inner workings of faith and the outer spheres of the world. Six months of time: hundreds and millions of awakening seconds and sleeping minutes. Six months of aching stretched out like the Sahara: lickety-split, snippety-snip, jiggity-jig. Six months of fading and blooming, stopping and starting. Six months of love: a breath, a deluge, an eternity; a single flake of snow.

7 The Centre is Everywhere

Siân was travelling the breadth of the world, hoping for the circle to close. Should she cry now, after so much? Should she walk to the edge of the earth and agree to fall? What childishness was this? What stupidity? To leave everything behind just to see the sun rise the other way around. Just to see a man who will strip you bare.

Standing on the platform at Chester station, the connections were already beginning to slip away. The centre of Siân's life was being dragged from her and scattered. Nerys was holding her, weeping silently, as if the sorrow inside her was so great she could only hold on to it for so long before finally letting it go like a life-sized breath of air. The brothers Huw and Owen were standing by the bags, looking at her with a mixture of wonder and dread: *Go on then*, they seemed to be saying, *Go on then, if that's what you want. Run into the dark. See if we're going to follow you.* And Bryn, who sat across from her all the way to Euston and then to Heathrow, watched from beneath the broad expanse of his forehead until the aeroplane floated down the silvery runway, up, up and away, until his daughter finally disappeared like a prayer into a cottony wedge of sky.

All the eleven hours to Bombay, the Indian businessman sitting beside Siân put his pillow up against the window and slept soundly. Then, as the plane began its descent, he awakened as if by some internal tuning, cleared his throat, adjusted his tie and lifted the shutter to look outside. 'Ah,' he sighed, with great satisfaction. 'Back home at last.' And then looking over to Siân, 'Your first visit to India?'

'Yes. Yes, it is.'

'And what is the purpose of your visit? You are coming in search of God? Some spiritual adventure? You are looking for Maharishi Mahesh Yogi, or someone like this? Something you cannot find in the West?'

'No. It's nothing like that.'

'You are coming to travel, maybe? I hope not alone. Pretty lady like you travelling alone, not a good idea.'

'No, no. It's not like that.'

'I see. Then what? Tell me, please. I am very curious. I am meeting all kinds of people in my profession, people from all walks of life. Basically, I am statistician.'

'I'm getting married,' said Siân, smiling despite her wish to remain aloof, because it was the first time she'd said it aloud to someone of no consequence; someone who couldn't berate her or try to alter her decision.

'Really!' the statistician gawped. 'Really! Well, that's wonderful news, just wonderful. Tell me, why isn't your "To Be" accompanying you? Are you going to be having some romantic English wedding in the jungles? Back to the Raj and all that?'

'No. I'm getting married in Gujarat to a Gujarati man.'

'My God! Don't tell me. But I'm also a Gujarati man. Devesh Shah is my name.'

'That's nice,' said Siân, trying to look beyond him to the country that was finally taking shape beneath her in broad swathes of brown and green, flanked by the ocean on one side, and by a cherry-silk sky on the other.

Siân and Babo were moving closer together. They were nearly there; ready to meet in a cluster of seven islands on the edge of the Arabian Sea. Bombay – queen of all India's cities: a city of cages and slums, film stars and vagrants. A city Siân would want to forget about as soon as she landed in it because it wasn't the India of her imagination. She'd imagined tree-lined avenues and mint-green houses. Lizards and peacocks. Not this. Not this.

Babo was standing in the arrivals lounge *sans* family, smoking cigarette after impatient cigarette. He had the keys to a new, orange-coloured Fiat Padmini in the top left pocket of his favourite linen shirt and a single red rose in his hand. His hair and beard remained uncut, untended, and by virtue of his unconventional but rather debonair look, a small gathering of uniformed airport staff had huddled around him trying to determine which famous person he could be.

Siân saw him first – *and it was gone* – just like that. The pain in her abdomen, the last thin line of crossing, the ability to be this and that, her whole previous existence. *Gone*. Because she was going to fall into this man. She was going to wrap her legs around his waist and drape her body around him. He was going to be so full of her that he wouldn't be able to remember what his life had sounded like before she came to him.

'Look at you!' she cried, running towards him in her home-made maxi and headband, looking every bit the hippy spiritual-seeker her fellow traveller had suspected her of being. She was moving fast, faster, faster, until she was upon him, bony shoulders and all. And Babo, smiling and crying simultaneously, said, 'Look at you, look how much more beautiful you've become!'

By the time Babo collected Siân's bags and packed them into the dickey of the car, it was time to drive off appropriately into the sunset. *I must not get lost*, thought Babo, trying to concentrate on the roads, which seemed to have altered now that the light was fast disappearing. Siân, who had been talking incessantly about the flight and the journey from

London, had suddenly gone quiet. She was looking out of the window, on to the streets.

Babo removed his hand off the gear lever and reached into Siân's lap to extricate one of her hands. 'You mustn't get upset. You promised not to get upset.'

'Look at them,' Siân whispered, as they drove. 'All of them settling in for the night together. Tiny children, dogs. Whole families. Who could imagine such a thing? And they have nothing. Not even a cardboard box for shelter.'

'I warned you about this, Charlie. Didn't I tell you it would be this way? Madras isn't as bad as Bombay, of course, but still, it's there. It's everywhere. There's no escaping it. Don't worry, you'll get used to it eventually.'

'Oh, I don't think I could ever get used to this,' said Siân, looking back in the direction she'd just flown in from. 'How could I?'

And then, as if to cement the tremendous displacement she was already feeling, Babo drove his new car into the entrance of the very opulent Taj Mahal hotel. 'Oh my!' said Siân, looking up at the façade of the building, at the turbaned men with twirly moustaches who were greeting people as they stepped out of their chauffeur-driven cars. 'I don't think I've ever seen a hotel as grand as this in all my life, never mind stayed in one.'

'Well, don't get carried away,' said Babo, 'It's only for one night. Tomorrow we drive to Anjar, where things are, shall we say, more rustic. And after the wedding, we go to Sylvan Lodge, which is no five-star hotel either. I decided to splurge on your first night in India since my monetary privileges have been reinstated.'

As they walked through the lobby and took the elevator upstairs to their room on the fifth floor, Siân finally unpursed her lips. 'I feel like everyone's staring at me.'

'That's because they are,' Babo grinned.

'Why? Do I look funny? Have I got something stuck in my teeth?'

'No, silly. Because they like staring in general, and because you're beautiful.'

Inside the room, Siân removed her shoes and walked past the bed on to the balcony, which had wooden shutters and which looked out on to a large archway.

'That's the Gateway of India,' said Babo, positioning himself on the bed with a beer from the minibar. 'Built to commemorate the visit of King George V.'

Siân stood there and watched, hypnotized by the pigeons and by the horse-carriages that were taking young lovers for a ride. All along the horizon ships were putting down their anchors in the harbour, and to the right, the streetlights glittered, defusing all the darkness of the pavements below. 'There's so much life,' she said, turning to Babo, 'So much – it feels like it's bursting from within. There can't be any place like this in the world.'

'Come here,' said Babo, 'Come, sit by me.'

But Siân continued to stand pensively on the balcony, trying to reconcile herself with her surroundings. It was so strange. She was finally here. Babo was sitting just metres across from her, looking as though the six months between them had never happened, as though they'd always been together. But Siân could feel the distance growing in her again, she could feel that little something in the pit of her stomach, quieter now, but there.

'Come here,' said Babo, suddenly standing on the bed, doing his best cave man imitation, beating his chest and howling. 'I want to devour you. I'm ready to devour you now. I'm going to have my way with you,' he said, leaping off the bed to grab Siân, who squealed uncontrollably as he pulled her away from the balcony and flung her down on the pristine sheets.

Now that he had her underneath him, Babo burrowed his face into her and said, 'I'm going to say it again. Look at you, you beautiful thing. Coming here so bravely all by yourself. All the way to India to marry ME! I must be the luckiest man in the world.'

'And the hairiest,' said Siân, giggling. 'I have to say, this is pretty sexy,' she murmured, running her fingers through his hair. 'But this,' she said, tugging his beard, 'This is pretty scratchy, so there's going to be no devouring until this is gone.'

That evening, before the first of three sha-bing sha-bang sessions and a romantic room-service dinner for two, Siân led Babo to the marble bathroom where she made him sit on a stool, shirtless, in front of the gilt-edged mirror, while she lathered up his beard and snip snipped it away. Babo felt nothing but her hands and the hot soapy water. He felt the sharp grazing of a razor against his cheeks, clearing and clearing, until a soft, new brownness shone through.

In Anjar, Ba was waiting for them to arrive. She could smell the Welsh girl coming closer. They were making a picture again: Babo and Siân in their orange Fiat – the 'Flying Fiat', as it would later be known. Siân was wearing a peacock-green sari that Trishala had picked out for her, and which one of the receptionist girls had secured into place with safety pins. Babo was trussed up in a bodacious rust suit with a rose in his buttonhole, Nehru-style. He'd had the mane mushrooming around his head tamed by the hotel barber, and then they'd set off. Babo and Siân: ready to rattle the cage of the world.

The rest of the Patel family were in a train moving towards Anjar, too. Meenal and Dolly, who had been playing wedding-wedding for weeks on the red-brick terrace with the neighbourhood girls – each fighting to be the beautiful foreign bride – twitching and chirruping in their new chanya cholis. Chotu – sole boy, coerced into playing his brother at these make-believe weddings – dressed for the first time in long pants instead of half-pants, spinning a cricket ball in his hands. Trishala, seriously practising what her husband had taught her to say, 'Hellooo. Nice to meet you. So nice to meet you.' And the children, giggling themselves silly, hearing the stiff English words from their mother's mouth.

Here they were: Babo, clean-shaven, triumphant; Siân, glorious and soft like buttered honey. Shoulder to shoulder, clear and bright. Meenal, Dolly and Chotu, watching from the dark pupils of their eyes, wondering if their lives were going to have as much masala as their brother's. Trishala reconciled: 'Pretty, quite pretty,' she conceded to her husband, who was busy outdoing himself, because hadn't Babo warned them? Hadn't he written to say: *If she doesn't feel right, if it's all too much, if she feels the slightest bit of discomfort, you'll have to let us both go.* And didn't they want to hold on to their son now that he was standing here in his grandmother's house, open like a kingdom, showering the village of Ganga Bazaar with his requited love?

Where was Lilaj-bhai? Shouldn't he have been taking pictures? So that later, their children could marvel at their parents: *how young and beautiful and strong and proud.* Later, wouldn't they want to see where they came from? Which nose, which stubborn chin, which forehead, which finger, which wisp of curly hair, which touch of eye and skin and blood had mixed and mingled to make them?

Because they were standing now: Babo, Siân, Prem Kumar, Trishala, Meenal, Dolly, Chotu, Ba. And here were the missing spaces: Nerys, Bryn, Huw, Owen. This is how it was on that chilly brand-new 1 January morning in Ganga Bazaar, Anjar, in 1970, with the family gathered around. A wedding of miniscule size but momentous proportions.

Here was Ba watching from the bamboo grove, thinking *finally, finally.* Because these two looked to her like a dream from another life. She took them aside and told them three things: *look to the sky every day* – for the sun and the moon signify eternal devotion of husband and wife; *look to the sea* – for love flows deep and you must be prepared to flow deeper; *journey like the fish and the birds* – because it is only those who agree to their own return who can participate in the divinity of the world. She poured honey in their palms and made them drink from one another so they could give sweetness to each other all their lives. Then she revealed a lore for fulfilling desire in seven nights.

To Prem Kumar and Trishala she gently reminded that he (or she) who disturbs a marriage is reborn as a mosquito.

So this was a beginning here. An opening of a window. A letting go.

For Siân there was much learning to be done, much forgetting.

'Don't forget where you've come from,' Bryn had said, 'Don't forget about us.'

But there were so many new things to learn. How to wear a sari properly; how to cook and care for your clothes, jewels, skin; how to choose the best vegetables in the market; how to make sanitary napkins; how to serve the men first; how to store water and save electricity. How to how to how to.

On their first night together as husband and wife, on cotton mattresses in Ba's back room, Siân couldn't get certain things out of her head – her mother and father, her two brothers, her aunts and uncles, Ronnie and Gwen and Dee. Where were they now? Could they feel her thinking of them? Was this how it was going to be from now on? *One foot in, the other foot out*. Would it always feel like you never belonged no matter where you went, who you found to love? And Babo, lying next to his wife, felt all this. Felt her blue-green veins fill up with a certain kind of sorrow that hadn't been there before. It was something to do with time and distance, love and separation. It spread through her transparent skin and shone through her like snow.

'You know what?' she whispered to Babo. 'My father bought me a round-trip ticket to India and back. He said, "If that young man isn't there to pick you up, you get on the next plane and come right home." He called you that – *young man*.'

And Babo, understanding it all, held her and said, 'I've got you now, Charlie Girl. I'm never letting you go again.' He knew if this was going to work, they'd have to make a world of their own together, because Siân couldn't begin to understand this world right now – all the millions in it. The beggars who went about with slippers on their palms because they had no feet to walk on. The young men – brown and black-bodied, like ribbed horses – ready to fall upon their destinies like torrents of rain. And most of all, these women of Ganga Bazaar who were like jungles – dark wombs from which all life seemed to have emerged. How could Siân hope to gain entrance to their world of renunciations and wanderings? When they watched from beneath wooden beams with the keys to their houses gently pressing against their hips – ka-chink ka-chink ka-chink – which secrets would they agree to share with her, and which would they keep?

8 All I Want is a Room Somewhere

In the early days, Siân poured her life into letters. She wrote every week, telling her parents the things she was slowly discovering about herself and this country, about Babo's peculiar neighbours and extended family. She steered clear of religion because she knew it would upset her father. So she said nothing of how Selvam, on Prem Kumar's instructions, pasted a poster of all the Jain symbols on the godrej almirah in their bedroom so they could contemplate it every morning. Nothing of how she accompanied the family to the Jain temple in Kilpauk every Sunday and joined them with folded knees and hands to pray for the purity of their souls. Nothing of how she was learning to be the perfect Gujarati daughter-in-law from Meenal, who had been in training for years: wearing saris, rolling faultlessly round chappathis, knowing when to be silent and when to speak.

On the first Sunday of every month Siân booked a trunk call to her parents in Nercwys. Then she waited for Bryn's measured voice and Nerys's barrage of questions. It was the only way for her to pass through the bubble, to reach out and touch a life that used to belong to her. She never allowed herself to cry, never told them about the fear that continued to live in her, that it might have been a mistake after all, because here, in this country with its own raggedy beauty, there were times she could barely find herself, barely pick through the complicated layers of her young life and find the beginning which began, not here, but *there* – where they were. Elsewhere.

How different it is to live in a city by the sea. The air is filled with salt, with comings and goings. There are no fields, but cows everywhere! And people, thousands of them! Babo and I have claimed the second floor of Sylvan Lodge, which lies at the end of an avenue of yellow, holly-hocked portia trees. We have a large bedroom with bath attached, and there's an adjoining terrace where I often go to watch the sunsets. It's strange to be surrounded by people all the time, and still experience a kind of loneliness; different from my London existence, at any rate.

She wrote of her daily battles in the kitchen with batter and dough, her attempts at creating a tiny patch of Tan-y-Rhos in the back garden of Sylvan Lodge, which were repeatedly thwarted by Selvam, who hurried out every time he saw her putting her hands in the mud. 'Madam, no no. I am mali, I will do for you.' *For the better, I suppose, because roses wouldn't do very well in this climate, wisteria never flowers, and geraniums only bloom in the cold season, which is hardly cold at all.*

I'm always a beginner here, she wrote, trying to get to the heart of the melancholy that had set in ever since they'd taken up residence in Sylvan Lodge. *I am always beginning because I cannot surrender a part of myself. It's difficult to explain. Everyone has been more than generous, more than patient, and yet, it's a feeling of being marooned, of not having quite reached my final destination. I miss home, of course, and the both of you, and yesterday I saw two young lads cycling with the sun on their backs, and they looked to me so much like Huw and Owen – only darker, more carefree. I miss the smell of things. I really miss bacon. But listen to me go on. You mustn't think I spend my days being morose. Far from it. Most days are so full with the business of living, I scarcely have a moment to myself. And there's this country – so incredibly beautiful, and different from anything in the world. I can't wait to go exploring.*

Later, when Babo's devotion to Siân was momentarily superseded by his new Minolta Hi-Matic F, Siân sent regular packages of photographs home by registered post, hoping it would make things clearer. The pictures were square with thick, white borders: Siân and Babo in cycle rickshaws, in rowboats, on elephants and camels; Siân with ropes of jasmine and jewelled slides in her hair; Babo in bellbottoms leaning Hindi-movie-hero-style against rocks and pillars; the both of them posing in front of the Taj Mahal with their gleaming teeth – jhill mill, jhill mill.

What the pictures didn't show was how in the early days Siân saw more of Trishala and the children than she did of Babo because Prem Kumar was always whisking him off to work. Everything that year was forced to take second place to Prem Kumar's new company, which he named Sanbo Enterprises (an ingenious combination of Siân and Babo), as a sign that Patel & Sons were truly entering the spirit of a new generation. For that whole year the talk revolved only around permits and licences, overshadowing all other topics of conversation. Even Meenal's upcoming marriage to the shipbroker, now that it was confirmed he didn't have a limp, wasn't given any priority, which is probably why the event itself turned into a decidedly damp squib affair.

'Will you be all right, Charlie?' Babo asked. 'Have you got enough to keep busy with . . . you know you could always come and type up some letters for us if you're getting bored.'

How could she tell him that what she wanted was the freedom to open the gates and jump into an auto rickshaw to Mylapore or Broadway to get the things she needed without someone constantly escorting her? To find a place where she could walk because she was tired of sitting around all day without moving, and God knows all the magazines Ronnie sent her from England said you needed to walk at least 8,000 steps a day if you didn't want to turn into a fat cow? But there was no chance of solitude in Sylvan Lodge. Even closing the door to their bedroom didn't ensure privacy. Anyone could open it at any time, and they frequently did. 'Bhabi, come let's do each other's hair, no?' or 'Bhabi, Mummy is calling you because Harsha-behn is here from Baroda and she wants to meet you – yes, yes, you must put on a sari.' Or 'Bhabi, tell us egg-zactly what happens on your marriage night?'

Meenal and Dolly didn't give her a moment's peace. They wanted to experiment with her make-up, fawn over her whiteness and coloured eyes, try on all the modern clothes hanging in her almirah. Surprisingly, it was Trishala, despite the language barrier, who was most empathetic to Siân's situation. 'Stop following her like a tail,' she'd bark at the girls. 'Maybe she wants to read by herself without being stared at by you two.'

Trishala knew that the first years of marriage were the hardest. Hadn't she spent two years with vegetables in her lap, wondering what it was all about? And Prem Kumar, rushing off to his silly factory at the crack of dawn and coming back late at night to eat and make small talk, as if it was easy – this making-a-family business. Trishala was convinced that it was a universal truth, regardless of where you came from and what the circumstances of your marriage were. Because, see – this daughter-in-law of hers, who was so full of love for Babo, who had travelled all the way from England to be with him – didn't she look so fragile and sad sitting on the kitchen floor learning the names of vegetables in Gujarati as she sliced them up for lunch? To Trishala she looked like an orphan who'd been dumped in a house of strangers, and it worried her to see her like this. Besides, she was growing thin, too thin. Not good for childbearing prospects.

'Ask if she wants to go shopping?' she'd instruct Dolly, who was the appointed interpreter. 'Ask if she wants to phone her mummy-daddy? Ask if she's not liking the food? We can always make what she likes. She can teach us.'

Even Chotu, who had taken longest to adjust to his foreign bhabi, mainly due to his pubescent shyness, ran to her as soon as he came home from school, in an effort to cheer her up. 'Come, bhabi, you can help me fly my planes,' he'd say, pulling her by the hand up to the terrace where the two of them would test Chotu's contraptions – each of them sailing beautifully over the railings and then promptly nose-diving to their death in the clump of ashoka trees below.

Only when Babo came home from work did something change in Siân. He continued to be the only space that didn't need filling. Babo and Siân, holding hands in the darkness of night, disappeared to a different place – to a city with no name, a city where they knew no one and no one knew them. Where they understood their lives and each other. It was a place where Siân could hold him and he became the same Babo she'd held months ago, when they were alone and unattached to their families, when they were listening to the trains screech by her blue-walled Finchley Road flat. And when Siân needed this feeling again, she'd curl into the walnut shell of her husband's body and say, 'Oh love, can't we go somewhere? Just the two of us for a while?'

And then they'd be off, escaping in their orange Flying Fiat. To hill stations and tiger sanctuaries, to the palaces of dead queens. Whenever Babo managed to disentangle himself from work, they'd be up, up and away like blistering bandits. Here they were on a houseboat in Kashmir, standing atop a desolate Rajasthani fort, tearing into chicken sizzlers in a lakeside shack in Ooty. Here they were in the coves of the Andaman & Nicobar Islands, deserted and spectacularly blue. Babo raising himself against her: sha-bing sha-bang.

They made love in places they fell in love with, in places that would soon disappear. They made love even if they thought someone was watching. They made love. They made love. They made love. If they didn't, there was always the threat that they'd fall apart. That something would come in to divide their bodies, to sever the string that connected them.

Some days, the connection was so light – barely a peacock feather distance of blue electricity between them. Other days it was like one river meeting another at the ocean's mouth. And when they came back to Sylvan Lodge, it was always a slow trudging back. Slow, because Siân longed for a place of her own, for their two-year time limit to set them free, so she could fill showcases with things of her own choosing: not pictures of emaciated Jain saints, not glass ballerinas with fans.

In the summer of 1971, while Bangladesh was struggling to be birthed into existence, and the Russians and Americans were racing to see whose space orbiter would return to Mars first, Siân made two discoveries. The first was that she was pregnant. The second was a place called The Garden of Redemption, where a man called Manna preached every Friday.

The Garden of Redemption was a place full of birds: parakeets, kingfishers, sparrows, mynahs; and there were 100-year-old trees that provided sanctuary to the flying foxes and common jezebels and all the places of worship that lay tucked in the different corners of the compound. It was a community of sorts, 'Nothing cultish,' Siân was quick to tell Babo, who was wary of communities in general, and religious communities in particular. It was a place where Siân could walk; where she could try to understand the length and breadth of her new life.

So, Siân walked. Every day she watched the smouldering Madras sun set across the Adyar River, and it filled her with the hope that she was finally getting closer to finding her place in India. Sometimes, a surreptitious Redemptionist riding a bicycle in their customary crisp white uniform would gently sneak ahead of her, nudging her off the red paths, or a shy mongoose scurried by – a sign that money was coming your way. And always, when the moon was waxing, the jackals down by the river lifted up their heads and howled at the sky.

These walks were nothing like her walks back home, where all she'd had to do was step out of Number 10 with Aunty El's dog, Gwythur. She'd been losing herself then, trying to find Babo in that cold, craggy air. It was all a bit ridiculous now that she thought about it – gathering bluebells and tramping across streams singing 'Yesterday', with Dylan Thomas tucked under one arm and a morose-looking black and white photograph of Babo under the other. How could she ever have thought to find Babo there, when he so clearly belonged here, amongst these moist mud paths and humid air, these brazen trees and flowers? Here it was easy: all she had to do was pick a single one of these flowers – jasmine, mimosa, frangipani – and crush the heady smell of it in her palms to feel like she was touching the inside of Babo's smooth brown skin.

Siân continued to walk throughout the duration of her pregnancy even though every Patel woman she knew berated her about her daily exercises and offered their own individual dietary advice instead. She should be lying down, eating ghee-filled delicacies, having oil baths, painting, reading, singing, anything but *this* – putting her swollen feet into walking shoes and making half-blind Selvam drive her to that cracked community of Redemptionists.

'Why?' Trishala wanted to know. 'Why must you jeopardize the baby? Why must you drink coffee when I keep telling you it will damage your uterus? Why won't you understand that pregnant women are meant to be fat?'

Trishala, fluttering around Sylvan Lodge with all her nervous energy, thought *she* knew better than anyone else what the dangers of bringing a child into the world were, especially one born of mixed-caste, mixed-country, mixed-colour desire.

'At least drink more milk,' she'd say, indicating her own pitcher breasts. 'Otherwise your child will go hungry.'

And even Ba, all the way from Ganga Bazaar, pestered her with regular missives. Was Siân soaking fenugreek seeds overnight and applying them with orange and lemon peel so that her breasts would grow? Did Trishala have rock salt at hand to hasten the delivery? Had Babo found roots of the gular tree, washed and cleaned them and inserted them into Siân's vagina to see if they came out whole or if they broke inside? If they came out whole it would mean the birth of a son, if they broke inside they could be sure of a girl.

Siân broke and broke inside.

She persisted with her walks because there were still gaps she couldn't understand, gaps that had something to do with her family – distant and untouchable. It had been a year and a half since she'd seen them, and when Siân thought about it, a feeling so oppressive grew inside her, making her run, tamarind underfoot, all the way down to the blue-gabled house on Dooming Street where an old lady played the piano, and parrots shrieked in the laburnum trees.

Siân made her first friend in Madras with the old lady who lived in the blue-gabled house. Her name was Ms Douglas, and after weeks of watching the young, pregnant foreigner with pink cheeks, leaning at the gate, listening to her play, Ms Douglas finally walked out and said, 'Why don't you come in and have some tea, dear?'

Siân discovered that Ms Douglas's grandfather had arrived in India as a young missionary from England, and had almost instantly been distracted from his calling by a vivacious singer from Calcutta. The legacy of that marriage and the journey of how its descendants landed up from Calcutta to Madras was an intricately gloomy tale that Ms Douglas managed to tell within the first five minutes of meeting anyone. 'It's a difficult thing,' sighed Ms Douglas, when the story was finished, 'To grow up with the idea that home is a place you've never been to. But we were raised in a way to believe that England was always the better place, the place to return to.'

Listening to Ms Douglas practising her Nocturnes and Hungarian Rhapsodies were the only times Siân gave herself properly over to homesickness. It was something about that Eastern European music wafting out and communing with the tropical Madras air – something sad and ruinous – that made her think it was really her father playing for her, saying in his own mysterious way how happy he was that a little rosebud was growing inside her.

Every Friday, Ms Douglas and Siân sat across from each other in planters chairs under the magnificent white buttresses of the house, drinking Earl Grey tea and eating Marie biscuits. Ms Douglas told Siân all the secrets of her life: how her father had installed the Steinway in the front room when she was six years old with the purpose of making her into a world-class piano player like Chopin (who had also been six when he began lessons, and eight when he was touring and giving concerts). 'But,' sighed Ms Douglas dramatically, whenever she tried to explain her unsuccessful career as a pianist, 'Without a proper teacher to guide me, failure was inevitable. And after Daddy died, well, I simply lost the will.'

Ms Douglas had had a brief affair with a man called Felix D'Souza who sang in the Santhome Cathedral choir with her, but three weeks after their engagement, when he got run over by a water tanker, she gave up all illusions of *that kind of life*. Then she met Manna and joined the Garden of Redemption, and it was here, she said, that she understood her life was meant to go in another direction.

'I just took it as a violent sign from God, dear, so I took off my engagement ring and locked it in my grandmother's ivory box and waited for salvation of a different kind! I still play, but nothing like a world-famous pianist. Besides, look at that poor Chopin. He died of TB in Paris when he was thirty-nine, and had to have his heart despatched to Warsaw in an urn – quite a sad ending for him, wasn't it?' .

Siân in turn told Ms Douglas about Sylvan Lodge, about the demented Parsi neighbour, Darayus, who sometimes sleepwalked all the way out of his house to knock on the front door and say, 'Have you seen my son? I think he's trying to kill me.' About the thing she loved best about India – seeing the fisherwomen walking to the markets with their husbands' catch on their heads, silver bells jingling around their dark, supple ankles. She told her stories about Nercwys, her father and mother and brothers. Over and over again, because Ms Douglas was slowly losing her mind and sometimes forgot who Siân was and where she'd come from.

Ms Douglas wanted to know if they had a piano at home? Had Siân or her brothers ever played? She wouldn't believe that they'd not had a bathroom or electricity in the house till Siân was seven years old, or that Siân hadn't been to a restaurant till she moved to the city of London. Because Ms Douglas believed that only India was made for the poor: not England, never England.

After tea, they sat under the banyan tree listening to Manna dissect the complexities of modern life. Manna, who was born with a smooth, ageless face and destitute cheekbones, who told them not to divide their life between living and dying.

'Can you be free of Time?' Manna asked. 'Can you really know anything when you are so busy thinking and despairing? Take this sunset. So beautiful, you want to capture it and put it in a box for later. But can't you just enjoy it now? Can't you just appreciate the colours, the sudden beauty of it? And then let it go. Sorrow stems from the same place as pleasure.

To understand it you have to hold it, and grapple with it, not try to run away from it.'

Afterwards Siân walked Ms Douglas back to her blue-gabled house, and left her feeling lighter, safer, sliding back into her life with all her stories and memories intact.

'Wouldn't it be sad if you came here one day and I didn't recognize you, dear?' Ms Douglas asked.

'Oh, it's not going to be like that with us,' Siân said, and then she was off, through the gates, past the golden circle of laburnum trees, out of the Garden and into the world.

9 A Welsh Interlude

In December 1971, while India and Pakistan threw bombs at each other for thirteen days; while ten million East Pakistani refugees crossed over the border, and Prime Minister Indira Gandhi called for a long period of hardship and sacrifice, Babo and Siân boarded an Air India flight to London via Bombay and Rome to visit Siân's family for Christmas. All the way over, Siân was anxious. She kept thinking back to those three silent months in Nercwys before she came to India, and of that one night when Nerys, barely raising her head from her knitting needles, had asked, 'And what about children? Have you thought about what they'll be like?'

What they'll be like.

Siân had run up to her room and wept. She'd written to Babo about how she couldn't wait to have children because they'd be so beautiful that people on the streets would have to stop and stare. *Would they, though? Would they?*

Trishala had voiced her concerns too. She'd spent a lifetime thinking about this matter of progeny. She wanted clarifications on how the children were going to be raised. 'Don't be airy-fairy about these matters, Babo,' she warned. 'What kind of names will they have? What God will they pray to? What traditions will they follow?' These were Trishala's burning questions. To which Babo had said, 'We'll cross that fence when we come to it.'

Well, the fence was here now, and Siân was getting ready to scissor-jump it. 'Love,' she said, linking her fingers through Babo's, forcing him to turn his head away from the window to look at her. 'I've been thinking about the baby, and about us, and I think regardless of how things go in Nercwys, I'd like us to stay in India – on a permanent basis, I mean.'

'But Charlie! That's never been the plan. It was always going to be two years in Madras and then back to London. You know Fred is holding a place for me at the company. I don't understand.'

But Siân's mind was made up. After spending nearly two years in India, she was convinced it would be easier to raise a family there rather than anywhere else. 'Besides,' she added, 'I couldn't bear it if our children were teased because they were mixed race. It isn't easy in England, you know.'

'Charlie Girl, what are you talking about? You know I never experienced any ill feeling when I was in England. Besides, you talk as though everyone in India were so forward thinking, when you know they aren't! People there stare, you know they stare. Their job in life is to stare. That's as bad as name-calling, isn't it?'

'No, love, it's different. You went to London as an adult. You were in highly controlled environments – at work, at the Polytechnic, at the YMCA. People weren't always expressing the truth of what they felt. Of course you were going to be fine. But you didn't have to go to school in England, did you? You didn't have to deal with children. And besides, when people stare in India, it's not done with any feeling of menace, it's out of curiosity. For God's sake, Babo, when we go to Nercwys, you're probably going to be the first brown person they've ever seen! And let me tell you, it's going to feel a whole lot different from how I felt as the first white person in Ganga Bazaar.'

'Yes. Well, that's 300 years of colonialism, isn't it? The adoration of white skin.'

'The point is, it makes practical sense to stay in India. You're starting this thing with your father. Why don't you stick with it? Why would you want to go and work for some company when you can be your own boss?'

'Oh, I'm not even going to pretend I'm the boss,' Babo said, turning back to face the window, out of which he could see the sun setting resplendently behind the aeroplane wing. 'Can we just think about it, first? Can we just see how we feel after this trip? We can always change our minds later.'

'I'll want my own house, of course,' Siân pushed on. 'Our own little place. We can find something nearby so your parents don't feel too abandoned. Just think, love – no one to bother us, our own little place.'

'You know what I think,' Babo said. 'I think you quite like being a memsahib. Why would you want to live in London where you'd have to do everything for yourself, when you've got a galley of slaves to do everything for you in India?'

Siân squealed. 'That's not fair, you terrible man! You know it's not. I'm busy learning languages and how to make dhoklas and what not. It's not like I'm lying around like a beached whale all day eating bonbons.'

'Thank God for that,' said Babo laughing, drawing his wife into him. 'Thank God for that.'

Babo never forgot his first image of Nercwys: a village of matchbox houses under a shroud of snow. There was something about the quality of light that winter afternoon – meagre and ancient, the way it trickled through the coverlet of clouds in long oblong shafts of grey. It made him wistful, as though he were returning to a place he'd known in a previous life. And even though Babo didn't believe in that sort of thing, it was a feeling that would recur every time he re-entered the village of his wife's childhood.

The drive to Nercwys was long and haphazard. Siân sat in the front seat of Bryn's old Morris Minor with her brother, Owen, while Babo sat in the back, watching the countryside pass by in a series of muted black and white frames. He thought about their journey up until this point, how at every stage they'd been received and sent off by someone. In Madras, Prem Kumar had insisted that the whole family, even Chotu (who was in the throes of preparing for his board examinations), be present for a formal send-off at the airport. In Bombay, Meenal and her shipbroker husband had picked them up from the domestic terminal and taken them to their flat in Andheri, where Siân and Babo slept fitfully for six hours before waking again and making their way across the city in darkness to the international airport. At Heathrow, they'd been met by Babo's old Polytechnic friend, Bhupen Jain, and his wife, Mangala. All the way to Euston, Bhupen talked about how bad life was for immigrants in the UK, and how difficult it was to run the post office. 'All these young goons and hooligans,' he complained. 'I can't leave Mangala alone at the till for even one moment. It's just not safe.' Bhupen talked and talked right until they reached the carriage doors, asking how business was in India, and if Babo was still drinking and eating meat, until Mangala cut in and pointed to Siân's belly. 'Nothing you've said about the good news. What a man you are. Don't ask how I put up with him,' she said to Siân, producing two tinfoil-wrapped rolls from her handbag as they clambered on to the train. 'Train food is no good and too expensive. See you on the way back, and may God shower many blessings on your baby.'

When they finally arrived in Chester, Babo expected to see the entire village of Nercwys on the platform waiting to greet them, but there was only Owen, looking serious and a bit stunned, shuffling towards them with a bouquet of red holly berries in his hands.

The drive to Nercwys seemed longer than it actually was because it was done mainly in silence. Every once in a while Siân asked a question about someone in the village, to which Owen replied monosyllabically – married, dead, moved away, sold, miner, alcoholic. A few times Owen had to pull over because Siân thought she was going to be sick. 'I'm used to Indian roads now, aren't I?' she laughed, 'I need those extra jolts and bumps. This is all much too smooth for me.'

Outside there were trees, the names of which Babo didn't know, bare of leaves, lining the entrance to the village like a row of ceremonial soldiers. Beyond, where he couldn't see, ran the River Terrig. They were nearly there now. Siân was pointing things out – The Crossing House where Mrs Bivins lived with her spinster daughter, Rhianne. The Tin House and Nercwys Hall. Hendre Ucha, the house with the first grass tennis court in the village.

Siân wanted Owen to drive all the way down the street, past the post office where she used to buy liquorice rings as a child, past the chapel, and The White Lion, and the old school house, before turning around and driving back up the street. As they crawled up and down the main street, it seemed to Babo that all the inhabitants of Nercwys had gone indoors to watch quietly from behind their curtains. There wasn't a soul to be seen except one man walking across the fields, his footprints like a trail of crumbs in the snow behind him, and the cows, standing disconcertedly in clusters, chewing the cud. 'Here we are,' Siân said, turning to give Babo a nervous smile as the car came to a halt outside Tan-y-Rhos.

'How's Mam been, by the way?' Siân asked. 'Agitated?'

'You could say she's been a wee bit panicked,' Owen grunted, as he helped Siân out of the car and steered her through the gates of the house.

Inside, Babo could smell chicken roasting. The first thing he saw was an antique barometer on the wall, whose blue needlepoint rested between 'Change' and 'Fair'. There was a narrow, carpeted stairway that presumably led to the bedrooms on the first floor. Babo deposited their suitcases at the foot of the stairway. To the right was the front room with large windows that looked out on to Nerys's famous rose garden, currently protected with a hill-up of branches, leaves and straw to insulate the plants through the winter. The wallpaper in the room was a dizzying mustard diagonal print, which overshadowed the upright pianoforte against the back wall and the modest collection of poetry and philosophy books stacked above it.

Bryn was by the fireplace, poking at the coals. 'Hello,' he said, dusting off his hands before walking over to shake Babo's hand, settle him in his eye, fix him somehow, before allowing Siân to fall into his arms.

Nerys, standing in the doorway of the kitchen with an apron tied under her ample bosom, eyes wet with tears, spatula in one hand, came over and took hold of Siân, kissing her on both cheeks repeatedly. 'My girl,' she said, crying, 'My girl.' Babo stared at them for what seemed like a very long time, before Nerys, recovering herself, extended one dainty hand and said, 'Very nice to meet you.'

'Likewise,' Babo said, 'Sorry it's taken us so long.'

Siân followed Nerys into the kitchen, their voices gaining in pitch and tempo until it sounded like they were speaking a different language. Babo, left to stand uncertainly in the centre of the room, looked out of the window.

'Sit.' Bryn indicated the chair next to his with a short nod of his head.

Hello, sit: two words.

Babo sat beside his wife's father and took note. He took note of the meticulous dark suit, the thick tortoiseshell glasses, the hair – whatever was left of it – combed back without any fuss, the neatly trimmed fingernails. He took in the lips, an anomaly on his face, somehow – sensual, a woman's lips, his wife's lips, blooming like crimson petals in the harsh desert of his face.

'Geoffrey Boycott is looking lethal,' Bryn said a few minutes later.

'He certainly is.'

And so it went. This little dance between Babo and Bryn, of economy and restraint. Afterwards, Owen said that seeing the two of them slumped in their chairs watching the cricket was the most natural thing in the world, like watching two old geezers who'd known each other all their lives.

They had all been curious about Babo, of course. All they'd seen were photographs with inscriptions scrawled along the backs. For all they knew, Siân could have taken up with a jungle warlord, and they'd have been none the wiser.

Treat him like a regular person, Siân had written to her parents. *Just remember to speak slowly and clearly*.

But it was difficult for Bryn and Nerys, who had only ever been out of Wales once, to Dublin in 1959, which didn't help at all in trying to imagine a country like India and what life there could possibly be like.

At suppertime Nerys made the rare exception of allowing everyone to fill their plates from the kitchen so they could eat in front of the television. She brought over a plate for Bryn, with an extra portion of roast potatoes and sausages, the way he liked it. 'And what can I get you?' she asked Babo.

'Oh, that looks nice,' Babo said, looking over at Bryn's plate of roast chicken and sausages and more of Trishala's forbidden things. 'That'll do me nicely.' Not knowing that in that moment he had absolved himself, because if he'd said, 'Something vegetarian, please,' all Nerys had were the potatoes and sprouts, and a tin of baked beans.

For the next few weeks Babo and Siân fell into different patterns. Most mornings Siân woke before anyone else and went for a long walk across the fields. By the time Babo came downstairs, respectably shaved and dressed, she would be sitting by the pile of old newspapers, helping her father roll painstakingly precise firelighters. After Bryn left for the quarry, Nerys and she sat with their knitting and embroidery or busied themselves in the kitchen with pastry or whatever the cooking endeavour of the day was. Babo occasionally went into Mold with Owen, and while Owen balanced accounts at Lloyd's, Babo walked about town, whiling away hours in the pub doing crossword puzzles. Gradually, he felt the need to engage in something a bit more physical, so when Uncle Norman from next door complained about the state of his shed, Babo spent a week helping him fix it up and paint it. After seeing what a good job he'd done, Aunty Eleri, Bryn's sister, got him to come around and put shelves in the greenhouse for her dianthus. By and by, the entire village had some odd job or the other for Babo to do, and soon, he was waking as early as Siân to make the most of the light, and to fulfil all his neighbourly obligations.

At nights, Nerys, Bryn, Siân, Babo and Owen played Scrabble on the kitchen table after supper. 'It's quite embarrassing,' Nerys said without fail after losing, 'Even though English isn't your first language you're better at this than any of us!' Babo told her how he'd become a Scrabble champ during his YMCA days in London, when he and the other young men played till four in the morning because it was a time in their lives when they were more in need of friendship than sleep. 'The trick is to know all the two-letter words,' he said, 'We memorized the whole list, and of course, the J, Q, X and Z words.' The talk would then veer from vegetarianism to the IRA, and inevitably, to the situation between Pakistan and India, until half past ten, when Bryn, inspecting his pocket watch, politely excused himself from the table. 'Some of us have to work tomorrow,' he'd say, retreating from the room like an army general, his back straight, his slippers treading noiselessly up the stairs. He must hate me, Babo thought. How can he not hate me for unravelling the very core of his life? How do you possibly get over your only daughter moving all the way across the world just because she falls in love?

By Christmas, the days had grown even shorter. Siân's older brother, Huw, and his wife, Carole, drove up from Brighton to spend a week with them, and were going to stay in a hotel in Mold before the idea got beaten out of Huw's head by Nerys. 'You can stay with Owen, who has a perfectly good spare room in his house down the street. I've never heard such nonsense in my life. A hotel!'

Babo liked his wife's brothers. They were solid, upright men, easy to get along with. Huw was the city slicker, full of opinions and used to being right. He could talk for hours about football or the insurance business if you let him, and only Carole seemed to have the power to reign him in. But it was with Owen that Babo really bonded. They spent many evenings at The White Lion together (drink being forbidden in Tan-y-Rhos), and during these sessions Babo managed to draw out some details of Owen's love affair gone wrong with an English school teacher, who disappeared soon after the engagement to take up a teaching job in New Zealand. Babo learned that what Owen really wanted was to be a farmer, working the land, watching his trees grow. 'So why are you working in a bank?' Babo asked, shocked that anyone would attempt to live life by avoiding his greatest desires. 'It's what's expected of me, isn't it? Either I'm a quarry man like my dad, or I go and do something properly modern like Huw.'

When Siân's friends Gwen, Ronnie and Dee arrived for their three-day reunion, Tan-y-Rhos nearly burst at its seams with all the extra people and the multitude of shopping bags filled with baby things. For three nights, Babo watched Siân get all trussed up in maxis and beads. Her cheeks seemed to have filled out along with the rest of her body, making her look younger, less sad. Babo watched her with her friends – their laughter, their endless easy chatter, and he thought he had never seen his wife look so happy before, so giddy and complete. He wanted to ask whether she really wanted to go back to India after all, because wasn't this her life, here? *Don't do it for me*, he wanted to say. *Because I am at home in the world anywhere you are. But you are different. Perhaps you need these things.* Later, in bed, when he tried to bring it up, she put her finger against his lips and said, 'Shush, love, it isn't that way at all. You'll see.'

On their last night in Nercwys, Babo and Siân walked through the falling snow to Aunty Eleri's house at the top of the village where everyone had been invited to cram into her front room for supper. Aunty El stood at the door, dressed in her Sunday best, welcoming people into the haven of her home as though she were the village pastor. 'Come in, come in, find a place to sit, help yourself to a drink. Aye, we serve alcohol on these premises, not like your father-in-law, Bob. We folks on this end of the village are a little less God-fearing.'

After everyone settled in with a plate of food and a glass of sherry, there was a long, painful silence, broken by Aunty El's dog, Gwythur, who was trying as usual to hump one of the guests' legs.

'Doesn't this remind you of the Queen's coronation?' Siân said, giggling. 'Aunty El was the only person in the village who had a TV in 1953,' she explained to Babo. 'I remember all of us squeezing in here to watch it. I'll never forget it.'

'Aye, what a night that was,' Aunty El said, cheering at the memory. 'Everyone stayed well past midnight, drinking whisky and having a merry old time – even the young ones here,' she said, pointing at Siân and her brothers. 'These were here till I booted them out. And these scallywag boys, they just darted out of here like bats out of hell, leaving poor Siân to find her way home alone.'

As more memories of that night began to be exchanged, Babo felt the village of Nercwys relax. Backs sunk lower into chairs, old lady legs that had been primly crossed, slackened, and in some cases, even deigned to rest side by side rather than one on top of the other. After a few rounds of drink, handbags were tossed under chairs, pipes were lit up, and there was enough noise emanating from Aunty El's front room to rival the crowd at an India–Pakistan cricket match.

It reminded Babo strangely of one of Prem Kumar's Sunday card-playing sessions where aunts and uncles – carbon copies of one another – congregated to crow like cocks and hens in a farmyard. There was something very similar here, except in this Welsh-chintz version the sideboard was heaving with devilled eggs instead of dhoklas. And instead of the sizeable paunches and behinds that middle-aged Gujjus succumbed to, these men and women were powerfully stocky, more uniform in their roundness. But there was the same parochial pride and failings on display. The same aunts berating an unmarried girl to hurry up and get on with it. The same know-all uncle complaining that a son was spending money like a man with no arms.

'You eat meat then, Bob? I thought Hindoos weren't supposed to eat meat?' Uncle Rhys wanted to know. 'And you're not averse to a bit of a snifter here and there?'

'No, sir, misfit on all counts, I'm afraid.'

Aunty Idella, one of Nerys's fourteen siblings, wanted to know about Siân's earrings. 'Did you get those done in India, then, love? Do all the ladies pierce their ears?'

'Oh yes, even the wee babies have their ears pierced,' Siân said. 'It's considered auspicious.'

'Gosh,' Aunty Idella remarked, 'My Angharad asked me if she could pierce her ears when she was sixteen, and I told her she could wait till she was married in a house of her own if she wanted to do a thing like that.'

'That's only the half of it,' Siân started, and then she went on to tell her family all about their wedding in Anjar and Babo's grandmother, Ba, who lived alone in a house of peacocks and lizards, and the jeweller, Hira Lal, who put a needle through fire before putting holes in her ears. Siân talked and talked, she couldn't help herself. It was an unburdening. But Babo sensed that the more she talked the less comfortable she was making her aunts and uncles. There was only so much newness they could take.

'Why, yes, dear,' they nodded. 'Mmhmmm. Of course.'

But really, they were thinking, El was right! Only Siân could do a thing like that – go off to India and marry some bloke no one's ever met, put hoops in her ears, and come back to tell tales like this.

Babo, looking at his wife that night, tried to imagine her growing up in the village of Nercwys. He thought of the picture he had on his desk at Sanbo Enterprises: Siân at four years old in her Welsh outfit – everything from the striped flannel petticoat to the apron, shawl and high black hat. There was a surreal quality about that photograph – her cheeks were touched up to match the candyfloss pink strap of the bag across her chest, and the ringlets that bobbed under the hat, though wild, seemed perfectly in place. To Babo it seemed that nothing about the four-year-old in that pewter frame corresponded to the woman sitting beside him.

Babo leaned back in his chair and wondered how things came together after all, how two beings fit, where all the movement and chaos of the world began. Because watching his wife that night, amidst her family, it seemed to him like she'd sprung from another place entirely – arrived chup chap

105

from the realms of some other floating world to descend like a migrating bird softly into this one. He realized as well, that she'd been right after all. Their destiny was in India. And it was lying patiently across the horizon, waiting to be made.

10 He not Busy being Born is Busy Dying

The following summer Babo, Siân and their four-month-old daughter, Mayuri, moved into a house with orange and black gates at Number 20 Rutland Lane. Waiting at the gates was a dark, sturdy woman wrapped in a green polyester sari, with two giant gold studs shining on either side of her nose. The woman announced that she was Selvam's sister, and that she'd come from the big house to help the foreign madam. Her name was Selvi, and Trishala, convinced that Siân would be incapable of being a good wife, mother and ayah all at once, had sent her along as a parting present. 'Besides,' Trishala confided to Babo on the phone, 'Before this, Selvi worked with a Christian lady, and she converted also, so now she speaks very good English.'

'I don't believe she's related to Selvam,' was all Siân would say, because this woman was a good foot and a half taller than wizened old Selvam. Babo joked that perhaps it was the teachings of Jesus or the sudden intake of beef that had given her the additional boost over her brother. 'Perhaps she'll turn out all right, Charlie,' he said, in an effort to cajole his wife, who was loathe to have a stranger lurking around her new house at this early stage in their adventure. On the subject of child-rearing though, Trishala would not be contradicted, so there was no option but to drag Selvi's steel trunk through the orange and black gates and into the house for good.

In the house of orange and black gates, Babo and Siân ate bacon for breakfast. They made love on mosaic floors. They

107

stayed up late watching cricket matches telecast from across the world – the black and white images from their shiny new television set coating their young bodies with a hazy, sepulchral light. Sometimes, the baby would murmur in the nursery, and Siân would hurry over to check, as she had done nearly every night since becoming a mother, to see if the child was still alive, still breathing. After putting her ear close to her daughter's chest, feeling the reassuring up and down rise and fall of it beating against her ear, Siân would pad back to where Babo lay – sprawled out in his white kurta pyjama like some exotic brahminy kite, legs and arms instead of wings – and she would try to find a place among her husband's entanglements: a safe, warm place which she could call home.

Babo and Siân discovered rhythms of living in this house which had been entirely impossible at Sylvan Lodge: days spent cocooned in the comfort of an air-conditioned room with Ella Fitzgerald moaning softly in the background, a paperback mystery novel or a dated *Good Homes* magazine in hand; the new baby, so small and pink and impossibly fragile, lying between them on their king-sized Kashmiri bed.

Selvi was given a room of her own behind the kitchen, which she kept neat and bare, except for two adornments – a poster of Baby Jesus in his crib which reassured her every morning that Jesus loved her, and a picture of her favourite movie star, MG Ramachandran, future Chief Minister of Tamil Nadu, dressed in a cowboy outfit, leaping mid-air into the words *FIRST KING OF STYLE*. Her presence in the house, which had initially seemed overly invasive, soon tempered into something more tolerable. Not only was Selvi able to translate everyday Tamil phrases for Siân, she also maintained a scrupulous account of all household accounts on scraps of notepaper which she updated every Friday and kept paper-clipped in the fruit bowl in the kitchen. Whenever there was any discrepancy in the dhobi's chit, or if ever the ironing man bungled up, like the time he misplaced Siân's favourite Mangalgiri sari, Selvi would storm out of the house with a knife in hand, cursing and shouting, until the guilty party, for fear of losing the precious ju-jubs between his legs, beat a hasty retreat and avoided all future accounting errors.

Besides her ferocious temper, Selvi also had the extraordinary talent of throwing together the most arbitrary scraps of food to create delicacies, which once made, could never be repeated. Part of Siân's emancipation from the tyranny of Sylvan Lodge had been to make forays into non-vegetarian Indian cuisine. Being a master chappathi-maker wasn't enough. She wanted to know how to make kebabs and spicy meat curries, because Babo and she had just made a new circle of friends, and if they were ever going to do any entertaining at home, they were going to have to come up with something a little more exciting than daal and rice.

For a whole year, Babo and Siân's life in Rutland Lane unfolded in a slow continuum of days, rooted around the brilliant orange flame-of-the-forest tree that towered between the gates in the front yard of the house. Siân's days began and ended with Mayuri's delicate powder rose smell, Selvi's heady coconut oil and jasmine flower combination, and Babo – his layers of earth and mimosa, his Gold Flake-smoking fingertips. These smells began to permeate Siân's consciousness so strongly that they came to replace her early memories of Sylvan Lodge, and define, somehow, the beginning of her real relationship with India and her new phase of motherhood. She began to understand how Babo and she were inextricably tied, how between them, they held the power of creation.

Those initial years passed seamlessly, without disaster or disease, punctuated only by the seasons that the city of Madras had to offer: summer, monsoon, a few months of cool reprieve until the January harvest season, and then summer again. There were no road trips in the Flying Fiat, no explorations around the countryside with Mayuri in tow. There was only the need to ground themselves into this house; learning the habits of the upstairs Singhania family, the next door Punjab Women's Association and the kingdom of cats that populated the walls between them. There were Sundays at Sylvan Lodge, and an annual visit to Ba in Anjar. But other than that, it was just Babo, Siân, Mayuri and Selvi in the house of orange and black gates, and Siân would never remember a happier, more content time in her life.

By the time Apollo 17 landed on the moon, Siân had already joined the Overseas Women's Club of Madras and made her first proper friends in India. There was Darlene Malhotra, née Adams, a paediatrician from Tennessee, who had met her husband, Praveen, at an Elvis Presley concert in Las Vegas, and after an intense LSD experience decided to get married and take six months to travel to India overland. And there was Janet Krishnamurti, née Miller, from Plymouth, who had been sufficiently seduced by Keshav, a Merchant Navy man, in 1956, to follow him on a ship all the way back to India, even though he warned her she'd have to share him with his overbearing, widowed mother who had always lived with him, and would continue to live with him until one of them died. The relationships that Babo and Siân forged with these two couples would become the core friendships of their lives. Twice a week at least, they'd meet on the lawns of the Madras Gymkhana Club to drink G&Ts and discuss everything from the situation in Vietnam to the new Bond movie playing at Casino. These were happy nights, filled with music, dance and drink – freedoms Babo and Siân had only ever experienced together in London.

This was also the time Siân threw herself into a blitz of charity work. Through the many social and charitable arms of the OWC, Siân found a way to deal with the overwhelming

110

guilt she had carried around ever since she'd arrived in Bombay and seen those families sleeping on the pavements. She knitted blankets for the sick and taught English to slum children. She held the wrinkled hands of men and women abandoned by their families, and made embroidered table mats with the Little Sisters of the Poor. Siân loved them all, visited them in mental institutions and cancer wards, wept when she heard stories of how they were chained to their beds at night, felt delirious shivers of joy when orphaned children came scampering out to greet her, crying, 'Aunty Aunty'. It seemed incongruous that her own child was no trouble at all; seemed happy to be slathered down with mustard oil everyday, and be bounced about on Selvi's hefty thighs to the tune of old Tamil film songs.

It was at this relatively peaceful stage in their life when Siân discovered she was pregnant again. During this second pregnancy, things went much more smoothly. This time, in the privacy of her own home, Siân could sit for entire mornings in her kaftan reading *Dr Spock's Baby and Child Care* manuals, while Mayuri played with blocks on the veranda under Selvi's vigilant eye. The barrage of advice from the ladies of the Patel clan was somewhat deflected towards Meenal, who was also expecting – her first – and who had come home a few months before the delivery, as custom dictated. With Meenal absorbing the full force of Trishala's attention (and in truth, she was only too happy to be able to put her feet up and be hand-fed till she bloated out like a pot-bellied pig), Siân was free to continue with her everyday routines as long as she deposited Mayuri at Sylvan Lodge once a week with her small overnight case, so her grandmother could lavish undivided attention on her, and so Mayuri could play with her new friend – Darayus's grandson, Cyrus, a gangly child with weak eyes, whose parents lived in America. In the evenings, Siân went walking in the Garden of Redemption, and every Friday she sat with Ms Douglas under the banyan tree and thought about what Manna was saying: *Do you know a thing just by naming it?* At nights, when Babo returned to her and they lay down with each other away from the pushing, poking and pulling of the outside world, Siân could finally consider quietness, and what it really meant in this country.

In those late midnight hours, she thought of her mother and father, who were waiting, growing patiently old, waiting for her. *Won't you come again?* they said. *Soon, soon*, she whispered. *Soon, we're all going to climb on a plane and cross the seas and come to Nercwys because it's time now, isn't it? Time for you to meet Mayuri and the new baby*.

Ever since they'd moved into the house of orange and black gates, Babo had spent a lot of time thinking about the choices a man makes: about where he begins and where he ends. He dreamed of London – all the excitement and movement he'd experienced there – of waking up every morning with a sense of conquering something. He thought of his old flame, Falguni, and wondered how husband-hood would have felt with her. Meenal had reported that Falguni was now living in Nairobi, married off to an ageing vegetable oil-producing millionaire. Thinking about her now, and her tear-stained letters, produced little jab jabs of guilt in Babo's heart. Would this new phase of fatherhood have been different if he'd been a dutiful son? If he'd done all that had been expected of him? Would it have been any easier to understand? What would their life have been like if they'd gone back to London like they'd originally planned? If he'd accepted that job that Fred Hallworth assured him was always waiting at Joseph Friedman & Sons?

How delicately balanced this intricate choreography of living was. And yet, how little anyone really thought about it. Certainly *he* hadn't had time to think about any of the choices he'd made so far. Everything had been react, react, react. And the worst thing about all these reactions was that they seemed to have pulled Siân and him in different directions. All of a sudden, *she*, who had been most plagued by separations, had suddenly found her place. As if *this* was what she was meant to do: spawn children, save the world. When in fact, there hadn't been any time for planning at all. Babo hadn't even got down on one knee to propose marriage. It had been decided: either-or, together-apart, and bang, they were married in Madras, ready to welcome baby number two.

As always, when Babo found himself struggling in unfamiliar territory, he turned to his grandmother for advice. 'Ba,' he moaned petulantly on the telephone, 'Why is it that nobody can talk about anything other than the baby? Papa has gone mad – I'm sure of it. He was never so concerned with us when we were children, but you should see him now, smiling away like a king. And of course, Ma is beside herself. Two more grandchildren on the way, I don't think she can stand the excitement. It's as if her whole life has been leading up to this moment of becoming a grandmother!'

'What's the matter?' Ba asked. 'Don't like being a daddy?'

'No. It's not that.'

'Then, what? Your wife kicked you out of bed?'

'No.'

'Then? Just being a silly, spoilt fellow. Don't like all the attention being diverted from you, is it?'

'No, Ba. It's none of that. I just didn't imagine it to be like this.'

Babo's whole life, now that he examined it in this new light, had zoomed ahead without him, and just as he was getting used to nourishing and protecting one extra being with her own set of chromosomes and aspirations, another one threatened to come along and make more demands of him. Siân was back on the yoga mat doing pranayama every morning, playing Mozart to the bump in her belly, bringing out her father's Dylan Thomas poetry books for evening recitations. It was too much. All this change. For what? What did it really mean?

Babo had only been able to view fatherhood, so far, in terms of abstractions. When Chotu gleefully pointed out that Mayuri had the same grey eyes as Babo and Trishala had, and as Trishala's mother, Gurvanthi, the temple cleaner, Babo supposed there was something quite magical in the way things continued. Having children was the closest humans came to immortality, he thought. But instead of feeling empowered by this idea, Babo felt diminished. He could feel the sand in his clock trickling down very quickly. He had only just started enjoying being young and reckless, staying up till three in the morning to drink with his friends, talking and dancing in each others' houses without having to explain anything to anyone. How could all that possibly continue when there were two babies that needed looking after?

Besides, nothing in his own body had forced him to recognise the eventuality of actual birth. No hormones or glandular changes, no little alien in the womb feeding off his food and water supply for nine months. Throughout the entire pregnancy saga, Babo had been the sidekick, the sperm that had come up with the goods, the errand-boy who delivered kati rolls from Tic-Tac or jam doughnuts from Spencers, depending on Siân's desires. And none of that really prepared him for the moment when he had to reach into the cradle and pick up his child for the first time. With Mayuri, it had been a feeling of being set afloat on the open seas without any compass to guide him. And the idea of having to do it all over again so soon petrified him.

It had taken a long time for Babo to carry Mayuri with confidence, before he could, like Chotu, toss her up and down in the air without worrying about breaking her into tiny pieces. The rewards had come slowly to Babo: hearing Mayuri say her second word, for instance, *Daddy*, sweetly and unexpectedly after her first word, *Mama*, showing right from the beginning Mayuri's earnest will to furnish her parents with equal amounts of love. And when Mayuri was brought to him after her bath for her night-time Daddy snuggle – the soft, innocent sheen of Wipro Baby Shampoo emanating from her entire being – it was true, it touched a chord in him that nothing else could.

These were things Babo gradually came to enjoy, even depend upon. But nothing, nothing about the birth of his first daughter prepared him even remotely for the birth of his second daughter – Beena Elizabeth Patel, who from the beginning would only be known as Bean. When Bean burst upon the scene, Babo experienced something he'd experienced only once, long ago, in a canteen in London. It was something that reached far into the depths of his body, to that thin sheaf of muscle that lay like a leaf across his stomach. It went beyond fireworks and cataclysms. It was love at first sight, and it went something like this: ba-ba-boom, ba-ba-boom, ba-ba-boom-boom-boom.

On 15 August 1973, in rooms 305 and 306 of the Lady Wellington Hospital, Siân and Meenal gave birth to two healthy girls. Meenal's daughter, hereafter known as Unibrow number one, clocked in at the reasonable hour of 16:23, while Bean took five hours longer, tearing through laboriously at an impressive nine pounds nine ounces, her arrival inconveniencing not only her poor mother, the delivery doctor and the night nurses, who were unable to enjoy their Independence Day holiday, but also shattering her grandparents' dream of a grandson.

'Oh God,' said Chotu, when he heard the news. 'Three nieces! Why won't someone have a boy for a change?'

'She *should* have been a boy,' scowled Trishala. 'But I suppose God changed his mind at the last minute.'

'Mama, can't we put her back?' Mayuri wanted to know.

In the beginning Bean was an angel. She didn't need lullabies or Tamil film songs. She just slept. As long as she was fed at regular intervals at her mother's breast, she was happy to lie like a slug in her cot, sucking brutally on her thumb. No matter what time Babo and Siân put her down, she slept through the night till eight the next morning, at which time she peered out of the bars noiselessly, waiting for someone, anyone, to lift her up and feed her.

'Bean,' Babo would whisper, while she lay curled on her side, thumb in her mouth, completely oblivious to the world. 'Hey, little Kidney Bean, look! Daddy's come to say hello.'

It amazed him how self-contained she was: a complete universe to herself. She didn't care if she was cuddled or not, if the lights were left on or not. As long as she had her thumb and her stomach was full, she never made a peep. Everything about Bean's birth was so much less of a fuss. With Mayuri there had been telegrams and presents, non-stop visitors, photographs, sweets, this, that. But with Bean, things were less exuberant. There were a few cards in the post, and a few telephone calls, but nothing really that Siân could wrap up in pink tissue and put away in her jewellery drawer for later, when Bean grew up and wanted to see how small her fingers and ankles once were. Apart from the staple gold bracelets from Trishala and a silver Tiffany cross from Bryn and Nerys, there was nothing like the booty Mayuri collected.

Six months later, Babo, Siân, Mayuri and Bean boarded the Navjeevan Express to Ahemadabad, and took a night bus to Anjar for Bean's naming ceremony at the Amba Mata Temple. Ba's house in Ganga Bazaar had been swept and scrubbed till the black stone floors shone like onyx stones. Jasmine garlands hung from the pelmets in the room of swings, and little brass urns filled with water and frangipani stood in every corner of the house. Ba, waiting on the front steps, could smell them long before they arrived. There was Babo's rain cloud and bakul smell, which was the strongest, most intoxicating smell she knew. There was the smell of his Welsh wife – acres and acres of fresh cut grass. There was her great-granddaughter, Mayuri, who smelled of roots in mud – a potent, stubborn smell as hard as rubies. And there was the new smell, so nostalgic and varied, it brought tears to Ba's creamy, diabetic eyes because it rose from the ashes of her own childhood. It was the smell of spices – her mother at the grinding stone, mixing chilli, turmeric and jeera for the entire year's cooking; the smell of lolly ice – sweet and synthetic on a summer day; the sharpness of river water, brass, sex, blood.

By the time they walked into the courtyard, Ba felt as though she had relived her entire life. It had been like a drowning, chapter after chapter of small enlightenments and giant disappointments. 'You took too long,' she berated Babo, before he could touch her feet and ask for her blessings. 'You forget I'm an old woman. You think I'm going to live for ever? Where's Beena? Let me hold her. Put her in my lap so I can learn what I still see.'

Ba held Bean in her hands for a long time, inspecting her toes and fingers, marvelling at the roundness of her utterly bald head. Mayuri standing by, still unused to all the attention the new fat baby was drawing away from her, leaned over to whisper into Ba's ear, 'I don't like her one bit, Ba. Selvi calls her a big fat bonda bajji, and she is.'

'You should take some rest after this,' Ba advised Siân.

'I think I will. There isn't much age difference between these two as it is.'

'No,' said Ba. 'I mean, you will need to take some rest after this one. Perhaps you should stop. You see, there are only three kinds of women in the world: earth, water and fire. Mayuri is going to sink her roots deep. She will know what she is and what she wants, always. But this one, this Beena, she will change from earth to water to fire, again and again. She will want to move like water, forever taking a different shape, but she will also long to stay still. And she will have a temper. Oh yes, you will have to do something to reduce the fire in her. No doubt about it, this one will keep your hands full.'

Bean, who seemed to be listening intently, enthralled by Ba's diaphanous hair, chuckled. Her first proper laugh.

Ba carried Bean to the Amba Mata Temple, where the priest chanted her name over and over again, birthing her into the world for a second time. Then, she was taken back to the house, bathed and dressed in new clothes, and arranged in Siân's lap at a previously arranged auspicious hour so that Hira Lal, the jeweller, could daub her lobes with coconut oil and put golden circles in ears. Bean squealed so terrifyingly even the peacocks on the tin roof were stunned into silence. Only Ba, taking Bean into her ancient lap, had been able to stop her crying. 'Laadli, oh mari laadli,' she cajoled, sliding a soft, sugary bit of gur into her lips to silence her.

Babo, standing in the back yard by the well, smoking cigarettes and listening to the shrieks inside, felt a numbness spread through his body. He had spent all day walking around the gulleys and lanes of Ganga Bazaar, thinking how it was only four years ago when he had grown his hair and come here as an act of protest, when his whole life existed only in the imagination, in the future. When everything depended on the slim blue letter Neeraj-bhai, the postman, would or would not bring. He remembered the many hours at his table in Zam Zam Lodge, drinking endless cups of sugary tea, writing till his pen ran out of ink; the evenings with Ba, listening to stories of the love affair between Trishala's parents, the great drought that followed, the many failing and restoring qualities a family could offer.

Looking through the window grills and the open doors of this grandmother's house now, where garoli lizards plop plopped off the walls, Babo could see his wife sitting in a majenta silk sari with a big red bindi in the centre of her forehead, cracking coconuts and anointing the baby, as if she'd been practising her whole life to assume this role. He could see his grandmother in her widow's white sari, holding his two daughters, perfect as jewels, and his heart suddenly lifted. This was a surrender after all, wasn't it? Love was a surrender, and he had been resisting.

Babo walked inside the house and removed his Minolta camera from its dusty cover. He stood with the light of Gujarat at his back and took pictures of these four important women in his life. He stood for a long time at the door, listening to the shutter whirr, framing the white and majenta, the small dark eyes, the points of light. He thought about the rest of his family: Trishala, Prem Kumar, Meenal, Dolly and Chotu – how not so long ago, they'd been standing at the gates of the Meenabakkam Airport, waving goodbye to him the first time he left for England. How young he'd been; barely a trace of a whisker above his lips. But he'd known then that his life was for ever going to be changed. He had wanted to go to his family and claim them, each one of them, while things were still the same. Babo, overcome with a similar feeling now, wanted to tell his wife, *I understand. This is our life, our future has become our present. These two girls, this country. This is what we're about.*

PART TWO

The House of Orange and Black Gates

1974–1995

11 So this is Where

So this is where they begin. This is where they really begin. This is where Siân gives birth to two girls who enter like winds: one warm, one cold, one squealing, one quiet. This is where they call themselves family: Babo, Siân, Mayuri, Bean.

Outside is the flame-of-the-forest tree that stands as a witness to their life.

Next door is the Punjab Women's Association on whose walls a whole generation of tabby cats make love and brawl through the night.

Down the street is the Okay Stores where Mr Mustafa sits and smiles with gold glinting out the back of his red gums; where Selvi buys kitchen supplies, and the girls fight over mango magic popsicles.

Upstairs are the Singhania family, whose young boys kneel by the white, paint-chipped grills to see Bean prancing out of the bathroom like a naked fury, whose red bicycle Mayuri borrows to teach herself the lesson of perseverance.

Outside are the orange and black gates that guard the comings and goings, the growing limbs and broken toenails, the girls and boys, boys and girls.

Babo, Siân, Mayuri, Bean: always seeking, trying to claim the beautiful things of the world as their own. They swing on the gates and open them when they should remain closed, slip out and slip back in, thinking no one has seen and nothing has been taken amiss.

Every Sunday they go to Sylvan Lodge, where the girls run first to the staircase to kick off their shoes before marching into Prem Kumar and Trishala's bedroom. Trishala Ba gives them brand-new one-rupee coins and an Indo-Burma notebook each, and Prem Kumar smiles at them, only slightly, with his betel-stained teeth, and asks if they've learned how to make chappathis yet.

Dolly Fie, before she gets married to Chunky Fua in Baroda, takes them in her lap and tickles them in turns until they nearly wee their pants and have to run and do half-bum half-bum on the potty upstairs. Chotu Kaka, who is always playing cricket in the maidan, or on the terrace, flying planes, takes them on his strong shoulders so they can try to see the sea from where they're standing. But what they see won't be the sea, but the long, portia-lined avenue of Sterling Road, dotted with yellow rickshaws and cars and motorbikes and bullock carts. And, outside the gates, half-blind Selvam painting another sign in chalk-dust to keep the demons away.

Next door, Darayus Uncle teaches his grandson, Cyrus Mazda, what each tool in his garage can do. Cyrus, with the protruding, coconut-scraper teeth and soda bottle glasses. *Cyrus the Great, born on a plate*. When Cyrus is done working in the garage, he climbs over the wall and begs to be allowed to join the Sunday Club, of which Mayuri is president. Mayuri charges Bean and Cyrus twenty-five paisa membership fees and makes them swear an oath of allegiance. Then she makes them write down all the gory things that happened in school that week: *Lalit poked his finger with a compass on Monday. Kaveri got hit in the head by a shotput. Mrs Subramanium fainted in assembly*. When they get tired of writing they race up and down the red-brick terrace till the girls are out of breath and pink in the face from trying to keep up with Cyrus's ostrich-long legs.

Afterwards, they sneak downstairs to get water from the earthen pot, and they find everyone sleeping as in Sleeping

Beauty's kingdom: Prem Kumar and Trishala Ba lying tidily on different sides of the bed; Mama and Dolly Fie in the air-conditioned room; Daddy and Chotu Kaka on brown sofas in the living room, snoring like fire engines – rim zim, rim zim.

Mayuri slides her hands into Babo's kurta pocket and steals the keys to the orange Flying Fiat and asks Cyrus and Bean, 'Do you want to do something grown-up and fun?' Then she opens the doors and puts them in the back seat and winds up all the windows, leaving only the tiniest crack of air to come through. She makes them sit like this for half an hour till sweat pours down their foreheads, and Cyrus's soda-bottle glasses steam up, and Bean starts to whinge. 'If you don't let us out I'm going to tell Daddy, May-May.' And Mayuri says, 'You want to be grown-up and see how it feels like in a sauna, don't you?'

Finally, Mayuri opens the doors and lets them out and they all tear around the pista-green walls, pretending to be trains. They go fastest at the back of the house where the servants' quarters are, and the washing stone, and the washing line, and the drain that runs along the house where Prem Kumar cleans his teeth with neem sticks every morning. And when Cyrus decides he's had enough of Mayuri's tyranny, he leaps over the wall and goes back home. The girls tear around some more till Siân calls them in for Bournvita and bread-jam, and sure enough, Bean has dirtied her clothes and scuffed her knees, while Mayuri is pristine – plaits intact, pockets full of change.

Inside, the grown-ups sit around the oval dining table with sleep marks on their faces. Trishala picks pomegranate seeds for them – one by one, painstakingly pink and small – which they stuff in their cheeks all at once and C-R-U-N-C-H, till the sweet juice comes running down their throats. Babo and Prem Kumar pour milky-brown tea into saucers and shluck shluck from them like goldfish. Siân rushes in and out of the kitchen in her sari because Sunday is not only Sylvan Lodge day, but sari day and beach day. And when Babo says it's time to go, they run up to the top of the stairs and whoosh down the wooden banister so Chotu Kaka, standing at the bottom, can catch them. They grab their shoes and run out of the door waving, *Aujo aujo, goodbye goodbye, see you next Sunday*.

And they do this and do this and do this till they're grown up and changed, but for now everything is still light, featherylight.

For now Babo drives them to Marina Beach, where they buy paper windmills and balloons. Mayuri and Bean strip off their clothes and dash into the waves while their parents sit holding hands on the shore, warning them not to go in too deep. Then Babo drives them to The Drive-In Woodlands, where they sit on the bonnet of the Flying Fiat in their swimming costumes and towels, their wet, childish hair sticking out around their faces in all directions. They shovel down iddlis with coconut chutney and sambar and run to the monkey bars in the playground while Babo and Siân sit in the car and eat their dosas demurely like film stars. And after all of it, Babo comes for them again, scoops his girls into his arms and lets them choose ice creams from the Dasaprakash counter: a different flavour every time for Bean, the same steadfast vanilla for Mayuri.

As they drive back to the house of orange and black gates, Bean and Mayuri pretend to be asleep in the back seat like snails, legs and arms interlaced. At the gates, Babo beeps and beeps till drunken Bahadur gets up from his cane chair and lets them in. Then Babo and Siân lift them, one for one, and take them up the marble steps, through the front door, straight to their bedroom with the matching cane beds and the blankets that came all the way from Nain's knitting needles in Nercwys. Siân draws the floral curtains. Babo switches off the lights and says, *Goodnight, little beanstalks, goodnight*, pretending he doesn't know that his girls are really

126

awake, suppressing their smiles, giving chori chori looks to each other across the dark. In the morning Selvi will take a jar of oil to their mangled, sandy hair. Siân will take a comb to it. But for now they're left to sleep in the islands of their beds, their young bodies surrendering quickly to sleep. These are the nights without nightmares, when no one has to run anywhere to feel safe, and morning, when it comes, is cool and dry and peaceful.

12 There are no Divine Beings who Threaten us

It was a Sunday in April when Bean saw her first ghost. She was six years old, hiding in the ashoka grove in Sylvan Lodge. The grown-ups were inside, sitting around the dining table drinking tea, and Mayuri and Cyrus Mazda were playing a restaurant game on the terrace. Bean felt safe in the grove, alone, among the warm green leaves, her bare feet in the mud. She decided to sit there for a while, drawing noughts and crosses in the sand, until someone noticed she was missing and came to find her.

Bean had been running away for some months now. Usually because Mayuri was being mean, or the upstairs Singhania boys were being pains in the bum. Sometimes the desire for attention was nothing Bean could name – it was just a feeling of such utter isolation that when it hit her, the only thing to do was to run out the back door, past Selvi's room and over the wall to the Punjab Women's Association, where she hoped to find solace with one of the kindly hostellers.

The first time Bean ran away, it was by accident. Her best friend, Mehnaz, invited her to come home after school to play in her apple-shaped swimming pool, and Bean, unthinking, had happily clambered into the car-pool van behind her. Three hours and many mutton pakoras later, Mehnaz's mother, Aunty Sherize, came home from shopping and shrieked when she discovered that Bean hadn't informed anyone of her whereabouts. She made a couple of necessary phone calls, and then said to Bean, 'Sweetie, you're always welcome here, but you *have* to ask your mother first.' Then she despatched Bean home in one of Mehnaz's father's Rover cars. When the Rover car drew up to the house of orange and black gates, Babo came running out to gather Bean into his arms and press his bearded face into her chlorinated hair. 'Never do that again,' he said. 'If you love Daddy, and don't want him to have a heart attack, you're never to do that again.'

Siân marched her into the bathroom and said, 'You never think it through, do you? Why don't you think about other people for a change, and the trouble you put them through?'

Bean thought about that first transgression as she watched the last of a fiery Madras sun disappear behind apartment buildings. *Of course* she felt bad about worrying everyone, especially Babo and Siân, but there was also something so wonderful about knowing you'd been missed.

'Did you think I'd been kidnapped too, May-May?' she'd asked her sister as they lay side by side in their beds that night.

'You're a STYOOPID-EEDYOT girl,' Mayuri shouted, sitting upright, flicking her two plaits impatiently behind her head. 'Do you know that while you were having a gala time at Mehnaz's house, Mama and Daddy were in the police station filling out forms, thinking you might be dead? And that while all the teachers went searching the school compound for you I had to sit in the princie's room with mosquitoes biting and nothing but a Thums Up to drink?' As Bean leaned back to digest this information, Mayuri fired her parting shot. 'And anyway, you're adopted, Bean, so who cares if you get kidnapped?'

Bean scooped up a handful of leaves and sighed. It was so hard to know where you belonged. She had spent hours in front of the full-length mirror in her parents' bottle-green bathroom, examining her face, searching out the similarities between Babo, Siân, Mayuri and her. It was all a mystery, the way features blended into one another; why this way and not another? *Why? Why? Because the sky's so high*. How come Mayuri had inherited Babo's grey eyes and she hadn't? How come neither of them had Siân's auburn hair? How come she had got stuck with boring brown eyes and boring brown skin?

'Baby-kutti,' a voice whispered, interrupting Bean's reverie. 'What are you doing hiding in there? Come out, I want to show you something.'

'Go away, Selvam, I don't want to see,' Bean said, drawing the corners of her mouth as low as they could go.

'Are you sure you don't want to see?' Selvam said, poking aside the bushes with his walking cane. 'It's a ghost, baby-kutti, one of Yama's creatures. I'll show you if you come here.'

Bean wriggled out speedily, wiping the sand off her overalls. She had never seen a real live ghost before, but the Singhanias' servant girl had told her all about them – the midgets in the pantry who hid in the biscuit tins, and could swallow up your soul in one bite if you let them; the chudail who slept in the cobwebbed cradle in the attic; Madhavi Rani, who chased cars at midnight, her face like a plump pumpkin at the driver's window. Even though Bean unreservedly acknowledged the presence of ghosts in the world, to this day she had never actually seen one.

Parking herself on the sand next to Selvam outside Sylvan Lodge, she waited expectantly. At first Bean couldn't see anything, only the long row of yellow-flowering trees that were slowly being enveloped by dusk. But, 'Sshh baby-kutti, watch and see,' Selvam persisted, and sure enough, a woman emerged from the branches, floating by with blue-green fingernails and grassy hair. The ghost had ribs like an old piano board, rotted black, shifting darkly under the torn shreds of her sari. Her breasts poked through the folds like withered fruit, and her eyes bored straight down the length of Sterling Road right at Bean.

'See her feet?' Selvam hissed, grabbing Bean into his bony lap. 'See how they're turned backwards at the ankle? That's how you can tell she's from the netherworlds.'

'Ma,' the ghost said, stretching out her skeletal hands as she came towards Sylvan Lodge, dragging her feet behind her. 'Maaaa. . . .' But before the ghost could get any closer, Bean sprang up from Selvam's lap screaming, 'Getawaygetawaygetaway', running through the gates, all the way up to the front door, ringing and ringing the doorbell because even though she wasn't talking to Mayuri or Cyrus Mazda, she had to tell them all about this.

'Oh, please!' Mayuri said, when Bean gestured for the fifth time how the ghost's feet were twisted at the ankles. 'You're such a baby, Bean, to believe everything Selvam tells you. But fine, if you want me to go and see, I suppose I can.'

To Bean, Mayuri was like the girl with the curl in the nursery rhyme. When she was good she was very very good, but when she was bad she was horrid. When Mayuri was good, the sisters could play together for days without any flare-ups, transforming their bedroom into any place they wanted. With Siân's bundle of old saris and scarves they could be damsels in distress, or twins separated at birth, changing outfits every few minutes, exactly like the heroines in the Hindi movies. Mayuri's world was all about fighting dacoits and making up skits for the Sunday Club like *The Tailor of Baghdad* or *Calphurnia's Adventures in Abyssinia* – all more exhilarating than anything Bean herself could ever imagine. But all it took was for one of Mayuri's school friends to come over and *poof*, the spell was broken. Mayuri would lock herself in the guest room with all the toys and Abba tapes, and if Bean begged to be let in to play, she'd scream like a banshee through the keyhole, 'Don't AGGRA-VATE us, Bean, go and find your own game to play.'

It was worst when they were with the hybrids. It wasn't just that Bean had to get dressed up in a proper frock and patent leather shoes, and sit patiently at a table on the lawn of the Madras Gymkhana Club while Siân and Babo talked to their friends. It was that Mayuri ganged up against her with the hybrid Rachel. Rachel was Bean's nemesis. She was a first-ranker, a high-jump champion and could blow a Big Fun bubble gum twice as big as her face, and for all these reasons Bean hated her.

Rachel's mother, Aunty Jan, had come to India from England a long time ago, and had made the two-week journey by ship. 'I cried all the way, every day,' she once told Bean, 'thinking I was making the biggest mistake of my life.'

Bean thought she probably *had* made quite a big mistake, because she'd never been able to go home since – and all to get married to Uncle Keshav, who had a face full of fur and tattoos of his old girlfriends etched like poison ivy into his arms. Every time he saw Bean he got hold of her cheeks as if they were doorknobs and said, 'Hi, girl, can I get you a drink?'

The person Bean liked most in the Krishnamurti family was Rachel's brother, Rahul, who was a full twelve years older, with dark blond hair and sea-blue eyes. Every once in a while, when Mayuri got too uppity, Rachel would take hold of Bean's hand and say, 'Come on, let's you and I go and spy on Rahul,' and the two of them would creep up to the window grills of the billiard room (where only people over eighteen were allowed) and watch Rahul playing snooker with the other big boys. Usually, though, prissy Ms Rachel had no time for Bean, and so Bean was left with the other hybrid child, Shyam Malhotra, who belonged to Aunty Darlene and Uncle Praveen.

Aunty Darlene was American, so she spoke different from Siân and Aunty Jan. She was super-tall with frizzy hair, and she always had something funny to say. Her husband, Uncle

Praveen, by contrast, was dour and sausage-bodied, and even though his eyes crinkled up when he laughed, he often looked like someone had just died. Everyone always said how strange it was that the two of them should produce a child like Shyam.

Bean once overheard Selvi describe Shyam as the ugliest half and half she'd ever laid eyes on. 'Sometimes, all this mixing gives bad results,' Selvi snorted to the Singhanias' servant girl, who concurred that Shyam was the saddest specimen of a little boy she had ever seen.

Siân said that the reason Shyam was sickly and grey in complexion like old people was because he was a 'surprise baby'. When he came into the world, it was much earlier than expected, and he very nearly died. This is why he was small for his age and plagued by an overall thinness: thin in body, eyes, nose, ears, and especially thin in the lips, making him look like a mean little matchstick. But Bean didn't give two hoots about Shyam's appearance. He was still the best tree climber she knew, and besides, he always took her side in everything.

Bean wished Shyam was standing with her right now outside the gates of her grandparents' house so he could help her find the ghost and prove to Mayuri and Cyrus Mazda that she was not a liar liar lipstick. Selvam, her only alibi, had conveniently laid himself out on the floor of the servants' quarters for a quick nap before his night duty, and there was nothing in the world that Bean could say or do to make Mayuri believe her.

Every night after the sighting of the ghost on Sterling Road, Bean stayed up listening for the sickly scrape-scraping sound of ghosts signalling their entrance into the human world. But all she could hear were the cats mating on the wall of the Punjab Women's Association. To Bean, they sounded like an orchestra of babies dying. Keening and wailing with horrific intensity, equal in revulsion, only to P. Vetrivel scratching his nails down the blackboard in class. There were other sounds too – rustlings and slitherings in the corners of the bedroom, making it impossible for her to sleep. When her eyelids finally succumbed to exhaustion, she fell into a sleep so deep and troubled, that inevitably, at some point in the night, her legs parted gently for a warm stream of wee to pass between her pyjama legs.

When Bean slept, even the most benign things took on a malevolent nature. Her toys, who were so gentle and unmoving during the day, threw off their sheets and threatened to poke her eyes out with sticks. Even her favourite story-book character, Dick Whittington, on his way to becoming Mayor of London, stood like a sentry at Babo and Siân's bedroom door with his billowy knickerbockers and his menacing cat, holding a spear in case she should try to sneak by him. Bean, quivering in her non-existent boots, spent most of her nights edging around her sheets, looking for a dry patch to sleep in, and only when she was on the very brink of despair, did she rise up in a brief spurt of courage and make for her parents' door, launching herself squarely between them in bed.

'For goodness sake, it's all rubbish.' Siân always said. 'You're too old to sleep with us now.'

Babo would put on the lights and say, 'See, there's nothing to be afraid of. Try to dream of beautiful things.'

Sometimes, she even tried her luck with Selvi, stretched out on her jute mat on the dining-room floor. But Selvi wouldn't have any of it either. 'Lord, what kind of craziness you got in your head, child? Just off the light and go to sleep.'

But Bean knew that ghosts could hide from grown-ups. They could fold themselves in half and slide into a chest of drawers, or casually slip into the thin space between the wall and the bookshelf, ka-chink ka-chink ka-chink. Or they could shimmy through the window grills and hide in the flame-of-the-forest tree until there was darkness in the house again. Really. It was no use. Once you knew that you lived in a house of ghosts, once you could see and hear them plain as day, there was nothing to do but live in a constant state of torment, until they came to get you.

And if the ghosts didn't get you then the Boochie Man would. It was Mayuri who told Bean about the Boochie Man, who climbed the walls of their room at night. When they lay next to each other after lights out, it was Mayuri who began telling the scariest story of all. *See, there on the toy shelf where Teddy and Panda are sleeping? The Boochie Man is creeping among them, slipping daggers into their throats, and Bean, he's going to get you next!*

Mayuri told her these things and then dreamed of fairies and Ferris-wheels. She woke like a perfect child in crisp, white sheets with sugar at the corners of her lips, while Bean woke up in a cold patch of wee, the soggy evidence of shame between her legs.

13 Love in the Time of Chicken Pox

Upstairs, in his bedroom in Sylvan Lodge, Chotu lounged in bed and scratched his armpits languidly. For two weeks he had been confined, with only regular visits from his mother and sister to relieve his boredom. Trishala spent the morning anointing him with various concoctions of oatmeal and calamine, allowing herself to be temporarily distracted from her main task in hand: to find Dolly a husband. When Dolly came home from candle-making or chocolate-making class, depending on which day of the week it was, she filled Chotu's ears with all the obsessions of her not-so-young life: why was her hair falling out so much? Who did so-and-so think she was wearing a miniskirt to the movies? What would the effect on her figure be if she ate only one meal a day for the next three months? When Trishala and Dolly collided in his room, they bickered as women do when they have lived under the same roof for too long. Only for a few hours in the afternoon, when the house rested, and late at night, after Prem Kumar had stuck his head round the door to give him work updates and news of Babo and family's vacation in Anjar, did Chotu have time for himself. This he used to watch Hindi movies and re-read his favourite *Hardy Boys* books.

On this bright July morning, the opening day of the Summer Olympics in Moscow, Chotu lay in bed examining the remnants of the dew-shaped welts that had until recently covered his legs, back and arms like a swarm of rose petals.

It hadn't been as bad as Jignesh-bhai, the fat-lipped family doctor, had predicted. He had missed cricket, of course, and for a few days he thought he would die from not being able to scratch his wounds, but after the itching subsided, and his body made its slow way to recovery, Chotu reflected that this illness had forced him to put his life into perspective.

Chotu looked around his bedroom at the things that normally brought him joy: his cricket trophies, smartly lined up in a specially built glass showcase; his latest model aeroplane, lying unfinished on the desk by the air-conditioner; a poster of Zeenat Aman from *Don* hanging sexily next to his most prized possession – a framed autograph of Lancelot Gibbs, the greatest bowler in the world, whom Chotu had met in a lucky encounter in the Taj Hotel in Bombay. If he had to name the feeling that was rising in his chest that morning, Chotu's first inclination would have been to say despair. But after letting the weight of that word settle on his tongue, he decided to slide it to one side, and replace it with another word: frustration. Because he was twenty-three, and what had he achieved? Nothing, really. He had graduated from college with a mediocre 78 per cent. He might have had a stellar cricket career if Prem Kumar had allowed it, but instead, he was looking at a future of working indefinitely at Sanbo Enterprises – a thought that brought him no comfort.

There was nothing about Sanbo Enterprises that Chotu liked. Not its location, in a dead-end off a turning from Hunter's Road; not the yellowing office building and its grimy floors; not the neighbours – a wig-making factory and a religious printing press; not even the monkeys that frolicked in the guava trees between the properties. Everything about his job was distasteful to him. He didn't like having to wear good clothes to work and then change into paint-smeared, soiled trousers and shirts like Prem Kumar and Babo. He didn't like the proximity of his desk to the canteen. He didn't like his father's old-fashioned notions of running a business. And he didn't like how Babo conveniently shut himself in the invention room, leaving Chotu to deal with boring administrative details. The only saving grace that Sanbo Enterprises offered was the secretary, Bhanumati, whom Chotu had been carrying on with since the beginning of the year. But even that, in recent times, had lost some of its zing.

Chotu had not been lucky in love. Like many of his college friends, his first sexual experiences had been with the whores of Fifi's House of Spices. After he learned what he'd gone there to learn, he had had a couple of discrete affairs. First, there was Uma, an Assamese girl with a moon face and diminutive but dextrous hands, who came to Sylvan Lodge once a month to give beauty treatments to Trishala and Dolly. Uma's specialities were eyebrow threading and pedicures. For one whole summer Chotu pursued her hotly, following her to her permanent place of work, Cuts and Curls, marvelling at how tenderly she'd handle the fat arms and legs of the housewives who came to her. For days he watched as Uma stood above them, threading away all the unwanted hair, massaging the rolls in their necks. He loved the way she put their feet up on her lap – scrubbing, filing, pumicing, picking out the dirt, smoothing, painting, making them as beautiful as they could possibly be, and he would have watched her for all eternity if Pamela Anne, proprietor of the beauty salon, hadn't told him to bugger off unless he had some serious intentions.

At the time Chotu's intentions were serious, very serious. He waited till Uma finished her shift, and then took her to Marina Beach, where there were groping sessions and passionate declarations of lust. Once, very delicately, during a late-night movie, Uma put her magical hands down Chotu's pants in the dark, which excited him so much he spilled Campa Cola all over himself. But in the end, they both agreed, it wasn't anything close to love, and there had been no consummation.

Then there was Soumya, the yoga teacher at the Madras Cricket Club, who was svelte and snub-nosed, and could bend herself into all kinds of pliable postures. Soumya was married to Major Narayanan, but this didn't diminish her enormous sexual appetite. She went through pool boys, cricket players, retired servicemen and mah-jong players as efficiently as if they were part of her daily yoga practice. With Chotu, the fling lasted a fortnight, more than her usual allotted time. 'You're eager,' she told him, when he had her pinned against the wall of the clubhouse like a butterfly. 'A bit too eager.' And shortly afterwards, his ardent overtures were spurned in favour of a restrained spin bowler from Saidapet.

And then, of course, there was Bhanumati. Bhanu could type seventy-five words a minute and whip up a mean masala tea. She was the last person Chotu expected any kind of romantic liason with until they attended an industry conference for Resin and Pigments at the Congress Grounds, where she was taking shorthand notes. When Bhanu laid a hand on his knee and said, 'Boss, if you want we can go somewhere else,' Chotu discovered she had a far wider array of talents at the disposal of her scrupulous, click clacking fingertips. Underneath her demure exterior, Bhanu was a fairly standard, sex-obsessed convent school product. For six months they went at it every chance they got in the cobwebbed archival room and the middling hotel rooms Chotu hired for the purpose. Everything was perfect until Bhanu started getting kookoo ideas about marriage. The day she showed up with her astrological chart, Chotu had to tell her the truth: that while he enjoyed *being* with her, there was no way that he could *be* with her. And with that another door closed.

Chotu had emerged from these dalliances with no delusions. He knew he hadn't experienced love, nothing even close to

139

love. They had merely been episodes to relieve the monotony of masturbation. What he really yearned for was not marriage, but a grand love affair, something like what his brother had, that could sweep him into another sphere of understanding. But how could that ever happen living in a house like this, with parents like this?

Chotu got out of bed and stood in front of the bathroom mirror in his shorts. He examined the growth of his two-week beard. It made him look older, distinguished, capable of greatness. He had lost a couple of kilos from all the inactivity; his shoulders looked smaller, and his biceps a little deflated, but it was nothing that a hundred one-arm press-ups and a month back in training couldn't fix. He slathered on a layer of shaving foam, relishing the minty softness of it against his face. Just as he was about to dip his razor into a mug of hot water, he changed his mind. *Let's make it a day to remember*, he thought, rinsing the foam off. He stood underneath the cold shower for a few minutes and then buttoned up a long-sleeved shirt he had no intention of changing from once he got to work 'From today we stand our ground,' he muttered. 'From today things are going to be different.'

In Anjar, Ba was remembering the dream she had had on the morning of Chotu's birth. It was a bottomless, frightening dream that involved the mythological serpent, Ananta, coming upon the vast waters of creation and refusing to grow wings. 'See,' she had cried out in her dream. 'These are the waters of creation, even the reptiles will one day sprout wings and fly like birds. Why won't you fly? If you don't fly, this child will never fly.' But the serpent, Ananta, in his wicked, limbless way had only smiled and said, 'We cannot *all* be vehicles of the gods.'

Ba had woken to see a cobra coiled in the branches of the jamun tree, and she had known then that this last grandchild would be serious and quiet, and worse, would know the failure of flight.

That morning, while the Patel family settled around the table to eat breakfast together for the first time in two weeks, Ba had that sensation again, of a thundercloud passing over a parched field, refusing to shed any drops. 'Dear God,' she muttered, as she made her way to the back of her compound to the bamboo grove. 'Something will have to be done.'

For years the entire Patel clan had been trying to persuade Dolly to get married. But as Prem Kumar correctly noted, she was as stubborn and hard as a pellet of goat dung, and if any man was stupid enough to marry her, then God help him. As the years passed by, though, he was beginning to understand that if they waited any longer, the person to suffer most would be himself.

'No more time-wasting now, Dolly,' he said, at the breakfast table, 'All your options have run out. After all these chocolate- and candle-making classes are over you're going to Anajr to look for a boy.'

Among the many problematic and failed life choices Dolly had made so far was a stint at an ashram near Pondicherry, an entrepreneurial bakery venture with one of the famed dames of her college which collapsed after three months when the famed dame ran off with the head baker, and a half-hearted attempt at working with a deaf and dumb children's project which Siân spearheaded for the Overseas Women's Club. Dolly had even considered retiring from life entirely and becoming a Jain nun, but even she knew she wasn't pious enough for such a vocation.

'You know what? Fine! But I don't want anyone short or fat, and he has to be rich and look a bit like Rajesh Khanna.'

'Excuse me!' Trishala said. 'Have you looked at yourself in the mirror recently? You're quite short and fat, and you don't look like any great film heroine yourself, so you better say yes to someone soon, otherwise you're going to be an old maid. How will you catch up with your sister?'

Chotu sat quietly, squirting lime over his papaya. *Sooner or later*, he thought, *Dolly will buckle, and then? Then, it will be just the three of us*. 'Papa,' he said aloud, 'I want to discuss my plan for England. Have you thought more about what I said?'

'Oof,' Trishala groaned. 'If it's not one child giving problems it's the other. Started again! Want to go to England! Want to go to England! As if it's such a great place?'

'Son,' Prem Kumar said, clearing his throat. 'I have thought about it, and your mother and I have decided that instead of going for studies – you're too old for that now, no one does studies at this age, why don't you go for a holiday instead?'

'But I don't want to go for a . . .' Chotu started, hating the whine in his voice.

'Just listen to me, Chotu. We already looked into all the details. Trishala, go and get that pamphlet. Go, go. It's all done. Just think of it as an "in lieu of" trip. In lieu of studying, you get to go for holiday. Lucky, na? Just say when you want to go and we'll book you for a full European vacation: twenty-one cities in twenty-one days. Imagine that!'

Dolly looked at her father and scowled. 'I don't believe this. I have to waste my time meeting and greeting one pathetic character after the next to possibly spend my life with, while Chotu gets to go abroad for a holiday, if you please! Such unfairness in this house, I tell you.'

'If you're lucky your husband will take you to Europe on your honeymoon, so stop complaining,' Trishala interjected, thrusting the pamphlet into Chotu's hands.

Chotu received the Big Ben Travel brochure like a blessing. He opened the first glossy page and examined the groups of brown faces standing in front of familiar world landmarks: the Eiffel Tower, the Leaning Tower of Pisa, St Paul's Cathedral.

The itinerary proposed on the following pages was staggering: Amsterdam, Paris, Rome, Bonn, Prague, Lisbon – in out, in out. Chotu studied the pamphlet intently, his bearded face getting smaller and tighter. Then he pushed his breakfast away, got up and walked out of Sylvan Lodge without saying a word.

14 Sometimes Summers and the Question of Suffering

Every three years Babo, Siân, Mayuri and Bean got on an aeroplane and flew across the ocean to see Nain and Taid in Nercwys. Mayuri and Bean loved their sometimes summers even though they were under strict instructions to mind their Ps and Qs, eat with their knives and forks, not talk with their mouths full, help clear up the table and wash up because there was no Selvi to help. It didn't matter because everyone made a big fuss over them. Uncle Owen took them horseback riding in the fields everyday, and Aunty Eleri secretly slipped them change to buy Smarties from the post office.

On Sundays Taid played the organ at church and Nain took them to Sunday School where they had to sit still and be on their best behaviour. If they were good Nain made hot Ribena as a treat and gave them two chocolate McVities biscuits from the Cadbury's tin when they came home. But they weren't to run around without shoes or make too much noise, and most of all they weren't to bother Nain when she was knitting in her chair or working with her roses in the garden because if they did, she'd screech 'Siân, Siân,' and then Siân would come rushing out and say 'For heaven's sake,' and bundle them up in sweaters and send them to the playground down the street.

The playground down the street had bigger slides and better swings than those they were used to in Madras. Bean and Mayuri walked down the street on either side of

Siân, dressed in matching army-green overalls but different coloured jumpers – Bean's hair cut short like a sugar bowl with a fringe, and Mayuri with two chestnut braids down her back. In the playground they played with the neighbourhood children who were white and ginger-haired, or white and blonde-haired; whose skin freckled in the sun, whose nails were so impossibly pink. They played as if in a crater of the moon, swinging and sliding about while the black and white cows watched from afar. Long after the other children left, Mayuri and Bean continued to play until Babo came to fetch them. 'It's late,' he'd say, 'NINE-O-CLOCK! Way past your bedtime. Wee Willy Winky's been looking for you.'

They laughed at him and called him a liar-liar, because the sky only looked like a 6:30 blue. But Babo showed them the face of his watch, and the girls, seeing proof of his claim, understood that Time must live where Ba said it did after all – in that invisible space between the eyes. It could be whatever you wanted it to be. A million years could pass like a second. A day could seem as impossible to get through as all of the seven oceans.

Babo walked with them under the summer Nercwys sky which was so big and full of stars, so much more than in Madras, or even in Anjar, that when they asked why it was so, he said it was because the stars in Wales were actually rabbits; they multiplied like rabbits.

Mayuri and Bean couldn't understand the machinery in this country. The watches lied and the televisions were magic. Mayuri wanted to take Nain's TV back to Madras so she could watch *Rainbow* instead of *Wonder Balloon*. Bean wanted to take the big kitchen clock back so she could get rid of the nights in the house of orange and black gates, because in Nercwys the nights were never long, and there were never any nightmares.

In Tan-y-Rhos Mayuri and Bean got to take baths together in a proper tub with soap bubbles and face towels, not like their bucket baths at home. Here, they could sit till their skin pruned, till Babo and Siân dragged them out, creamed them up and put them to bed – Mayuri on the top bunk because she was the oldest, and Bean on the bottom because she slept so hard she often fell off the edge.

In the mornings, before anyone woke up, Bean was at the window, pulling apart the curtains to see what kind of day it was going to be. And it was on one such day in the spring–summer of 1981, when Mayuri was asleep with a fever and the rest of the house was sleeping too, that Bean peered outside the window panes and saw the world changing colours right in front of her eyes. She ran straight to Babo and Siân's bedroom even though she had been told to stay out.

'Daddy, Mama, wake up! I think it's snowing!' she screeched.

Siân turned over crossly and said, 'What are you talking about, Bean? It's April!'

But Bean pulled Babo by his hands and took him to the window even though he was only wearing his VIP underpants, and when he opened the curtains, he could see too – the green fields were being covered with a blanket of white. 'Yes, indeed!' Babo laughed, 'You're right, Kidney Bean. It's snowing. Imagine that!'

Bean put on her woollies and raced outside without even bothering to bring in the newspaper or milk bottles for Taid. She left Mayuri and her melon face inside to sulk on Siân's lap in the front room.

Nain, Taid, Uncle Owen, Babo and Bean made a snowman, using bits of coal for his eyes and a turnip for his nose. It was wonderful – just like the scene from *The Wizard of Oz*, where Dorothy and Lion are sleeping in the deadly poppy fields and snow starts falling all around them. 'Unusual weather we're havin, ain't it?' Lion says to Dorothy. And Bean, all that April day, even though the snow stopped falling almost as soon as it had begun, kept singing, 'Oh we're off to see the wizard, the wonderful wizard of Oz,' until Mayuri said if she didn't put a sock in it, she would never let her use her make-up glitter again.

Later that night, after Babo and Siân had wiped down the girls' faces with hot towels and put them in flannel pyjamas, Bean wriggled up the ladder to tell Mayuri that playing in the snow hadn't been so much fun without her after all. She pushed the little coal button snowman's eyes into Mayuri's palms, and Mayuri took them and slid them chup chap under her pillow, but still said nothing.

Even when Mayuri was feeling better, and Taid drove her into Mold in his Morris Minor to get her a present for missing out and being a good girl about it, even when Mayuri had her new doll, Tessa, tucked permanently under her arm, and they all watched Lady Di get out of a glass coach like a real princess in a bouffant lace gown with puffy sleeves, Mayuri wouldn't forgive Bean, and she wouldn't return the snowman's eyes either. This was Bean's first lesson in suffering.

When they returned from Nercwys that summer, all Bean could think about was suffering. Everywhere she looked it was there – staring her in the face. She couldn't help noticing how the people in Madras had very little compared to the people in Nercwys. She thought about all the suffering in the world: the pictures on TV of families standing on the roofs of their houses, caught up in cyclones and earthquakes; families living in countries of war, living among the ruins of their homes with broken faces and bloodied hearts. She thought about the stories Trishala Ba had told her, of Gautam Buddha and Lord Mahavir, who renounced their kingdoms and went in search of Enlightenment so they could ease the suffering of the world. She thought of how it must have been for Siân to leave her house and family and country behind to come zing zing zing all the way to Madras. Most of all, she thought about how it would be if something terrible happened to Babo, Siân and Mayuri, leaving her all alone in the world.

'You're just being morbid,' Babo said, when she asked about Babo's final will and testament, his life insurance policy, what the back-up plan was in case the house of orange and black gates burned down in a fire. 'You've got an over-active imagination, Bean. Nothing's going to happen.'

But Bean saw things happening around her all the time. Every day, on the way to school, when she wasn't forced to sit between the crater-faced Singhania brothers because Mayuri insisted on sitting in the front with the driver, she looked out of the window and counted the number of unfortunate people she saw: beggars, lepers, raggedy children, monkey-men, snake-charmers – there seemed to be an awful lot of them in the city of Madras.

And then there were the gypsies who lived by the Aavin Milk 'n' Ice Parlour past the Adyar Bridge, where every Friday after school, they were allowed to get creamy pink softy cones. The gypsies sat huddled around cooking fires under mango trees, and their children – barely as old as Bean – went about with hardly a scrap of clothing on them. The girls wore grubby panties, and the boys walked around starkers, showing off their little Mr Whatsits. And the boys and girls, both, had long, bright, sun-bleached hair that shone like knotted haloes around their heads. How could they live like this? thought Bean. Where did they sleep at night? What did they eat?

Mayuri said that the gypsies ate squirrels and whatever else they could lay their catapults on. Cyrus Mazda confirmed this: he'd once seen a gypsy bring down three squirrels – tup tup tup – from the tree outside his bedroom window. Besides which, Cyrus also confirmed that it was the gypsies who had stolen Mrs Jhunjhunwala's beloved Persian, Fluffy, and eaten him for dinner. The thought of poor Fluffy being skinned and roasted on one of those cooking fires made Bean feel quite ill.

'A man's got to eat,' Babo said. 'It's a dog eat dog world, Bean, and a man's got to feed his family.' Babo was always saying things like this – that people created situations for themselves, that an awful lot of despair in the world was due to *just-plain-laziness*, that fatalism was the noose around which the masses of this country were kept in poverty.

For all his talking, though, Babo never *actually* did anything. It was Siân who spent her days with the underprivileged – which meant people who had less than them. It was Siân who dragged Mayuri and Bean to the Andhra Mahila Sabha school, where she taught English to kids with no arms and legs. Kids who came crawling out any which way they could, on trays and in wheelchairs, lolloping along the floor like strange animals. 'See how they're smiling?' Siân always said, bending to pick one of them up – little Venkatesh, usually, who was her favourite, and had a weird thing bumping out of his back. 'Even though they have no mama or daddy to look after them. See how brave they are?'

Bean smiled and patted one or two of them casually on the head, but what she couldn't bear to say to her mother or Mayuri, was that it horrified her. *They* horrified her, just as the ghost she'd seen scraping along Sterling Road with its twisted feet had. She knew it was awful and unforgivable, but if she was really honest about it, what she'd like to do more than anything, was to never see the AMS school again, and to play with her best friend Mehnaz in her room of toys for ever. But Bean couldn't say it, because she knew that admitting this would mean disappointing Siân, and somehow, disappointing her mother was far worse than disappointing anyone else in the world, even her father.

Bean had heard all about the love story of her parents from Ba in Anjar. How Babo met Siân in London, how they had a testing period of six months apart before Siân finally came to India to live happily ever after. *But Mama was the braver*

149

one, Bean thought. No matter how much she loved her father, *Mama was always the braver one because she left everything behind to be here with us*.

Siân really was like no other mother Bean knew, and it was mainly to seek her approval that Bean persisted in her quest for goodness. She shared all her toys with Mayuri even though Mayuri didn't share back, and she put aside half her pocket money to give away to the blind children at the Clarke's school, because they didn't give her the creeps as much as the AMS kids. But every now and then, Bean had a serious lapse. The capitalist side of her nature unleashed itself, usually at Shastri's Fancy Stores, where the object in question was another thing she didn't need – a stainless steel kitchen set or a mask-making kit. Bean began with little hints, a bit of loving fingering, a few tears, and when none of that worked she went for the floor – thumping her fists and arms, wailing that for all the good things she'd done, this was just a small thing Siân could do for her in return.

Whenever this happened Siân disappeared with Mayuri following like a tail, leaving Bean hollering on the floor as if she wasn't her child. Ten minutes later Siân would return. 'Are you done? Ready to go home now? Ready to behave?' And Bean nodding, subdued, would take her mother's hand out into the world, where suffering was inevitable and where her selfishness was exposed for all to see.

In September 1981, on a perfectly ordinary Madras day, while Bean and Mayuri were playing Lady Di, wrapping mosquito nets around their heads as veils and clip clopping around on Siân's high-heeled shoes, a phone call came in the middle of a Saturday morning that altered life in the house of orange and black gates for a long while.

'It's Uncle Owen,' Mayuri said, putting the telephone receiver to one side, and marching up to Babo and Siân's bedroom door. 'He says he needs to speak to Mama. Something bad has happened.'

Mayuri and Bean stood outside their parents' door, wondering what to do. Saturdays were off limits to them. It was the day Babo and Siân locked themselves in their bedroom doing God-only-knew-what for hours and hours. Sometimes, the girls didn't see their parents till evening, when they rolled out in kaftan and kurta pyjama to drink tea on the veranda before getting ready to meet the hybrids at the Madras Gymkhana Club. Often, the only evidence that any kind of life carried on inside that room, was the low, consistent drone of the air-conditioner, and the occasional glimpse of a long, white arm reaching for one of the breakfast or lunch trays that Selvi left on the floor outside their bedroom.

Mayuri and Bean stood at their door and knocked.

Nothing.

They knocked harder. Wham bam. Wham bam.

'Mama,' Mayuri screamed. 'Telephone call for you. It's Uncle Owen and he says something bad has happened. Can you hurry up and come out, please?'

Knock knock knock.

'Mama. Hurreeeee.'

Finally, Siân emerged, wearing one of Babo's shirts, and Babo followed with a bath towel wrapped around his waist, the scanty curls of hair on his chest glistening. They ran into the dining room where the red telephone receiver still lay on its side. Siân picked the phone up and held it close to her ear, her auburn hair falling in jagged shafts across her forehead. 'Oh my God,' she said. 'Oh my God,' she kept saying.

The girls watched as Babo stood behind their mother and put his arms around her shoulders.

'Of course, I'll be there, I mean, I have to . . . wait for me.'

When Siân put down the telephone she told Mayuri and Bean to wait for her in their room. Then she took Babo's hand

and walked back to their bedroom, where they locked the door for what seemed like a whole day. Mayuri told Bean she was 99 per cent sure they would not be going to the Madras Gymkhana Club for dinner that night, and she was right. By seven o'clock Selvi had laid the table for two, and Mayuri and Bean were eating chicken frankies with tomato sauce under the whirring Khaitan fan. When Babo and Siân finally came to them, fully dressed, Siân's eyes were red, and Babo had that look on his face when he'd done something wrong, like smoked cigarettes inside the house, or called someone a bloody basket.

'Sit down, girls,' Siân said, indicating the matching cane beds. 'Now listen to me. Mama's got to go away for a while. I've got to go home because Taid has died. Do you understand? I've got to go home, because my family needs me.'

Home, Bean wondered, *Isn't this home? Here, with us. Aren't we family? Babo, Siân, Mayuri, Bean?*

15 All You Need is Love

All the way over on the flight, Siân kept thinking, maybe it's not true, maybe it's like the time Prem Kumar tricked Babo into coming back to Madras, saying Trishala was in hospital. Maybe Bryn hadn't really cycled home from work one day to sit down in his favourite chair and die without even having a cup of tea first.

Bhupen Jain picked her up at Heathrow and took her hand in an honest, heartfelt way. He told her what a difficult thing it was to lose a parent you had abandoned. He had left his own ageing parents in a dilapidated house in Baroda. He could understand what she was going through. *Could he, though? Could anyone?*

Bhupen told her that life had been hard for him too. The paint course he had done with Babo at the Borough Polytechnic had come to no good. Nobody wanted to hire someone with no technical experience, and no one was willing to give him that experience unless he worked for free. But how could he work for free when he had two children to support? Indrani, who wanted to take ballet lessons instead of bharatanatyam, and Deenu, who was more interested in Spanish than Sanskrit.

And if that wasn't bad enough, they'd had another robbery at the post office. They were thinking of selling up, moving to some other line of business, but what were they equipped to do other than this? They were unskilled traders who knew only what their fathers and their grandfathers had done before them – how to convert one rupee to five to fifty to a hundred by means of the slow diligent qualities of persistence and parsimony.

Bhupen hadn't had much luck converting his money. He wondered why he had ever come to a country that was so cold and unforgiving in the first place. So his children could take ballet and Spanish, of course. So he could write to his parents in Baroda and tell them he was a proud house-owner, upstanding pillar of the community, President of the Jain Association.

Siân wanted to tell him it was different for her. She had learned the secret of surviving in a foreign country. It had something to do with love. She'd been on the brink of understanding for so long. And what she had discovered was this: love can't be fear, love can't be violence, love can't be anything we name or anything we can't bear.

The two weeks Siân spent at home after Bryn's funeral reminded her of the time she spent in Tan-y-Rhos pining for Babo all those years ago. Except this time, there was no Bryn to take her away for poetry and picnics, only her friend, Ronnie, returned to Nercwys to marry Ken Davies, owner of The White Lion. Huw and Carole came up from Brighton with the twins, and Owen was there too, grown suddenly old and more withdrawn. There were no fervent letters from Babo at his makeshift desk in Zam Zam Lodge, telling her that the whole world hinged on their love. There was a phone call instead: *Come home soon, Mama, we miss you.*

There were still spaces and spaces between her mother and her, still so many silences. Every morning, she and Nerys worked in the rose garden, their gloved hands deep in the earth. *If you dig deep enough, you'll get all the way to China.* Isn't that what Bryn used to tell her when she was a little girl? Siân had dug and dug but reached India instead.

Siân spent her days looking for Bryn. She wandered to their secret places alone, at twilight, waiting for her father to appear in the half-light, half-dark. She wanted to know if the God he believed in and loved so much had saved him in the end, or if on the last day, he had given up his ideas of eternal life and everlasting punishment. She kept looking for him in valleys with midnight-blue ridges and silver flowers, wondering if he'd found a home in the roots of the black poplar tree or if he was that ancient owl staring at her from a solitary branch. Was he happy to be something so simple and unrecognizable?

Never forget where you've come from, Bryn had said. *Don't forget about us.* But Siân had allowed everything to fade; she had packed it all away in the bottom drawer of her heart and began a beginning halfway across the world. And now that she was back in the house her father had brought her to, a month after she was born, in the coldest winter of the century, there was nothing to do but run to the graveyard in the chapel where he lay under the earth; to sit by his side and weep.

She sat in that autumn scene, tracing the letters on Bryn's headstone, reciting *Under Milk Wood*, in spite of herself, the rhythm of the lines falling like a field stream, like a long, suffocating snowdrift from childhood. She wondered about her daughters so far away in Madras, how they were ever going to remember their grandfather or guess at the breadth of his generous, patient love.

When Siân finally returned to the house of orange and black gates she was a changed woman. Everyone could see it. Not just because of her new hairstyle – a perm, which Babo, Mayuri and Bean jointly hated. It was something more, as if someone had climbed inside her and switched off all the lights. She was always tired, sleeping well into the morning and going to bed right after dinner, barely able to make it through the one episode of *Mind Your Language* the girls were allowed to watch. When she wasn't resting she exhausted herself by marching around the house with a duster, or getting on her knees with an old toothbrush to clean the cracks between the bathroom tiles.

In the first week of her return she removed every piece of fabric in the house and gave it to the dhobi. The mosquito nets from the window grills, the curtains and lambrequins, the upholstery covers and antimacassars, the sheets, pillowcases, bedspreads, blankets – all were bundled up and sent away, leaving the house looking a little forlorn and bare. She got the rubbish man to collect the old newspapers and bottles that had been piling up in the storeroom for months, and she made Selvi sit on the veranda and polish all the brass pots and figurines till they shone.

Siân couldn't catch hold of this new feeling. She wondered if it was grief, this dull, insistent thing that circulated in her blood and refused to leave. But grief couldn't last this long, could it? Grief expelled itself in intense gut-wrenching fits, and she had done most of that already in Nercwys after seeing her father laid out in a coffin, after understanding that she would never hear his voice again. This was different. This was re-entering your life and being suffocated by it.

Siân started to feel it as soon as she landed in Madras – that cruel, oppressive struggle of the day-to-day. The wave of humidity that immediately deflated her new curls – so buoyant in Nercwys, limp and frizzy here. The stale sweaty smell of porters, the nausea of bidis and spit and smoke. Everything she had once admired about India – the persistence of life, the triumph of the human spirit – wilted in the presence of so much grot. Now it all seemed like a mindless scramble to survive. And for what? As she drove home from the airport, the poverty hit her with renewed vigour – those mothers with scrawny babies at their breasts, who came up to the car and tapped at the windows, the outcast and the maimed, the rag-tag children. What on earth could be done for them?

Even in the sanctuary of her own home, everything looked faded and a little sad, despite her and Selvi's cleaning binge. Siân surveyed her home. Every object was there because *she* had put it there, lovingly, and with pride, and yet, it all seemed so inadequate. The golden-yellow settee and glass-topped table, the Wedgwood plates on the dining-room wall, the twenty-five-volume *Time–Life* nature series, sold to her by a charismatic door salesman, stacked in the rosewood cabinet. Even the framed print of Brueghel's *Landscape with the Fall of Icarus*, which she had bought in London a long time ago because it enchanted her, positioned now between the girls' matching cane beds; even those pale white legs disappearing into water couldn't restore her.

And it wasn't just in the things. It was Selvi's pomposity in taking charge of the household, and Mrs Singhania's malicious gossiping, and Bahadur's perennial drunken stupor; human flaws which she'd put up with quite happily before, suddenly setting her on edge. It wasn't the individual failings that bothered her, but her dependence on them. The fact that she needed them, along with the driver and the ironing man and any number of other people, just to get things done. Her whole life seemed suddenly crowded, impinged upon, eternally dusty.

And then there were those letters, hers and Babo's. Babo's sprawling notebooks and her faded blue aerogrammes, all neatly filed in chronological order in two Sanbo Enterprises folders in the bottom drawer of the rosewood cabinet. Did she dare go there now? *Of course we'll have children, darling, and they'll be so beautiful, people in the streets will have to stop and stare*. Really? Really? Because here was Mayuri looking distinctly unbeautiful, walking into the house for the umpteenth time with no shoes on her feet and broken toenails from riding that infernal bicycle. And Bean, pouting in the corner, going on about her imaginary ghosts. Siân wanted to scream, *Can't you just be quiet and listen for a change? Selfish creatures! Can't you just do something right?*

'You're spoilt,' she badgered them. 'That's the problem. You think Selvi's always going to be around to do things for you. Well, let me tell you, you'll have to learn eventually. From now on you're going to make your own beds. I always did, so why can't you? And you can hang your towels on the line to dry instead of throwing them on the floor.'

'But Daddy doesn't even step into the kitchen to make his own tea!'

'Daddy is also the only person in this house who has a job and makes money, so let's not forget about that. Besides, you're children. Children don't get to make the rules.'

Babo felt this new brittleness in his wife, but he waited, because the hunger between their bodies was still raw, still present. At nights, when he held her, she wouldn't speak of her father, or his passing. 'Not yet,' she said, when he pressed her, 'I can't just yet.'

She wanted to preserve an idea in her mind, that being this far away, she could pretend Bryn was still alive, taking pleasure in the things that brought him joy. 'Because the awful truth is,' she finally told Babo, 'I loved him best. I always loved my father best.'

She sat with Manna in the Garden of Redemption, hoping to make sense of things.

'If we understand our own births and deaths,' Manna said, 'We'll know what to erase and what to put forward.'

Siân didn't know what that could possibly mean. She was thirty-four years old. A wife, a mother, a half-orphan. She didn't know what erasing or putting forward had to do with living or dying. 'When we disappear, what kind of spaces do we leave behind?' she asked.

'What are you seeking, and why?' Manna countered. 'The minute you think you've found something, haven't you already lost it?'

Wasn't it simple? Wasn't what Manna saying simple?

All beauty created by man is destined to disappear with him.

A month after her return, Siân shut herself in with her best friends and talked about what exactly they had given up when they decided to get married and live in India. They sat in Darlene's living room, huddled around a low wooden table on divans, talking about their losses, their fears of the future.

Jan hadn't been home since she got to India in 1958. Initially, it was because they couldn't afford it, but afterwards, the need, which had seemed so visceral at first, diminished into a wistful fancy. Her parents had died early, in quick succession, and after getting over the shock of that, there was no need, really, for going back. 'My life is here,' Jan said simply. 'I wouldn't know where to begin if I went back to England.'

It was different with Darlene. She came from a family of six, and all her brothers and sisters had married and bought houses within a five-mile radius of her parents. They got together as often as they could – Thanksgivings, Christmases, birthdays, even just regular weekends, and they often telephoned to tell her how much they missed her, and how much she was missing out. 'It just kills me,' Darlene said. 'To think if anything happens, I'm two whole days away from Tennessee.'

'Well,' said Jan, 'I've thought about it, and God forbid, if Keshav goes first, I'm going to stay in India. I'll probably take to the hills and preside over the local library. And if I'm lucky, my children will come and visit once a year. But I'm quite sure I'll die in an ivy-trellised cottage full of cats with no one but my manservant to watch over me.'

Darlene sighed. 'I suppose we all die alone, no matter where we are. No less lonelier here in India than anywhere else.'

'You're right, of course,' Siân said, patting Darlene's hand. 'You're right.'

Siân told them how, only the day before, she had taken Bean and Mayuri to see her old friend, Ms Douglas. They had been fidgety the whole time, begging to play in the garden rather than sit in Ms Douglas's blue-gabled house and drink tea from chipped cups and saucers. 'I suppose there's something eerie about that place if you're a child, but still, I've always found solace there, and I guess I kind of hoped they'd feel it too.'

Siân supposed there was something about Ms Douglas herself that didn't exactly endear her to children – so thin and corroded, always repeating herself, slapping those twiggy wrists of hers, the dentures slipping in and out of her mouth.

'But all they wanted to know as soon as we left was how come Babo hadn't sent someone to paint her house, and why did Ms Douglas have so many jars of Champion oats in her kitchen, and wasn't it sad that Ms Douglas was losing her mind and was she going to die soon?

' "Why's it sad?" I asked them. "Where else is she going to go? She's got no family. Her brothers are dead. She manages on her monthly pension, what's sad about that?" And then I said, "What do you think is going to happen to me when I get old?" And they both looked at me, incredulously, as if the thought had never occurred to them, and you know what Mayuri said? She said, "It's different with you, Mama. It has to be. You have family. You have Daddy and Bean and me." '

Siân thought about this as she drove back to the house of orange and black gates. When she walked through the front door, she saw Mayuri and Bean dancing in their nighties to the new *Top Ten* tape she had bought them. She watched them jiggle their limbs like marionettes, jerking their hips this way and that, singing, *I love a rainy night*, their faces shiny and clean like plums. When they saw her, they immediately stopped dancing and ran to her. 'Mama, you're home! Read to us. Read to us.'

'OK!' Siân laughed. 'Let's get into bed and read together, OK?'

Siân leaned against the pillows and started reading aloud from *Anne of Green Gables*. She struggled to keep her voice steady as she read, because *this* was something, wasn't it? Mayuri and Bean, their two damp heads pressed close on either breast, their thin brown legs lying protectively over hers. They relied on her to explain things. This is what she had chosen. And all she could offer them was some hope of beauty, some way of seeking it. Because they loved her as simply and unconditionally as Babo did. And this fierce, this maddening love was the only true thing in her life.

Here's another picture: Siân in a red dress and gold sandals waiting on a beach where Babo has arranged for a cottage and a hammock for the night. Babo is driving out into the streets of Madras with Mayuri and Bean on the back seat of the Flying Fiat, kissing them at the gates of Sylvan Lodge, where Trishala is breezing about like a bonfire, saying, 'Come in, my little laadlis. See what I've made for you.' Babo races back along the shoreline of the city, going further and further south till it narrows and clears, until it's almost desolate. Later, when the dark and pale of their undersides are gleaming like crabs in the moonlight, he whispers, 'Tell me a secret.' And there's nothing to tell, because he holds all of her entirely, completely, in the endless summer of his palms.

16 Ignatius and the Unibrows

The marriage of Dolly Patel to Chunky Shah took place over three pomp-filled days in Anjar, Gujarat, culminating in a teary reception in Ba's house on 5 July 1982, a day before the longest lunar eclipse of the twentieth century. At the start of that month Ba's house was invaded by women. Trishala and Dolly arrived first from Madras, fat and flush with wedding fever. Then a band of spinster sisters descended from Bhuj to present themselves in all their miserable spinsterly glory as examples in case Dolly should try to back out at the last minute. Then, to everyone's surprise, Trishala's old friend, Meghna-behn, mother of the lovely, lisping Falguni, made a courtesy call to deliver sweets to celebrate the arrival of her fifth and final grandchild: a boy. It was the first conversation the two friends had had since Babo broke off his engagement in 1969, and the tension between them was enough to stun both the red garoli lizards and the peacocks sauntering along the tin roof. Besides this, there were the usual constants in Ba's life: the thoroughfare of Ganga Bazaar ladies who came unfailingly every evening for their daily activities, and, lately, Ignatius.

Ignatius: a lady-boy hermaphrodite of startling beauty, with padded bosoms and a fake plait.

Of all the assaults on the sanctum of Ba's house, Ignatius was the only one whose presence Ba tolerated, in fact, relied upon. 'Save me from this madness,' she whispered, when

Shakuntala-behn started up on the benefits of a purely milk and mango diet, or if the triplets Rukku, Munnu and Tunnu began arguing about who was eldest, and therefore whose word should be taken as final.

Ignatius worked as a seamstress at the New Pinch Boutique in town, and had for the last few years taken up residence in a thatch shack in the thicket of the bamboo grove in Ba's compound. To his name he also had a small room on the top floor of Hira Lal's jewellery store, where he sat by the east-facing window grills and did most of his intricate stitching work. He moved between these two residences constantly and effortlessly, so much so that if Ba hadn't been in possession of her rarefied sense of smell, she'd never have been able to monitor his comings and goings. But as it was, Ignatius signalled his arrival with a never-ending testosterone trail of male admirers, who crept past the sides of Ba's house after midnight and left their slippers outside Ignatius's makeshift door.

The relationship between Ba and Ignatius was something of an enigma to the women of Ganga Bazaar, who held Ba in the highest esteem – not just because her hair had turned completely white in her fifty-third year, conferring upon her an automatic mantle of wisdom, but because she had meticulously shown over time the merit of her unconventional ways. By contrast, Ignatius was boisterous and uncouth, always flirting shamelessly with their husbands and sons. And while it's true that he had the remarkable talent of being able to fix anything from a broken television to a broken heart with his lady-boy fingers, there was something about him that unsettled them.

Ignatius, conscious of their discomfiture, always absented himself from Ba's evening sessions. 'Who wants to hear a bunch of old women cackle?' he'd say, disappearing to perform his ablutions at the well. After they left, Ignatius would reappear, freshly powdered and flowered, to help Ba roll the mats away. 'Finished dispensing with advice, oh holy one?' he'd tease, before taking out dinner on two steel plates and resting them under the shade of the jamun tree.

For all his apparent irreverence, nobody doubted Ignatius's loyalty to Ba. She had saved his life when others had been happy to let him wither up and die. At the age of fourteen, when Ignatius ran away from the Catholic orphanage in Mundra where his parents had dumped him as a baby, he had been rescued by Ba, who found him half-starved and mute with fear at the bus station. She had brought him to her house and taught him how to make the hair fall away from his legs and arms; how to smooth turmeric and rosewater on his skin to soften it; how to pick the bristles off his beard without leaving any scars. And when the breasts wouldn't grow and the blood between the legs wouldn't come, it was Ba who comforted the disconsolate Ignatius and told him that a swan could never swim away from its own whiteness, meaning to say that he was what he was, and we are what we are, and because Ignatius was *unable* to bring life into this world either as man or woman, he was *enabled* with other powers that ordinary people couldn't have, and these powers had to do with preservation – that second most important principle of the universe.

When Ignatius turned seventeen and decided to leave for the big city of Bombay to find his destiny, Ba let him go, and told him that whenever he wanted to find his way back to her, all he needed to do was follow the wind. After five years of working at Bombay's VT railway station with a band of belligerent hijras, Ignatius, embittered and worn down, reappeared on Ba's doorstep ready to start anew.

Ignatius learned from Ba how women were the true inventors of the world: the original creators, the tillers and sowers, the nurturers and warriors. He learned about magic and science, and all the other ways to control illusion which

164

Ba used to bring the women of Ganga Bazaar back to their bodies after they'd worked in the fields and in the streets – bending, sweeping, spinning, swabbing. Because your body is your universe, didn't you know? *Your body is your universe*.

In the lead-up to Dolly's wedding, Ignatius's body went into overdrive. He sat in the back yard knocking pieces of wood together so that the guests would have tables and chairs to sit at after the ceremonies at the Amba Mata Temple. He constructed an elaborate thatch and bamboo covering over the tables and chairs to lessen the effect of the sun's intensity. He helped Ba and Trishala decide the menus for the various functions and, along with the triplets Rukku, Munnu and Tunnu, decorated the entire house with garlands of rose and marigold. Most importantly, though, Ignatius spent all night working under the light of an electric bulb, wearing the thick-framed glasses he was too vain to wear during the day, sewing real strings of gold into Dolly's wedding sari.

Six months earlier, when Trishala had arrived in Ganga Bazaar, determined to find Dolly a groom, it was Ignatius who had taken matters into his own capable hands. 'Trishala-behn,' he said. 'Is that daughter of yours driving you crazy? Don't worry about it. I'll find her a nice man. No problem. Chak-a-chak. Just send them to me and I'll inspect their goods before giving the thumbs up.'

For two weeks a long troop of possible candidates trotted in and out of Ba's open doors. Every day Dolly cried to Ba about how she hated Anjar. There was nothing to do, only old people sitting around chewing paan and gossiping about people she couldn't care less about. 'Sorry, except you, of course,' she added, with a touch of remorse. No cinemas, no shops, only Zam Zam Lodge with its limited enticements – an ice-cream counter with twenty-four flavours that was out of bounds for her, and a fortune teller with his parrot who sat on a faux-jewelled dais in the playground.

'How Babo-bhai ever managed to stay here all those months without dying of boredom, I don't know,' Dolly moaned.

Trishala was distraught and her dishevelled condition reminded Ba of that oh-so-long-time-ago when she had been struggling with Prem Kumar's flat-footed desire, trying to conceive a child. Ba had counselled her then; told her to put vegetables in her lap, and to dance in the rain. Now she had come with another problem: to make Dolly accept a match before it was too late.

Finally, they settled on a diamond merchant from Baroda by the name of Chaitanya, pet name Chunky, who wasn't chunky at all. In fact, he was unusually skinny, looming several inches over Dolly with his only film-star attribute – an outrageously untidy mop of Shammi Kapoor hair.

Now at last, the wedding that Trishala had hoped for Babo and then for Meenal came to fruition, with more hoopla and tha-ra-rum-pum-pum than even she could have imagined. For three days there was non-stop singing, dancing, praying, eating and almost no sleeping. Trishala basked in the envious congratulatory words that came pouring forth from everyone, and lied through her teeth to whoever would listen. 'I *knew* all along that Dolly would find a good husband. Nowadays thirty is not so old to get married. We have to change our mindset and be forward thinking, isn't it?'

In reality Trishala's relief was so immense that she felt the weight of all the jalebis she'd consumed in recent weeks drop off her sizeable saddlebags almost instantly. She floated around Ba's house, admiring her own granddaughters, who were behaving like good girls by diving at all the grown-ups' feet with reverence as she'd instructed them to do. She shouted loudest and most enthusiastically when Babo and Chotu lifted Dolly on their shoulders for the garlanding ceremony – where the groom and bride compete to see who gives in first to the garlanding, setting the tone for the rest of their married life; and she showed her delight by kissing both sons repeatedly when they held Dolly up long enough so she could win. Even Prem Kumar, who relished being difficult at the best of times, toed the line by shutting up about how much money all this was costing him, and when it was all finished, filled her heart with joy by saying, 'You did the right thing with this, Trishala. After all, love is an ideal thing, but marriage is a real thing.'

When Dolly finally departed with her new husband, taking with her an extensive wedding trousseau that included fifty-one saris, five gold jewellery sets and a sexy honeymoon negligee, the whole village let out a collective gasp of relief. Ba's house emptied out almost as quickly as it had filled up. Trishala, Prem Kumar, Meenal and her shipbroker husband, Babo and Siân, Chotu, the spinster sisters from Bhuj and all the other aunties and uncles, gathered up their belongings and departed in the space of a single morning. Only Ignatius and the four great-granddaughters stayed, all set to squabble for the remainder of their summer vacation.

After everyone left, Ba walked around her compound to survey the carnage of Anjar's grandest wedding. All around were torn pieces of paper and plastic; giant vessels which the ladies of Ganga Bazaar would scrub with Vim powder before hauling them back to the Amba Mata Temple; coconut husks and banana skins; branches, leaves, red garoli lizard skins, peacock feathers. Ba could smell the lingering camphor from the marriage pyre, the sickening smell of leftover vegetable oil, dying jasmine. She could smell Dolly's tears and Trishala's sulphuric gunpowder anxiety hanging like a shroud over everything. But rising above it all, there was another smell, the smell of fallen apples, a rich, sweet, failed smell of something unfamiliar, yet disturbingly familiar; a smell that permeated through the rafters of her room of swings, and stayed.

'Ruination,' Ba said to Ignatius, who had come out to look for her. 'Can you smell the ruination, Ignatius?'

Ignatius, finding Ba's hand in the dark, turned her around and guided her through the threshold of her front door. 'Perhaps that's life,' he said, 'Perhaps that's how life smells when something rotten is about to happen.'

For a fortnight after Dolly's marriage to Chunky, the cousins played wedding-wedding non-stop. They wanted to use Ba's old wedding sari, wrapped in tissue and naphthalene balls in the tin trunk as a prop, but Ignatius said if they dared go near it, he'd chop off their hands and feed them to the peacocks. Ignatius made them costumes instead: four garish, interchangeable swathes of mirrored cloth, which they slipped over their heads like pillowcases, and kept in place with ropes of silk around their waists.

Every night, while the cousins slept on mattresses in the front room where three long, wooden swings hung from the ceiling, Bean crept out on the veranda and manoeuvred her way into the soft, withered bow of Ba's body. For Bean, being in Anjar was like living in an Enid Blyton story, except instead of a magic faraway tree there was the tree of flying foxes behind the Amba Mata Temple. And instead of picnics on rolling green meadows with sticky gingerbread and ham rolls, there was dinner under the jamun tree with Ba hand-feeding them balls of spicy tamarind rice in turn.

The only problem with Anjar were her fatty bumbalatti cousins, who always wanted to know things like what *egg-zactly* did Mayuri and Bean eat at their British grandmother's house.

'First of all,' Mayuri barked, 'She's not BRITISH, she's WELSH, OK? And second of all, we eat whatever we eat here, STYOOPID.'

Unibrow number one, who shared Bean's birthday, who was already twice Bean's size, owing to Meenal's fondness for using liberal quantities of vanaspathi ghee in all her cooking, was especially probing. 'Tell me, nah,' she'd say to Bean, sensing a softer target while Mayuri was otherwise occupied, 'What do you *really* eat in your Welsh nani's house?'

Bean was petrified that one day, in a moment of confusion, she'd tell the truth; and that the truth would generate disastrous consequences. The mere mention of the words 'chicken' or 'fish', caused the unibrows, who were devout Jain girls, to make a face as though someone were strangling them. Imagine then, if Bean spilled the beans, exposing Babo, Siân, Mayuri and her as a family of meat-eaters! They'd fall into irreparable disgrace, and worst of all, no one would ever trust her with a secret again.

Every morning and evening, much to Bean and Mayuri's joint disgust, both unibrows demanded one hot tumbler of milk, which they claimed made them strong and fair, and which they chugged down in a single, steady glug. Afterwards of course, they suffered terrible gas, which they happily expelled by lifting their bottoms in the air – prr prr prr – so the smell could drift freely from underneath them.

'EXCUSE ME!' Mayuri would say admonishingly, pinching her nose with one hand, and waving the air around her frantically with the other.

'Huh?'

'You're supposed to say "excuse me". It's rude to break wind in public.'

'I'm not breaking anything. What are you talking about?'

Even though the unibrows were more fluent in Gujarati, the cousins spoke in English at the request of Meenal, who wanted her girls to be cosmopolitan. While Bean and Mayuri's Gujarati suffered as a result, their better command of English gave them the upper hand in most activities.

When the cousins got along, they had a grand time – bum-skating vroom vroom across Ba's black stone floors like meteors. They were allowed the run of the house and could play wherever they wanted except by the well in the back courtyard, which was out of bounds after the tragic incident of Sampurna-behn's drowned child some years ago. They played shop-shop in the pantry, and shipwreck-shipwreck in the room of swings. In the front courtyard, where the peacocks were always pecking at grain, the cousins drew hopscotch grids and played seven stones under the trees. And if they ever got too bored to move, or too worn out to imagine a new game, there were always the garoli lizards for entertainment. All you had to do was say 'SHOO MANTHAR' and they plop plopped off the walls like red crystal raindrops to the ground.

But that summer, as post-wedding gloom descended on the village of Ganga Bazaar, the cousins discovered that most of their childhood games had lost their sparkle, and try as they might, none of them could be resuscitated. It was in the wake of this stupor that Mayuri suggested a god-god skit at bathtime. The idea was good enough; they each got to choose whichever god they wanted to be, and instead of sticking to a mythological script, they could make up their own special powers. But when she presented her idea to the unibrows, they sat in all their hefty nakedness on plastic stools and knitted their eyebrows into one deep, flat hairy line apiece.

'My mummy says that God will punish you if you disrespect him,' Unibrow number one said.

'And you will die and go to hell,' added Unibrow number two for good measure.

The unibrows knew everything about God and God-worship. They'd been initiated at an early age at the Adishwarji Jain Temple in Bombay, so they knew exactly when to ring the bell, how many times to circle the garba griha, when to kneel and fold their hands, but most importantly, they had the words – the special words to prayers that tumbled

170

off their lips like waterfalls, gathering and gathering force, until Bean was sure they got channelled straight into the skies above and on to the gods sitting on golden thrones, who were ready to grant whatever you wished for, as long as you knew how to ask for it. It was like having the password to the Secret Seven: without it you couldn't be part of the club. But no matter how badly Bean wanted to be part of God's club, she'd rather die than have to ask the unibrows how to join.

'It will be fun,' Bean cajoled, 'You can be Sita or Lakshmi – the richest, most beautiful goddess in the world. Or you could be Durga on her tiger, wreaking havoc upon her enemies.'

But the unibrows, intent on resistance, folded their arms across their pippy, pubescent breasts and remained vehemently opposed.

'Mayuri, do you know that a day in hell is equal to one hundred human years?'

'I don't care what you think,' Mayuri said. 'My Daddy told me there's no such thing as heaven and hell, and that God is only something that people have made up to make them feel good about themselves. He says if he had a gun he'd line up all the religious leaders of the world and shoot them dead. And that all this religious stuff is a whole lot of mumbo jumbo jiggery-pokery.'

'Oh, really?' gawped Unibrow number one. 'If that's so then tell me, please, how did the world begin?'

'From the beginning, EED-YOT.'

'Who made it?'

'It was just there, already.'

'Mayuri, if you don't shet-up right now you're going to be reborn as a dog in your next life,' shrieked Unibrow number two.

'Fine. I don't care, because you've already been born as an elephant.'

And with that no words were exchanged between the cousins for three days and three nights.

When Mayuri and Bean returned to Madras that summer, long after Ba had brought them together and said, 'We should all make castles within ourselves from the stones thrown at us,' and Bean had penitently gone to her cousins and said, 'It's OK, we can believe in different things and still be friends,' Bean asked her sister if she really thought there was nothing out there.

'Don't you think that Taid is up in heaven with the angels like Selvi says?' she asked, as they lay in their matching cane beds.

Because deep in her heart Bean believed there was more to it. There had to be. She *felt* something when she went to the Velankini church once a year for Christmas mass, and when Trishala Ba took her to the Jain temple in Kilpauk. Even when Siân dragged her to the Garden of Redemption to sit under the banyan tree to listen to Manna – Bean thought, there *must* be something. It can't *all* be jiggery-pokery.

'I don't know all about what Selvi talks, Bean, but I believe what Daddy says. If you're good then nothing else matters.'

'But isn't not believing the worst thing? Doesn't it add up to being bad?'

'I don't think so, Bean. I think if there's a God he'd know these things.'

'But everyone believes in a God. Why can't we believe in one too?'

'Because the sky's so high. Good grief! Didn't you listen to anything I just said?'

'Sure I did, May–May. Sure I did.'

Then, Mayuri, in a rare act of sisterly grace, pulled the sheets over their heads and said, 'I know what, let's play caravan-caravan.'

And just like that, Mayuri and Bean were walking the desert sands, starving and thirsty, down to their last camel, struggling and suffering together against sandstorms and heat. They kept walking through this desert until they found a garden where they were offered fruit and water, a place in the shade to rest their broken bodies.

Mayuri and Bean, pretending they're a family together, read the map of the night sky and find their way across the desert. They climb out of their beds in vests and panties to lie down on the cool, mosaic floors. They lie down with flattened spines: head to foot, foot to head, pretending they aren't afraid of being afraid, of not being this or that. They wait like incy wincy spiders, to begin.

And later, when they grow up and walk about barefoot in their lives, when they're trying to understand the darkness and the divine beings that threaten them, this is what they remember: there was a beautiful time once; it was childhood. They carry it around inside them, thinking if only they hold on to it, if only they don't drop it in the sand, it will stay inside them for ever, and they'll be able to return to it whenever they need. Because Mayuri needs. Bean needs.

17 The Five Thieves of the Body

Almost three years after Prem Kumar's original 'in lieu of' proposal, Chotu, realizing the stubbornness of his father's will and the futility of continuing to dream of a foreign education, finally took him up on his offer. Before the onset of the 1983 monsoon, a week before his twenty-sixth birthday, Chotu, holding his first ever passport, took a flight to Bombay, and from there set off for the first stop of twenty-one: Paris.

The disaster of Chotu's 'in lieu of' European holiday was something only Ba could have predicted, and did. On the morning of his return, Ba had another dream. This time the serpent Ananta rose from the ocean with an aeroplane wing in its mouth, and Bean was astride its thick neck, trying to throttle it with her knees. Ba's first fear was that Chotu's plane had crashed; that his young body would have to be dredged from the ocean floor, charred and blackened beyond recognition. She thought about her grandson moving against the night sky, falling helplessly into an ocean, and a fear so deep gripped her she felt physically ill for the first time in a decade. After telephoning Madras and hearing from Trishala that nothing of the sort had happened – Chotu had arrived safely, and had even put on a few kilos – Ba spent the rest of the day reassuring herself that she had been overreacting. But the anxiety persisted, only now she began to wonder if it wasn't Bean who needed her help.

*   *   *

In Madras, Trishala gathered the entire family around the dining table for a welcome home dinner for Chotu. Prem Kumar sat at the customary head, Babo and Chotu sat to his left, Bean and Mayuri to the right, while Trishala, Dolly and Siân ran back and forth from the kitchen, serving them hot puris.

'How was Germany?' Babo asked wistfully, remembering that it was the place he and Siân were to go, before their dreams got cut short by Trishala's faux illness.

'Oh, it was good. Everything was wonderful,' Chotu said, staring at his plate of food.

'And what did you like about England?' Siân asked, nudging a rasgulla on to his plate.

'Bhabi,' Chotu said, 'to tell you the truth, I don't know how you ever left that place to come here.'

'Well, all's well that ends well,' Prem Kumar said. 'I knew this would be a good idea.'

After a while, Chotu got up to leave the table. 'I'm going upstairs to lie down. Maybe it's jet lag or something. I don't feel too well.'

Three days later, Trishala phoned Babo to say that Chotu was still doing the same thing: nothing. 'Not eating, only sleeping. Is it possible this jetting has affected him so much? Come and find out what the matter is.'

'Heavyweight, what's the problem?' Babo asked, as he sat on the red-brick terrace of Sylvan Lodge, smoking a cigarette. 'Why aren't you coming to work? What's going on? Is something bothering you?'

'Oh, bhai,' Chotu said. 'I don't know. I don't know what I'm doing with my life. Can I just tell you about my "in lieu of" experience? Please? Twenty-one cities in twenty-one days, in the company of middle-aged Gujarati couples from Bombay with a cook on board to make sure there was absolutely no need to try any local cuisine. All middle-aged couples with school-going children, except for one widow, Mrs Triveni, who I had the pleasure of sitting with for the entire journey. I don't know. It was ridiculous. I wish I'd never gone.'

By the end of the week the showdown that was threatening to happen, happened.

'You thought you were giving me the chance to discover the world by putting me on a bus with a bunch of old, conservative Gujaratis to explore two thousand years of European civilization in twenty-one days? Have you ever understood anything I need?'

Prem Kumar was confused. To think! All the things he had done to help this child broaden his horizons. All right, so he hadn't sent him to study abroad like he had sent Babo. But how could he have? After the irreversible loss of face with Falguni's parents, Kamal and Meghna Shah. How could he have sent his only other son to England for studies and risked him coming back with a foreign wife?

Chotu decided to adopt a form of protest previously employed by Babo: the no-negotiation tactic. He announced a leave of absence from Sanbo Enterprises, started coaching the junior state cricket team, ate all his meals at Balaji Snacks down the road and spent more and more time at Babo's house watching *Dynasty* with his nieces, which was the new family addiction.

'I take it you don't intend to become a partner with your brother in this business I've spent my whole life building?' Prem Kumar asked, cornering him one day under the staircase.

'That's right.'

'And how do you plan to support yourself? By coaching? Going like some second-rate schoolmaster from here to there, and then retiring with a pingy pension? What a sad life you're choosing for yourself, son, and what about family? Don't you want a family of your own?'

There was nothing further from Chotu's mind. Aside from Babo and Siân, who had managed to create an oasis for themselves, all the other married couples he encountered looked utterly bored and frustrated with each other.

'Well,' Prem Kumar said, when Chotu offered no reply. 'All I can say is, if every fool wore a crown, we would all be kings.'

'And all I can say is it's better to be one's own king rather than a slave of another,' Chotu said, before marching out and slamming the front door for the zillionth time.

'Chotu,' Ba shouted down the phone from Anjar. 'I hear you're going on a protest now, just like Babo. Very clever. Good idea.'

'Nothing like that, Ba. I just don't want to work with Papa in the office, that's all.'

'Good, good,' Ba said, 'I have a better idea for you anyway. I want you to coach Beena into a champion swimmer. Don't worry, you can still do your cricket coaching business, just spend a few hours with her in the morning. Your niece is nearly ten, and still wetting the bed. All this nakra about ghosts is just an excuse. She needs a proper hobby. Not all this one-day wonder business with painting class and all.

'And anyway, it's probably better if you don't go to work for a while. Take some time to think about your life. You're not a baby any more.'

'I know, Ba. That's what I've been trying to tell everyone.'

Ba wanted to tell Chotu about the serpent Ananta that had been visiting her for twenty-five years. She wanted him to understand that there was something beyond all this – there was bliss, there was beauty. She wanted to warn him about the five thieves of the body: greed, affection, desire, love, pride, who were always lurking around, ready to devastate the sanctity of the spirit and the mind.

'Whatever you decide to do,' she said, 'Never renounce the world, Chotu, because it will be the world that saves you.'

*   *   *

And that is how Chotu started coming for Bean in Prem Kumar's Ambassador at 5 a.m. every morning. He drove up to the house of orange and black gates and waited for Bean to hurry out with her school gear and Milo swimming bag. Bean, creeping out of the house, bleary-eyed, still straddling her world of dreams, sat up in the front seat beside Chotu as they drove all the way down the length of Marina Beach, which in those early hours, looked like a desert pressed against the city's metallic sky. Bean gave in to the desolate morning: the dismantled merry-go-rounds, the horsemen and returning fishermen, the morning walkers trundling like pilgrims across the endless biscuit-coloured sand. Chotu taught her the names of the buildings lining the promenade – the Ice House, Queen Saint Mary's College, the Senate House – while she counted the crows sitting on the statue of Gandhiji's shit-spattered head. *One for sorrow, two for joy, three for a letter, four for a boy . . .*

At the Madras Gymkhana Club, Bean struggled into her Lycra swimsuit, fixed the ridiculous chinstrap swimming cap over her head, spat into her goggles and threw herself in like a seventy-pound cannonball. Those first few warm-up laps were like arrows to her heart; icicles of terror; a stinging in her ears that went on and on like a pressure cooker whistling. But after a while, as the rhythm of her breathing settled down, and the solid push of her feet against the sides of the pool propelled her forward and forward, as the sun rose overhead, warming and tanning the backs of her legs, Bean forgot everything. She bolted through the water, up and down, up and down, until she could hear her heart beating in her ears. Chotu, standing at the edge of the pool with a stopwatch, shouted, 'PULL, BEAN, PULL.' And hearing his sweet, deep voice asking for something only she could give, Bean pulled as hard and fast as she could.

After the training session, while Bean hoisted herself out with a powerful two-arm press-up and tip tapped into the changing room, Chotu would lay his watch on the table and glide into the water to swim a few lazy laps. Then, after gobbling down a quick breakfast, with the sun beating down on the city of Madras, Chotu drove Bean to school in time for morning assembly, while she sat beside him, tummy full, arms and legs like jelly, head resting against the window – knock knock knock, all the way there.

For four years the measure of Bean's days began like this: a long, cool submersion into emptiness, where every fear she had in the world could be drowned. As much as she hated having to wake up with an alarm clock instead of Siân gently pulling her toes; as much as she hated the wet bathroom floor of the Ladies' Room, and the dank smell of talcum powder the ayahs at the Gymkhana Club liked to douse her with before she changed into her school uniform; there was something about her mornings with Chotu that gave meaning and importance to her life.

As Bean meticulously paced up and down the swimming pool – her shoulders growing broader, her hair more like straw – a miraculous thing happened: her prayers were finally answered. Bean's problem with the ghosts prowling along her bedroom walls finally dissolved. Siân put away the plastic sheets. Babo bought her a new, springy Blossom mattress. Selvi said, 'Child, you growed up finally, like a big girl.'

Even Chotu seemed to put the disappointment of his European vacation behind him as Bean went on to win bronze medals in the under-10 and under-12 state championships. He agreed to return to work at Sanbo Enterprises as long as he could be absolved of all administrative duties and collaborate with Babo in the invention room. He continued to indulge in harmless flirtations and threatened to move into an apartment if Trishala or Prem Kumar ever brought up the M word. 'When I'm good and ready,' he warned them, 'I'll find a bride of my own.'

For a long time Ba believed her timely dream had saved both Bean and Chotu. But when Bean, at the age of thirteen, decided to trade in her swimming cap for a tennis racquet, convinced that she was going to be the next Martina Navratilova, Ba saw that old, sad look creep back into Chotu's face. Even though Chotu told Bean, 'You have to do what you want to do, Champ, don't worry about me,' Ba knew that this new sorrow would give the five thieves a space to enter. Greed, affection, desire, love, pride. They had been standing at the periphery, waiting for their chance to slip through the gates of Sylvan Lodge, chup chap, when no one was looking. They had been waiting for a while; ever since Chotu had been given a tiny, tethered leap instead of a proper, fully-fledged soaring. And once the thieves forced their way inside your home, how could anything ever be the same again?

18 This Place is a Dream.
Only a Sleeper Considers It Real

On the morning of 31 October 1984, at 0900 hours, the precise moment when Prime Minister Indira Gandhi's security guards were pummelling her body with bullets, Trishala complained to Prem Kumar of an electrifying pain in her right breast. Prem Kumar, who was particularly partial to Trishala's right breast, it being the closest available to him for suckling, immediately summoned Jignesh-bhai, the family doctor, who scootered over to Sylvan Lodge with doctor's bag in hand.

After an hour of groping, Jignesh-bhai removed his hairy hands from Trishala's blouse and shuffled sadly into the living room to give Prem Kumar his diagnosis. 'I can't be knowing this for sure,' he said, spluttering through his sausage lips, 'But your wife has a cyst in her right breast which may or may not be cancerous, which may or may not be successfully operated upon in our clinic.'

Prem Kumar, hearing this news, allowed his knees to tremble slightly. At the gates of Sylvan Lodge, he exchanged a steely handshake with Jignesh-bhai, which Prem Kumar misunderstood as a sign of solidarity, but which in fact, was the doctor's way of saying that he was an inexperienced blunderbuss, wholly incapable of dealing with something on this scale.

In the bedroom Prem Kumar found Selvam sitting on the floor next to Trishala, weeping his half-blind eyes out while

Trishala consoled him gently, patting his bald head like a drum. 'I'm telling you one thing,' she snapped as soon as she caught sight of her husband. 'There's going to be no more doctor's hands going up this blouse again. If I have to go, then I'm going with my breasts intact.'

By noon the city of Madras had collapsed. Schools sent home children, workers fled from offices, shops pulled down their shutters, layabouts and workaholics vacated the streets to position themselves by a radio or a television to hear what further insanity would unfold in the capital.

Mayuri and Bean rushed around Sylvan Lodge in their blue and white pinafores, excited to be here on a Wednesday which felt like a Sunday; excited that they'd been made to leave school at break time while the teachers hugged each other and said *tragedy, tragedy* over and over again; excited that there were policemen on the streets, and death in the air. They were breathing it all in and whooshing down the banisters with it.

Babo, Chotu and Siân soldered themselves into the saggy, brown sofas in the front room, watching the television screen like hawks. It was confirmed: the country was going mad. Indira Gandhi had died after receiving sixteen bullets in her chest and abdomen shot by two of her Sikh security guards. Stores were burning, soldiers were shooting, thugs were looting, mothers were clutching children to their breasts.

Trishala, watching all this confusion, made Prem Kumar and Selvam swear to say nothing of Jignesh-bhai's visit that morning. 'There's enough to cope with at the moment,' she said stoically. 'Let's not add my worries to the top of the pile.'

So they sat together, a family bound to despair, eating dinner in front of the television in silence, while teary-eyed newscasters from Delhi gave them updated bulletins from the capital. They watched Indira Gandhi's sole surviving son,

Rajiv, being embraced by members of the Congress Party. He was telling the people of this nation, *his* people, to restrain themselves, to not let their emotions get the better of them.

Meanwhile, Sikhs were hiding, Sikhs were burning, Sikhs were cutting their hair and running for their lives.

This was 1984, the year of Orwell's black-white, outer-inner prophecy, when lies became truth, and ignorance became strength. This was the year the Patel family learned that justice was not equal for all. The year of massacres, mammograms and malfunctions. The year of the Bhopal Gas Tragedy. The year Babo and Siân woke up every morning to see things in the world dying.

It was the year Trishala slunk around the hallways of Sylvan Lodge, braless and sore, in tailor-made vanity blouses with big wads of cotton stitched into where her right breast used to be – her munificent right breast, which she'd agreed to relinquish only because they said there would be a chance to save the left one. When, after countless treatments which made her hair fall out and her voracious appetite dwindle, they took her left breast too, Trishala put her sizeably shrunken foot down and demanded to be taken home so she could die with dignity.

It was the year Trishala stopped speaking without so much as a goodbye speech except for a final word of warning about the romance that had begun to bloom between Mayuri and Cyrus Mazda from next door. 'That boy has the deceptive nature of a crow. If I were you, I'd nip this thing in the bud.'

A year of itching, burning, peeling, blistering silence.

A few weeks after Trishala's second mastectomy, Babo and Siân found Mayuri sitting in bed, refusing to go to school.

'When I grow up I want to be a maid,' she declared. 'You don't need maths or chemistry for that, do you?'

'And will you like being a maid?' Babo asked. 'Will you like mopping floors and cleaning toilets and living in a small, dingy room all by yourself?'

'Yes I will,' Mayuri insisted. 'That's exactly what I want to do.'

'What a relief,' said Siân. 'That means we don't need Selvi anymore. We can just keep you in the house for ever and pay *you* to do all her work. And Bean can have the bedroom all to herself.'

Mayuri's eyes brimmed over with petulant tears. 'What does it matter?' she screeched. 'I'm going to die anyway, so I won't be able to do any of those things because I've got a lump in my breast just like Trishala Ba, haven't I?'

Mayuri, at thirteen, was checking her panties every single day, hoping for a stain of blood because most of her friends had already had their period and had started wearing bras while she still wore girly cottony vests. It hadn't helped that Siân never sat her down to tell her any of the things she should expect from her impending womanhood. Mayuri's friend Sunaina's mother was a doctor, and she had given Sunaina a sex-education manual that explained *everything*, using all the proper words and diagrams. Why couldn't Siân be more like her, instead of all this la-la Redemptionist stuff? As far as Mayuri was concerned, it was all well and good for people to believe in whatever they believed in, but if she was dying, her parents had an obligation to sit up and take note of it, and understand that she had better things to do than go to school.

'If you *do* die,' Bean asked, patting Mayuri sorrowfully on the arm before she left for school, 'Will you leave me your party frocks in your will?'

'Don't worry,' said Mayuri sweetly. 'You won't be needing party frocks in the slums, because that's where you'll be when Mama and Daddy dump you after I'm gone.'

Jignesh-bhai was summoned to put his hairy hands up Mayuri's vest to examine whether her mosquito-bite-sized breasts did indeed contain a life-threatening lump that they should all be worried about. This, Jignesh-bhai did assiduously, while Mayuri turned a deep, self-conscious shade of magenta.

'I can see where you think you might have had a problem,' said Jignesh-bhai sincerely. 'But really, there's no lump growing in your breast. You are absolutely A-OK, Number One Fantastic, ready to go to school again. Nothing to worry about. No problem.'

'But,' he said, to make sure that Mayuri understood he was treating her case with utmost seriousness, 'You must conduct regular self check-ups, especially with your family medical history, if you know what I mean.'

Mayuri nodded wisely, buttoned up her shirt and walked outside to tell her mother and father, who'd been made to wait in the sitting room, that all was well with the world, her breasts were not infected, and she'd be returning to school the next day so she could aspire to be something higher than a common maid.

Afterwards, Siân took Mayuri to Fountain Plaza to buy her first bra – a 32 AA which was white and thick-strapped, and which sported an embroidered red rose in between its pointy boobs. Mayuri was so pleased with this purchase that instead of wearing it immediately, she placed it prominently on her bed so when Bean came home from school that day, she'd realize that her sister had finally, in the space of one eventful morning, become a woman.

In the months of Trishala's illness Babo stopped noticing the world around him. His skin developed moles in places where there was once only softness. His grey eyes became opaque, hardened with fatty deposits and disillusion, unable to receive light like they used to. His body began to lose elasticity, and hair started sprouting in new, undesirable places. He decided to quit smoking, swap cigarettes for Polo mints – which he ate compulsively, activating a dormant Gujarati sweet tooth, which led to a thickening in his once twenty-eight-inch waist. There was all this slowing down – slow and slower.

Babo, in those months, found himself looking up diseases in books, imagining tumours and mutations growing inside him. His nights were filled with pictures of bodies ridden with ailments so complicated and cruel, their names fell down on him like heavy trunks, opening and closing: leprosy, leukaemia, kaposis sarcoma – opening and closing, showering all kinds of malignant portents on top of him. It was an unleashing: a mad, furious thing that kept going and going – dhishoom dhishoom – kicking, ripping, denting.

Prem Kumar spent those final months in consultation rooms and doctors' offices. Long after his wife resigned herself to dying, Prem Kumar continued to believe that a miracle would change everything. Every morning he woke with a new plan: urine therapy, heat therapy, reiki, pranic healing, acupuncture, castor oil, vegetable juice, soup. Trishala, lying depleted and dispirited on her side of the bed, told him to leave things be. 'Let me go,' she said, 'We will meet in our next janam.'

Something old and sad began to grow inside Prem Kumar, tugged like a root, following him everywhere he went. The future loomed ahead like a black cloud devoid of any shape or substance. It was unforeseeable, to imagine living without this woman who had berated and cajoled him for forty-five years. He had chosen her so long ago, in the village of Anjar, for the simple reason that she had eyes through which the light of God could be seen. Trishala had had little by way of dowry or prospects. Her father had lost all his money in senseless stock speculation, and her mother had died giving birth to her. But her misfortunes had given her a bit of fire that none of the other girls had. And of course, there were those eyes; those gauzy, grey eyes.

Towards the end Trishala kept her eyes closed, hoping to prevent her loved ones from seeing anything like fear or anguish in her. All she asked for was a bit of morphine, which Jignesh-bhai administered once a day, to ease the unbearable pain. At nights, Prem Kumar lay awake listening to his wife's laboured breathing, and wondered how tricky a thing love was after all: to arrive where it had never existed. He stretched his hand out in the dark to touch the body which had once been so plump, the breasts so full. 'My love,' he whispered, when he was sure she could not hear him, 'How good you have been to me, and how little I have given you.'

On the night of Trishala's death, the planet Mars was closer to the earth than it had been in 60,000 years. If you'd been standing on the red-brick terrace in Sylvan Lodge, you would have seen it shining like a star with its own red halo, the whole surface of it – deep, subterranean red, with rivers running through it like the unwritten desires of the body.

The dogs of Sterling Road barked through the night. They stood at the gates of Sylvan Lodge and howled and howled at the red planet in the sky. Darayus Mazda, next door, sensing always the terrible immanence of death, stood on his balcony waiting to see what further mischief his family were planning for him. Ba, all the way in Anjar, could smell it too – the smell of fallen apples. She knew, before anyone phoning to tell her, that the five thieves had come for Trishala's body.

Downstairs, in Trishala and Prem Kumar's bedroom, the family were praying – reciting Navkar Mantra, bowing down to the liberated souls who had reached a state of non-attachment: the sadhus and sadhvis, the upadhyayas who taught the scriptures, the arihants and the thirthankaras. The family's heads were all bowed low, even those of Babo and

187

Siân, asking those supremely unattached people to guide Trishala to that spotless holy region, free from all the suffering of the world.

The granddaughters had been made to wait outside. They were holding hands in a line, standing in front of the showcases in the sitting room, in front of Trishala's beloved emaciated Jain saints and glass ballerinas with fans. In the last days they had seen Trishala Ba lying in bed, very thin and very quiet. It was as if Trishala Ba had been taken away and some other woman had been made to lie in her place with a piece of gauze tied around her mouth so she wouldn't swallow some microbe by mistake while offering her prayers. No more Indo-Burma notebooks or one-rupee coins. No more Sunday skit costumes from her Singer sewing machine. The granddaughters were praying, in whatever words they knew, that Trishala's journey would be peaceful, that it would be filled with music.

Trishala was leaving her anger behind. She was removing all the garments of illusion and strapping on a girdle of wind, so she could fly all the way across samsara – that terrific deception of the human world – to the abodes of the gods. She was removing all the layers of karma, all the dust that coated her soul, before setting off on her final pilgrimage. She was cutting each tie, severing each painful connection: limb, child, husband, body, pista-green house, until she could cast off the memories and cross over the wilderness. Trishala, doing as her faith commanded, entered that unblemished land where purity was instantaneous.

19 When Your Heart's on Fire, Smoke Gets in Your Eyes

Only once in all their long years of marriage did Babo and Siân lose each other. It began a few years after Trishala's death, in the summer of 1987, when Mayuri finally allowed Cyrus Mazda to put his tongue down her throat, and it only really got resolved towards the end of that year, when Nerys got over her fear of flying and climbed on an aeroplane to visit her daughter in India.

The summer of 1987 was unrelenting. Madras in July was like a desert – heat thrashing down on a city gone dry, with no promise of coolness or reprieve. Every morning Babo scoured the newspapers, looking for a story that would reinstate his faith in humanity. But it was always more of the same: biscuit bandits on the run, mass suicides by farmers because of failing rains and rising debts, politicians destroying libraries, old folk dying of asphyxiation. Rampant thuggery, abscondings.

As if all this were not enough, his girls were going to Anjar for a whole month, leaving him alone in the house of orange and black gates. Babo, standing at his bedroom window, looked out of the grills. He saw his wife and daughters moving around briskly, oblivious to the heat. Everywhere, women were barking orders: Selvi, Siân, Mayuri, Bean. Young Cyrus, who had grown tall and handsome in an awkward, endearing way, was loading the car with boxes and bags. He was flashing smiles here and there uninhibitedly with his recently emancipated unbraced teeth. The girls were laughing with him: jhill mill, jhill mill. They were swatting mosquitoes off their summer-brown legs and laughing. Life was going on without him.

Babo wanted to rush over to his children and cradle them in his arms. He wanted to carry them high into the orange crown of the flame-of-the-forest tree, deep into its petals of fire where Bean once used to see ghosts hiding. He wanted to tell his daughters how they had come from him, how they *were* him, and he was them. How these were the ways people found to continue: to bear children – little bits of silver – who would carry the same noses and chins, the same foreheads and eyes, the same weaknesses for love. Because he could feel them moving away from him – Mayuri's footsteps tapping out of the front door and tapping back in, only so she could drive around the city with Darayus's long-faced grandson in his fancy cars; Bean, talking on the phone from morning to night to Mehnaz because *her* life was the most important thing in the world, never to be discussed with family, only with friends.

And his wife – he wanted to call her that – *his wife*, and tell her to come back to their city of refuge because she'd become a stranger in his life, in the house they shared and the bed they slept in. It had been so long since they'd touched each other as if their existence depended on it; so long since Babo had ba-ba-boomed like a firecracker. He wanted to carry her away too, and save her. But Siân didn't need saving. She was busier than ever with her weekly commitments and charity cases. She now had a colour-coded timetable pasted up on the fridge in case she should forget where she needed to be, and with whom: pensioners and craft class biddies, swimming and bridge, SOS, AMS, Cheshire Home, Ms Douglas, Manna and the Garden of Redemption. Monday through Sunday chock-a-block.

Where's the colour-coded box for me? thought Babo. Where's the alone time with husband in all of this? Babo, looking out into the front yard, felt something he hadn't felt since he was twenty-one, when he left his family behind and zing zing zinged all the way to London to discover alcohol and meat for the very first time. It was a strange feeling of disconnection. Of walking down the streets and discovering that there was nothing you could claim, nothing that belonged to you; that if you were to lift yourself out of the scene, it would continue on without you.

It was like lying down on the soft, immaculate Tokyo hotel room bed during those weeks when he had entertained the idea of expanding Sanbo operations overseas: the TV blaring in an incomprehensible language, the yukata, the green tea, the curious red bean sweets. He'd been adrift then, in a world where he couldn't make his mark, and he'd known then, as he knew now, that without his girls he was nothing.

He knew, because he'd already found *it* all those years ago in the canteen of Joseph Friedman & Sons. The moment he'd seen the whirl of ribbon in Siân's auburn hair – he'd caught hold of that moment and planted it in the ribcage of his soul, pinned it there like a spotted butterfly wing. Such beauty! And without it, such absence.

But lately it had been like waking up in a foreign country all over again. His family were here – scattered in the front yard, getting ready to abandon him without the slightest pang of thump thumping remorse. He wanted to go with them, so they could escape the mosquitoes and flies together. He wanted to load them up in his Flying Fiat and take them away like he used to: to Kanyakumari, the tip of India, where the Bay of Bengal, the Indian Ocean and the Arabian Sea all joined together, or two hours down the coast to Pondicherry just to eat fresh apple custard pies. Most of all though, he wanted to be able to sha-bing sha-bang with Siân like he used to – three times in a row, no problem, because at the heart of it, this was where things were falling apart.

Babo was approaching forty, and for the first time in his life, he was beginning to grapple with his mortality, his manhood. He could feel changes in his increasingly weighted-down, half-way-over-the-hill body – most of them having to do with Mr Whatsit. It had never been like this before. Babo remembered a time when just the sight of Siân's exposed collarbone got him all excited – ushering him almost immediately to the brink, like in those early days in the blue-walled Finchley Road flat. Or later, in Sylvan Lodge, when they used to make love so quietly and for so long, that sometimes when they woke in the morning, still fitted somehow into each other, it used to seem to him as if their bodies had been created for this express purpose – to realize these sweet configurations.

These days it took a while for Mr Whatsit to get aroused, and even longer for him to reach the brink. They hardly ever locked themselves in for Saturday afternoon sessions any more. In fact, they hardly ever touched. It was as if they no longer needed to make their own world together at the end of a day. Even when Siân slid into bed wearing nothing but her emerald green satin slip, her marble body endlessly accessible to him, Babo felt, not a diminishing of desire towards his wife, but a diminishing in his own capabilities. Babo couldn't understand how he'd grown so much older while his wife had remained so young, scarcely changed since the day she'd first arrived in India. The gap between her teeth had grown quarter micro-millimetre by quarter micro-millimetre, but the rest of her was still soft, achingly sexy. Yet most nights the only thing he could manage was to take hold of Siân's body and cling to it like a drowning man holds on to a river branch, falling asleep with relief against the milky white smoothness of it.

Babo put it down to stress. Now that his mother was gone he found himself in the crossfire zone of his family. Not just the temper flares and differences of opinion that had resurged between Prem Kumar and Chotu, but Dolly calling from Baroda, complaining that life with her husband, Chunky, was quite unbearable, and Meenal weeping about some new failing in her body – some lump or growth which convinced her that she'd be the next to go.

And as if the immediate family wasn't enough to deal with, Babo suddenly found that he'd become a magnet for maladies in general – ageing aunties called him from Bhavnagar and Porbandar to grumble about gallstones and diabetes, cataracts and colonoscopies. His father's Sunday rummy-playing group, who had only ever been interested in betel-chewing and political banter, suddenly wanted to confide *in him* about their inflamed prostates and calcified testicles. As though *he* could advise them in any way, or even swap notes with them about their ailments. As if *he* were about to join them and become part of that club any time soon.

Siân and he had lost a parent each, and yet neither of them could communicate the depth of their loss to each other. Things were changing rapidly around them, and the thing that had always come easiest to them – the sha-bing sha-bang that had saved them in the past and brought them back to the centre – *that* lay just beyond their reach in a country they'd once lived in, but to which they had suddenly lost visiting rights.

Once, when they were in bed with the door safely locked so there could be no chance of the children coming in, Babo said, 'Charlie Girl, what's happening to us?'

He thought at first Siân might try to pretend that nothing was the matter; that she'd say 'Hmm,' and push it under the carpet like she did with most problems. But Siân looked at him straight on, as though she were seeing him clearly for the first time. 'What's happening is that you're turning into your father.'

'No, I'm not.'

'You absolutely are. Look at you – you're even sticking out your lower lip in that stubborn way of his. What's happened is that you've lost all your spontaneity. When was the last time just the two of us went out to dinner? NOT to the club. When was the last time you surprised me in any way? You used to be all about those things. Now the only thing you're interested in is your precious Sanbo Enterprises and your fucking stock of Johnny Walker.'

It was Siân's use of the word 'fucking' that floored Babo. He'd never so much as heard his wife use the word 'shit' before, never mind 'damn' or 'bloody' or any of the other lower-ranking swearwords. It went against her strict Calvinist upbringing and sense of propriety. When, in the past, he made the mistake of cursing aloud, Siân always glared at him and hissed, 'THE CHILDREN,' as though he were pouring poison directly into their ears. So to hear her utter a profanity now, was not only an ominous sign of disintegration, it was in a crueller sense, a betrayal.

'Daddy,' Bean was saying, waving frantically at him, 'Aren't you going to come kiss us goodbye? We're leaving soon.'

Babo, turning to leave the bedroom, caught sight of his reflection in the mirror, and saw how his wife has been right as usual. Trishala's eyes, which had once been the centrepiece of his face, had sunk into the background, allowing Prem Kumar's intractably wide nose and lips to emerge to the foreground. He *had* turned into his father. What's more, this physical change had somehow made a difference to his very essence. It was why he could no longer sit through a late-night film at the Casino any more without his eyes closing halfway through. It was why he wasn't performing the way he should have been in bed.

Was this a fate reserved for every man? thought Babo. To slowly transform into the father they had always assumed was far, far away from them? Babo wanted to halt this movement in its tracks. He wanted to be the man he'd once been, the man who drove his soon-to-be-wife to a five-star hotel in Bombay when he could scarcely afford it, and ravished her three times in a row on those white, pristine sheets. He wanted to do that to her now, to drag her inside and tell her not to go away from him. But he couldn't, because he had become the kind of man he'd always despised: fearful and predictable.

It would happen this way, Siân would be in the kitchen or garden, and her mother's voice would swish up as if from underwater, out of the crockery cabinet, or from between the springs of the settee. And always, Siân felt she must *do* something; save her mother from something terrible. While Babo had been slipping away from her, Nerys's voice had increasingly slipped in – calling, prying, screaming, stammering – the same shrill, urgent supplication – *Siân, Siân!* – as though she were calling from under a trapped rock or had slipped on the bathroom floor, or worse, was drowning in the middle of the ocean.

Siân could hear Nerys now, as the train lunged up the west coast of India. *Siân, Siân*, following her like the wind. *What are those girls up to?* Siân thought. *Are they in her Sunday clothes? Are they stealing biscuits from the Cadbury tin? God forbid, are they pulling up her roses?* Even though Siân knew that the girls weren't doing anything of the sort. The girls were almost grown-up and playing dominoes on the way to Anjar, but it felt, for a moment, that she was back at Tan-y-Rhos again; that her world was intact: husband, children, brothers, mother, father.

'When you were children you used to like to stand at the door, watching the trees and telegraph poles rush by,' Siân said to Mayuri and Bean, who were sitting on the berth across from her. 'Shall we go do that now?'

'Oh, it's too hot, Mama,' Mayuri said, looking up, giving her fringe a little flick with her fingers.

'And anyway,' Bean chimed in, 'We're in the middle of a game now, Mama, please!'

Siân turned to watch the countryside as the wheels of the train laboriously zigzagged across little villages and towns. She wanted to catch hold of one of those sparkling images out there – that woman squatting by the wood fire with a covered head and a jewel-box face, that lone man riding his bicycle between fields of bright golden mustard – because everything felt tentative now. Her daughters teetering threateningly on the brink of adolescence. Babo temporarily lost to her. Even her mother calling to her. Siân wanted to bring them in from the world: the outside world that dimmed and glowed, hissed and spat, tore and restored.

On the morning after Babo's family left for Anjar without him, there was a harsh, incessant ringing at the doorbell. Selvi, who had taken a few days off to settle some land affairs in her village, had left him all alone in the house, forcing him to rise from his bed and answer the door himself. At first, Babo thought that it was Siân returned, saying the girls could manage on their own; Ba was there to look after them as she always was. But when the ringing persisted, Babo knew it couldn't be Siân because she had her own key, and if she really wanted to surprise him, there were simpler, sexier ways of doing it.

So Babo dragged himself to the door preparing to vent his anger at the milkman or whoever the imbecile was, for disturbing his sleep so early in the morning. But there in front of him, was a stranger – a young sardarni with a face like a peach, her never-cut hair spread like a bed sheet around her face, black kohl from the night before still in her eyes. She was standing barefoot in the frame of his front door in a loose kurta and pyjamas.

'Do something about your cats,' the sardarni said, jabbing her fingers towards the wall that divided the house of orange and black gates and the Punjab Women's Association. 'I can't sleep. It's impossible. I tell you, I can't sleep with all the racket they're making.'

Babo noticed, then, that the sardarni had a slight lisp – a slow, seductive 'sss' that rolled off her tongue when she said '*ssss*leep'. He noticed as well the substantial curve of breasts under her kurta, which in this strong morning light, and because they were unencumbered by a bra, he could see swelling through as peachily as her face. Obviously she'd come straight from bed without bothering to put slippers on, to march up to his front door to complain. Both the lisp and the epic dimensions of her breasts reminded Babo of Falguni – his old love, whom he'd ditched most cruelly in London, and never seen since. But it was more the pleading nature of the young woman – the *promith me that ssomorrow you will only danth wiss me* look, that was making the sardarni, at that moment, utterly irresistible.

In the seventeen years that Babo had been married to Siân, he'd not so much as glanced at another woman, never mind entered into any kind of compromising fantasy involving himself, his wife, another woman, or any combination of the above. Siân had been the first and only woman to take true possession of Babo's heart, and when they'd taken claim of each other, there had been no place even for the actresses that Babo had once so ardently loved – the Liz Taylors and Madhubalas – even they had faded into a shimmery kind of haze never to be called on again to say, *Akele akele kahan ja rahen ho?* Even the light flirting that always carried on between their hybrid friends – Darlene particularly, who after

197

a few drinks always liked to position herself in Babo's lap and drawl, 'You're sooooo lucky, Siân, you don't know what you got, girl' – even *that* was harmless, and for Babo at least, had been as enticing as one of his sister's landing themselves in his lap.

The point is, Babo had never strayed, never wandered, never so much as peeked in a direction away from his wife, because for all these years his wife had been the breath and the life, the everything. This morning, though, with this agitated sardarni standing in front of him, Babo felt desire building in the hitherto dormant Mr Whatsit, and this reaction – while it was positive, anatomically speaking – was certainly not a sign made in the right direction or at the right time. In fact, the mere occurrence of it shook Babo to his very foundations, for he was nothing if not a principled man.

'But they're not my cats,' Babo said, discreetly adjusting his kurta. He ran his fingers distractedly through his curls and wished more than anything for a cigarette right then. 'They live in your compound and they come and go as they please. They aren't our responsibility at all.'

'But how do you stand it? I've been here a week and I haven't been able to sleep. Not a single night.'

Stand. Sleep. Single. Sssss-sss-ssss.

'One minute,' said Babo, leaving the sardarni at the door, and re-emerging with a box in hand. 'At one point, when my daughter was young she had the same problem. In fact, it was very serious. She had nightmares for years because of those cats. So our family doctor gave us a large stock of earplugs hoping they would relieve the situation. Maybe you can try them and see if they help?'

'Oh!' the sardarni said, lowering her eyes, suddenly looking very bashful. 'You don't look at all like you could be the father of grown-up children. You're very youthful-looking. Thanks for these, though, really,' she said, taking the box gingerly, and then turning to go back the way she'd come, her peachy buttocks swaying gently from side to side – dhamak dhimak, dhamak dhimak – as she disappeared slowly from sight.

This encounter was the closest Babo ever came to cheating on his wife for the entirety of their marriage. The effects of the desire that the sardarni stirred up, though, were far-reaching, extending well beyond that long desert of Babo's fortieth year, when she appeared like a mirage to stir him from his mid-marriage crumblings. Later, whenever Babo heard the sound of cats mating, Mr Whatsit would respond Pavlovian style to the peachy memory of the sardarni's front sides and back sides, filling with such desire that he'd turn straight away to his wife's body, no matter what time of night, and sha-bing sha-bang.

More immediately, though, the sardarni's ego boost left Babo simultaneously so refreshed and guilty that he was left with no other option but to change his life in the only way he knew how: by listening to what his wife and daughters had been telling him for some time now. Not to, not to, not to.

He stopped sitting out on the veranda with his scotch and sodas every evening, eliminated fried foods and restricted his intake of high-calorie snacks to a handful of cashews. He started waking up at six in the morning to go walking in the Loyola College compound. When he met their hybrid friends at the Gymkhana Club at weekends, he steered clear of the biscuit-layered chocolate cake and nutty-boy ice creams even though this seemed to disappoint Keshav and Praveen more than his recently adopted teetotal habits. 'What's got into you, yaar? Don't tell us you're missing your wife so much? Or that in this old age God is finally finding you? Is this some kind of religious fast?'

Even Chotu, who was increasingly retreating into a world of his own, noticed a radical change in his brother. 'Bhai, why are you losing weight like this? Is Selvi not feeding you at home? Do you want to come and stay with Papa and me in the meantime?'

'You silly goat,' Ba said, bellowing down the phone all the way from Ganga Bazaar. 'It's your birthday in one week. Why are you going to sit in your house all alone when your family is here? Is that what you make so much money for? So that you can sit on it like a hen hatching eggs?'

So Babo, without too much deliberation, packed a small suitcase and told Selvi to go off to her village for the week. He left Prem Kumar and Chotu to throttle each other at Sanbo Enterprises if they wished, and got on the first flight to Bombay, from where he would take an onward train to Anjar – all so he could surprise his wife and save their marriage.

By the time he arrived in Ganga Bazaar, Ba had already smelled the bakul flowers in his hands, and the rain clouds that inevitably followed her grandson wherever he went. 'Come and see,' she shouted to the girls, who were lounging about on the swings with magazines. Siân came, too – drawn to the front door not by any discriminating sense of smell, but to a voice that had been calling for some time now.

It wasn't necessary for Siân to say anything. Her eyes gave Babo all the approval he needed. She was looking at him the way she'd looked at him when she'd got off the plane in Bombay after those six terrible months apart, and wrapped her body around him, determined to be the only light in his life. But now, instead of running towards him, she stayed rooted to the spot and said, 'Well, well. Don't you think your daddy looks handsome, girls?'

And just like that, the inevitability that one day they would both be orphans, that they might allow that peacock-feather connection of electricity between them to slip away, all those weights lifted, and it was like rose petals falling from the sky again. And Ba, who heard them in the corners of her house, softly rocking the earth of Ganga Bazaar into a million pieces, marvelled that they had the same jhimak jhimak sheen as when they drove into Anjar all those years ago, showing the villagers their first motor car and their first white person. It was a fearlessness then, and it was a fearlessness now: the ability to dissolve into love.

We must all be ready to die for impossible love, thought Ba. *Because love shouldn't need proof of time or remembrance. Love should always be new. Love should be an eternity.* And when Babo and Siân left with their two daughters amidst thunderstorms to go back to their city by the sea, Ba understood how Ekam was always Ekam. *They have been through fire. Now they will lift each other up and fly again.*

That Christmas, when the Chief Minister of Tamil Nadu, M.G. Ramachandran, India's first actor-turned politician, husband of three and father of none, went tottering into the sunset with his furry cap and dark glasses, leaving in his wake a spate of state-wide riots; when the Patels' most faithful vanguard of domesticity, Selvam, disappeared for ever without so much as a *hello – goodbye – excuse me please*; when Nerys took to the air and came all the way to India, the voices in Siân's head finally stopped.

Babo and Siân drove to the airport on a tropical December Madras night with Mayuri and Bean giggling with excitement on the back seat, holding garlands of fresh jasmine and bouquets of red roses. Babo, Siân, Mayuri and Bean stood at the arrival gates of the Madras Meenambakkam Airport, watching as Nerys arrived in India for the very first time in her sixty-year-old life, wearing a brand-new Debenhams knee-length polka-dot dress and a wide-brimmed sunhat even though it was the middle of the night.

Nerys, who said she'd never fly because she didn't trust anything with all that metal up in the air. Nerys, who was never afraid, who was only amazed by this huge and devastating country: how she could put something on to wear for just a few hours, and how, by the next morning, the thing was washed, cleaned, ironed and ready to wear again; this movement of people: watchmen, ayahs, drivers, sweepers, gardeners – who worked mostly invisibly in some magical cycle of constant renewal – how all this sustained itself. Nerys, who returned to Nercwys after three months in India, content never to leave her village again, content to know how her granddaughters slept every night, how they looked under those blankets of hers, how her daughter lived like a princess after all. Content with the things she could tell Bryn to ease the furrows in his brow if he should ever come back to her.

Siân ran towards her mother, who was striding bravely past the sea of brown faces of taxi drivers and parking ticket collectors as though it was the most natural thing in the world. Her mother was finally saying 'Siân, Siân' in a voice that wasn't haunting or calling for help. Nerys was standing in front of her, miraculously, allowing her two worlds to meet for a moment. And Siân held this moment – this picture of her teenaged girls draping their Nain with flowers, her clean-shaven husband walking over and stoutly planting two polite kisses on either side of his mother-in-law's face.

Babo manoeuvred them away from the crowds and drove them back to the house of orange and black gates, which was decorated with silver tinsel and lit with lamps. Inside, Perry Como was singing, 'There's no Christmas like a home Christmas', and the girls, even though they no longer believed in Santa, scattered the idea of Christmas all over the house with their glistening eyes and their bodies and minds as pure as bells.

20 Love is Always Love

When Bean was sixteen she began to sneak out of the house every night to sleep with a boy called Michael Mendoza. Every night she sat in the bay window of the room she no longer shared with Mayuri, her eyes drifting between wakefulness and sleep, waiting for Michael to flash his torch light against her window so she could hurry outside and they could up, up and away.

Michael came for her on his Yezdi motorbike, riding down Rutland Lane with the engine switched off, slithering up to the orange and black gates like a silent creature from the sea. He never told Bean exactly when he was coming, and if Bean asked, he'd say she must wait without questions. If she really loved him, she'd wait without questions.

Bean would wait, because there was nothing like falling into the sinful layers of his body. It was terrible, really. Didn't everybody say it? Didn't she say it herself? *What a fool. What a fool.* What a fool for letting him do what he did to her. And what did he do? He saw her floundering; saw it in her eyes. It was easy. She was so young, so compliant. She was dancing at her first party in a low-waist leopard-print dress with padded shoulders, her grown-out hair pushed away from her large forehead in a bright red headband, her strong swimmer legs stuffed into distressingly white ankle boots.

She was dancing with Mehnaz, who was dressed from head to toe in tangerine orange. Bean and Mehnaz, who had put away their dolls, who had spent three straight days in front of the mirror deciding what they were going to wear, who were pretending to have the time of their lives, pretending not to be terrified.

So it was easy for the boy to come over and put his hands on Bean's skin, to take hold of her heart and slip it into his pocket, to take it out whenever he wanted to squeeze squeeze squeeze. Because Bean had been brought up to believe that there was no life possible without love; that love, when it came, would be devastating and difficult.

If Prem Kumar had known, he'd have said it was the same old story again – of a fish trying to swim on land. If Ba in Anjar had known, she'd have said that this was a danger a long time coming.

But Ba didn't know and Bean didn't know any better. For now Bean was sitting in the bay window listening for noises and dreaming of giving herself to Michael Mendoza. She was listening out, not for the Boochie Man or Dick Whittington on his way to becoming Mayor of London, but for the sounds of sleep.

Here was Mayuri in what used to be the guest room – sleeping with the sheets pulled up to her neck, her economics and accounting books piled neatly on the study table, pictures of Cyrus Mazda looking uncomfortably down at her from the walls. Here were Babo and Siân, spooning like old times in their Kashmiri bed. Here was Selvi stretched out like a corpse on the dining-room floor, her bountiful chest rising and falling under the Khaitan fan. Upstairs were the Singhanias, snoring like a family of water buffaloes. Outside was Bahadur, drunk as a skunk, in the cane chair under the flame-of-the-forest tree.

Here was Bean, sneaking past them all so she could slide behind Michael Mendoza on his motorbike and ride back to the house of his divorced mother; to the dark shrine of his room with the Black Sabbath and Skid Row posters, the tightly drawn curtains, the salty smell of teenage sex and testosterone.

Bean lay down amongst it. She laid her young body down on his filthy bed and allowed him to touch the space between her legs, to carry that space away for ever.

The first time 'it' happened, Bean was so ashamed she made Michael leave the room and sent him a note under the door. *Don't you think we've done something wrong?*

Afterwards, when Bean couldn't get enough, when they were fucking in the bed, on the floor, in the shower, in cars, in corners of parties, Michael Mendoza would remind her of those early concerns in his most plaintive voice possible: 'We shouldn't, we shouldn't, really, we shouldn't!' While Bean, wrapping her legs tighter around him, begged him to shut up and do it, just do it.

If Michael had loved Bean, she'd have been sailing. She'd have been out on the open sea with dolphins. Because all Bean had ever wanted in life was affirmation: from her family, from God, from the world. All she really believed in was life-affirming love; something like the love she saw between Babo and Siân.

So when Michael Mendoza, a half-Goan, half-Malayali boy, made her sit on his bed in her bra and knickers, and said, 'I like looking at you like this,' it was inevitable that Bean would fall; fall hard.

And when he took her from behind, saying it was better than racing his bike, better than smoking weed, better than anything in the world, Bean came to believe that he was the only person who could banish the never-ending worries. Bean believed that as long as she was ready and willing, Michael Mendoza would arrive at the gates every night to help her escape.

But after every escape there had to be a return. And the return was always trickier. The return made Bean's heart quiver like a whiskered bulbul, darting this way and that. Any minute now, she thought, *any minute* Babo would appear before her, blocking the door in his striped pyjamas; eyes bleary, curls dishevelled, saying, *Bean, what is it? Where are you coming from at this time of night? What have you been doing?*

And after six months of sneaking out and sneaking back in, six months of exacting deception, six months of *I'm going to see a film with Mehnaz, I'm staying over at Mehnaz's, Menhaz and me are going shopping* – there was trouble.

When the trouble arrived and Bean had to push her breakfast away to run to the toilet to retch, it was Mehnaz who made the appointment at the Jayalakshmi Ladies Clinic in Alwarpet; who got into the auto rickshaw with her; who told her to make up a name and lie about her age. And when the urine test came back, when they found out that it was really true – that Bean was undeniably pregnant at the horrifyingly inappropriate age of sixteen – it was Mehnaz who scavenged the money and stood beside Bean while they anaesthetized her and removed what needed to be removed.

'Don't you think we should tell your mother?' Mehnaz asked, even though she knew there was no way Bean would ever tell.

'How?' Bean replied. 'How can I disappoint her? I can't.'

And when it was all over, and Michael Mendoza arrived to see her in the hospital room, in his usual hoodlum gear – in torn jeans and bracelets around his wrists – smiling his irreverent smile, trying to rub her there between the legs, saying it was OK now, it was all OK; and Bean, seizing that poignant moment to get some clarification – because this *would* be the moment to hear it – asked, 'Do you love me, Michael? Do you?' and Michael Mendoza said, 'I'm not sure I know what love is, but you're the closest I've come to it,' when all this bullshit was going on, the usually placid Mehnaz was standing outside, fuming.

I'm not sure? I'm not sure? Meaning to say what? she wanted to ask. Meaning to say that it wasn't enough for someone to give her body and soul like this in return for some measly words. Meaning to say that if you could lie about other things with such sophistication, couldn't you come up with something better than this? Michael Mendoza – you good-for-nothing son of a second-rate weasel.

So it was Mehnaz who gently suggested to Bean that perhaps she should stop seeing Michael Mendoza because it was no secret he slept with other girls. Perhaps it wasn't cool any more for Bean to be the Queen Bee in his harem. Perhaps she should aim higher.

It was Mehnaz who walked her out past the nurses in their starchy green uniforms, Mehnaz who took Bean to her own pink-papered room and tucked her into bed, and helped change the cotton wads between her legs where it was bleeding – where it would bleed for several days. It was Mehnaz who allowed her to sleep till midday, who brought her buttered toast in bed, and returned to the house of orange and black gates with her, because they had to put on a show for Babo and Siân. They had to pretend that everything was all right, especially for Siân, who always knew when something was wrong.

And later, after exhausting themselves with phoney laughter, after Mehnaz had to go home because Aunty Sherize complained she never saw her daughter any more, Bean, following an early instinct for security, walked into her parents' bedroom and found her mother sitting in the corner, crying for only the second time in her life.

'I hope we raised you right, Beena,' Siân said, not looking at Bean but somewhere beyond.

And Bean, holding back the tears, buried her face in her mother's shoulder and said, 'Of course everything's all right, Mama. I don't know what you mean. Of course everything's going to be all right.' But knowing in her shattered sixteen-year-old heart that nothing was right, that nothing would be right for some time to come.

Bean would have liked to tell Mayuri the truth. She would have liked to tell her sister how the first time she felt something *down there* was when they were watching *The Key to Rebecca* in Babo and Siân's bedroom on the sly, and Mayuri had gone chi chi and switched it off just when it got steamy. Or how it felt when Michael Mendoza put his head between her legs. Or something about the trouble that followed.

But Bean couldn't bring herself to say anything, because Mayuri, who went through the world with a sense of indignation, with an angel's sense of right and wrong, would have looked at her as though she'd betrayed the universe, as though she'd utterly failed as a human being.

Mayuri, whose love for Cyrus was so above-board and acceptable that no one had to ghus phus about it behind closed doors; who walked with Cyrus as though they'd been married for twenty years – standing respectfully apart, with only the occasional leaning in, to tuck a strand of hair back into a braid, or to sweep a straggling crumb away from the lips. Everyone who witnessed these two, carrying on without any of the usual teenage dramas and jealousies, with the quiet dignity that only comes after years and years of comfortable adult intimacy, thought it was so sweet, so unbelievably sweet that two childhood friends should become lovers.

> *Mayuri and Cyrus sitting in a tree.*
> *K I S S I N G.*
> *First comes love, then comes marriage,*
> *Then comes the baby in the baby carriage.*

Except that Mayuri and Cyrus weren't lovers, not even close. Despite the fact that Mayuri regularly came home with

Cyrus's trademark coconut scraper love bites on her alabaster neck; despite the fact that there may have been moments of weakness over the years when Mayuri inadvertently allowed Cyrus to put his hand up her shirt to fondle a breast or two, there was no doubt that Mayuri was resolutely and vigilantly holding tight to her virginity.

How did Bean know? Because she'd been rummaging around in Mayuri's room and discovered five years of Indo-Burma notebooks hidden in her chest of drawers. Five years of meticulously dated shenanigans between Mayuri and Cyrus, inscribed in Mayuri's, virtuous, soldier-straight fountain pen handwriting. Everything from Mayuri's early tyrannical days to the miracle of first realizations: first hand-holding and first under the table knee-touching. These notebooks were an unfolding of love. Everything from Mayuri despairing about having to change her name to Mayuri Mazda (if and when), and Cyrus telling the unhappy story of his parents on an upturned boat one full-moon night, to their first disastrous attempts at tongue-kissing in the ashoka grove at Sylvan Lodge. There were softenings and hardenings, gentle rubbings against each other in the ocean, light tracings of inner thighs and hands held over the gear lever driving home. There were simmerings and bubblings. There were even a few midnight expeditions to sneak out and lie down with each other on the beach, but there was absolutely no record of a first sha-bing sha-bang, of a hello Ms Sunshine, of any kind of explosion. Bean, after combing through 350,000 words, searching for something to justify her own chicanery, was quite sure that nothing in the lifelong romance between Mayuri and Cyrus had ever come close to penetration.

It made no sense at all. Cyrus went to an all-boys school, he had no sisters, his female cousins lived in America; the only access he had to girls other than Mayuri and Bean were the mighty-shouldered, moustachioed he-women who rowed with him at the Madras Boat Club every morning. By all accounts, he should have been gagging for it like any regular eighteen-year-old boy. He should have been pursuing Mayuri like a sex-starved rabbit, but he wasn't. In fact, if Mayuri's account was to be believed, Cyrus wasn't very interested in any of the normal eighteen-year-old activities: parties, smoking, drinking. The occasional party he went to, on Mayuri's insistent cajoling, he moved about disconnected from the crowd, taller than anyone else at 6ft 3, with his hands stuffed in his pockets, while everyone around him drank and threw up and fought and danced. Cyrus never drank or fought, and if he ever danced, it was in a carefree, non-sexual way – not trying to rub his you-know-what against you like other boys.

Cyrus got his pleasure from other places: Cyrus rowed and played tennis and fixed cars in the garage with Darayus and lifted weights and even took yoga lessons to stretch out his gangly, giraffe limbs.

Cyrus was in a constant state of work and movement, sweating in dirty jeans and half-sleeved shirts. It was as if he was trying to pretend he wasn't the son of a millionaire textile owner who'd emigrated to America and left two Jaguars in the garage for his son to play with. It was as if he was trying to pretend he hadn't had a life of privilege, that his grandfather wasn't senile, that his parents really loved each other. Because Cyrus would have swapped his life of privilege in a flash. He would have preferred a life of hard work and diligence, and parents who were the salt of the earth, rather than high-faluting society types.

So Cyrus forced his Parsi white body to turn golden brown in the sun, and worked his hands till they were permanently calloused and smeared with engine oil, and drove a revamped Maruti 800 like all the other upper middle-class kids his age. Only late at night when he was alone, or occasionally if Mayuri was with him, would Cyrus take the old Jaguar

E-type or the XJS out for a spin with the roof down, when there was no one in the streets to ooh and aah with envy. And even then, he tried his hardest not to enjoy it: the V-12 engine, the sleek bonnet, the oval headlights, the utter thrill of driving a machine that was so fast and so beautiful.

Ah, Cyrus! With his toothy smile and eternally uncombed hair. When you looked into his extravagantly lashed, wounded deer eyes, now that the soda bottle glasses had been replaced by contacts, you'd see how Cyrus Mazda had the ability to make you fall in love with him. This was a simple truth. Not mad falling in love in the way Bean had fallen for Michael Mendoza; something truer than that. If you walked into a room of strangers, Cyrus would be the one you'd go to. If you were lost in the street looking for directions, Cyrus would be the one you'd seek out, because there was something so good in Cyrus, something so solid and inevitable about him, that he could melt even the strongest, most stubborn hearts.

Babo and Siân, for instance, who had strong, stubborn hearts, and every reason to be wary – they were putty in Cyrus's hands. Whenever Cyrus came over to pick Mayuri up, Babo and Siân made sure they were both available in the sitting room. 'Have you got something for me to eat, Aunty?' Cyrus might say, 'I hope it's better than what you gave me last time', Mayuri and Bean, never having seen their mother like this – all bashful and giggly over a teenage boy, scampering into the kitchen to bring out a lemon meringue or Victoria sponge on her best china, with a dessert fork and an embroidered napkin. Siân, who tut tutted about his cheek, but who was secretly pleased that this boy was in her house, this boy with the long, sad face like her father's.

And Babo, who had been a love-struck father from the beginning, who found it difficult to relinquish any control when it came to his girls – Babo tolerated Cyrus at first, then warmed to him, then began to adore him. Babo talked about

211

the prices of land or the abysmal state of Indian cricket, not caring that Cyrus didn't really know anything about any of these things. He always asked how Darayus was getting on, and Cyrus always told him the truth: that his grandfather was getting more and more senile by the day, but was still doing the things he loved – messing about with his cars, feeding the local beggars. And finally, Mayuri would have to take him by the arm and drag him out the door, otherwise they'd be there all day, because this boy, who shone and beamed and didn't threaten to rob you of anything you might hold precious – your money or your daughters – opened his arms to the world, and the world embraced him back.

And even Bean, who'd known him since his gawky ostrich years when Mayuri used to persecute them both; who'd sweated buckets and opened pores with him on the back seat of the orange Flying Fiat – even she had to admit that there was everything to love about Cyrus Mazda, and that Trishala Ba, in her dying days, must have got it wrong.

21 Chotu's First and Only Flight

The speed and authority with which Rinky Damani appeared in Chotu's life, destroyed it and then disappeared, was nothing less than remarkable. She appeared in foggy conditions on an early morning flight from Madras to Delhi in the late December of 1990. Chotu was 13,000 feet in the air, looking down at the world. He'd been in a state of philosophical pondering – a state he often found himself in when he was up in the sky. And the predominant feeling he'd been having that morning was this: that perhaps it was possible to live in the quiet, uncomplicated way he'd been doing, without the need for entangling himself with another person, without the need for ownership or belonging.

Because *look* – just look at the world below! The entire superstructure of a city reduced to a mere toyscape. Little toy cars moving about on little toy roads – noiselessly, aromalessly; little toy trees and little toy people. A city with a thousand years of history reduced to a view from a window. All its gates and gardens and towers, its monuments and markets, its politics, its ugliness, its many irregularities reduced to a fine palimpsest of design. *This* was the undeniable miracle of flight: not that it allowed you to travel great distances in small amounts of time, not the actual physics of getting 200 tonnes of metal to stay up in the air. No. It was the miracle of perspective. The fact that down there could be anywhere. Down there, where things were happening, where people were marrying and fighting and working and sleeping and defecating and cooking and crying and dying – down there where all those things that made up life were happening – could be anywhere in the world. And from where Chotu was sitting, it was a world without demarcations, a world perfectly capable of saving itself.

It was while Chotu was looking out of the window and thinking these thoughts that Rinky Damani appeared in his peripheral vision. What Chotu felt when he came in contact with this vision was that he'd finally arrived at the entrance of the world.

'Sir,' Rinky was saying, 'Sir, could you please put your seat forward, we're about to land.'

And when the vision leaned over to do it herself, to tweak the lever and push the headrest forward, Chotu, who could smell the perfume on her and see the tremendous shape of her beneath the constricting Indian Airlines uniform, felt something he hadn't felt since he was twenty years old, about to visit Fifi's House of Spices in North Madras for the very first time. He felt a rush of pure, unaccustomed lust.

Chotu had had his affairs, but he'd emerged from these affairs with no delusions. Those encounters had ignited nothing but a renewed conviction that man and woman weren't meant to share their lives in the way they currently did – under the bonds and ties of legal documentation. He only had to look around to see the unhappiness, the oppression that marriage brought – binding people to each other senselessly on and on and on. What did it all matter when the world was threatening to fall apart? What madness was it to bring children into this world? For Chotu, the idea of having to sleep and wake up in the same bed with the same person day after day, night after night, was enough to make him want to jump out of a plane without a parachute, to fall into that dollhouse splendour and sink slowly into oblivion. Until. Until.

Until Rinky Damani appeared before him with her painted talons and multi-ringed fingers. Rinky Damani, who was like a Chola bronze – a Parvathi whose hips and breasts defied the mountains, who was ready for 10,000 years of coitus or more. Rinky, who could easily match those shalabhanjikas of yore – those tree nymphs who were so fertile, they could, with their mere feet, kick saplings into fruit-bearing trees; who as long as she kept kicking, would be surrounded by a jungle so thick, a vegetation so dense, the world would never have to worry about deforestation again. Rinky, whose face was all eyes and lips – mascara-caked eyes and lips that lay across the bottom of her face like two fertilizer-fed worms, perfectly pursed above the olive birthmark on her chin. When Rinky laughed it was like she was inviting you into her special world – the nostrils flaring ever so slightly and the head thrown back in abandon – thrown back despite the dark rings, the uneven skin, the double layers of foundation. Thrown back because she was a ball-buster and she knew it. Rinky Damani: the most sexually provocative thing Chotu had ever encountered.

The affair between Chotu and Rinky Damani was a relationship of noteworthy lopsidedness. Granted, Chotu had never been in love before, so it was impossible to know what to expect. But no one in his family expected this: mild-mannered Chotu, disposed to bouts of sulking and flashes of anger, suddenly giving voice. Babo couldn't understand it. Was this the same brother he'd grown up with? Little Chotu? For the life of him, Babo couldn't understand his brother's attraction to this woman: she was brazen, tedious, rude, and it had to be said, a whole seven years older than him. Clearly, she was controlling Chotu in the most basic way possible: through sex. Chotu must have been getting it all the time, frequently, and in exciting locations. Why else would he alter his matador hairstyle and start wearing see-through designer

Delhi shirts? Why else would he run circles around the country for this woman while she continued to insult him and his family on a regular basis?

As usual, Babo became the centre for complaints. 'Did you know, bhai,' Meenal said from Bombay, 'The first time she saw the girls she asked them if they had a hormonal imbalance? Can you believe it? HORMONAL IMBALANCE. And when they said no, why? That witch told them that *these* days there is laser surgery to get rid of facial hair for ever. Can you believe it?'

Sitting around the dining table in the house of orange and black gates, Rinky Damani actually said to Siân that she was surprised she'd lasted so long in such a crackpot family. 'I mean, both your sisters-in-law look like Ladies Club treasurers. And your father-in-law, oh my God, don't get me started on him. He's the worst. He treats Chotu like a child. I mean, Chotu – is there any worse way to stunt a man's maturity? What a ridiculous pet name. Why not just call him Tejas? Why not just let him do what he wants to do?'

Never mind that Rinky was a pet name for Renuka. Never mind that Rinky was forty years old.

In spite of all her complaining, Rinky agreed to move to Madras and live in Sylvan Lodge as long as there could be a Delhi flat as well. She was full of ideas to renovate the top floor and redesign the whole look of the house. She even got Babo to invent a new shade of salmon pink paint with silver flecks so she could replace Trishala's pista-green legacy. She went on shopping sprees, tried being vegetarian on Mondays, agreed to hand in her resignation a few months before the wedding, but most importantly, she spent hours and hours painstakingly planning their honeymoon because Rinky, who had never flown internationally before had only ever had one ambition in life: to walk into a Rolex shop and to be able to afford anything in it. Rinky was planning Switzerland because Switzerland was the playground of the rich; Switzerland was cuckoo clocks and Swarovski and everything India was not. And Chotu, all the while, kept handing her bundles of Rs 100 notes, despite Prem Kumar's protests and Babo's raised eyebrows, because he'd never been happier in his life.

And yet, on Tuesday 21 May 1991, the same day Prime Minister Rajiv Gandhi was assassinated by an LTTE suicide bomber, in the small town of Sri Perumbudur, fifty kilometres outside of Madras, barely six months after the love affair between Rinky Damani and Chotu had begun, it was officially over. Just like that. While the country revisited the turmoil it had seen after Indira Gandhi's death, Chotu's life fell apart.

On the Friday before the assassination, Rinky met the International Head of Nestlé Marketing on the Delhi-Bombay sector. By the weekend, she had vanished, leaving Chotu a wedding trousseau of considerable value, the gold and diamond Titan watch he'd bought her to rectify her tardiness, and two round-trip tickets to Switzerland. On the Tuesday of the assassination, the one-line note of apology arrived.

Dear Tejas,
> *You know that in the end, it wouldn't have worked out.*
Renuka

But Chotu didn't know. How could he know? He felt like he'd been thrust into a cave, a cave emptied of light and filled with Rinky's absences. How could he get used to the darkness and the shadows again after he had bathed and frolicked and made love to the light? The cave was full of despair, and the problem with this despair was that Chotu couldn't give vent to it. It was there – every minute of every day – following him like a brooding thundercloud wherever he went. So there was nothing for him to do but wait in the cave surrounded by her

217

things, waiting for a phone call that might come miraculously to save him, to confirm that it had all been a terrible mistake – that Rinky was being held for ransom, or had been taken seriously ill – anything but Rinky Damani heartlessly and deliberately abandoning him for another man.

And after months of sitting by a silent phone, and checking the letter box seventeen times a day, and the Indian Airlines office telling him that they really had no information about their previous employee Ms Damani – after months and months of soul-destroying despair, there was anger. Anger, because this was his life, and suddenly, it was diminished. Gone. Suddenly, he was left to confront the reality that was left: the insomniac father with the torn vest and dhoti sitting around the table with a *why don't you ever listen to me* look in his eyes, the football sisters and pitying brother shuffling tentatively around him, waiting to catch him if he should fall.

Prem Kumar couldn't begin to know how to deal with yet another lovesick son. He was older now, feeble and worn down, working only half-days at the office, and struggling through the endless nights by listening to religious songs on his Walkman. 'Come and help him,' he instructed his first-born.

But when Babo came over to Sylvan Lodge and tried to smooth over some of the madness that Rinky had left behind, Chotu, who wasn't in the mood for reconciliation just yet, said, 'Bhai, it is what it is, just let it be,' and disappeared upstairs.

Inside his half-renovated room, Chotu's suitcases lay about in the hope that Rinky Damani would summon him up as she used to summon him up before. Chotu lived in this state of transition for a few years – unable to stay, unable to go, unable to work, unable to fly. The only time he got any kind of comfort was at the Madras Gymkhana Club with his sister-in-law and his nieces. There, while the girls dived off the springboards and canonballed in the deep end, he remembered an earlier, purer time, when Bean and he spent their mornings patiently trawling up and down the length of this same swimming pool, and he tried to replicate that feeling now, by swimming his way into a state of meditation. And after unsuccessfully trying to swim the idea of Rinky Damani away, he'd come out of the water and sit with Siân under the sun umbrella with a fresh lime soda and say, 'Bhabi, I really loved her. I know she was difficult at times, that she was overpowering and maybe spoke her mind too openly, but you know, she could be adorable. You should have seen the way she ate ice cream – like a little girl – letting it dribble all the way down her neck. And even though she ate meat, she really did love animals – in her heart, she did.'

And on and on and on till the memory of Rinky Damani, although it never entirely vanished, began to take the shape of a dream life – a kind of underwater swimming without breathing. And what he felt when he was holding his breath on those long concentrated Saturday morning swims, was how his life had always been evading him. Sometimes, it was there – right at the bottom of his throat, in the base of his lungs, threatening to explode. It was trying to remind him of what Ba had been telling him all along – to leap into the sunshine and let the world save him. Because after Rinky disappeared, leaving a one-line note that would tear into his heart for ever, Chotu was left with the realization that love was more powerful than flight – it was its own soaring, its own bird-like keening in the wind that required no glider, no motor. And now that he had loved and lost Rinky Damani, there was nothing for him to do but flounder in the dark, trying to remember what it had been like when it was light, when he could fly, when there had been a possibility to escape the world.

22 What Goes Up Must Come Down

A picture then, of the Patel-Jones family at a crucial point in their history, five years before the start of the new millennium. Mayuri and Bean are standing at the edge of the world. They're about to change their lives and leave the house of orange and black gates for the very first time. Mayuri and Bean, aged twenty-three and twenty-two, on a balmy New Year's day in 1995, have decided to do what Babo and Siân always knew they'd do but hoped they wouldn't. They've decided to leave home and go exploring for a while.

The family has congregated on an isolated beach one hour south of the city of Madras for Mayuri's wedding. The women are dressed in glitter and gold, sequins and silk, shimmer and shine – jhimak jhimaking like the blood-orange sunset falling across the sea. All except for Ba, who's in her usual widow's white, who has left Gujarat for only the third time in her life. The men are in ties and blazers, embroidered kurta pyjamas and safari suits. There are an unusual number of children. Who knows where they've come from – but they are here – running around in birthday-cake dresses and baba suits with flowers in their hair.

Darayus first: who's standing towards the back of the scene, surveying everything. He's keeping an eye on the caterers, making sure they've got their gloves and aprons on, making sure none of them has the look of death about them. Darayus is watching everyone, especially his estranged son Neville and his daughter-in-law, Farah. Yes, they're here too. All the way from New York City for the first time in thirteen years. They're standing with the other faraway guests – the Welsh contingent – Owen, Huw, Carole and the twins Gareth and Ed – all dressed like they're going to church, except for Carole, who looks like she's dressed for the races in an extravagant fuchsia feathered hat and a too-tight fuchsia suit. The faraway guests have formed a clique already. They're sitting on the colourful mattresses laid out in the sand, waiting to be told what to do. Darayus will keep an eye on them, and only if there's something very urgent, something that can't wait for later, will he go to Cyrus so *he* can deal with it. But Darayus will not move. Darayus will stand at the back and not get paranoid, and behave and watch.

Prem Kumar and Ba next: who've been given places of prominence up front in two plastic chairs owing to one's weak knees and the other's weak eyes. Nothing is said between mother and son, nothing audible at least. Maybe Ba is complaining about Prem Kumar's beige safari suit, which is a ditto copy of the same old safari suit he always wears for important occasions; only this one doesn't look new, this one is hanging on him in that sad, old-man way, with one leg hitched into his socks, and some of the buttons undone. Maybe she's wishing Ignatius had come, so he could sit beside her and entertain her while all this marriage tamasha takes place. But Ignatius had said, 'No, thank you. God knows how those Madrasis will take to someone like me. I'll stay here and look after things.'

Prem Kumar isn't speaking. He's saying nothing about the picking up and falling away that's been going on in his life: his granddaughters growing up and not knowing him, Mayuri getting married to a boy Trishala disapproved of, and Bean planning to go away to London – that place where all the trouble began years ago. He's saying nothing of his youngest son who he's certain is paying for the sin of fornicating with an unworthy woman. For years all he has heard is Rinky this, Rinky that – Rinky dink dink. Prem Kumar knew right from the beginning that Rinky Damani wouldn't have made any kind of daughter-in-law. Imagine! Walking around in those high-heeled shoes like a beauty queen. His youngest son seems to him like an electric blue kingfisher caught in mid-air: a small, precious tear against the sky. Prem Kumar is saying nothing about this; not to Ba, not when the family is gathered together in a way they'll never be gathered again.

Dolly and Meenal and the unibrows next: they are brighter than anyone else – the unibrows especially, who were married within a year of each other; who've got rid of their menacing unibrow and are reasonably attractive after all; who've vowed to battle their fatty bumbalatti genes by becoming border-line anorexic and eating like ants. They are thin. Will remain so till their first babies. Then genetics will prevail; then the curse of the pear-shaped body will rear its ugly bottom. But for now, they're both wearing bright yellow, still in their first flush of marriage – one to a computer engineer, the other to a music producer in Bollywood – hauling the bride's make-up kit between them like two yellow ducklings across the sand.

The aunts Meenal and Dolly are rushing about despite their heaviness, in rust and ochre Gujarati-style saris, with stucco-like make-up caked to their faces and elaborate hairstyles involving ringlets, both. They're taking charge of the things that should have been assigned to them in the first place. *Where are the coconuts, where are the pendas, where are the silver coins that Mayuri needs to give away, where are the garlands, and where on earth is the pujari?* Periodically, they must scrunch down in their saris next to Prem Kumar to see if he needs anything, more so he feels attention is being paid to him than anything else, because his night-nurse Sonam is never very far away. Sonam, with her oversized eyes and oversized body, is talking to the secretary Jyothi – the third and final secretary of Sanbo Enterprises – a severe, bird-like woman whose loyalty to the family overrides her mediocre abilities as a typist. So, Sonam and Jyothi – an Indian female version of Laurel and Hardy – a choti and a moti, standing with the other helpers.

Selvi is the head of the helpers. She's wearing a turquoise-blue striped polyester sari that a big-busted woman really shouldn't wear, with her hair tied back in a scraggly bun and the gold studs in her nose flaring ferociously because she can't get the group to pay attention to her all at once. This is the drill: first the ceremony has to finish, then the guests will eat, then all the helpers, *including* the drivers, are to come in as quickly and quietly as possible to sit at the long tables that have been laid out for dinner. There's plenty of food for everyone – all vegetarian, of course, but at least five different kinds of sweets. For now, drivers must drink their coffee and go. *What about booze?* No booze, you cheeky son of a whore. Booze only comes later, after the ceremony, when there may be dancing of some kind. Booze and dancing strictly off limits for the drivers. *Oh really?* And I suppose you think you're a sweet-smelling lily, you filthy pubes of a stray dog. *Not you*, she quickly turns to the young mechanics standing around – the young men who are clearly out of their depth – who work with Cyrus sir in the garage. *You are guests here*, she says, pushing them into the centre. *Go sit. Go and sit on the mattresses. It's all going to start soon.* The young mechanics with the trim moustaches who've made an effort with their cleanest shirts and their best pair of jeans, but who still have their hair slicked down with coconut oil and the look of the labourer about them – they pick up glasses of Pepsi from a passing waiter and sit opposite the faraway guests.

The friends: the friends belong to Bean and Mayuri. They are college-going or just-finished college-going girls. Bean is rounding up the dance crew to go through the routine again. There are seven of them altogether, with a cameo entrance by Cyrus at the end that no one knows about, not even Mayuri. *That* will be the best. *That* will be hilarious. Cyrus has no hips to speak of and is totally uncoordinated, but he's going to give it a shot. They've been practising for a whole month to last year's hit song 'Pehla Pehla Pyar' every single evening on the redbrick terrace of Sylvan Lodge because it's the only place where there's some privacy and some space, but where they had to shush and keep it down because Chotu Kaka was right next door. There's no keeping it down here.

There's much tittering and wittering going on in the friends' group. Mehnaz is here from Bombay with her fabulously rich and ugly husband Ali, who is, for the moment, standing with the faraway guests. Mehnaz has rounded out like a soft balloon: wide-hipped, ample-breasted, in a light peach antique Benares sari wrapped efficiently against her glowing skin. Bean's lesser circle of friends – Parvathi, Immaculate and Saira – are there too, along with Mayuri's maids of honour – Sunaina and the hybrid Rachel – all dressed in shades of green, from pale sweet pea to bright parrot. Rachel is engaged to a boy in America, and because of this she now talks with an American accent. Bean and Mehnaz talk to each other in the same affected accent when they think she can't hear them.

Bean is the only one who isn't in a sari. She's in a traditional Gujarati chanya choli – a long, flouncy, burgundy skirt that flares out like an umbrella when she twirls, a skimpy silver tussar silk blouse, and an embroidered odhni that keeps slipping off her shoulders. Around her neck are Trishala's rubies – they are her only real ornamentation. But she's overdone it with the jasmine; rather, Pamela Anne's girls at Cuts and Curls have overdone it. They've given her a beehive, which she didn't want. She merely wanted it up and away with a bit of hairspray to keep it off her face. By nightfall the pile of jasmine on her head will have sagged halfway down her back like a ball of frayed rope, and she'll have broken most of her burgundy bangles, but for now she's faultless, complete.

'Hello, gorgeous,' Rahul says, coming towards her with his mousy Maharashtrian wife. A few years ago if Rahul had called her gorgeous in public, Bean would have blushed for days and noted it faithfully down in her diary: *Saw R today. Guess what? He called me gorgeous in front of everybody. He's soooo adorable!* But ever since his disappointing marriage to the mousy Maharashtrian Bean hasn't been so enamoured with him, because Rahul's gone and done that thing that lots of young men do: he's turned into an uncle before his time. Looking at him now, you'd never have thought he was once the school hurdles champion, that with his dark blond hair and sea-blue eyes, he was once Bean's Bonnie Bobby Shaftoe. It's funny how the tables turn, Bean thinks, as she blows him a kiss, feeling beautiful as she does so, and then dodges quickly out of sight because she can see Uncle Keshav trundling towards her like a steam engine, getting ready to tweak the hell out of her cheeks.

Babo and Siân next: who are standing together smiling hesitant half-smiles. Who should be walking around making people feel comfortable, at this, the wedding of their eldest daughter, but who are frankly at a loss. Surely they should be talking to their counterparts Neville and Farah, or over with Huw and Owen and the boys. But no, they're with their hybrid friends instead: Keshav and Praveen, who are swilling whisky robustly from hip flasks, and sallow-faced Shyam, desperately trying to keep up with them. Jan and Darlene are dressed in saris, looking like has-been hippies – their skins have sagged, worn down with liver spots after years of exposure to the Madras sun, and they look old, unlike Siân, who as Dolly rightly points out to the girls, 'Has really maintained, no?'

Siân and Babo, who've been married twenty-five years to the day. Twenty-five years! Would someone like to tell them exactly what they've been doing for a quarter of a century? And how they've come to this particular moment in their history? They are the most beautiful thing on this beach. They can't help it. Babo, who had to go to Syed Bawkher thrice for his suit fitting, while Siân ribbed him the whole time, saying he'd better cut down on those scotch and sodas, and those nutty-boy ice creams. He'd better get his cholesterol checked, he'd better start his morning walks again, he'd better better better. Babo, who listens and smiles, but does as he pleases in his new charcoal-grey suit with a pink shirt against his walnut skin and a rose in his buttonhole. His hair's been cut so close to the scalp there's no evidence of his once-bounteous curls. His grey eyes are hardening, hardening because he's determined not to become emotional. He's got his lips on the Macallan's because he needs it if he's going to stay composed, if he's going to address all these people gathered here. He's been preparing for weeks, carrying his little speech around in his wallet, so that he could whip it out to practise whenever he had a free moment alone. He's learned it all by heart, but he's going to stand up and read from the paper just in case. Of course, he gets emotional; his voice cracks on the very first sentence: *Some of you have come from a long way away. Siân and I are so pleased to see you all here ...*

Siân, who decided on a sari, thinking it wouldn't look right in the pictures if she was in something Western and the girls were in something Indian. Siân is in maroon – a rich maroon with fine zardosi worked sparingly over it. She's wearing gold, not diamonds – not too much – again, she doesn't want to over-shine. But Babo and she sitting together – they always over-shine – it's unavoidable. They're standing so close, making such a fine picture with their jhill mill gleaming teeth. They're at the summit of something; anyone can see. It's not youth, it's not beauty – it's something like adoration, an ultimate and complete adoration. A summit, which is such a fatal place to be, because what goes up must come down.

Chotu next: who's made it in spite of. Chotu, who's in a regal black sherwani, who's sitting on the mattress in front of the Singhania family, his legs curled under him, making him look quite small. The sisters Meenal and Dolly are squatting down on their fat knees to ask if he needs anything. One brings coconut water; the other brings lime juice. 'Stop it,' he barks. 'Go and see if that damn pujari has arrived yet. Go and do something useful.' The sisters leave him laden with beverages before waddling back into the crowd. Chotu picks up the lime juice and drinks it. Is he happy? Yes. It's a happy-sad moment for him. He doesn't once think of Rinky Damani. This, he is proud of. He thinks he has banished her so forcefully from his body and mind, he doesn't realize she's always going to be there – as soon as he wakes and before he sleeps – running through his blood, mocking him, because he lets her. But not here, not this evening. Not while they're all waiting to witness something beautiful again, like they'd done on a cool January day in Anjar twenty-five years ago.

Mayuri and Cyrus: finally. Mayuri is going to become Mayuri Mazda. It isn't as funny as she thought it would be. She can't quite believe it. She'd decided this so long ago. She'd loved this boy for ten years! Ten long years. And there had never been any guarantee that it would come to this. It might never have if she hadn't brought things to a head: 'And how long do you think we're going to keep this teenage thing going?' *What do you mean?* Cyrus, sweet Cyrus. Never thinking that she might want things differently. That they might have to grow up one day and do things for themselves. 'Well, either we live together or we get married. I'm tired of running between your house and my house.'

227

So they lived together for a while in Cyrus's room, in Darayus's house next door to Sylvan Lodge, which was all a bit too close for comfort and not really what Mayuri wanted. Not those cupboards with the doors taken off the hinges and the helmets and the bags of tools lying around and the car posters on the wall, for chrissake. She wanted her own place on the beach, with long French windows and a veranda that opened out to the sea. Wood, windows, glass. She wanted to fill it with things from all over the world – the world they were going to travel soon: talavera plates from Mexico, enamel ware from Italy, lamps from Indonesia, bougainvillea everywhere. They'd get a dog or two, and Cyrus could have his garage with a broken-down jeep or a jag or whatever he wanted to put in there. And they could sit out at nights – she with her glass of red, he with his apple juice, and listen to the ocean and work out what they were really meant to be doing.

But for now it was all going to begin, because here she was, sitting cross-legged in her great-grandmother's wedding sari – the exquisite red and gold sari that Bean had been determined to have, aired of its naphthalene, covering her long, chestnut braids. Here she was with a nose-ring and hennaed hands and feet, with tiny, traditional red and white dots painted along her forehead and down the sides of her face. Everyone is watching her and Cyrus, who's the cleanest he's ever been, who is this minute being excommunicated for marrying outside the Parsi community. But who cares? His parents are here – Neville and Farah – strangers in a way; ready to perform their parental duties as always, ready to accept whatever Cy demands, because they're too busy living their own lives. *Cy wants to stay with his senile grandfather?* Fine. *Cy wants to get married?* Wonderful, we'll be there. *Sigh. Sigh.*

Cyrus, who at this moment isn't thinking about his philandering father or his mother, who's holding on for all the millions he's worth; who isn't thinking of the grandfather who's doing as he's been told to do for a change; who isn't even thinking of Mayuri sitting next to him, even though she's gleaming in that extraordinarily beautiful way of hers, looking at him as though he were the only person in the world. Cyrus is thinking of his life – the bigger picture of his life. He's putting a ring on Mayuri's finger. He's drinking honey from her palms.

So the family is all here. There is only one missing space: Nerys.

Nerys, who has just had her second stroke, is sitting in her wheelchair in Tan-y-Rhos with Aunty Eleri, who's trying hard not to look at the left side of her sister-in-law's face. Nerys, whose three children have been taking turns to look after her – even Siân all the way from India. Nerys, who will die soon, as will Darayus, peacefully in her sleep, without any resistance.

Nerys will wait for Owen to return to Nercwys with the photographs. There'll be no videotapes because Mayuri had wanted it intimate and private; she hadn't wanted those camera fellows shoving lights into people's faces while they were eating dinner. So what Nerys will see is not the continuity of that evening, not how the rain came down as if the skies were falling after it was all over – pulling up the shamiana and the bamboo poles as though they were tufts of grass. She'll see imprints instead: of that bruised Madras sunset, snippets of bright colour, teeth and tears, a ring of seven girls twirling sticks – Bean heading them. Bean, who'll be in London soon. Bean, who'll come too late.

She'll see the priest holding Cyrus and Mayuri's hands, one on top of the other over the fire; Cyrus and Mayuri with flower garlands as thick as ten snakes around their necks; Cyrus and Mayuri bending at Ba's feet, at Prem Kumar's feet, at Babo and Siân's feet, at Neville and Farah's feet, at Meenal and Dolly and Chotu's feet. Bending for blessings. Bending, bending, bending.

But Nerys won't see the heavy salt air coming in from the ocean; the triangular patches of sweat spreading underneath the ladies' arms despite the deodorant; the odd assortment of people who seem to appear out of nowhere – aunties and uncles from the Madras Gymkhana Club, employees of Sanbo Enterprises and Neville's textile factory, Mr Mustafa from the OK Stores with his glinting gums, Manna with his destitute cheekbones floating through the crowds like a cloud, Ms Douglas in one of her grandmother's lavender scarves, cornering Bean and saying, 'You don't have your mother's auburn hair, do you?'

Nerys won't see how the family gathers around the fire as the light of the first day of 1995 begins to diminish. She won't see what happens when Owen brings out her silver locket for Mayuri – the one she's worn around her neck ever since she was married – with the thumbnail picture of Bryn now safely removed and kept under the magnifying glass on the bureau downstairs. She won't see how Siân, who's been holding it all together until then, begins to weep, to convulse into tears. How this starts up an ululating from the women who've been practising for centuries, who know this deep inside them – this *too-muchness* of emotion – which try as they might they cannot contain. How it is this way sometimes at Indian weddings – whole ceremonies devoted just to this: to crying, to tearing your guts out, to saying goodbye to your daughter. Because there's nothing as devastating as saying goodbye to your daughter. No. Not even saying goodbye to your son. It cannot be. Your sons will devastate you in different ways.

But when your daughters decide to do as Mayuri and Bean have decided to do – to change the direction of their lives, to pick themselves up and out of the house of orange and black gates – when they decide to do this simultaneously, it is about as devastating as it gets. When Siân starts up this wailing and cannot stop till it's all washed out of her, the other women begin to think about their own private sorrows and they let it out and let it out until there isn't a dry, smudgeless eye on that beach.

Mayuri, who's the one they're supposed to be crying for, is crying for all the changes that lie ahead, all the painstaking tiny red and white dots blotching her satiny face. Bean, who hardly ever needs an excuse to fall into self-pity, is holding her mother and crying. *Sorry*, it means, *I'm sorry*. Mehnaz is crying too, for something lost, never to be recovered, ruining her peaches and cream complexion. The aunts, the unibrows, the helpers, the hybrids, the friends, the faraways – every single woman on that beach is wailing as though the love of her life has just died in the most horrific way possible.

Every woman, that is, except for Ba. Ba is *not* crying. Ba has gone looking for Babo, who's sitting by himself, watching the inky sea. He's thinking about the first English love song he ever heard – Nat King Cole's 'Love is a Many Splendoured Thing.' He's thinking how that song used to play in his head over and over when his daughters were little, when they used to strip off their clothes and go running into the waves at Marina Beach while Siân and he held hands on the seashore. He's remembering leaning over to his wife and saying, *Life really did begin in the ocean, didn't it?*

When Ba finds him she lowers herself on to the wet sand beside him. 'Nobody said it was going to be easy,' she says.

Babo lays his head in her lap.

'Only fools and lovers never learn how to let go,' Ba says, opening her mouth to the rain, moving her fingers out of habit through Babo's non-existent curls.

'It's not what you think. It's not that I don't want them to go away from home, find love, live their lives as fully as they possibly can. It's not even that I want them to remain

231

eternally innocent. But what I want, what I really want to know is what I'm supposed to do with the space they leave behind? What am I supposed to fill it with?

'You fill it with love,' Ba murmured. 'Like you have always filled it. With love and more love.'

PART THREE

Lewisham to Ganga Bazaar

1996–2001

23 One Foot In the Other Foot Out

The night before Bean left for London Babo sat on the tiled floor of the bottle-green bathroom and cried. He couldn't sleep. Something resembling a dream, but refusing to behave like one, kept sliding in and out of his consciousness. He wanted to wake Siân and say, 'Are we mad? For allowing our baby to go away? Off to stay with Bhupen and Mangala Jain in the city of London, the city we might have made our home a long time ago?'

Babo and Siân had thrown a barbeque bon voyage party that evening. The usual crowd – the Krishnamurtis and the Malhotras, plus the upstairs Singhania family, whose boys were also about to flee the nest. For the hybrids it was an emotional night. Shyam was leaving to embark on a five-year doctorate in neuroscience at Johns Hopkins University in Baltimore, and Bean was going off to do God-only-knew-what in London. Babo could not know that only a few hours earlier, Shyam had sweet-talked Bean into fucking against these very same walls. *A sympathy fuck*, Bean would tell Mehnaz later. But a fuck, nevertheless. Shyam Malhotra wasn't the kind of boy Babo imagined his younger daughter with. Not that he could imagine either of his daughters with any man. But if he had to describe the ideal man for Bean, he would have aimed for someone taller, stronger, a little less clever.

Babo kept thinking about the evening. Three sets of cronies out on the veranda, eating kebabs and knocking back G&Ts

and scotch sodas. Cyrus expertly manning the barbeque, while Mayuri and Siân soldiered back and forth from the kitchen with trays of skewered vegetables and marinated pieces of meat. It seemed like they'd been doing this for years: sitting on that veranda, telling the same stories. These were their mythologies in a way. How they had upped and left one country, fallen in love in another country, and then up and marched right back to the place they started from. Perhaps it's inevitable, Babo thought, that our children suffer a similar displacement; that in order to understand the pattern of their lives here, they must go elsewhere.

More and more these days, as Prem Kumar and Chotu's bickering escalated, Babo sat at his desk at Sanbo Enterprises and reminisced about his inauspicious London beginnings – getting gypped by that sardarji taxi driver as soon as he arrived, the whole brouhaha with Nat and Lila, the cafeteria ladies trying to fatten him up with cheese sandwiches and double helpings of custard. He yearned to feel all that again: the newness, the anonymity, even the utter loneliness.

Babo wondered about Bean's reasons for upping and leaving the house of orange and black gates. Part of it, he knew, must have had something to do with that dreadful boy, Michael Mendoza, whose name was forbidden in this house, and who Siân had confirmed had disappeared with his divorced mother to live in Australia. Part of it must have had to do with the boredom of college life, where for four years Bean went and came home with a dull look in her eyes, with no new boyfriend or best friend of note, and a degree in English literature which she didn't know what to do with. There must have been other reasons too, but Babo, struggling against the effects of too much alcohol, couldn't guess at those just yet.

Babo got up from the floor and walked cautiously into the darkness to Bean's bedroom door. Once, both his daughters had slept in this room in two cane beds under their grandmother's knitted blankets. Then Mayuri became a teenager and insisted on claiming the guest room for herself, and for the past year and a half, ever since her wedding to Cyrus Mazda, she only ever came to spend the night when her husband was out of town. Tonight, after many years, Babo saw his daughters sleeping side by side again. He lingered in the doorway, watching their shapes on the bed. He thought of the old days, when Siân and he used to come home late from parties to find Mayuri and Bean sleeping on the floor with dolls in their hands, surrounded by remnants of a midnight feast. Sometimes, they were really asleep, exhausted from the excitement of being able to stay up as late as they wanted. But most times, they were only pretending, having seen the wash of lights from the Flying Fiat beam up against the grills of their bedroom window, keeled over any which way, knowing that Babo would pick them up and put them in their beds.

Standing there, on the night of Bean's departure, Babo wondered if his daughters were giving chori chori looks to each other across the dark. *I can see, you know!* he wanted to say. *I'm not a fool.*

As he turned to go back to his wife in bed, Babo caught sight of Bean's suitcases standing upright by the door, and the knowledge that all her most precious belongings had been carefully packed and locked away like this almost made him cry again. In a few hours Bahadur would pack these cases in the dickey, Selvi would stand at the gates and beat her big breasts in grief, and Babo would drive his girls through the still-sleeping streets of Madras all the way to the Meenambakkam Airport.

Bean rolled over a few moments later and opened her eyes. She couldn't sleep either. Every time she closed her eyes, images of Shyam bombarded her retinas. Shyam whispering how much he had always loved her. Shyam promising to write to her from Baltimore. What had *that* been about, anyway? A last-ditch effort to be filled by something – to be able to touch and take something as hers? Because nothing filled her any more. Nothing at all. Not her family, not her life, not this city of Madras, which had become, in recent years, a city of absences.

Bean couldn't say herself what her reasons for leaving were. There was a vacancy in this house of her childhood that she couldn't get used to now that Mayuri was living with Cyrus in a house of their own. Mehnaz was off, pursuing motherhood with a vengeance in Bombay. Her other friends – Parvathi, Saira and Immaculate, were all either married or on their way to being married. And the unibrows – well, they were already certified aunties, which left Bean as usual, hovering, waiting for someone to point the way.

Instead of waiting for something to happen, Bean had decided it was time to seek it out; to go off on her own adventure like Dick Whittington and his cat, on a quest to conquer the city of London. All Bean really knew of London were bits and pieces patched together from childhood memories – riding atop the red double-decker buses with her cousins Gareth and Ed, ice-cream cones from the ice-cream van, walking into Hamley's, with Siân saying, 'Behave, don't be greedy now,' and Bean, nodding and saying 'Yes yes,' but breaking her promise instantly because she'd never in all her life seen such beautiful toys.

What Bean was really hoping when she left Madras in that August of 1996, was to find love: the kind of love Babo and Siân had found in London. And for the first three months that she lived with Babo's old friends Mangala and Bhupen Jain in their modest, three-bedroom, red-brick house with attached sunroom and garden in Lewisham, this is what Bean went looking for: love, pure and simple. Ba-ba-boom, ba-ba-boom, ba-ba-boom-boom-boom.

*   *   *

Bean should have known. She should have known the minute she saw Mr Jain's sourpuss face at the arrival gates in Heathrow to welcome her. The minute Mr Jain, after briefly enquiring about the state of everyone's health and wealth in Madras, started complaining about the exorbitant cost of airport parking. The minute he launched into his litany of rules.

If Bean had known she'd have to live in a freezing, cheerless house where nobody smiled and everything was counted; if she'd known how difficult it was going to be to get a job and open a bank account; if she'd known there'd be so much to deal with during those first three months – not just learning bus routes and rushing home to sleep in sweatshirts and socks, but Nerys and Darayus Mazda passing away in their sleep, within days of each other. If Bean had known that at the end of all this there would be still be the incident with Mr and Mrs Jain's forty-year-old son, Deenu, to contend with, she would have turned right around and flown back home.

But it was too late for that now. Because now she was busy looking out of the window where it was raining a soft, swish swish, late summer London kind of rain. She was letting Mr Jain's words fall over her with the sounds of Kishore Kumar playing from the Oldies Goldies Sunshine radio station, where in between the firstly, secondly, thirdly and fourthly, Mr Jain was allowing himself briefly to digress and croon along, 'Yeh tere pyar ki hai jadugari.'

Mangala Aunty was standing at the door of 32 Sunnydale Road in a chiffon floral sari and pink wire-rimmed Gandhi glasses, smiling goofily, waving a rose-coloured kerchief that had seen infinitely better days.

The house was nothing like Bean remembered it to be. It looked smaller, squashed between two similar houses in a crescent at the end of a shaded street. Bean remembered a palace of spices, of coming here during her sometimes summers after all the weeks of having to use knives and forks at Tan-y-Rhos, after all the steak and kidney pie. Here, Mayuri and she were allowed to tear chappathis into deft little triangles with their fingers, to mash rice balls, ping-pong size, down their throats until Siân said, *No more, no more, you're going to be sick*, and sent them up the carpeted stairway to sleep in the guest room till it was time to wake up and fly zing zing zing all the way home to Madras.

'How was journey, Beena?' Mangala Aunty asked. 'All fine? You must be hungry. Shall I make you some garam-garam hot-hot bhajjiyas? Come in, come in. Last time you were still a baby, such a beautiful girl now. Come in, come in.'

Mr Jain unbuttoned his coat and hung it carefully in the closet under the stairway. He looked distinctly older – hair all gone, body stooped over at the waist, almost frail. But there was nothing frail about Bhupen Jain, Bean would soon discover.

'You may not be used to having deadlines with your mummy and daddy in Madras,' he started again, just in case she hadn't been paying attention the first time around. 'But in this house you are AUW-ER responsibility. Anything that happens to you is AUW-ER responsibility. So, let me repeat again: latest time of arrival at night is 9 PEE EM.

'Tomorrow we go to corner shop and buy you travel card. I take you on the bus and train to London Bridge. We sit with *A-Z* and you begin to understand how to move around the town.

'Don't be forgetting about phone calls, Beena. Phone is very expensive in England. Ten minutes incoming, five minutes outgoing. No international calls direct from here, please.

'Don't worry, we buy you phone card for best rates to India so you can call your mummy and daddy, and Mayuri. How is Mayuri? Enjoying married life?'

While Mangala Aunty disappeared into the kitchen to make the bhajjiyas, Mr Jain showed Bean her room upstairs and advised her on the order of morning ablutions.

'We are not rich people, Beena, not like your daddy.' Cackle cackle. 'So, we are having only one bathroom with commode in separate room. In the morning time, Deenu will go first, myself second, then you, then aunty. OK?

'After shower, you take this cloth from sill and wipe down bath. You want I show you how? Same like morning window wiping in your room. Why? Because panes get condensation, wood gets wet, then rotten, then very costly to replace. I show you how. Very easy. Come, I show you how.

'On weekends, you can teach me computer and help Aunty with house-cleaning. Any doubts, you just ask me, OK?'

No rules of any sort had been discussed with Babo and Siân before leaving. In fact, the only advice they'd given Bean was not to get too discouraged by Mr Jain's *apparent* sourness, because he was exceedingly sweet and generous underneath. Bean supposed they were right. After all, he was opening his house to her, feeding her, helping her find her way and refusing to take a single pound in exchange, all because she was his best friend's daughter, who was like his own daughter. And as long as she, *unlike* the real one, abided by the rules of his house, all would be well.

In the kitchen Mangala Aunty was popping batter-covered potatoes into spluttering oil and reassembling the crispy concoctions on a single neat square of paper towel to soak up the oil. Mr Jain directed Bean to the far end of the kitchen bench and squeezed himself beside her. Mangala Aunty brought the bhajjiyas to the table and parked herself directly facing them. These would be their permanent places.

Mr Jain ate his bhajjiyas like a goldfish, dipping them in a circle of tomato ketchup and glubbing them down without any evidence of masticating. Bean, avoiding his watchful gaze, swirled her two bhajjiyas around on the plate in front of her.

'Dieting or what?' Mangala Aunty said, smiling her goofy smile again, plonking two more bhajjiyas on Bean's plate.

'Puppy,' Mr Jain told his wife. 'Don't give if the girl doesn't want.'

And then turning to Bean, 'It's not nice to waste, is it, Beena?'

Bean, reeling from the use of the word 'puppy' between sourpuss Mr Jain and his wife, managed to croak back, 'You're absolutely right, Uncle. My grandfather always says, the less we waste, the less we lack.'

For the first few weeks, Bean spent every evening with Mr Jain at the kitchen table with the evening papers, circling all the possible jobs she could apply for. 'Don't be so high and mighty, missy,' he scolded, if Bean grimaced at the word 'secretary' or 'receptionist'. 'When you're starting out you can't afford to be so choosy.'

During the day, Mangala Aunty took her around the neighbourhood: 'This is Woolworth's, this is Boots (your mummy loves Boots), this is Waitrose (too expensive), this is W.H. Smith (you might like because of books, no?), this is bingo place for old people, this is local leisure centre (Mr Jain and me get for free because of senior citizen), this is library, this is job centre. This is Sainsbury's – we do shopping here. Anything you want, just put in trolley, OK? Don't feel shy, OK? Everything all right?'

Bean bought a monthly travel card for six zones. She rode in double-decker buses and took long walks in all the different hills of the city: Primrose, Notting, Muswell, Denmark, Parliament, Lavender, Haverstock, Herne, Forest, Tower. She browsed through second-hand bookshops on the Strand, and sat in pubs writing long letters home, sketching the old men around her who had nothing to do but drink beer and watch football all day.

From Ba in Anjar, Bean felt a distance she had never felt before.

Ganga Bazaar is the furthest place in the world from London. If I close my eyes and try to remember your house, try to imagine the warmth there, it's impossible to do. I'm going to come and see you soon, don't worry. I just don't know when. I've started working, so I suppose I should stick with it otherwise I'll be called a one-day-wonder, as usual. But I don't know, Ba. I'm still trying to find my place. I remember you once telling me that there were only two mistakes to make on this journey of life: not going all the way, and not starting. So, here I am, trying to make a start. It's difficult, but it's a beginning.

She missed her bedroom in the house of orange and black gates; her mother and father and Selvi; but most surprisingly, she missed her sister. Bean had never imagined that she and Mayuri could be friends; that time and distance could change a person; that after all, the bonds of blood were thicker than water.

Mayuri had transformed from a tyrannically hard child to a soft-spoken woman, unafraid of admitting her dependencies, of finally saying to Bean, 'Of course, I need you too.' How was that possible? What's more, Mayuri didn't seem to remember any of the cruelties of childhood. 'Did I really do that, Bean? Did I really say that if you wore lipstick your lips would turn black? Did I really say that if you touched the whiskers of a buffalo you'd get thrown to heaven seven times and back? How bizarre! I don't remember any of it.'

More, more, Bean wanted to tell her. You were mean beyond belief. But nothing mattered now that they were grown up and changed and wandering about in their lives, because Mayuri was the only one who had known her from the beginning. And Bean wished she could summon up her sister now, even if it was just for a cup of tea in a nearby café, even if they could sit wordlessly under a midnight-blue sky heaving with stars, multiplied like rabbits, just so she could understand how she had travelled that long distance from there to here.

Do you remember coming here when we were little, May? It's funny how memory works. I remember this house being such a glorious escape, such a comfort. Now it all feels a bit jaded. Everything's shrunk, including aunty and uncle, with all the misfortune they keep going on about.

Mangala Aunty is sweet, but she's been trained well. I have to tell you about the umbrella she lent me as soon as I arrived. My first day of work, and it's pissing down with rain, so Aunty very kindly offers me her brolly. The saddest thing you ever saw – all the spokes going here and there, turned a million times inside out in the rain. And it was so carefully packed up in this Tesco bag, it must have been fifteen years old, at least! Anyway, I went out and bought two new umbrellas that day, and you should have seen her face when I presented one to her – tears in her eyes. Of course, misery-moo was like, 'There's no need to waste money Beena, you should be saving for the future.' A fucking umbrella for godssake!

It's really depressing in a way, having to think about money so much when you've never had to think about it before. And London is such an expensive city, ridiculously so. I wish I could get my own place, but at the moment, I just can't afford it. So I'm going to have to deal with the Jains – all of them. Did I tell you about Deenu, the son? You remember him? Well, anyway, I'm pretty sure he's gay – he's got this love of all things designer, and he overdoes it on the cologne like nothing. Besides, he's forty and still living at home with his parents! Anyway, he's the prince of the house – comes and goes as he pleases in his BMW. Runs a restaurant in Richmond. I hardly see him. Sometimes we collide in the kitchen at breakfast and he says the exact same thing to me each and every time, 'All right, Beena? Getting on OK?'

The daughter, Indrani, from what I gather (because they don't talk too much about her), still hasn't returned from her get-rich stint in Guatemala with the English boyfriend. Mama said that she disappeared with a chunk of Mr Jain's retirement money a while ago – so I guess she's done a runner.

Anyway, they've still got her pictures all over the house – graduation pictures of both kids – at least four in every room, in case you missed the point. Oh, and the mantelpiece, I have to tell you about the mantelpiece in the sitting room. It's got this giant Taj Mahal in the centre, flagged by the Eiffel Tower on one side and the Statue of Liberty on the other. It's TOO tacky.

Every Indian family's living room I've been taken to so far is exactly the same. LOOK, they all seem to be saying, see how far we've come – all the way from our village in the boondocks. But we've been to Paris, we've been to New York, we own a house in London. God! Don't ask how I'm going to survive the next few months because every time I walk into this house I feel like I'm on high alert, like they're watching me all the time to see what I've been using and how much. Only yesterday, I was up in bed early, reading with my lamp on, and who pushes the door and walks in but old sourpuss himself. Guess what he tells me? Beena, I hope that light hasn't been on ALL night. And that's just the tip of the iceberg! They make me watch TV with them every night. There's this quiz show – Who Wants to be a Millionaire – and it's hilarious because whenever any of the contestants decide to risk their money and go for the jackpot, Uncle hides his head behind a cushion and says, Puppy, I can't watch any more! Is the answer correct?

Bean wrote all this to her sister, imagining the delight on Mayuri's face when she saw her letter sitting in the jute bag that hung on the gate of the house she and Cyrus had rented by the beach. A small white house with two-bedrooms and a garden where they grew tomatoes and basil and sometimes threw fancy-dress parties. Bean could almost see her sister shaking with laughter, and then sitting down at her writing desk.

Mayuri's news from home was predictable at first, about the heat, or the difficulties she was having with the children at the Montessori school where she taught. And then slowly, as the distance between them grew wide enough to accommodate the truth, she began to reveal things Bean could never have imagined.

Sometimes, when I'm lying across from Cyrus in bed, it's as if I don't know him at all. I can recognize all the parts of him – the long, gangly legs, the pale arms, the nose he hates so much. It's a picture I know and love, but sometimes, how can I explain it? I'm standing outside this picture. I'm looking at this man I call my husband, and he's a stranger to me. Do you know how terrifying that is? Sometimes, when he has his arms around me, I have to move out from under them and retreat to my own side of the bed. Just so I can breathe. This happens only in flashes, of course. On a daily basis, we move and work like one of his well-oiled cars, knowing exactly how to please and irritate one another. But when it does happen, it's the saddest thing in the world. I used to believe in destiny, but I don't know any more, Bean. Now I only believe in what you create.

Sometimes I think of Mama and Daddy, about those Saturday afternoons they'd lock themselves in the bedroom. I remember us standing outside and hollering for them, and Daddy coming to the door, all dishevelled, saying how we had to run along and play because this was their "alone time". I wonder if they ever had their moments of doubt. They must have, but how amazing that they never once made us feel it. But tell me about you. Have you met any nice men? There must be lots of nice men in London.

Oh, there were men. Men and more men. Everywhere Bean looked there were men. Bean watched them on her way to work, dressed like crows in their dark suits and briefcases, and she wondered whether there was a life to be made with any one of them. With that man reading the paper so devoutly – that fine-looking, upstanding man who might be cheating on his wife with a young girl in the office who totters in on spiky heels with blow-dried hair? Or how about that stranger there – leaning against the pole, devouring his just-picked-up photographs from Snappy Snaps? If it wasn't for the way he clutched the leather satchel under his arm, or the stoutness of his fingers, Bean might have approached him and said, 'Let's get off at the next stop and walk the streets together. Let's build a house and start a life.'

Bean was looking for someone to come rushing in to meet her at the end of the day in a blue long-sleeved shirt and ironed trousers. Someone who would gather her into his arms and take her to a place they could call home. She was waiting for someone to push open the door and enter her life, but it hadn't happened yet. Not yet.

Once a month Bean went to visit her Uncle Huw and Aunty Carole in Brighton, and allowed her cousins Gareth and Ed to parade her around town as the exotic cousin visiting from India. Or she took the train to Nercwys and stayed with her Uncle Owen, who was suffering terrible arthritic pains, but was still spending all day in the garden watching his trees grow.

In Nercwys Aunty Eleri wanted to tell her stories of when her mam was young and daring and had dashed off to London and then dashed off to India. 'Look here, love, that's her before she went away,' Aunty El said, pointing to her favourite photograph of Siân, standing at the gates of Tan-y-Rhos, looking at the fields ahead of her – her hair so long and beautiful that Bean, looking at it, wanted to say, *Mama, Mama, why did you ever cut it?* 'Your mother's something else, I tell you. All the rest of us getting older by the minute, and she just looks the same. Hasn't changed a jot.'

Bean pored over Aunty El's immaculate photo albums, searching for pictures of her sometimes summers. There were so many that when Bean looked through them, she couldn't remember the exact order of what happened when. There were pictures of her first trip when they were all standing like a row of perfect pins at the front door: Babo, Siân, Mayuri, Nain, Aunty El, Taid and baby Bean in Taid's arms. There were old black and white ones of Nain and Taid: Nain with her curls so tight they bobbed up under her hat like springs; Taid looking exactly like Siân in a man's suit with that same long, serious look. There were pictures of Uncle Huw and Owen with their heads full of hair, smiling as if one of them had just told a joke. There were so many pictures of Bean and Mayuri in smocks and frocks, sitting on wombles and bicycles and on their uncle's shoulders, in swimsuits at the Sun Centre in Rhyl, on ponies at the beach in Kinmel Bay, that when Bean looked at them she could never remember ever having been so small, so precious.

At her grandparents' grave, Bean sat trying to work out how part of them were part of her, how part of this village was part of her. Because if she understood *this*, she thought, perhaps she'd understand where she fitted into the rest of it – into this mist and rain, these houses and cars, these people walking their dogs, leading their lives.

And my life? Bean wanted to ask. *Where's my life in all of this? Is this my real life or is it just a prelude to something before I return . . . Return to where? Why do I always feel like I'm visiting wherever I go?* Why? Why? Because the sky's so high. *Is this how you felt when you first came to India, Mama? Is it possible you still feel this way?* One foot in, the other foot out.

24 A Great Sin Can Enter
Through a Small Door

Within a month of her arrival in London, Bean signed up with a temp agency called Working Angels, who were so impressed with her words per minute and Excel skills, they immediately sent her out to financial and media organizations all over the city, where she stuffed envelopes, despatched media packages and updated computer databases; where no one bothered to learn her name because she was only going to be there for a few days or a week, tops; where by the time she worked out where the fancy pens were stocked and who in IT to call if there was a problem, she had to wave a quick adieu and disappear through the revolving doors.

As it grew colder, Bean began to learn the city underground. The elaborate connect-the-dots system, which had at first seemed confusing, now began to appear in her dreams like a giant earthworm, burrowing under the surface – picking people up in one place and spitting them out in another. For a long time she travelled like a slave to those dots, going from point to point without having any idea how it all connected above the ground, finding out only later how sometimes it was easier to just get out and walk: Green Park to Piccadilly Circus for instance, or Holborn to Chancery Lane.

Bean loved the trains and the people who travelled in them. What possibilities there were lurking under each of their lives, what chances escaping into the air! What amazed her most was the sense of decorum that prevailed; nothing like India with all its abundance of chaos and noise. Here, nobody complained if the train halted for five minutes between stations. At most, there were raised eyebrows, a brief glance up from the columns of the newspaper, but otherwise, people seemed oblivious, little islands unto themselves. Once in a while, though, there were slip-ups – some poor fool trying to jam himself into the carriage while the doors were closing, thinking those two minutes between trains were going to change his life. And once, at Baker Street, Bean saw a man try to kill himself by jumping on the tracks – an incident that rattled her so badly, she quashed all her dominant Indian sensibilities, stopped elbowing to be first and began standing far behind the yellow line until the train came to a complete and final stop.

By the end of September, Bean was assigned to a small publishing firm in Islington called Stonewell's, who specialized in bed & breakfast guides to the British Isles. Bean's job was to phone each of the B&B owners to find out if they still held the same accreditation, if they had any new information they wanted to add and how many, if any, of their clients in the past year had mentioned Stonewell's as their major source of information. It was a boring job, but steady.

Al Stonewell, proprietor of Stonewell's, was an amiable, unkempt sort of man who stormed in late every day with his pug Lizzie and disappeared under the mountain at his desk, only to emerge in the afternoon to make tea for all his employees – an act he'd later bring up casually in the pub to prove he was a man of egalitarian principles.

There were only two other employees at Stonewell's: Tom McDonald and Allegra Edwards. Senior editor Tom was a young, Oxford-educated man, always dressed in collars and V-necked sweaters. If you could get him to talk about classical music or tennis, his face lost its usual constipated look as he burst into a torrent of unexpected enthusiasm, but his modus operandi was to sit quietly in the corner, tap tapping away on the computer in a dispassionate and dull manner.

Allegra was a web designer by profession, but a portrait painter (of fluctuating talent, it has to be said) by inclination. She was one of those vigorous, voluptuous women that Bean always thought, if she were a man, she'd be attracted to. She was tall and striking in a Meryl Streep kind of way, besides which, she took nothing too seriously, and was so heavily endowed with that excellent English quality of self-deprecation, that Bean spent many an afternoon at her desk with her legs clamped, recalling those long-ago days in Sylvan Lodge when Mayuri and she, having worked themselves into a frenzy of laughter, would have to race and do half-bum half-bum on the potty upstairs.

After a month at Stonewell's, Al sat down with Bean and told her that Working Angels was charging him £10 an hour to hire her but paying Bean only £8, so how about they eliminate the temp agency and he hire her for £9?

Bean acquired a routine. Angel Station every morning. Past the hairdresser, Abel, who asked her to come away with him to Paris every weekend. Past Sergei, who flirted madly while making her tuna and sweet corn baguette for lunch. Past the glass doors of the two-man architect's firm that Bean could see straight into if she leaned towards the left-hand side of her desk.

Bean spent many hours leaning on the left-hand-side of her desk, spying on the raven-haired Spanish architect with the muddy green eyes. She knew how many cups of coffee he drank, how he cleaned his fingernails while talking on the telephone, the way his compact body eased in and out of his golden Vauxhall. She knew at the end of the day, if she walked slowly and pointedly enough, maintaining eye contact through the glass, he would see her and give her a little smile.

Allegra and Bean made wagers about the Spanish architect: could they get him to wave? Did he have a woman? Did he even like women? What was the width of those sturdy calves beneath his jeans? They began an ever-evolving list of possible names for him on the weekly ideas pad: Raphael, Francis, Enrique, Fernando, Juan, Gabriel, Jorges.

Bean began to feel that this had always been her life. She put weekly cheques into her first-ever bank account. She had drinks with everyone after work at The Fitzroy Tavern, always hoping that the Spanish architect would walk in. Always missing him, because she had to rush home to Lewisham, where Mr Jain would be standing at the front door, tapping his foot impatiently because Bean was a little past the 9 PEE EM curfew, saying, 'This is England, missy. ENGLAND.'

Bean would do this and do this for three months until the incident with Deenu happened. Then, Bean would pack her bags and flee to the uber-posh Euro-Trash area of South Kensington to live with Allegra, who offered her the spare room in exchange for a monthly contribution of £400, plus one nude sitting a week – a deal that Bean, given her circumstances, couldn't possibly refuse. Bean would change from a girl to a grown-up, throw her incy-wincy fears up in the air – and fall in love like never before. Russian rocket scientist, Brazilian dancer, Greek musician, English actor, Nigerian investment banker, Canadian rock-climber and finally, Spanish architect. Bean, with her own set of keys for the first time in her life – ka-chink ka-chink ka-chink – coming and going as she pleased.

The incident with Deenu happened in November 1996. The Stonewell's crew had started early at the pub because Tom was going back to Oxford to take up a job with the NHS, and Bean was going to train up to take his place. There were celebrations all around.

'Fuck the old man,' Allegra said, when Bean got up to leave at eight. 'Fuck him, fuck him. Just go home when you damn well please. What's he going to do anyway? Tom,' she bellowed, 'Get Senior Editor Bean here another Chardonnay.'

Bean, carried away with the idea of possible revolt, downed her third glass of wine, and her fourth, thinking it would be OK, just this once, owing to her promotion and all.

For the first time, Bean stayed out till last call, till they were rolling out of the pub towards the tube station. The Spanish architect hadn't shown up, but his English partner, George, the not so exciting half of the two-man team, had.

'I just knew he wouldn't show, darling,' Allegra slurred, 'This just isn't his thing – he's too old for this, probably has a nice Spanish girl to go home to.'

Bean saw how the city changed at night; how people weren't decorous at all; how with a little bit of alcohol in them, English people were suddenly emboldened and set free.

By the time she ran up the length of Sunnydale Road it must have been after midnight, because when Mr Jain opened the door, letting her freeze out in the cold for a bit, he looked down at his watch and pronounced, 'Three hours ten minutes late,' his face all pinched up like a garden tool – corroded and cruel.

Bean unzipped her boots in the dark corridor, leaving her socks on to keep her warm. She hung her coat in the hall closet and put one light on in the kitchen, where her plate lay like a solitary moon on the table. She ate the food cold, without joy; rinsed out the dishes, soaped them down and stacked them on the draining board. She walked upstairs, feeling her way in darkness to the bathroom, where she washed her face with cold water, brushed her teeth and wiped down the sink. Then she went to the lavvy, pulled the flush shortly and waited for the gurgling to subside before opening the door. Again, in darkness, she padded back to her room, put on her pyjamas, jumper and night socks, and climbed into bed. Bean slept. She slept like she always had, with difficulty and some dread.

Later, there were sounds of flushes and taps. This house was so cold, so unsecretive. Bean, shivering in bed, could hear Mr and Mrs Jain next door – their symphony of snores and windbreakers. Later, much later, the door opened, scrape scrape scraping against the carpet. *Ah*, thought Bean. *Someone's come to fix the heating. Finally.* But this man hadn't come to fix the radiator. No. He got into bed and started smoothing down Bean's hair. Bean couldn't understand it. Why was Deenu cradling her as though she were his child?

Did I ask for you? Did I call out your name for you to be here?

Bean was awake now, looking at him with charcoal eyes. She could smell the aftershave on him, the toothpaste and alcohol.

'All right?' he asked.

'Yes. Yes.' Bean said, automatically.

He touched her cheek, and then gently, again, 'Are you all right?'

Nothing. Bean couldn't speak.

'You're wonderful, you know? So wonderful.'

Nothing.

Deenu turned his body towards Bean; she could feel him harden against her leg. Bean wanted to choke, scream, something – but there was only a bird caught in her throat, saying, *no no no*. Deenu must have heard the bird, too, because he looked at her confusedly and said, 'Do you want me to leave?'

'Yes,' Bean said. It was all she could say.

'Sorry,' he muttered. 'Sorry.'

Deenu rose from the bed, turning so the bald plate of his head shone through his thinning hair in the moonlight. He scraped her door open and shut, scraped the door to his room open and shut. Bean heard him shuffle over to his bed on designer socks. Then there was only noiselessness.

'I'm telling you, it came out of nowhere!'

Bean was standing in the telephone booth by the Lewisham Leisure Centre, trying to tell Siân about the incident with Deenu.

She was trying to explain to her mother that she had done nothing to encourage such behaviour from Deenu. NOTHING. From the beginning, their relationship had been perfunctory: *All right? And how are things going? And do you need help with your CV?* Nothing more than that. If anything, Deenu had seemed apologetic for his parents: for his mother's careful storing of plastic bags and counting of vegetables in the fridge, for his father's fussing about in the garden like an old clockwork toy in his frayed sweaters and 1970s trousers.

Deenu of the no-curfew – who existed outside the framework of his father's rules; who paid the mortgage and provided two off-season annual tickets to Baroda; who, compared to the runaway daughter, shone.

'Hush, hush,' Siân said. 'Sweetie, listen, we have some really bad news to give you.'

But Bean wasn't listening to her mother. She wanted Babo. She wanted to ask, *What are you going to do about this, Daddy? Tell me, what are you going to do?*

'Baby, listen to me,' Siân said, 'Please, listen. Chotu Kaka is very ill. He started having trouble swallowing a few months ago, and the doctors, they did all these tests on him, and, well, it's really serious, Bean. Cancer of the oesophagus. He's on his second round of chemo, but the cancer has already spread.'

'Bean?

'Bean?'

There was that bird again, stuck in Bean's throat. 'Why did you wait so long to tell me?' she whispered.

255

'We wanted to, we really did, but it was all so sudden, and you were trying to settle in. It's just been a nightmare, the whole thing. Daddy's practically living in the hospital. The prognosis isn't good, love. Six months. The doctor said six months, if he's lucky.'

'I want to speak to Daddy. Can I please just speak to Daddy?'

Poor Babo, trying to deal with his dying brother, trying to deal with the news that his daughter had been violated by his oldest friend's son. What could he say? *Maybe Deenu really was sleepwalking like he said. Maybe it really was a terrible misunderstanding. Couldn't Bean work it out? Couldn't she?*

What could he offer? *Come home? Come back? Go and stay with your Uncle Huw? Go and stay with your Uncle Owen?*

No more uncles. Bean was adamant.

Well, what are you going to do then, Bean? Tell me what you want to do.

Bean was going to pack her bags and get on the next flight to Madras.

25 Where There are Graves
There are Resurrections

In the six months it took Chotu to die, the only person he wanted close was Babo. 'Bhai,' he'd say, 'Don't leave me. When are you coming back? Why don't you stay?'

Babo didn't know whether he was coming or going, but he was moving all the time: from home to hospital to Sylvan Lodge. His days were measured out between tea breaks and radiation sessions. He suffered a brief but intense lapse into smoking. It was his only respite from the claustrophobia of the hospital and its waiting rooms.

Every morning at the Apollo Cancer Hospital the well-wishers arrived. Babo began to recognize them over the days – their penitent faces, their paltry comforts of pillows and magazines. The well-wishers went first to the temple on the ground floor to beg a miracle of God, then to the pharmaceutical counter to buy the promise of a miracle and then to talk to the doctors, who reminded them this was final-stage cancer they were talking about – better not expect miracles, better prepare for the inevitable.

How practical the avenues of death were, Babo thought, sucking on his Gold Flakes. After all, no matter how bad it got, someone had to think about settling the final papers, paying the hospital bills, filing the obituary with the newspaper, organizing the death certificate. Someone had to do all that and still manage, despite all death's dehumanizing, to grieve.

Babo watched them all – those who were alive and those on their way to dying – people who used to be lovers once, who at some point in their lives must have thought they were invincible. At night, when he lay beside his sick brother in a hospital bed, Babo thought about ruined bodies, a mad unleashing of them – dhishoom dhishoom.

'What do you think of Dr Rangaraj?' Chotu wanted to know. 'Do you think we should go with his diagnosis, or should we try something different?'

Chotu was all about trying. Every evening, after all the daily reports and test results were in, he held the sheaf of papers in his hands, stroking them as though they were maps waiting to be deciphered. He spread them out on the bed in front of him, the coloured graphs and X-rays, and surveyed them. As if life could be as simple as that. As if all you had to do was lay all your cards down and choose: which way should I send this?

In those days there was no talk of Rinky Damani, no talk of the past. 'When I get out of here, bhai, I'm going to travel. I'm going to see the world. I should have done it a long time ago.'

'Oh, there'll be plenty of time for that, heavyweight,' Babo said cheerily, 'Plenty of time.'

When Dolly and Meenal came to relieve him in the afternoons, Babo went home to shower and change, to lie down with Siân on their king-size Kashmiri bed and sha-bing sha-bang. After all the lovemaking, Babo wanted to talk about his childhood. He wanted to name the events, single them out and name them, because he thought if he didn't, they might disappear along with Chotu.

So Siân listened to how Babo got punished for the time he carried two-year-old Chotu on his shoulders all the way to Marina Beach just so they could see the fishermen going out in their catamarans. How they used to play cricket in the gullies around Sylvan Lodge, and sometimes, if there were enough of them, they went to the ground in Barnabas Road where they could have proper boundaries and stumps. *Before going to England*, Babo sighed, because whether it was true or not, *this* event had been identified as the turning point for his entire family. *Before going to England*, Babo used to take Chotu to play against the Akash Ganga Colony boys and they'd thrash them hollow, even though Chotu was only tiny then; broomstick-legged tiny.

'And you remember when we took him to Bombay, Charlie? When we saw Lance Gibbs in the lobby of the Taj, and Chotu went up to him for his autograph. You remember what we saw afterwards? That man with the rogallo glider jumping off the Express Towers? You know what I told Chotu when we saw that? I said, "It makes you want to believe in something, doesn't it? A man flying in the sky like that." And do you know what Chotu said? He said, "Of course, bhai, what's there not to believe in?" '

But Babo didn't know any more. He wondered what there was to believe in now that they were losing people in speedy succession: Bryn, Trishala, Nerys, Darayus, and now Chotu. The sadness pulled around his eyes and cheeks, dragged at the corners of his mouth, stole years and years from him, just like that.

It was the same look Prem Kumar harboured behind his bottle-thick glasses, sitting in the front room all day, welded into his dilapidated brown armchair. Now that work had been suspended at Sanbo Enterprises, there was nothing for Prem Kumar to do but hold court in Sylvan Lodge with the despondent relatives who passed in and out like a procession of deadbeats. He refused to go to the hospital. 'I'll wait till my son comes home,' he insisted, even when Babo told him there was a chance Chotu might never be well enough to come home. But hadn't he done all this before with Trishala? Hadn't he wandered around the corridors of hospitals only to listen to the lies of doctors? Did he have to go through all this again with his own son?

No. Even if Trishala hovered around his insomnia-plagued nights, bristling like a typhoon, admonishing him for his fears; even if his mother, all the way in Anjar, kept phoning to tell him he would never die in peace, never reach siddhashila – that place where all the pure jivas went to experience their true nature – if he didn't go and spend at least one night by his son's bedside, he still couldn't do it.

In the mornings, after Sonam, his nurse, brought him his neem stick to chew on, he imagined going to the hospital and surprising Babo, imagined telling him, 'Son, go home, eat, shave, rest – get that horrible smell off you.' But then he thought how it would be to see Chotu, propped up in bed against a hard-backed pillow, looking like all the air had been sucked out of him, and he couldn't do it.

Babo told him that the kidneys were threatening to give up, that Chotu had refused a bedpan. Would he be able to help his son – a grown man, to the toilet? Prem Kumar's knees shook violently at the thought. What would he say to Chotu, anyway? Chotu, who was more stubborn, more self-righteous than Babo, more like Prem Kumar than either of them cared to admit? How were they going to continue after all of this was finished? This long nightmare that started with Trishala's breasts and now lived in the corroded walls of Chotu's oesophagus.

No. It was easier to sit cross-legged in the armchair in his frayed vest and dhoti with his betel-nut box by his side. Babo could continue to bring him reports – *every blessed word* – the doctors uttered. And in the evenings, when the conversation turned increasingly maudlin, and Dolly and Meenal cried so much, killing off their brother before he was ready to go, Prem Kumar could gruffly steer everything back to his own ill health and failings – his urinary infection and the insomnia which was making his daily life so very painful.

In November, Ba came to stay. The whole family needed to be together now, more than ever. It was monsoon season in Madras, and the roads were damp and porous from all the rains. They seemed to swallow ideas as if they were nothing.

Dolly and Meenal, who had left behind their diamond merchant and shipbroker husbands, shared their old bedroom downstairs in Sylvan Lodge. Ba was given the room next to Prem Kumar's. Siân and Babo shut up the house of black and orange gates and moved into Chotu's half-renovated room upstairs; the room where they had spent their two-year trial period in Madras.

Siân fell into long-forgotten patterns: knowing when to be silent and when to speak. She was a young bride again, wearing saris, shelling peas on the kitchen floor, looking for solitary places of comfort in the house because the doors could never be closed. Someone was always ready to storm through them to say, 'Come, bhabi, let's play cards, let's *do* something.' Or 'Bhabi, come and help Meenal and me sort out Mummy's old jewellery boxes – there's such a lot of junk.'

Babo, when he came to her, no longer smelled of Gold Flakes or mimosa, but of formaldehyde – a clean smell of death.

Sometimes, in the middle of the day, Siân would panic because she couldn't remember what Chotu had looked like when she first arrived in India. Nothing of what he was now reminded her of the shy, knobbly twelve-year-old he used to be. Now he was a stranger under sheets: thin lines for legs, and a face with no rim zim in it.

Ba found Siân huddled in secret corners. 'It's a terrible thing,' she'd say. 'Terrible and unnecessary – all this madness with hospitals. Tell Babo to bring him back home. Chotu should die at home.'

For weeks, Siân had been telling Babo to call Bean. *She deserves to know. Now. Before it's too late*. But Babo hadn't called. Saying it aloud meant squashing the only hope that perhaps everything would be OK.

Normality crashed into their days. There were still clothes that needed washing, food that needed cooking. Sometimes it began to feel like they were on one of their long, stifling family holidays – maybe Dolly and Meenal should call one of the Cuts and Curls girls to come and give them pedicures, maybe they could go sari shopping – because there was still boredom to deal with, endless hours of waiting. Only Chotu was missing, gone off on a trip somewhere, swimming with Bean, or on his 'in lieu of' European holiday. He'd be back soon, they were sure of it.

And then the guilt would strike. One of the sisters usually, sitting at the dining table after lunch, would crack open and let lose a store of remembrances, until Ba got up, pushing her plate away, and said, 'This isn't the way. This can't be the way.'

In the evenings, Prem Kumar's old card-playing buddies came to sit in the saggy brown sofas and slurp tea from saucers, talking of business and politics, never of death. Mayuri came later, after teaching at the Abacus Montessori School, to rescue Siân. Mother and daughter sat on Chotu's bed, doing cross-stitch patterns – creations that wouldn't be framed and hung on the walls, but folded away uselessly in some bottom drawer. It helped pass the time, and it helped not having to speak. Cyrus came for Mayuri after work at the garage, his long, sweet face and fingers smeared with engine oil. 'Do you need anything, Aunty? Why doesn't Mayuri stay with you? Really, it's all right. Tell us, what can we do?'

But Siân wouldn't allow it. This wasn't the time for it in their life. Hadn't they already had to deal with Darayus dying? Darayus, who had to be bathed and wrapped in white and packed in a cool box direct to Bombay so he could be taken to the Towers of Silence. 'You go on home, love, both of you, get back home.'

Siân thought about her mother and father. They were in the cemetery in Nercwys, lying under the earth together, united in death: a stack of bones with wild daisies sinking roots into them. *Is this how a thing must end?* she thought. And Babo, and herself? How would they be united if she was buried and he was burned?

'I want to be cremated,' Siân told Babo, as the time drew nearer. Because she knew there was nothing that survived this world. Didn't they know this already? Hadn't their two daughters vanished – whoosh whooshed down the great banister of Sylvan Lodge, pushed open the orange and black gates and disappeared?

Babo told Siân, like he used to in her blue-walled bedroom in Finchley Road, how he didn't believe in ideas of redemption or guilt. He remembered telling Trishala once, in a fit of adolescent anger, that the idea of reincarnation was the biggest escape of all. And he still believed it: after we died, there could be nothing. *A man is born and dies alone*. But he was carrying around a new hope these days: that in the ultimate dissolution on the funeral pyre, *something* would be left. Babo, after years of unbelieving, began to believe in the idea of the phoenix, in resurrection and ashes.

Siân found him under the stairs of Sylvan Lodge rearranging Chotu's shoes, holding each of them close to his chest, marvelling at their size. 'How did he get so much bigger than me?' Babo asked. 'And when? How did he grow to wear such big shoes and then shrink so much?'

When Chotu died they laid him out on the dining-room floor with turmeric sprinkled around to keep the ants away. The priest prepared Chotu's body for death; created a passage for all the impure elements to pass through, so his soul could flee from the crown of his head. They had a funeral in the rain that lasted for hours, until fire won over water and the body burned to ash.

Bean was there to watch it all. She saw Prem Kumar totter over to Chotu on the dining-room floor to place the final garland of flowers on his wasted body. She saw Ba pouring honey over Chotu's feet. When the men carried Chotu away, Bean slumped against the pista-green walls of Sylvan Lodge along with Mayuri, Siân, her aunts and the unibrows. After the funeral, she watched as Babo waded out to sea, knee-high in water, scattering the remains of his brother – the garlands, incense, ash, the burned-down cancers, burned-down rotten kidneys, burned-down stubbornness. She saw her father with his head in his hands looking up and down the dirtied shoreline of a city he had once loved, knowing it to be lost to him, just as his brother was now lost; weeping because it had to be on a day of rain.

Bean observed her aunts Meenal and Dolly, women who used to be girls once, slender as any beanstalk, grown sideways, expanded like planets with multiple rings. The aunts told Mayuri and her to look upwards. They gave them prayer beads and told them to pray for Chotu's soul because if Chotu's soul was still caught in the house, if it was still unhappy, then all kinds of terrible things could happen. Her aunts said that it was only after a man died that his soul could think about the acts of his life that had caused him pain or pleasure; only afterwards could he think about escaping the multiplicity of sorrows. Because a man must leave all that behind if he wants to move towards purity, and they must help him along, counting prayers on their fingers, clickety-click clickety-click, so his soul could know which way to turn, so his journey could be safe.

Bean and Mayuri sat on the red-brick terrace with prayer beads in their hands. Now that they were within touching distance of each other, they couldn't really speak. Not of the letters, not of the fears. They couldn't even speak of Chotu, whom they had watched in the final days, disappearing and disappearing until there was nothing left.

Back in the house of orange and black gates, Babo held his wife in all her hard and soft places. His daughters slept in the room next door. For a while, Babo had all his girls under the same roof again. In the mornings, after breakfast, Babo went to stand at the edge of the newly installed fish pond in the garden. There he lovingly drizzled nourishment down on its green surface, waiting for the little flashes of gold to come shluck shlucking from the reeds. 'They're waiting for me,' he said happily, to Mayuri and Bean, counting their sparkling bodies to make sure the cats from the Punjab Women's Association hadn't been up to any mischief.

Babo found solace in rituals. At 11 a.m. he left for Sanbo Enterprises with his tiffin carrier and battered briefcase, *The Hits of John Denver* on automatic replay in his car stereo. After lunch, he called his wife, as he had done everyday of their married life, and said, 'Charlie?' expectantly, waiting for her to fill the silence with something, anything, that could take him from now till when he was home again. At nights Babo held his wife, and wondered how they'd shared their blood after all, secured their own immortality. Babo, who knew that making children was like making your own religion; who knew that darkness was an indispensable part of beauty.

And inevitably, when Mayuri moved back to her house on the beach, and Bean said, 'Daddy, it's time to go back to London now. Do you want me to stay? Just tell me, because if you do, I will,' Babo wished she hadn't asked, because it meant he couldn't say yes. *Yes, stay with us, don't ever leave*. Because losing this brother had been something like losing his own life, and the tears he wept into his wife's marble body at nights were selfish tears of his own losing, separate from the temporary space Chotu had created.

Babo wanted his daughters to understand that the world was changing – lickety-split, snippety-snip – without his consent. All the roads had shrunk in size, suddenly merging into a single stony path leading surely and abruptly over the hills. He wanted to tell his girls that this is how he felt – *over the hill* and quite far away from where he really wanted to be, which was travelling somewhere in the world with Siân. Lying under a night sky bludgeoned with stars, with nothing to tie them to the earth except their own bodies. Nothing to drag them downwards. Nothing but the single thread of love between them, which had always been enough, more than enough.

26 If Something Ain't Right It's Wrong

Bean had been having dreams again. She was walking through
the rooms of the house of orange and black gates with Mayuri,
lying on the mosaic floors: head to foot, foot to head, learning
to walk in darkness.

When Bean woke from this darkness in London there was
still the same *shame shame puppy shame* between her legs; her
sheets were still wet, but they were wet from other things.
Every morning Bean clambered out to wash herself because
love in this city was dangerous. There were men everywhere
she looked. Men who needed and demanded, but who never
stayed long enough for Bean to think, this is *it*, this is the
Ekam Ba was talking about. After everything, when one of
them got up to walk through the door, there was always a sigh
of relief; it was never anything unbearable.

'Give it a chance,' Allegra was always saying, and she was
right, because Bean blew through them like the wind; all her
love affairs were so brief and second-rate, they may as well
have never happened at all.

The Brazilian dancer was the oldest: forty-three. He had
the most beautiful body Bean had ever seen – carved from
gold, lithe, hairless. It was like a woman's body, except instead
of fully-fledged breasts he had two pale pink rosettes, ideal for
suckling. When they made love the Brazilian dancer wanted
Bean to suck hard on those rosettes, 'Bite me, baby,' he'd say,
because it helped him come. At his age it took longer. Not like

the Nigerian investment banker or the Greek musician, who were young and greedy and always ready to go. Not like the Russian rocket scientist, who liked to have sex once before dinner and twice afterwards when they were nice and giddily drunk.

The Brazilian dancer didn't drink. He loved his body too much. He was always following some kind of stringent diet, compartmentalizing his food, weighing it out according to textures and colours.

'Don't you miss it?' Bean asked.

'Oh no,' he said. 'There was a time when I drank every day, smoked packs of cigarettes, and had endless shots of espresso. I've had my share of being nervous and high. Things are much clearer now. My body not only dances, it sings. But,' he conceded, 'It does help for flirting. It's much easier to flirt with alcohol.'

The English actor knew all about flirting. He loved the bodies of women. He was always touching Bean in public, tracing the inner part of her thighs or the backs of her knees in taxis, gently guiding her along with one hand placed firmly on the curve above her bum. 'This part is my favourite,' he'd say, in bed, lifting Bean's hair away and scraping the back of her neck with his perfectly-square, stubbly jaw. The backs of things, curvatures. After three months of solid courting, after fucking Bean vigorously and efficiently in every room of his Notting Hill mansion, he said, 'Well, this has been so nice, hasn't it? I'm going to miss you when I'm away.' And then he disappeared to shoot a film, phoning once a week, then once a month, then dwindling down to nothing, until the memory of him faded into a pale litmus blue like the rest of them.

Only the Canadian rock-climber refused to leave in a hurry. He really fell for Bean. The first time they had sex in his flatmate's basement bedroom, when he saw little drops of sweat form between her breasts, he told her she was the woman he'd been waiting for all his life. The rock-climber wasn't the kind of man Bean usually went for. His body was stringy and powerful, marked with lusty patches of dark hair.

'I didn't think hairy was my type,' Bean told Allegra. But what difference did 'type' make when it came to chemistry?

The rock-climber believed in making out like an avalanche: strong, hard and all of a sudden. Things between them might have lasted longer if it hadn't been for the fact that he held Bean at nights in the same way – enveloping her so tightly, she could barely breathe. 'I'm going back home to India,' she finally lied. 'My parents have found me someone to marry. I'm sorry.'

And then, finally, *it* happened. After months and months of walking past the glass-windowed office, willing the raven-haired Spanish architect to make eye contact with her, they were introduced at a party in Kensington on a rooftop with flamingos. Bean was wearing a turquoise dress that showed off the bones in her shoulders and the bronze in her skin, and he was in dark blue jeans, a long sleeved shirt and a corduroy blazer. Bean was so thrilled to learn his name. Javier. HA-VEE-YAY. Nothing Allegra or she had guessed at.

Javier and Bean sat side by side without eating. Wry, compact Javier, who whispered in Bean's ear after seven vodka and tonics. 'I want to make love to you. Where can we go so I can make love to you?'

Javier, who held her, who rubbed and touched, but wouldn't kiss, wouldn't fuck, not yet. 'What soft skin you have. Almost too soft, as though you aren't really here. And what a nice bum!' Tops off. Chest against chest. Skin on skin. 'I want to fuck you, and I don't.' Javier and Bean, saying each other's names to each other again and again in Bean's bed that very first night. 'You're unbelievable, do you know? Where did you come from, to land in my life like this?' Bean, leaning on her elbows, glowing.

Their first weekend away in Barcelona, Javier's home town, they barely left the hotel room. Bean waited for him, perched on the edge of the bed with her skirt up to her thighs. *Don't you know what that does to me?* Javier, touching her, putting his hand in the space between her legs, moving her in a way she'd never been moved before.

When Bean and Javier made love they kept their eyes wide open. Javier on top of Bean, the weight of his sturdy body falling like a wave upon her. Bean straddling him on the edge of the couch, rocking her hip bones into his, her small breasts dancing up and down like fruit. Afterwards, they lay spent, their thighs interlinked, staying in the moment for as long as they could. They ordered up expensive bottles of wine and plates of calamari, took long baths together, soaped each other's backs and downtheres as though they'd been lovers for centuries. They sat on the balcony in fluffy white robes watching the sunset, discussing how and when they were going to take the next step.

'Can't we go and see Gaudi's skulls and bones building? Won't you show it to me? Or Miró's museum. I can't leave without seeing anything.'

'There's so much time for that, mi alma. There's the rest of our lives.'

Mi alma. *My soul.*

When it was time to fly back to London, Javier cried. He laid his head down in Bean's lap and cried like a baby. There was so much in his heart, so much he wanted to change. 'I love you,' he said, 'It's simple. I can't imagine not having you in my life.'

'So don't,' Bean whispered. 'It *is* simple. You have me. I'm here.'

Sometimes the desire for him was so strong, Bean had to stop looking through the glass windows from her office desk. It was a desire that stopped her in her tracks, made her sit down in a chair, throbbed between her legs. It took the breath from her. Bean couldn't understand it. It was nothing to do with his body because she had seen bodies more beautiful than his. It wasn't his intellect or sense of humour or any one specific thing. It was the way he allowed her to drown in him, demanded that she stand at the centre of his life, and she in his. It was the constant text messaging and phone calls, the *I can't get through the day without you*. The incredible need.

Javier put rings on her fingers and laid himself bare. 'I want to tell you everything about my life. I wish I had met you when I was younger. I never expected this in my lifetime, this kind of love.' He was ten years older than Bean. 'When I'm not with you my blood feels like it's flowing the other way.'

Javier wanted to know all about her old loves, so Bean summoned them up. Michael Mendoza led them with his painted jeans and Metallica rings. The lovers were holding out pieces they'd claimed and carried, pieces that had prevented others from walking through: a pierced navel, a lower lip, a hip bone, a tear-shaped birthmark, a night spent weeping in the bay window of a room. Bean was collecting all those missing pieces because she had to be whole if she was going to give. And she wanted to give to this one. She wanted to reassemble herself to be as she was at sixteen: so pure and un-inundated that this man would want to walk with her for ever.

'One day we'll go to Madras,' Javier said, rolling his 'r' like a bird's trill. 'Do you think your family will like me? Who do you look like, your mother or your father?'

Bean opened her albums and showed him pictures of Babo and Siân when they were young, driving around India in their Flying Fiat. She told him the story of their love affair, which began in London nearly thirty years ago. How they found each other in a canteen, and how they'd been chasing each other ever since. She showed him pictures of Ba in Anjar, and Chotu. 'Isn't it scary, how one minute we're there, the next minute gone? And this is Mayuri, don't we look like sisters?'

'Was it a magical time for you, your childhood?' Javier asked. 'It must have been.'

'I'd like my children to be born in India,' Bean said, looking seriously at him. 'To grow up there.' Bean had never thought of having children before, never mind where they were going to be born and raised. But Javier had already imagined them. A boy and a girl with olive-brown skin and shiny white teeth.

From the beginning Bean kept Mayuri updated. *I can't explain it. I've never felt anything like this before. It's chemical, immediate. And, May, I willed it, months before we actually met, I willed this to happen. He's everything I could want in a man. Strong and kind and gentle. And he loves me. He loves me so much. He knows me. Even though we come from two completely different cultures, we are both home here in London. All of a sudden, nothing seems strange or difficult any more. He wants to marry me. He said this right at the beginning, the first weekend we went away together. He went out and bought me a diamond ring, and said, I wish I could marry you.*

It isn't going to happen any time soon, though. He says there's still so much he needs to work out. But I'm so happy, I'm willing to wait as long as I need for this to happen. When a love like this comes into your life, you have to believe in destiny after all.

What Bean doesn't tell Mayuri is what she hardly tells herself: she cannot marry Javier. Not yet. Not while his petite blonde wife in loafers and the three children with matching muddy green eyes are still in the picture.

The nights Javier can't get away Bean imagines him tucking his children in bed, making love to his wife. She imagines him occupying all those things that belong to him, solidly, *his* house, *his* children, *his* wife. All the things he had to call his own. And what did Bean have? Bean had Allegra, who said, 'Be careful, Bean, it's a delicate situation. Take it slow.'

But it was too late for slowness. Because Javier was close, so close. This was Ekam. Bean was sure of it.

27 All Men Shall be Sailors then Until the Sea Shall Free Them

In the summer of 2000, two years into their love affair, Bean and Javier spent a weekend in the Lake District to decide on things once and for all. Like most of their weekends away, it was fraught with emotion: intense sessions of lovemaking alternated with crying. Javier told Bean it was tearing into him now, the guilt. Sharp as knives, twisting in his stomach. 'I don't know what to do about it,' he said. 'Sometimes I wish she'd just accuse me, then I could admit to it.'

'Why don't you just tell her?'

'I can't do that. I'm the first love of her life. The only man she's ever known. We have three beautiful children together. And her father is dying. How can I do this to her now?'

Javier and Bean walked around Lake Windermere, holding hands in the rain. 'I miss home,' Bean said, taking in the landscape, which reminded her somehow of Anjar. The terraced green hills, the long blue horizon.

'You know, I'm so fed up of all this. It isn't simple at all. I want to be able to share my life with you, entirely. I can't live like this any more – stopping and starting. My whole life on pause. I keep waiting for something to change, but it never does.'

They made their way back to the city separately. Bean took the train, and Javier the motorway. That evening, there was no customary text message from Javier, no phone call to make sure she had reached home safe. Nothing. *Let's see how long it lasts*, Bean thought, going to sleep, fully confident that there would be a text from him in the middle of the night, or first thing the next morning, saying, *Mi Alma, I can't live without you, you know this. Let's work it out*.

But in the morning there was still nothing. At work, when Bean looked through the glass, she saw only George, manning the phones, pacing up and down like a caged animal. All day Bean waited for something, a sign, a peep. 'Something's happened,' she told Allegra. 'I can feel it. It's his wife. She knows.'

Bean imagined all sorts of things. Javier coming home and realizing the futility of his double life; his wife discovering one of Bean's many love letters and confronting him; Javier breaking down in a moment of weakness, confessing everything. In every scenario that Bean invented, Javier eventually came back to her, because they had already decided it, hadn't they? A love like theirs wasn't easy to come by. No matter how difficult it got, they were going to do this.

But that night, when there was still no word from him, Bean began to worry. For the entire duration of their relationship, it was the first time that twenty-four hours had passed without any kind of contact. It was surreal, as if she had just dreamed up the last two years of her life with a man who had suddenly vanished. In bed, unable to sleep or cry, Bean dialled his mobile number. His wife picked up. 'Hello,' she said. 'Hello, who is this?'

The next morning, still nothing from Javier. Bean stared at the glass, willing Javier to suddenly materialize. Every time the phone rang Bean pounced on it, expecting it to be him with some kind of explanation. 'I don't understand,' she said to Allegra. 'Why hasn't he just called to say what's going on?'

Bean moved through the day feeling like a robot. Tears threatening to fall any minute to spoil the illusion of calm. She walked home, talking to herself the whole time. *Like a crazy woman*, she thought. *I've become one of those crazy women.* Finally, at midnight, when she had resigned herself to sleep, her mobile rang, vibrating heavily on the side table. 'Where are you?' she cried, 'What's happened?' Breath returned to her body. To hear his voice meant everything was going to be OK. Things would return to being as they were.

'There was an accident,' Javier said, sounding different; muffled and far away. 'It's OK, I'm all right. Nothing happened to me. A miracle really.'

Javier, driving home from the Lakes, had found himself on the side of the M6, sideswiped by an Asda delivery truck, his golden Vauxhall smashed like a Pringle's potato crisp, his body intact and untouched.

'I didn't see my life flashing before me,' he told Bean. 'Nothing like that. I only thought if I died, my wife has no other husband, my children have no other father.'

'What are you telling me?'

'I told Renatta everything when I got home. I showed her your pictures and letters. I told her how much I loved you. She threw me out of the house and screamed, and oh my God, the children. Rosie, she's old enough to understand these things. She said, "Daddy I don't want you to move into another house." It was awful. It's been two days of torture. I begged Renatta to listen, to understand. And we talked. We talked like we haven't talked in fifteen years.

'Mi alma?

'She wants to give me another chance. I have to give my family another chance. Have I let you down? Tell me, have I let you down?'

Bean pictured Javier crying and pleading, saying he didn't know what had come over him. It was something to do with the middle of his life, something to do with the way Bean appeared before him on a roof with flamingos. It was such an easy thing to fall into. There had been so much beauty. He was terrified by having it, and not having it. Javier, weeping all the sadness out. Bean knew how his head bent when he wept, how the sadness curved out of him and settled in your fingers. Because Javier knew how to let go of things. Bean didn't.

'You have to do what you think is right,' Bean said. Of course, it was betrayal, but Bean wasn't going to say it. She wasn't going to say, *This is what happens when you give yourself away, when you had no business giving. Do you know how I feel right now? Like I've been abandoned, left to stand by myself in the darkest corner of the room.*

'She knows I'm talking to you now. I have to tell her everything, otherwise it will never work with us again. I don't know what to do. I'm so confused. I feel like every action I make, every time I open my mouth, I'm hurting someone. She said I could call to explain everything, but we leave for Spain tomorrow for a few weeks, maybe more. To try and work things out. I think about you every day.'

Bean wondered at it all. How a man, who couldn't get through the day without her, had suddenly set himself free. How a woman, who knew her husband had loved and touched another woman could even dream of taking him back. *Isn't it a tainted thing?* She wanted to ask. *How can you possibly build on something so shattered?*

Bean sat with Allegra and explained it away. She had already recognized him for what he was long before all this. A few weeks ago at the park, sitting shirtless on a wooden bench, the river flowing by – he wasn't the young-old boy she loved. There was the slight belly, the beginnings of hair on his stomach, the pale skin from too many hours in the office. No. she couldn't imagine any kind of permanence with him at all. And what kind of man did this to you anyway? Made you believe in something and then dashed it to the ground?

'I won't say I told you so,' Allegra said, 'Actually, I will. I *told* you they never leave their wives, Bean. Never. And three children? Forget it!'

When Bean let go it wasn't a procedure, it wasn't slow. It was immediate: an epiphany. Because it was the only way she knew to confront her illusions. This was how the universe explained itself to her: in one second, between breaths. Not with a whimper, but a bang.

Bean could see her life ahead, waiting for her to catch up with it. She was going to pick up her skirts and race across the sand to where it was dancing, where it was saying, *Where have you been walking without me?* She was thinking of going back home and staying.

Home. Home. Mayuri writing to her from across the sea with terrible news of her own. *I've had another miscarriage, Bean, the second this year. I don't know what's wrong with me, but Cyrus is desperate to have children, and I'm not even sure I want them. The whole thing is so tedious – having to have sex at a particular time, and in particular ways, the constant checking and worrying. I don't know, it takes the joy out of everything. And if the doctor says that I can't, for whatever reason, carry a baby to term, Cyrus wants to adopt. But I don't know, Bean. I want my own flesh and blood. I miss having you here. Don't you miss home? Won't you come home?*

As though home were something so solid and fixed into the ground there could be no denying it. As though you could just say the word and know exactly what it meant.

Bean knew how it would be when she finally wandered into that Madras city air smelling of dust and tobacco, rosewater and jasmine. Everything would be familiar again: that old woman selling coconuts with the broken voice, that man with the hernia sitting at the corner of their street, those children playing in the gutter with sticks. *Home again, home again, jiggety-jig.*

But a part of Bean was still standing outside looking in, saying. *There's no such thing as home. Once you've forsaken it and stepped out of the circle, you can't ever re-enter and claim anything as yours.* How could you? When you've portioned off yourself in such a way? It was always going to be like this: when you walked down the cobbled streets of one city, your mind was always going to be in the folds of another. Hadn't Bean tried? Hadn't she gone away to recover parts of herself, and failed?

Bean had been losing the lines and boundaries for some time now. She wanted a place that was magical and warm, and even though Babo and Siân were calling her back to the house of orange and black gates saying, *Come back, come back, we have things to talk about*; even though Mayuri kept saying, *Cy and I miss you*, Bean knew she couldn't go back to Madras just yet.

Bean needed the heartbeat of another person to help her through the night. She wanted something definitive to happen to her. Something like an Asda delivery truck swiping you off the road, allowing you to understand your whole life for one shining, brilliant moment. She wanted to go to Ganga Bazaar, where the doors were always open, where Ba would be sitting like a white-haired goddess with ointments to soothe her soul.

'I've left him, Mayuri. I've finally come to the end of it. I have to leave this place.'

'Sometimes the right thing is the harder thing to do, Bean.'

'There's something else.'

How to say it? Isn't it ironic? I'm knocked up again. There's a little seed growing inside me, Javier's little seed, and this time I'm going to keep it.

'Promise you won't tell Mama and Daddy. I don't want them to know, not yet.'

'Have you told him, Bean? He deserves to know.'

278

There was a beginning of a dream that came to Bean before she left London. It was thin and transparent and she could see herself and all the future glistening like soft, glowing lamps behind its curtains. Javier was walking along a shore. He was holding lilies in his hands, bringing them to her. It was Bean's chance – to look at that picture and let him go. To take the flowers and say, *Let's not do this now*. There, in one of the coves, the wife was demanding explanations, the children were crying. *It's OK*, Bean wanted to tell them. *Because Daddy's taken his mid-life crisis and throttled it*. Bean saw him walking away, smelling of lilies and light. She took this image of him: those long sleeves rolled up to the elbows, those changeable hands through which she'd fallen. He was floating by.

28 Living After the Fall

This was a strange kind of wilderness, this in-between place of no places. Bean was travelling the world; flying to the city of cages and slums, the city of Bombay that Siân had wanted to forget about as soon as she landed in it because it hadn't been the India of her imagination. Bean would leave it too. She'd hop on to a train to Ahmedabad and take a night bus to Anjar exactly as Babo had done as a young man, stopping to pick rain clouds along the way for Ba.

To reach the village of Ganga Bazaar you had to pass through long stretches of silence, through desert mounds of rubble and stone, past caves and lightless caverns. You had to steer your way through the dreams of childhood. Bean, accustomed to these surreal terrains, settled herself by the window to witness them. She unwrapped her dinner – jeera aloo, pickle, chappathis and a packet of buttermilk. For weeks, ever since her morning sickness had passed, this is what she'd craved most: the taste of dry, homemade spice on her tongue. Her fellow passengers were spreading newspaper squares and eating too, anxious to fall back on the hard plastic length of their seats.

Bean ate quickly and made her way down the corridor to catch the last of the sun. She wanted to stand at the door and watch the countryside go by. In this light she could barely make out the difference between the shady babul trees and the handsome, cylindrical teaks – but they were out there, under the vast skies along with the umbrella jamuns and their deep, purple-black fruit. When they were children, going to Anjar for the summer, Mayuri and she had stood like this, by the open doors, with Siân standing right behind them, telling them to hold on tight.

What Bean saw now was an endlessness that went on and on: cotton and groundnut fields, unruly grasslands, temples, mosques, minarets, tombs. It was a landscape that belonged to no one – no king, no one moment in history. Bean stayed enraptured in this spell until they stopped, and the overpowering stench of urine and rush of hawkers invaded, but the minute they were moving, it was hers again – this entire swaying, intoxicating country, pulling away as they rushed forward.

At nightfall, Bean returned to her seat and tried to sleep. She had been travelling so long now, out of the lush forests of Maharashtra into the desert of Gujarat. Such dryness, impossible for the mind. Bean wished for rain. For overwhelming flood and deluge to come crashing through this place. For tiny streams to carve the hide of this parched earth. Because she'd already left one desert behind – the hissing urban desert of London. She'd left Javier on the front lawn of his house on Elsworthy Road, carrying Rosie around on his feet like a penguin carries its chick. Javier, in the faded English autumn light, who kept stepping in and out with his ideas of love and marriage.

Suppose Javier had been able to convince her that *Love was always new, Love was an eternity*, would Bean have been able to make her life there? To leave her home and family like Siân had done for Babo all those years ago? *For sure she would. For sure.*

Bean wouldn't have had to think about it. Bean, who was so convinced she was Daddy's girl, but who had none of Babo's steadfastness, who in the end, had turned out exactly like Siân, plagued by separations. It was why Siân was always saying 'Behave' to Bean, never to Mayuri, because Siân knew if someone said to Bean, *Come to where I am, make my life sparkle*, Bean would do exactly what she had done. She'd abandon them all and go. But Mayuri was different. Mayuri wanted to stay rooted to her earth, bound to her blood. *Blood. Blood.* Bean didn't believe in blood.

Ba explained it all to her later. She told Bean you could never be afraid of your own blood; that you could have a yearning for someone long after they'd disappeared from your life, but you could also yearn for them before they were born: Javier, her unborn child. Ba told her to recognize these two worlds as one; to be easy and light so when the moment came you'd be ready to plunge. You wouldn't have to go stooping around the edge with no fizz fizz in your step. You could dive straight in without smashing your head on rosewood floors. You could come back up to the surface with pockets full of pearls.

Otherwise, it was always going to be this way, wasn't it? Chasing close, but not close enough. All this time between the picking up and letting go. Wasn't it through these cracks that a human being could fall? Like Icarus – too close to the sun: melted wings and pasty-white legs, disappearing into the water for ever.

In Amroli the bus halted for a late-night toilet stop. An old woman across the aisle held out her hand and asked if Bean could help her outside. The woman's hand felt soft to touch, pruned, as if it had come from water. Bean took it and guided her to the thatched hut on the other side of the road where cows were usually kept, where they would have to squat, one in each corner, lifting their skirts to relieve themselves.

When they were finished, Bean took the old woman's hand and led her back across the street, where children had abandoned their skipping ropes for the day. On the derelict verandas, mothers and fathers slept on charpoys, hoping for a soft caress of midnight breeze. The only sound came from the night birds – spotted owlets and nightjars – and from the laughter of young men playing cards under dusty peepal trees. Back on the bus, Bean relinquished the old woman's hand and watched as she faltered back to sit by her husband, a wizened, slack-jawed reed of a fellow, and Bean, seeing them side by side together, thought only this: how tired they must be of living with each other.

All night, as they moved towards the village of Ganga Bazaar, Bean felt the old woman's hands on her. They humbled her with their deterioration. Chotu Kaka's hands had felt like this in the end, except his deterioration had been quicker, crueller.

The bus arrived in Ganga Bazaar at dawn when the jackals were returning to their lairs and the first rays of the sun were lighting up the periphery of the village like a smudgy line of burning coals. Bean got off with the other passengers and dragged her suitcase through the familiar crepuscular lanes, over potholes and along skinny drains, past the Amba Mata Temple with the sugar-cane fields blowing softly in the distance, past Zam Zam Lodge, past rows of concrete, tin-roofed houses where all the doors and windows were open, and where the tulsi plant grew copiously in courtyards, filling the air with its magical powers.

Everywhere Bean looked there were women: picking stones from rice, hanging their bright skirts and odhnis to dry, oiling and combing each other's hair, waving a greeting as she passed by.

In the old days the women of this town would have had a field day ghus-phusing; they would've closed their doors and averted their eyes if they'd known that an unmarried woman with child was among them. But Ba had trained them well. Ba, who had understood the true nature of reality in her fifty-third year, and who had been teaching the women of Ganga Bazaar ever since; whose sister eloped with a Muslim boy, and whose grandson married a white woman. Ba would teach Bean too, how to separate love from betrayal, anger from abandonment. She'd pick up all Bean's broken pieces and help her find her way home.

Bean felt like she was entering a mirage. These women looked to her like they existed from before time began: as if they had sprung, as the myths told, from cremation grounds, from the mouths of conches and the undersides of oars. These women walking about busily with their hair unbound, with keys ka-chink ka-chinking from their hips, with charcoal kajal in their eyes and bright red kumkum in the centres of their foreheads – they looked to Bean as though they really turned into tree-sprites and blue-faced boat women at night; as though they could spring lotuses from their necks, part their oblong legs and give birth to all the vegetation of the world.

Ba, sitting on the front steps of her house under the shade of the jamun tree in her white widow's sari, was cutting pomegranates, carving the red seeds out of the skin and placing them in a steel bowl beside her. Her creamy eyes squinted in the light. Her diaphanous knee-length hair lay plaited loosely down her back like a rope of glistening snow.

Everything around her was abundant, mysterious, despite the dryness, despite the heat. In the courtyard, peacocks milled about, pecking the ground for grain. Through the open doorways Bean could see red garoli lizards chewing plaster from the walls. The morning sun was rising like a siren, beating down on the tin roof with her curled up fists, extending rays of light to the bamboo grove and Ignatius's shack all the way at the back of the compound.

'The wind has been good to me today,' Ba said, smiling her crooked, bow-shaped smile.

Bean dropped her bags and went to sit with her face against her great-grandmother's breasts. She stayed there for a long time because there was something old and safe there, something like sitting cross-legged on the kitchen floor in Sylvan Lodge with Trishala hand-feeding her and Mayuri in turn; something like hiding in Selvam's lap while the ghost with grassy hair and her feet turned backwards at the ankles scrape-scraped along the portia-lined avenue of Sterling Road.

Every evening in Ba's front room of swings, jute mats were spread along the black stone floors so people could come and exchange bits of gossip and information, or simply to sit and listen, as Bean did. Most of the visitors were women: Shakambari and Shakuntala-behn, Malini-behn, Durga-behn, Bhavna-behn, the triplets Rukku, Tukku and Munnu. The occasional man passed through too – Vinod-bhai the goldsmith, Moti Lal Mehta, the village head, who came for an elixir to soothe a bout of indigestion or for counsel on how to silence his nagging wife. But the person who came everyday unfailingly was Ignatius. Ignatius, who had taken it upon himself to be the father of Bean's unborn child.

'Do you think she'll mind that her father's a girl?' Ignatius asked one day, cackling in that paddy-husk voice of his. 'At least I'm a pretty girl, no, Beena? If I was ugly I would understand; it might be difficult for the child to accept. But I think I'm quite pretty, maybe even prettier than you. What do you think?

'Arre, stop looking like you've swallowed a spider. You think *your* trouble is the end of the world? Just because some bastard fellow didn't leave his wife and family for you, you think it's the worst thing that's going to happen in your life? Let me tell you something – you try waking up and realizing that everyone is different from you; that the whole human race is divided into those who have cocks and those who have pussies, and very few who have a mini cock and a mini pussy. You think you have problems being half and half? Try being me for a day. See what you can do with these useless shrivelled-up pieces of flesh. Then see the walls come tumbling down.

'Let me see what he looks like, anyway. This hero of yours. You have a photo? Let's see what's so great about him.'

'Arre, no!' Ignatius squealed, when Bean took out the only picture she had kept of Javier and herself, standing by Lake Windermere in anoraks – Bean's face blurred in profile, kissing Javier's cheek, Javier looking straight at the camera, smiling his uncertain half smile.

'This is him? Now I understand what they say about true love being blind,' he chuckled. 'A bandicoot is lovely to his parents, and a mule is pretty to its mate. But surely, Beena, you could have fallen in love with someone a little younger, no? I think you should be happy that you're rid of the motherfucker. He would have treated you exactly as he treated his wife. Such men are never to be trusted, always thinking with the snake in their pants. I'm telling you, Beena, be happy that you're having a baby. What a blessed thing, to be having a baby.'

In the many months Bean spent in Ba's house, she felt her twenty-seven-year-old body expanding and changing, slipping through the moorings that connected her to the outside world. Her body transformed day by day, moved with a heaviness she'd never felt before. There was a substantial boost to her breasts, her bum. *Oh no!* thought Bean, *The fatty bumbalatti genes have arrived*. Everyday, she measured the circumference of her thighs and hips. What would the Brazilian dancer have said about this assassination of the body? Her mood swings grew so erratic that the only person who could talk to her without setting off a flood of hysterical laughter or tears was Ba.

'This has been happening since the very beginning, Beena. There is nothing new about what you're doing except it's the first time you are experiencing it. But this is old. As old as it gets.'

'I don't understand anything any more, Ba. I can't sleep. I can't concentrate. I feel inconsolably sad most of the time. I thought there would be joy, so much joy. But mostly it's something like shame. I haven't been able to tell Mama or Daddy about it yet. Only Mayuri knows.'

'But there can be no shame in the body, Beena. Because the universe was born out of Desire. Desire was the first seed of the mind. When we procreate, we are creating universes of our own.'

Bean already knew this. She'd been hearing it for ever: what exists in the universe exists in the human body. *Your body is your universe*. There were rivers and stars, sun and moon, oceans and mountains and places of pilgrimage in the body. To know the body was to have the ability to realize great bliss. Bean knew all this but still she felt shame–*shame shame puppy shame* – unpurifiable shame. Not just the shame of Javier, but the shame from before.

None of the women of Ganga Bazaar had pestered Bean, not a single one. Ba had warned them well in advance. So, while they were all dying to conjecture whether she was going to have a boy or a girl, dying to lift up her blouse and touch the tight drum of her belly, dying to offer a pearl of their own wisdom in Ba's house, none of them did anything except for Shakambari, who slipped Bean some unnamed roots and herbs and told her to put them under her pillow, 'Don't ask *how-what-why-where* now, I'll explain to you later, just do it.'

Only Ignatius had been given free reign. He sat with Bean everyday, massaging her feet and shoulders, trying to get her to shake off her sadness, because this was the closest he was going to get to being a parent in this world and he'd be damned if he was going to let Bean ruin it for him.

In those blackest of black Anjar nights, Bean cried for Javier. When she first arrived, in the ninth month of the new millennium, when she had still been able to feel the rocking of the bus that brought her – the jabber and chatter – she'd felt him in her blood, refusing to go away.

My kids are lovely, you know. I love my children. They have my blood running through their veins.

Fi Fie Fo Fum.

When I'm not with you, I feel my blood running the other way. Have I let you down? Tell me the truth. Have I let you down?

When Bean thought about him now, all she could feel was the blood rushing to her head, exactly like that counting game Babo and she used to play; when he used to put her on his lap and lean her all the way down to his toes.

Down down down to the bottom of the sea, how many fishes can Bean see?

One, two, three, four, five, six, seven, eight, nine, ten, thirteen, fifteen, sixteen . . .

Yes. It was exactly like that childhood counting game, wasn't it?

It was like seeing monsters and angels walk hand in hand together, or a single white-tipped shark moving into the horizon of your eye for a second and then disappearing into whiteness. Like Javier standing in the doorway saying, *I see you everywhere*, and walking straight through him.

In those early weeks Bean asked Ba why love was so important. Why it bound us so. Because there was still a body blustering through her, and even though she'd let it go, Bean still wanted to bask in it, capture it.

'Love means to worship the deity in your body,' Ba told her. 'It means not to struggle with the world.'

How could Bean explain that her melancholy over Javier had been replaced with something far more serious? An anxiety more concrete: an earlier misdemeanour involving Michael Mendoza and the Jayalakshmi Ladies Clinic in Alwarpet? How could Bean explain to these preservers of the body that she'd laid herself out like a piece of meat to have something removed from her, something she was now trying to nourish and protect.

Sixteen. Bean had only been a girl. A little girl. And they had been so secretive and chup chap about it. Michael Mendoza and Mehnaz, taking her to the place where they shaved her pubis and shone light into her eyes. 'You won't feel a thing,' they said. But Bean had felt everything. She had woken up with cotton wedges between her legs the colour red: the colour of woman, of creation. Bean had run away from Michael Mendoza, she'd thrown away her rattles and rhymes. Chak-a-chak. She'd gone to sleep with a flat, childless tummy. Siân must've known. Mayuri must've known. But they wouldn't say anything because this was her family, and it had always been about sugar and spice and all that's nice.

Bean was worried because she thought they might have damaged something *downthere* when she was sixteen, when she'd been so eager to have everything removed. She was worried that there might be something wrong with her. Bean had thought she'd never tell anyone, but here, in the village of Ganga Bazaar, where anything was possible, she was going to tell because she needed to know from Ba and Ignatius: was she going to be able to have her baby?

Ignatius and Ba said nothing. They picked her up and took her outside. They removed the wooden planks that covered the well and lowered Bean down on a stool, shouting to her from above, 'Remove everything and stay there for a while – under the water. Hold on to the grips.'

'But what . . .'

'No buts, Beena, just remove everything and stay there under the water.'

Bean removed her tie-die bandhni skirt and cotton blouse, she lowered herself in the water till her new womanly breasts were submerged, till those fiery circles of her eyes were drowning. She stayed for a while in that deep blackness until she heard voices of children whispering under the surface of the water – a whole classroom of them, chanting, *All the king's horses and all the king's men, couldn't put Humpty together again.*

Michael Mendoza was there too, sitting in the dark cave of the well with his dimpled cheek and marcasite eyes, still holding on to her fist-size pounding heart. *Wasn't it strange to see him here?* But Bean was used to seeing people where they didn't belong. She was shrinking, falling back into that sixteen-year-old frame: the slim hips and soft spine. She was telling him how he'd drawn fire from her. She didn't know it at the time, but the first one who did that to you would haunt you for the rest of your life. 'You are a permanent ghost in my life,' she told him.

Michael Mendoza was sitting in his black T-shirt and painted jeans, smiling. *If we wanted*, he was saying, we could will ourselves back into that time again. She could be waiting for him in the bay window of her room. He could be that same boy for her, and this time, they wouldn't have to put cotton wedges between her legs; this time, they could keep it. But Bean wouldn't be ravished this time. She wouldn't allow him to wash in and out of her, licking the salty wounds of her body.

'It's all right, Beena, I'm bringing you up now,' Ignatius yelled from the top of the well – an apparition in an apple-red petticoat and blouse, drawing her body up with his lady-boy fingers and wrists.

Ignatius carried Bean inside the house where Ba was sitting with a pile of sundari mangoes, scooping out the flesh so Bean would have sweetness and strength. 'The seeker is the starting point,' Ba said, 'So don't try and escape it, don't doubt your ability to shine alone.'

Ignatius wrapped Bean in a cotton towel. He was telling her that everything was going to be all right because he had seen a child hiding in the hibiscus shrub. A little girl with knee-length hair and gauzy grey eyes, shedding all kinds of golden light.

29 All should Speak Apart to the Homesick Heart

In the house of orange and black gates, Mayuri sat in her parents' bedroom, waiting for Siân to return from the Garden of Redemption. It was time to speak of things; to tell. Three weeks ago, Babo, Siân, Cyrus and she had gone out to celebrate the new year and their respective wedding anniversaries. Cyrus had booked a table at the city's most expensive restaurant, where they ate miniscule portions of food with copious amounts of champagne. Mayuri had wanted to say something about Bean that night, but seeing her mother so radiant in a navy silk dress with chunky lapis lazuli beads gleaming around her throat, seeing Babo look at her so intently, made it difficult.

In an earlier time, it wouldn't have been difficult. Mayuri would have told because it was the right thing to do. But right and wrong wasn't what it used to be, and besides, her parents looked so happy and strong, now that the weight of Chotu's death had finally begun to lift. Babo and Siân had space for each other in their lives again. After years of staying put they were thinking of making trips – far-flung, romantic ideas like going on a jungle safari in Africa, or a cruise in the Mediterranean.

Of course, news of her miscarriages had hit them hard. Especially, Siân, who was dying for a grandchild. She had wept openly when Mayuri called her – the first time, when it happened in the middle of the night, and more recently, when the cramps and bleeding started at school. 'Maybe you should take some time off work and rest at home?' Siân said. 'You need to take care of yourself, love.'

Mayuri had told her that Cyrus and she were taking a break from the baby-making business. 'It's not worth it, Ma. It's ruining our relationship.' *And, Ma*, she wanted to say, *You're going to be a grandmother after all, except it's not going to be mine.* And then she thought of Siân's withering disappointment, of her disapproval of Bean taking 'that path' with a married man. What did she expect? What were people going to say? All of it. So Mayuri stayed silent.

But it was uncanny how mothers *knew* things. A few days ago, Siân had called to say how she felt things weren't right with Bean. She'd been trying to get in touch with her to have a proper conversation, but every time she got Bean on the phone, she quickly passed it to Ba or Ignatius, fobbing her off with some excuse about work in the kitchen. Since when did Bean set foot in the kitchen?

'It's odd,' Siân said. 'I feel like she's calling out to me, for help. I know it sounds like I'm stark raving mad, but it happened with Nain – before she had her stroke. For months, I kept imagining that I heard her voice, that she was calling to me. And it's the same now, except it's Bean's voice I hear. I could be walking, or just pottering about in the garden, and suddenly, I hear her calling, *Mama, Mama*. It's unbearable. I don't know. I just feel like she's in some kind of trouble, and she's not able to tell us. So Daddy and I have decided, we're going to go to Anjar to check on her.'

That would have been the moment to tell her. *Mama, you're right, Bean is in trouble. She's pregnant. Can you believe?* But even then, Mayuri let the moment go, thinking of her promise to Bean.

This morning, Babo had called to inform her of their plans. 'We're flying to Bombay tomorrow,' he said. 'We're going to

293

stay at Meenal's for a couple of days and then we thought it might be nice to hire a car and drive to Gujarat like we did for our wedding. It's been a long time since we made a road trip. We should get to Anjar in time for the Republic Day long weekend.'

'Have you told Bean?'

'No. Of course not. We're going to surprise her.'

'Oh.'

'And another thing,' Babo said, 'Could you come to the house every other day and feed my fish?'

When she heard the gates open and the car drive in, Mayuri got up to stand at the window. Outside, the flame-of-the-forest tree was lit up like a scarlet lantern. Mayuri looked at herself in the mirror, scarcely able to recognize herself. The day after the anniversary dinner she had made an appointment at Cuts and Curls to lop off her chestnut braids, in an effort to feel light and different. Pamela Anne had hovered around her with glinting scissors for half an hour, repeatedly asking, 'Are you sure, Madam, are you absolutely sure you want to do this, such beautiful hair, why do you want to cut it?' And Mayuri, gritting her teeth, had ordered her to get rid of it all. Now her hair was short, below her ears, opening her face in a way it couldn't before, and staring at her reflection, Mayuri saw how much like Bean she looked after all.

As Siân walked through the front door, Mayuri formed the beginnings of words in her mouth. She had things to say.

In the early hours of 26 January 2001, Bean and Ignatius climbed into Mansuk-bhai's taxi service with two overnight bags and a basket of waiting-to-ripen chikoos. It was still dark when Mansuk-bhai came for them, the exhaust of his 118 NE letting off a low, continuous rattle like the sound of a rodent scuttling home after a night of hunting in the sewers. 'Today is holiday,' Mansuk-bhai complained, 'Everybody gets to relax on Republic Day, but not Mansuk Kotadia. What to do? Because you are best customer I must drive you personally. But you will pay more, eh? You pay more.'

Ba, who had only just risen herself, was skulking around in her white sari. 'Here,' she said, sticking her head through the taxi window, 'Don't forget to deliver the chikoos to Chimanlal, and remember to bring back ten kilos of dates and almonds for the ghari. We need enough for Monday.'

'You can come too, you know?' Bean said.

'What for? To those modern buildings of death? No, dhikri, you take Ignatius and go and see Lola's photo. I'll wait for you here.'

Lola's photo was the main purpose for Bean and Ignatius's expedition into Bhuj; Lola being Ignatius's preferred name for Bean's unborn child, who had been kicking like Diego Maradona for three solid weeks. In the last few days, though, Lola's vigorous feet had fallen silent; hardly a flurry had fluttered up from the depths of Bean's womb, and this lack of energy had worked Ignatius into an unusual state of agitation.

'It happens at this stage,' Ba tried telling Ignatius, 'The head starts turning downwards. Lola is getting ready to come out.'

But Ignatius still thought it would be wiser to check. Besides, it was an excuse to go into Bhuj for the night, to pick up supplies for the New Pinch Boutique and see his best friend, Bablu – a one-time pearl-fisher from Jamnagar, now proprietor of the Aina Mahal Annexe Guest House, Bhuj's most popular establishment.

Bean and Ignatius had been making regular forays into Bhuj for months to see Dr Gladys Pinto, gynaecologist and child specialist. Dr Pinto's office was hidden away at the top of a rickety stairway somewhere in the mangled maze of the old city. On the walls above her orange neon name board was this sensible advice: *Do not spit or make urine here*. As you entered, to the left of the reception desk, was a children's play area with a conglomeration of wooden horses and toys to distract any toddlers who might have been dragged along. In the centre of the room, under the single slow-turning fan, was a round cane table stacked with outdated newspapers and film magazines. An Onida television sat perched precariously on the wall, perpetually switched off, and all along the peach-coloured walls there were framed scenes of idyllic beaches – fishing boats, white sands, turquoise waters, palm trees – to soothe the eyes, and to serve as daily reminders, perhaps, to Gladys Pinto of her home state of Goa, which she'd abandoned a long time ago in pursuit of a medical vocation.

Gladys Pinto had no associates, but she had an army of nursing sisters – five Christian converts who walked around in white uniforms with starched white hankies pinned to the top of the left side of their chests, and spotless white Bata trainers on their feet, padding softly along the tiled floors. These sisters were in charge of all operations at the clinic, including determining who got to see the doctor first, so there was always an ingratiating rush whenever any one of them appeared in the corridor. 'Sister, such problems, whole night vomiting,' or 'Sister, sister, please me next, I'm feeling faintish.'

Inevitably, the waiting room at Dr Pinto's was full of women, most of them spherical and hormonal, whether they were pregnant or not. Mothers, daughters, sisters, a high proportion of them Muslim, covered from head to toe in black burquas, peering out at Bean and Ignatius with accusing, if not slightly bewildered eyes. '*As if,*' Bean once hissed, when it got too much. 'As if they're all bloody Immaculate Conception cases. As if they haven't all laid down with their legs spread for some man to get them into this condition.'

'Arre, shush, Beena,' Ignatius was quick to reprimand, fearful that his deferential attitude, which had so far garnered some preferential treatment with the sisters, would go to waste.

Occasionally, a man would show up, a rare appearance, to sit beside his wife and patiently trawl through a ten-day-old newspaper while she clutched grumpily at her stomach. And once, just once, Bean saw a stick-thin underage girl walk in alone, her face as blank as a morning sky, and Bean instinctively knew that Gladys Pinto was going to help her to return home with a flat, childless belly just as the nurses at the Jayalakshmi Ladies Clinic had done for her all those years ago.

The last time Bean visited Gladys Pinto she'd complained of fatigue and headaches; she was eating all the time, but never getting enough sleep, and her belly was getting in the way of everything. 'The worst is nearly over,' Dr Pinto assured her. 'Just imagine, Miss Patel, your Lola can now sense light and dark in the uterus. She can hear your heartbeat, your digestive system, your voice.'

'What about *my* voice?' Ignatius interjected.

'Yes, Lola can hear your voice too. But not like how I can hear it. You have to imagine you're underwater, a muffled kind of hearing. Can you imagine it?'

'Yes,' Beena said, 'I can imagine it very well.'

Then, Gladys Pinto lifted Bean's blouse and traced the wide expanse of her stomach with gel, moved from rib to rib with the gentle undulations of a desert wind, while Ignatius, standing beside her in awed stupefaction, watched as little Lola inside stirred: eyelashes, fingers, toes, a heartbeat.

'Do you really think it won't be crowded today?' Bean asked, staring out of the window as Mansuk-bhai rattled along the mud path road out of Anjar towards the highway to Bhuj.

'Trust me, it will be just us.'

Bean watched as the beginnings of light slowly filled the day. It was a cool morning, the kind that reminded her of waking up early for swimming lessons with Chotu. Those lonely mornings in the house of orange and black gates when everyone was still asleep, except for Selvi – risen from her jute mat, hair sticking out of her bun, to thrust Bean's school bag and tiffin carrier into her hands.

'Arre, Mansuk-bhai,' Igantius grumbled, 'Are you determined to make whatever genitalia I have shrivel up and die? Close the window, old man, I'm freezing here.'

The day ahead of them was going to be long. Ignatius had already enumerated all that needed to be accomplished. There were ultrasounds to be taken and chikoos to be delivered, there was a three-course Chinese meal at Chopsticks to be devoured and the many crenulated gateways and gullies of Bhuj to be explored for beads and Patola silk, wood blocks and dyes. In between all this, they had to go to Dee Pee's around Harmisar Lake to buy the dried fruits for Ba. And finally, there would be the ice-cool glass of illicit Kingfisher beer with Bablu on the terrace of the Aina Mahal Annexe.

Bean's final thought, that Republic Day morning when the world changed, was how ladylike Ignatius looked when the muscles in his neck relaxed. Sitting in the front seat with his arms spread out and head stretched back, he almost looked like a swan in flight. Just as Bean felt herself drift into a similar oblivion, the taxi suddenly shook and swerved into a roadside tree. Ignatius instantly lifted that long neck of his and reached backwards protectively. Mansuk-bhai shrieked like a woman as the windshield glass scattered across his face. Bean, lurching forward in her seat, felt as though she were falling under the feet of the world. Wham bam, wham bam, until there was nothing.

30 Looking for Footprints of Birds in the Sky

It began with a shiver that moved beneath the surface of the earth, gathering force like a flame grows in the dark, ravaging the land like a forest fire. It was a falling like never before. The town of Anjar was turned on its head, torn asunder, as though an army of iron-armed marauders had ripped through, razing all the buildings to the ground, tossing the good men and women of Ganga Bazaar about like they were rag dolls, their houses, mere playthings.

Look – Zam Zam Lodge, where Babo spent six months writing epic letters to Siân: collapsed. The Amba Mata Temple, where the entire Patel family was birthed into existence, the New Pinch Boutique, Hira Lal's jewellery store: all fallen to the ground. Every single crepuscular lane of Ganga Bazaar, shattered like one of those new-fangled glass Diwali decorations, into a million pieces. The earth was spinning, swaying those hips of hers – dhamak dhimak, dhamak dhimak. And even though it was still the beginning of the day, everything was plunged into darkness.

Men ran out of their broken homes, coated with dust and blood. Children sat on heaps of stone, crying. In the streets, peacocks opened their feathers – jhat jhatta, jhat jhatta – fluttering like sheaves of silk paper, spinning blue light out of their crowns. And the jackals, who usually hid from dusk to dawn, stood boldly in the gutters with their supine faces, baying for the end of the world to end, and the beginning to begin.

Two days after the Republic Day earthquake registered 7.9 on the Richter scale at its epicentre in Bhuj, Gujarat, there was still no news from Ganga Bazaar. No phone lines going in, no phone lines going out. In Meenal and her shipbroker husband's Andheri flat, Babo and Siân sat with an assortment of newspapers spread around them. Babo spent hours going through every column inch of them, scouring them for bits of information that the BBC or NDTV wouldn't or couldn't give him. Siân sat transfixed on the sofa, while the TV spewed out one image after another; listening to the newsreaders repeat, in their grave but moderate tones, the stories that were saddest.

By now, everyone knew about the 350 school children from Anjar who had been crushed to death during their Republic Day Parade, whose families would receive Rs 100,000 as compensation because their children had died doing 'patriotic duty'. Their parents and grandparents had been interviewed, their baby pictures beamed into living rooms all over the country. The teachers who'd survived had been shown gushing like water hydrants, saying what good children they'd been, every single one of them – angels in human forms.

And the diamond workers from Bapunagar – what a story that was! They'd been interviewed too – telling the world how their employers had locked them in, actually locked them in, to make sure they wouldn't run off with their diamonds. The ones who were lucky to be alive, who hadn't panicked and jumped out of the windows – they were standing in front of the camera thanking the gods above, the firm ground beneath their feet and their female colleagues who'd had the good sense to use their saris as ropes so they could all slide down to safety.

Meenal's telephone rang non-stop. Mayuri and Cyrus from their beach house in Madras asking what news of Bean, what news of Ba. Sonam, the night nurse from Sylvan Lodge, saying, 'I don't know how he knows because the TV hasn't been on for days, but sir, he keeps asking for his mother. You better talk to him, I don't know what to tell him.' Prem Kumar, whose memory was hinging from one night to the next, asking for his wife, who'd been dead nearly twenty years, and then smiling quickly afterwards saying, 'No, no, of course, she isn't here. But where is Mayuri? Where is Beena? Someone tell me, where is my mother?'

Finally, after two days of negotiation, Meenal's shipbroker husband managed to find a driver. 'Bhai,' Meenal said to Babo, 'People are managing to get through. It's time for you and Bhabi to leave.'

Babo and Siân's hazardous journey to Anjar began in a sky-blue Ambassador outside the gates of Meenal's apartment building. While they waited for the driver, Prakash, to show up, Babo contemplated the pros and cons of another lapse into smoking. Siân and the unibrows stuffed the dickey of the car with boxes of medical supplies and crates of food and water, all organized by the local Jain Samaj.

At 11 a.m., Prakash arrived. He was a young man with a wide, honest face, marred only by a hooknose and a severe middle parting with equal amounts of frizzy hair pasted down on either side. The minute Prakash saw the sky-blue Ambassador, his wide, honest face closed up. 'Sorry,' he said, 'I can't do this.'

'Why not?' screamed Meenal. 'Good-for-nothing fellow. I told you we shouldn't have paid him money up front!'

'Madam, there is no god,' he said, pointing to the dashboard of the car. 'You want me to make a journey like this with no god?'

'But we don't believe in the keeping of idols in our car,' said the shipbroker. 'We are Jains.'

'Well, I don't believe in simply risking my life,' said Prakash, haughtily. 'If you want me to drive, you better put in a god.'

Eventually, a plastic Ganesh with fairy lights was procured from a nearby shop and hastily installed on the dashboard, and only after Prakash made a solemn show of folding his hands and bobbing his head several times, did the sky-blue Ambassador finally lurch forward.

'Go safely,' Meenal said, touching Babo's arm, reminding him of a moment they'd had years ago, on the red-brick terrace of Sylvan Lodge, when they had both been thin and innocent, and Meenal was pressing one of Falguni's tear-stained letters into his hands.

Babo and Siân sat in the back of the car, holding hands across the Rexene seat. Babo was wearing his great-grandfather's platinum locket – the one Prem Kumar had given him on the morning of his departure to London. The last time he had worn it was when he was flying home to Madras after Prem Kumar lied about Trishala's illness. Babo had noticed it while packing for this trip; it was lying in an old cigar box, and seeing it so forlorn and forgotten, he packed it in his shaving case thinking Ba might like to see it again.

It had taken them twenty hours just to get to Ahmedabad from Bombay, and they still had a way to go, up the coast, past the Gulf of Cambay, through Sanand, Surendra Nagar, Rajkot, Tankara, Jetpur – towns whose names evoked a long-ago thump thumping in his chest. Babo had known their rugged shapes once; they had been as familiar to him as the blue-green filigreed network of his wife's body. But all of it was strange now, alien territory.

The women of Ganga Bazaar arrived after days of searching. They came to sit on Ba's stone floors. 'What shall we do?'

they asked, not with tears in their eyes. There was no real energy for tears. But very simply, *Where do we go from here?*

During the day, they went sifting through debris searching for things that could be used. Some cooked in the big steel pots recovered from the Amba Mata Temple. Still others, who could hold down a limb and sew a neat line of stitches across gashes without any anaesthetic, went with the doctors. At night they sat together in circles and shared the stories of the day. They talked about the workers in the crematorium who had used up two years' supply of firewood already, and who were now just throwing bodies one on top of the other, burning them unnamed and unaccounted for. They worried about water. What they had wouldn't last much longer, and there were already outbreaks of cholera, typhoid and dysentery. They talked in muted whispers, trying to portion out the collective guilt of their survival. 'Why?' they asked. 'Why them, not us?'

Babo was going back now. *Back, back.* Past the sun-browned faces and salt flats. On and on till he was there, standing at the door of his childhood in Ganga Bazaar, where his grandfather was allowing him to count up his coins and organize them. Babo's rusty-faced Bapa, who was stingy with his affections and his money with everyone except his favourite grandson.

Babo was passing it all – the proud cows of Gujarat, whose horns were the most beautiful in all of India. The rivers Tapti, Narmada and Sabarmati, the marshes and low-lying ranns that isolated Kutch from the rest of the country.

Babo was remembering how his Ba and Bapa had taken him to the Rann of Kutch one winter to see the flamingos. If any of the other children had asked, they'd have been belted and made to sit in the storeroom for the day. But because Babo was the preferred grandchild, because he buttered up his grandmother and whispered that what he'd *most* like to do was to see the pink-coloured flamingos like the ones in Africa, because of Babo's desire, all of them – Meenal, Dolly, Trishala, Ba and Bapa – piled on to Suraj-bhai's bullock cart and made the two-day journey from Ganga Bazaar to Khavda village, where after the monsoon, tens of thousands of flamingo colonies gathered over the water marshes to breed.

Babo wanted to share this memory with Siân: how he had told his sisters that flamingos left pink footprints in the sky, and how he'd promised two annas to the first person who saw one. Meenal had grown bored easily. After an hour of straining her neck she'd forgotten all about the flamingos. But Dolly had persevered – she'd stretched out on her back, head in Babo's lap, eyes never leaving the sky in case a pink footprint should elude her. By the time they arrived of course, Dolly was crying because of a crick in her neck. When Trishala found out what had happened, she slapped Babo till he was pink in the face. 'Pink footprints! I'll give you pink footprints,' she shouted, 'Always making mischief.' But Ba had made her stop just as she was getting started, and Bapa only smiled and called him a little badmash. Bapa had put Babo up on his bony shoulders so he could get a better view of that glittering pink net of feathers and wings spread over the water, and Babo, all these years later, still thought it was the most magical sight he'd ever seen.

Babo closed his eyes and tried to recall that image in his mind now. He needed it fixed there as an anchor to prevent other thoughts from forcing their way through. Somehow it was safer to dwell in the past, because the future ahead frightened him so much. What he wanted to say aloud to his wife was this: that everything would be OK. It had to be. He had only just made peace with his brother's death. To even contemplate a world without Bean or Ba was impossible, unfathomable. Beyond any cruelty he could imagine.

Siân was looking out of the window stonily, the knot in her throat constricting and constricting, until he thought she would choke. All along she had refused to talk directly of Bean. She had stuck to the facts, to what the papers offered them.

The papers had talked of babies recovered from buildings, families clinging to each other with pinched faces and runny eyes, a man buried under his house, clutching a bag of 300 ancient gold coins. They wrote of the failures of electricity, water, medical facilities and telecommunications.

One reporter flying over the town of Anjar in a helicopter wrote how he'd actually been able to smell the dead. From all the way up there, he'd been able to smell the dead. And what he'd seen below was a broken land dotted with blue relief tents, vultures swooping and picking their way through the carnage.

But there were stories of hope as well. Babo had made sure to unearth those and present them to Siân. Stories of housewives who installed pandals in the open maidans and started community kitchens; phat-phatti drivers who converted their taxis and vans into ambulances; doctors who moved through the rubble day and night, treating victims with the few supplies they had; Hindus and Muslims lying down together to sleep on the floors of the houses that had remained standing.

And of course, there were the *just-plain-miracles*: a newly-wed couple who dramatically survived under the rubble of their four-storeyed apartment after thirty-six hours; an eighty-year-old man found lying in his bed under a mound of debris two days after the quake, complaining only of minor throat irritation and constipation; a twelve-year-old boy, Mohammad, who lost his entire family, and said it was an angel who spared him by singing in his ears day and night.

In all these miracles Babo hoped there would be his centenarian grandmother, a hermaphrodite called Ignatius, his pregnant daughter.

31 Ladybird, Ladybird

It was dusk by the time the sky-blue Ambassador rolled into the wrecked town of Anjar. Siân was thirsty. She hadn't drunk any water since their last stop in Amroli, where the Ganesh on the dashboard's lights had given out. She hadn't spoken since the night before, when they stopped the car outside Ahmedabad for a few hours to sleep. They drove in silence, snaking through a darkening countryside under cloudless skies. All around, as far as Siân could see, there was rubble. Cracked buildings and fallen pillars lining the streets like a scene from the underworld.

The entrance to the village of Ganga Bazaar was crowded with people. 'Are you sure?' Siân asked: 'Are you sure this is it?' Because she had never seen it like this before. People wore frightened looks on their faces, and the sound of screams and cries filled the air.

As the car turned in to the main thoroughfare a policeman stopped them and asked if they were with an NGO or an international agency. Babo explained that his grandmother and daughter lived in Ganga Bazaar; that they hadn't heard anything from them or their condition so they had driven here to find them.

'Oh,' the policeman said. 'You'd better park the car and walk the rest of the way. As it is, the gullies are so small, but with all the cheap cement they use here in the villages, most of the houses crumbled in the first tremor itself.'

Babo and Siân walked, carrying a box of supplies each. They made Prakash stay with the car. They walked past looters and tricksters, past villagers who were lining up to intercept any incoming relief goods, past soldiers who were using explosives to bring down teetering buildings, past mourners calling out to their loved ones with incense in their hands to mask the smell of death.

Nothing will ever be the same again. This was Siân's only thought as they picked their way through the debris. Babo took out a torch from his pocket and shone the light ahead so they could see where they were going. None of the street lamps were working, and while there were stars in the sky, it seemed like even they were holding themselves back, scattering their light into other, safer parts of the universe.

Finally they reached a structure that was the only one standing in the entire street. It was Ba's house, entirely complete except for the tin roof, which, Shakambari later told them, had flown off clean like a magic carpet. Babo and Siân walked towards the house, following a path illuminated by oil lamps. They entered the room of swings and saw it was filled with women. Circles of women sewing pieces of material together in weak light, mumbling like bees.

It was Shakambari who noticed them first. 'Thank God you're here,' she said, raising herself with considerable effort from the floor. 'Come and see Hansa-behn. She was injured by a falling wooden rafter. She's OK, but very weak.'

'And Bean?' Siân asked, 'What about Bean?'

Shakambari fell silent. 'I think it's better if Hansa-behn tells you.'

Ba lay in the corner of her room on a mattress, her body turned to face the wall. Above her a group of red garoli lizards chewed softly, keeping watch over her.

Babo was immediately at her side. 'Ba,' he said, touching her frail arm. 'I'm here.'

Ba turned to face him.

'I can't see you,' she said. 'It's dark. I can't see anything. What can I tell you? Ignatius and Beena left to see the doctor in Bhuj a few hours before the earthquake happened. We haven't heard anything. No one is able to get out. And Babo, I can't smell anything either. Everything is gone, vanished, just like that.'

That night, Babo and Siân slept next to Ba while the women lay on the floor of the room of swings like a line of suckling puppies, huddled together for warmth. Siân tried not to think about Bean, about the number of times she'd said to her, 'Behave, behave,' and the number of times Bean had done exactly as she pleased. Bean, who because she'd been born second, always thought she'd been loved less. Bean, who felt safest when she was sleeping between her mother and father, who had to be walked back to her bedroom in the middle of the night and have the lights switched on. *See Bean? There's no Boochie Man. No snakes. Try to dream of beautiful things.* Bean, who knew to drag and drag till every bone had been dragged out of you.

Where was her family? Bean had something to tell them. It started with a drumming – thrum thrum thrum – like an old black and white film coming undone in front of her. And then everything had speeded up, gone all Charlie Chaplin topsy-turvy on her. Cattle and long-haired pigs running about madly. A man emerging from the rubble with a mutilated child in his arms. She couldn't breathe, her heart refused to breathe in its cage. Thrum thrum thrum.

'Hold on, Beena,' Ignatius was saying. But what madness was this? Walls and ceiling crashing around her. Moving and shaking. People running in every direction. And then silence. Bean stopped hearing. She was on a boat out on the ocean, bob bobbing calmly, while underneath the surface all kinds of turbulent things were brewing.

Ignatius put her down in a place where there was still walls and a roof. He cleaned her forehead and shoulders with the end of his dupatta, and laid his ear down on her distended stomach. 'What a thing to have happened,' he said, click clicking his tongue, and then walked back out into that madness with a crowbar in his hands. Mansuk-bhai was going with him, sleeves rolled up to his elbows.

Are you going to war? Is this what's happening here? Bean wanted to ask. *Who are we fighting? Don't leave me alone. Come back!*

But Ignatius was gone already, his silver bangles clacking menacingly in the morning sun.

Bean needed to find Mayuri. She wanted to tell her that they'd been living their lives together after all. She wanted to go whooshing down the banister of Sylvan Lodge again with matching denim skirts so they could slide. Vroom vroom, so they could fall.

She wanted her father and mother to hold her hands and walk through the broken rooms naming things: table, chair, cupboard, mother, father, sister. Would it be that simple to learn them again? To make them whole?

What Bean smelled now was the smell of paint. Her father's factory during Diwali, a 500-wallah bomb going off for what seemed like hours – phat-a-phat phat-a-phat. Diwali. The God Ram bringing the Goddess Sita back to the kingdom. The triumph of good over evil. The unibrows, the lamps, oil baths, new clothes. Selvi and Selvam, dark and polished like coffee beans, collecting their gift-wrapped presents from Siân. It was about beginning the new year, about being protected. Her mother and father, Siân and Babo, an amalgamation of their names on cans of paint, spread on the walls of people's homes, surviving monsoons and marriages. And what of those houses now? Collapsed, crumbled. All fallen down. *Ladybird ladybird fly away home, your house is on fire, your children all gone*. Babo, in his paint-smattered shirts. Siân, the milky smell of love between her breasts. Mother. Father.

This was it, thought Bean. The moment I asked for: my moment of blinding clarity. Forty-five seconds of it. Bean hadn't thought of Javier. She had thought of her baby, of Ba. Of what Babo, Siân and Mayuri would do without her in the world.

For four days she'd been living in darkness. It reminded her of the Madras cyclone of 1984 when they'd been trapped in the house of orange and black gates. No school. No office for nearly a week. Only rain pounding down on telephone wires, hacking off branches of trees. Bean hadn't been scared of that darkness. Siân and Selvi had filled the house with candles. Babo had taught Mayuri and her how to play Rummy. All day they played cards, gambling with pistachio shells first, and then with twenty-five paisa coins. 'Never doubt the Gujju genes in these girls,' Babo had laughed when Bean and Mayuri cleaned him out. At night they slept together like a perfect family: Babo and Siân on either side of their Kashmiri bed, Bean and Mayuri tucked between them. And then the inevitable happened – the rain slowed down and finally stopped. The lights came back on again, uncomfortably bright. They fell back into their daily routines, slept in their own beds. Soon afterwards, Selvi found Bean at the power box, trying to disconnect the electrical mains. 'What's the matter with you, child? Gone mad or what?' But Bean couldn't help it. She'd fallen in love with the idea of darkness, even though it was the same darkness the Boochie Man roamed around in.

This was a different kind of darkness. Barely any food or sleep, the smell of rot and decomposing flesh around them. At nights, there was mostly quietness, but once in a while, a gurgle of laughter from some black corner, an illicit sound, almost. Strange, thought Bean, even at a time like this, we must laugh, and somewhere perhaps, a husband and wife, lucky to be alive, or a pair of lovers, were holding each other and making love, as they must.

Bean folded her hands across her stomach. She could feel the baby kicking inside. Soft, insistent thud thuds.

Forty-five seconds. That's all it took to change your life.

Bean didn't remember when Ignatius came back for her. It might have been a few hours, or a day. 'It's OK,' Bean told him, 'Lola is fine. I can feel her.'

'We're getting out of here,' Ignatius said. 'Now. Come on, let's go. I found someone to take us. An old lover. Trust the past to come up with a solution. Come on, Beena. There, I've got you.'

Ignatius carried Bean into a bright yellow Ashok Leyland lorry. It was daybreak, and even though the roads were piled high with stone, and the sky seemed to have holes in it, the sun still shone through as if nothing had happened. All around them was the aftermath of struggle. It was exactly like in that poem about suffering Bean had learned in school: the dogs go on with their doggy life, and everything turns quite leisurely away from the disaster.

Ba heard it first – a towering roll of thunder that tore through the air as though the sky were clearing its throat – khat phat, khat phat, preparing to regurgitate all it had been witness to. Then she began to smell. First an intoxicating drift of bakul flowers and wet grass, and then from afar, wafting over the long kilometres of rubble, past the bodies and howling jivas of jackals and peacocks, children and neighbours, there was the smell of spices and lolly ice, brass, sex, blood.

Ba threw off the covers and rose from the mattress she'd been lying on for so many days and nights. Her legs felt unsteady, like columns of water. She inched her way down the corridor, wondering about the walls of her house. These walls that were still standing. It must have been the red garoli lizards that saved them – chewing for all those years, leaving behind traces of their saliva along the walls, binding everything tightly together.

At the basin, Ba stood, unplaiting her long, white hair. The mirror above the basin had fallen and cracked. There was no water coming out of the taps, but there was a bucket of water on the floor, full to the brim. They had been rationing the well water: two mugs per person per day. It was all they had to drink, clean themselves with, clean wounds with, cook.

Ba pulled up a plastic stool to the bucket. She removed her clothes quickly and hung them on the bathroom hook. Then she sat down, her lungs making dangerous rattling noises as she lowered herself. She scooped up one mug of water and dipped her fingers into it. The water was cold. She dipped her fingers in again and splashed a few drops on her face. Her eyes stung with joy.

Ba remembered as a young girl, going to the river to bathe with her friends. Wading in fully clothed and then plunging their heads under the surface until their bodies were immersed. The feeling of water on your skin. Was there anything more sensual, more erotic than this? She wanted to feel that now; to dissolve into a similar kind of bliss. She poured a mug of water over her head. Then another and another, until her hair stuck to her body like a river plant. She gasped and shivered, the coldness of it, the cleanness of it. Again and again, she poured, until there was nothing left. Then she wrapped a towel around herself, reached for a clean blouse, which she put on with difficulty. The scars on her shoulder still hurt, and the gashes on her forehead and collarbone where the rafter hit, hadn't healed. Within a few minutes, she was dressed again: hooks fastened, sari retied.

Before leaving, she groped along the bathroom shelf for her comb and a silver box of kajal. She ran the comb through her

...ntangling the k...eling long s... come away in
...in Then she op...silver bo...stuck her ring,
...needed no...find t...rims of her
could he...king he...way th...ch the roo...swings
much chilli powder...re...ses...Durga-be...from o...She
Rukku saying, 'No, no not like...something...ould...ar
make as many tents as we can.'...ut it this wa...need...

When she was finally at the wooden door...trying to
position herself so she would...n't appear shaky, ...omen of
Ganga Bazaar suddenly noticed her and let o...collective
shriek. 'Hansa-behn, what are you doing? Wh...e you got
up like this?'

'Go and fetch Babo,' she said. 'Tell him not t...nywhere.'

Babo and Siân were getting ready to leave fouj in their
sky-blue Ambassador. 'What is it?' Babo asked, ...ing to her.
'Are you all right?'

Ba could hear the red garoli lizards plop pl...ing off the
walls. The tin roof was gone though, she was su...of it, taking
the peacocks with it.

'What do you think?' she said. 'They're c...ming, Babo.
They're coming home. I can smell them. Come sit with
me. Come,' she said, pulling Siân's hand. 'Sit with me, and
wait.'

Ba sat on her front steps, looking straight ahead, her diabetic
eyes curdling and stilling, her diaphanous hair unplaited, wet
and open to the contaminated air.

When those first drops began to fall, Ba knew they were
here, walking up to the front steps. Babo and Siân were up
and running, trampling over the surface of the earth as if it
were a carpet of butter-yellow pendant flowers. Ignatius was
coming towards her, raising those tender arms of his like the

wings of a dragon. Bean was wild, laughing though

the heavy shall rain... of rain. ... was done.

It would... all rat... to go... thous... Hee broken fields

to... would... ploughbodies... don't have to

The whemsee parch...

to alves acr... parch...

the... gain. Th... could cov... to the fallen wheat.

... own it open their...

li...

ACKNOWLEDGEMENTS

Thanks to my entire family in India and abroad, who made me understand how 'love, having no geography, knows no boundaries'; my friends who opened their hearts, homes and kitchens to me (you know who you are); Ameet Gheewala and David Miller, my first readers, who convinced me there was a story to be told somewhere in the morass of my first draft; my stellar team of editors – Gillian Stern, Victoria Millar and Audrey Cotterell, who helped shape and reshape my words when I could no longer bear to look at them; everyone at Bloomsbury, but in particular, Alexandra Pringle, who gently reminded me of the value of slowness, and who believes, like me, that breakfast is the most important meal of the day.

I must also thank Beatrice von Rezzori for a stay at the Santa Maddalena Foundation where I experienced the rare joy of two back-to-back 5,000-word days, and DW Gibson at the Ledig House International Writers Residency for providing me with a room of my own when I most needed one, and the Arts Council England for a generous grant.

Finally, thanks are due to those constant guides who have lent their philosophy, poetry and wisdom to many of the chapter headings and characters in this book: Arthur Rimbaud, Friedrich Nietzsche, J Krishnamurti, Epicurus, Bob Dylan, Dinah Washington, Leonard Cohen, The Beatles, Chandralekha, Gautama Buddha, Mahavir Swami, Harry Belafonte, Khalil Gibran, Rainer Maria Rilke, Dylan Thomas, Jalaluddin Rumi, Goethe, W. H. Auden, Li Po, Albert Camus and Bhavabuti.